Dan Brown is the bestselling author of *Digital
Fortress*, *Deception Point*, *Angels and Demons* and
The Da Vinci Code. He is a graduate of Amherst
College and Phillips Exeter Academy, where he
has taught English and creative writing. He lives
in New England. He can be found on the web at
www.danbrown.com.

Also by Dan Brown

DIGITAL FORTRESS
DECEPTION POINT
THE DA VINCI CODE

ANGELS
AND
DEMONS

Dan Brown

CORGI BOOKS

ANGELS AND DEMONS
A CORGI BOOK : 0 552 15073 8

First publication in Great Britain

PRINTING HISTORY
Corgi edition published 2001

32 34 36 38 40 39 37 35 33

Copyright © Dan Brown 2000
Ambigram Artwork © John Langdon

Set in 10/12 Palatino by
Falcon Oast Graphic Art Ltd.

Corgi Books are published by Transworld Publishers,
61-63 Uxbridge Road, London W5 5SA,
a division of The Random House Group Ltd,
in Australia by Random House Australia (Pty) Ltd,
20 Alfred Street, Milsons Point, Sydney, NSW 2061, Australia,
and in New Zealand by Random House New Zealand Ltd,
18 Poland Road, Glenfield, Auckland 10, New Zealand
and in South Africa by Random House (Pty) Ltd,
Endulini, 5a Jubilee Road, Parktown 2193, South Africa.

Printed and bound in Germany by
GGP Media GmbH, Pößneck.

Papers used by Transworld Publishers are natural, recyclable
products made from wood grown in sustainable forests.
The manufacturing processes conform to the environmental
regulations of the country of origin.

For Blythe . . .

ACKNOWLEDGMENTS

A debt of gratitude to Emily Bestler, Jason Kaufman, Ben Kaplan, and everyone at Pocket Books for their belief in this project.

To my friend and agent, Jake Elwell, for his enthusiasm and unflagging effort.

To the legendary George Wieser, for convincing me to write novels.

To my dear friend Irv Sittler, for facilitating my audience with the Pope, secreting me into parts of Vatican City few ever see, and making my time in Rome unforgettable.

To one of the most ingenious and gifted artists alive, John Langdon, who rose brilliantly to my impossible challenge and created the ambigrams for this novel.

To Stan Planton, head librarian, Ohio University – Chillicothe, for being my number one source of information on countless topics.

To Sylvia Cavazzini, for her gracious tour through the secret *Passetto*.

And to the best parents a kid could hope for, Dick and Connie Brown . . . for everything.

Thanks also to CERN, Henry Beckett, Brett Trotter, the Pontifical Academy of Science, Brookhaven Institute,

FermiLab Library, Olga Wieser, Don Ulsch of the National Security Institute, Caroline H. Thompson at University of Wales, Kathryn Gerhard and Omar Al Kindi, John Pike and the Federation of American Scientists, Heimlich Viserholder, Corinna and Davis Hammond, Aizaz Ali, the Galileo Project of Rice University, Julie Lynn and Charlie Ryan at Mockingbird Pictures, Gary Goldstein, Dave (Vilas) Arnold and Andra Crawford, the Global Fraternal Network, the Phillips Exeter Academy Library, Jim Barrington, John Maier, the exceptionally keen eye of Margie Wachtel, alt.masonic. members, Alan Wooley, the Library of Congress Vatican Codices Exhibit, Lisa Callamaro and the Callamaro Agency, Jon A. Stowell, Musei Vaticani, Aldo Baggia, Noah Alireza, Harriet Walker, Charles Terry, Micron Electrics, Mindy Renselaer, Nancy and Dick Curtin, Thomas D. Nadeau, NuvoMedia and Rocket E-books, Frank and Sylvia Kennedy, Simon Edwards, Rome Board of Tourism, Maestro Gregory Brown, Val Brown, Werner Brandes, Paul Krupin at Direct Contact, Paul Stark, Tom King at Computalk Network, Sandy and Jerry Nolan, Web guru Linda George, the National Academy of Art in Rome, physicist and fellow scribe Steve Howe, Robert Weston, the Water Street Bookstore in Exeter, New Hampshire, and the Vatican Observatory.

FACT

The world's largest scientific research facility – Switzerland's *Conseil Européen pour la Recherche Nucléaire* (CERN) – recently succeeded in producing the first particles of antimatter. Antimatter is identical to physical matter except that it is composed of particles whose electric charges are *opposite* to those found in normal matter.

Antimatter is the most powerful energy source known to man. It releases energy with 100 per cent efficiency (nuclear fission is 1.5 per cent efficient). Antimatter creates no pollution or radiation, and a droplet could power New York City for a full day.

There is, however, one catch . . .

Antimatter is highly unstable. It ignites when it comes in contact with absolutely anything . . . even air. A single gram of antimatter contains the energy of a 20-kiloton nuclear bomb – the size of the bomb dropped on Hiroshima.

Until recently antimatter has been created only in very small amounts (a few atoms at a time). But CERN has now broken ground on its new Antiproton Decelerator – an advanced antimatter production facility that promises to create antimatter in much larger quantities.

One question looms: Will this highly volatile substance save the world, or will it be used to create the most deadly weapon ever made?

AUTHOR'S NOTE

References to all works of art, tombs, tunnels, and architecture in Rome are entirely factual (as are their exact locations). They can still be seen today.

The brotherhood of the Illuminati is also factual.

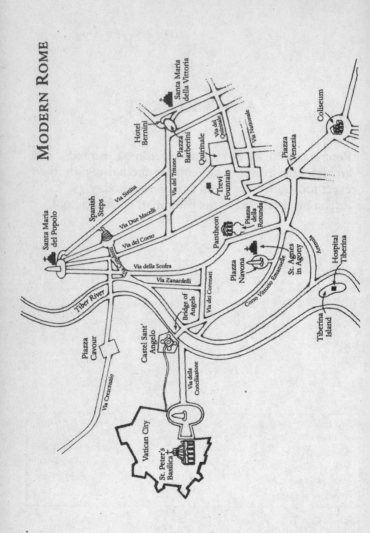

MODERN ROME

VATICAN CITY

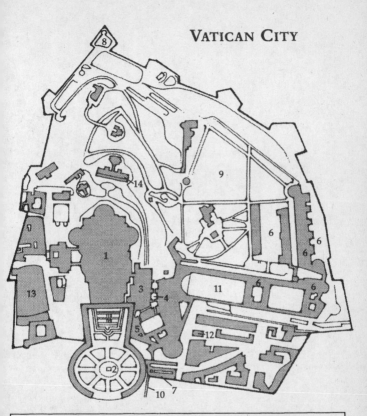

1 St Peter's Basilica	7 Office of the Swiss Guard	11 Courtyard of the Belvedere
2 St Peter's Square	8 heliport	12 Central Post Office
3 Sistine Chapel	9 gardens	13 Papal Audience Hall
4 Borgia Courtyard	10 the *Passetto*	14 Government Palace
5 Office of the Pope		
6 Vatican Museums		

ANGELS
AND
DEMONS

PROLOGUE

Physicist Leonardo Vetra smelled burning flesh, and he knew it was his own. He stared up in terror at the dark figure looming over him. 'What do you want!'

'*La chiave*,' the raspy voice replied. 'The password.'

'But . . . I don't—'

The intruder pressed down again, grinding the white hot object deeper into Vetra's chest. There was the hiss of broiling flesh.

Vetra cried out in agony. 'There *is* no password!' He felt himself drifting toward unconsciousness.

The figure glared. '*Ne avevo paura.* I was afraid of that.'

Vetra fought to keep his senses, but the darkness was closing in. His only solace was in knowing his attacker would never obtain what he had come for. A moment later, however, the figure produced a blade and brought it to Vetra's face. The blade hovered. Carefully. Surgically.

'For the love of God!' Vetra screamed. But it was too late.

1

High atop the steps of the Great Pyramid of Giza, a young woman laughed and called down to him. 'Robert, hurry up! I knew I should have married a younger man!' Her smile was magic.

He struggled to keep up, but his legs felt like stone. 'Wait,' he begged. 'Please . . .'

As he climbed, his vision began to blur. There was a thundering in his ears. *I must reach her!* But when he looked up again, the woman had disappeared. In her place stood an old man with rotting teeth. The man stared down, curling his lips into a lonely grimace. Then he let out a scream of anguish that resounded across the desert.

Robert Langdon awoke with a start from his nightmare. The phone beside his bed was ringing. Dazed, he picked up the receiver.

'Hello?'

'I'm looking for Robert Langdon,' a man's voice said.

Langdon sat up in his empty bed and tried to clear his mind. 'This . . . is Robert Langdon.' He squinted at his digital clock. It was 5.18 a.m.

'I must see you immediately.'

'Who is this?'

'My name is Maximilian Kohler. I'm a discrete particle physicist.'

'A *what*?' Langdon could barely focus. 'Are you sure you've got the right Langdon?'

'You're a professor of religious iconology at Harvard University. You've written three books on symbology and—'

'Do you know what time it is?'

'I apologize. I have something you need to see. I can't discuss it on the phone.'

A knowing groan escaped Langdon's lips. This had happened before. One of the perils of writing books about religious symbology was the calls from religious zealots who wanted him to confirm their latest sign from God. Last month, a stripper from Oklahoma had promised Langdon the best sex of his life if he would fly down and verify the authenticity of a cruciform that had magically appeared on her bed sheets. *The Shroud of Tulsa*, Langdon had called it.

'How did you get my number?' Langdon tried to be polite, despite the hour.

'On the Worldwide Web. The site for your book.'

Langdon frowned. He was damn sure his book's site did not include his home phone number. The man was obviously lying.

'I need to see you,' the caller insisted. 'I'll pay you well.'

Now Langdon was getting mad. 'I'm sorry, but I really—'

'If you leave immediately, you can be here by—'

'I'm not going anywhere! It's five o'clock in the morning!' Langdon hung up and collapsed back in bed. He closed his eyes and tried to fall back asleep. It was no use. The dream was emblazoned in his mind. Reluctantly, he put on his robe and went downstairs.

Robert Langdon wandered barefoot through his deserted Massachusetts Victorian home and nursed his ritual insomnia remedy – a mug of steaming Nestlé's Quik. The April moon filtered through the bay windows and played on the oriental carpets. Langdon's colleagues often joked that his place looked more like an anthropology museum than a home. His shelves were packed with religious artifacts from around the world – an *ekuaba* from Ghana, a gold cross from Spain, a cycladic idol from the Aegean, and even a rare woven *boccus* from Borneo, a young warrior's symbol of perpetual youth.

As Langdon sat on his brass Maharishi's chest and savored the warmth of the chocolate, the bay window caught his reflection. The image was distorted and pale . . . like a ghost. *An aging ghost*, he thought, cruelly reminded that his youthful spirit was living in a mortal shell.

Although not overly handsome in a classical sense, the forty-five-year-old Langdon had what his female colleagues referred to as an 'erudite' appeal – wisps of gray in his thick brown hair, probing blue eyes, an arrestingly deep voice, and the strong, carefree smile of a collegiate athlete. A varsity diver in prep school and college, Langdon still had the body of a swimmer, a toned, six-foot physique that he vigilantly maintained with fifty laps a day in the university pool.

Langdon's friends had always viewed him as a bit of an enigma – a man caught between centuries. On weekends he could be seen lounging on the quad in blue jeans, discussing computer graphics or religious history with students; other times he could be spotted in his Harris tweed and paisley vest, photographed in the pages of upscale art magazines at museum openings where he had been asked to lecture.

Although a tough teacher and strict disciplinarian, Langdon was the first to embrace what he hailed as the 'lost art of good clean fun.' He relished recreation with an infectious fanaticism that had earned him a fraternal acceptance among his students. His campus nickname – 'The Dolphin' – was a reference both to his affable nature and his legendary ability to dive into a pool and outmaneuver the entire opposing squad in a water polo match.

As Langdon sat alone, absently gazing into the darkness, the silence of his home was shattered again, this time by the ring of his fax machine. Too exhausted to be annoyed, Langdon forced a tired chuckle.

God's people, he thought. *Two thousand years of waiting for their Messiah, and they're still persistent as hell.*

Wearily, he returned his empty mug to the kitchen and walked slowly to his oak-paneled study. The incoming fax lay in the tray. Sighing, he scooped up the paper and looked at it.

Instantly, a wave of nausea hit him.

The image on the page was that of a human corpse. The body had been stripped naked, and its head had been twisted, facing completely backward. On the victim's chest was a terrible burn. The man had been branded ... imprinted with a single word. It was a word Langdon knew well. Very well. He stared at the ornate lettering in disbelief.

'Illuminati,' he stammered, his heart pounding. *It can't be . . .*

In slow motion, afraid of what he was about to witness, Langdon rotated the fax 180 degrees. He looked at the word upside down.

Instantly, the breath went out of him. It was like he had been hit by a truck. Barely able to believe his eyes, he rotated the fax again, reading the brand right-side up and then upside down.

'Illuminati,' he whispered.

Stunned, Langdon collapsed in a chair. He sat a moment in utter bewilderment. Gradually, his eyes were drawn to the blinking red light on his fax machine. Whoever had sent this fax was still on the line . . . waiting to talk. Langdon gazed at the blinking light a long time.

Then, trembling, he picked up the receiver.

2

'Do I have your attention now?' the man's voice said when Langdon finally answered the line.

'Yes, sir, you damn well do. You want to explain yourself?'

'I tried to tell you before.' The voice was rigid,

mechanical. 'I'm a physicist. I run a research facility. We've had a murder. You saw the body.'

'How did you find me?' Langdon could barely focus. His mind was racing from the image on the fax.

'I already told you. The Worldwide Web. The site for your book, *The Art of the Illuminati.*'

Langdon tried to gather his thoughts. His book was virtually unknown in mainstream literary circles, but it had developed quite a following on-line. Nonetheless, the caller's claim still made no sense. 'That page has no contact information,' Langdon challenged. 'I'm certain of it.'

'I have people here at the lab very adept at extracting user information from the Web.'

Langdon was skeptical. 'Sounds like your lab knows *a lot* about the Web.'

'We should,' the man fired back. 'We *invented* it.'

Something in the man's voice told Langdon he was not joking.

'I must see you,' the caller insisted. 'This is not a matter we can discuss on the phone. My lab is only an hour's flight from Boston.'

Langdon stood in the dim light of his study and analyzed the fax in his hand. The image was overpowering, possibly representing the epigraphical find of the century, a decade of his research confirmed in a single symbol.

'It's urgent,' the voice pressured.

Langdon's eyes were locked on the brand. *Illuminati,* he read over and over. His work had always been based on the symbolic equivalent of fossils – ancient documents and historical hearsay – but this image before him was today. Present tense. He felt like a paleontologist coming face to face with a living dinosaur.

'I've taken the liberty of sending a plane for you,' the voice said. 'It will be in Boston in twenty minutes.'

Langdon felt his mouth go dry. *An hour's flight* . . .

'Please forgive my presumption,' the voice said. 'I need you here.'

Langdon looked again at the fax – an ancient myth confirmed in black and white. The implications were frightening. He gazed absently through the bay window. The first hint of dawn was sifting through the birch trees in his backyard, but the view looked somehow different this morning. As an odd combination of fear and exhilaration settled over him, Langdon knew he had no choice.

'You win,' he said. 'Tell me where to meet the plane.'

3

Thousands of miles away, two men were meeting. The chamber was dark. Medieval. Stone.

'Benvenuto,' the man in charge said. He was seated in the shadows, out of sight. 'Were you successful?'

'Si,' the dark figure replied. *'Perfettamente.'* His words were as hard as the rock walls.

'And there will be no doubt who is responsible?'

'None.'

'Superb. Do you have what I asked for?'

The killer's eyes glistened, black like oil. He produced a heavy electronic device and set it on the table.

The man in the shadows seemed pleased. 'You have done well.'

'Serving the brotherhood is an honor,' the killer replied.

'Phase two begins shortly. Get some rest. Tonight we change the world.'

4

Robert Langdon's Saab 900S tore out of the Callahan Tunnel and emerged on the east side of Boston Harbor near the entrance to Logan Airport. Checking his directions Langdon found Aviation Road and turned left past the old Eastern Airlines Building. Three hundred yards down the access road a hangar loomed in the darkness. A large number '4' was painted on it. He pulled into the parking lot and got out of his car.

A round-faced man in a blue flight suit emerged from behind the building. 'Robert Langdon?' he called. The man's voice was friendly. He had an accent Langdon couldn't place.

'That's me,' Langdon said, locking his car.

'Perfect timing,' the man said. 'I've just landed. Follow me, please.'

As they circled the building, Langdon felt tense. He was not accustomed to cryptic phone calls and secret rendezvous with strangers. Not knowing what to expect he had donned his usual classroom attire – a pair of chinos, a turtleneck, and a Harris tweed suit jacket. As they walked, he thought about the fax in his jacket pocket, still unable to believe the image it depicted.

The pilot seemed to sense Langdon's anxiety. 'Flying's not a problem for you, is it, sir?'

'Not at all,' Langdon replied. *Branded corpses are a problem for me. Flying I can handle.*

The man led Langdon the length of the hangar. They rounded the corner onto the runway.

Langdon stopped dead in his tracks and gaped at the aircraft parked on the tarmac. 'We're riding in *that*?'

The man grinned. 'Like it?'

Langdon stared a long moment. 'Like it? What the hell *is* it?'

The craft before them was enormous. It was vaguely reminiscent of the space shuttle except that the top had been shaved off, leaving it perfectly flat. Parked there on the runway, it resembled a colossal wedge. Langdon's first impression was that he must be dreaming. The vehicle looked as airworthy as a Buick. The wings were practically nonexistent – just two stubby fins on the rear of the fuselage. A pair of dorsal guiders rose out of the aft section. The rest of the plane was hull – about 200 feet from front to back – no windows, nothing but hull.

'Two hundred fifty thousand kilos fully fueled,' the pilot offered, like a father bragging abut his newborn. 'Runs on slush hydrogen. The shell's a titanium matrix with silicon carbide fibers. She packs a 20:1 thrust/weight ratio; most jets run at 7:1. The director must be in one helluva hurry to see you. He doesn't usually send the big boy.'

'This thing *flies*?' Langdon said.

The pilot smiled. 'Oh yeah.' He led Langdon across the tarmac toward the plane. 'Looks kind of startling, I know, but you better get used to it. In five years, all you'll see are these babies – HSCT's – High Speed Civil Transports. Our lab's one of the first to own one.'

Must be one hell of a lab, Langdon thought.

'This one's a prototype of the Boeing X-33,' the pilot continued, 'but there are dozens of others – the National Aero Space Plane, the Russians have Scramjet, the Brits have HOTOL. The future's here, it's just taking some time to get to the public sector. You can kiss conventional jets good-bye.'

Langdon looked up warily at the craft. 'I think I'd prefer a conventional jet.'

The pilot motioned up the gangplank. 'This way, please, Mr Langdon. Watch your step.'

Minutes later, Langdon was seated inside the empty cabin. The pilot buckled him into the front row and disappeared toward the front of the aircraft.

The cabin itself looked surprisingly like a wide-body commercial airliner. The only exception was that it had no windows, which made Langdon uneasy. He had been haunted his whole life by a mild case of claustrophobia – the vestige of a childhood incident he had never quite overcome.

Langdon's aversion to closed spaces was by no means debilitating, but it had always frustrated him. It manifested itself in subtle ways. He avoided enclosed sports like racquetball or squash, and he had gladly paid a small fortune for his airy, high-ceilinged Victorian home even though economical faculty housing was readily available. Langdon had often suspected his attraction to the art world as a young boy sprang from his love of museums' wide open spaces.

The engines roared to life beneath him, sending a deep shudder through the hull. Langdon swallowed hard and waited. He felt the plane start taxiing. Piped-in country music began playing quietly overhead.

A phone on the wall beside him beeped twice. Langdon lifted the receiver.

'Hello?'

'Comfortable, Mr Langdon?'

'Not at all.'

'Just relax. We'll be there in an hour.'

'And where exactly is *there*?' Langdon asked, realizing he had no idea where he was headed.

'Geneva,' the pilot replied, revving the engines. 'The lab's in Geneva.'

'Geneva,' Langdon repeated, feeling a little better. 'Upstate New York. I've actually got family near Seneca Lake. I wasn't aware Geneva had a physics lab.'

The pilot laughed. 'Not Geneva, *New York*, Mr Langdon. Geneva, *Switzerland*.'

The word took a long moment to register. 'Switzerland?' Langdon felt his pulse surge. 'I thought you said the lab was only an hour away!'

'It is, Mr Langdon.' The pilot chuckled. 'This plane goes Mach fifteen.'

5

On a busy European street, the killer serpentined through a crowd. He was a powerful man. Dark and potent. Deceptively agile. His muscles still felt hard from the thrill of his meeting.

It went well, he told himself. Although his employer had never revealed his face, the killer felt honored to be in his presence. *Had it really been only fifteen days since his employer had first made contact?* The killer still remembered every word of that call . . .

'My name is Janus,' the caller had said. 'We are kins-men of a sort. We share an enemy. I hear your skills are for hire.'

'It depends whom you represent,' the killer replied. The caller told him.

'Is this your idea of a joke?'

'You have heard our name, I see,' the caller replied.

'Of course. The brotherhood is legendary.'

'And yet you find yourself doubting I am genuine.'

'Everyone knows the brothers have faded to dust.'

'A devious ploy. The most dangerous enemy is that which no one fears.'

The killer was skeptical. 'The brotherhood endures?'

'Deeper underground than ever before. Our roots infiltrate everything you see . . . even the sacred fortress of our most sworn enemy.'

'Impossible. They are invulnerable.'

'Our reach is far.'

'No one's reach is that far.'

'Very soon, you will believe. An irrefutable demon-stration of the brotherhood's power has already transpired. A single act of treachery and proof.'

'What have you done?'

The caller told him.

The killer's eyes went wide. 'An impossible task.'

The next day, newspapers around the globe carried the same headline.The killer became a believer.

Now, fifteen days later, the killer's faith had solidi-fied beyond the shadow of a doubt. *The brotherhood endures,* he thought. *Tonight they will surface to reveal their power.*

As he made his way through the streets, his black

eyes gleamed with foreboding. One of the most covert and feared fraternities ever to walk the earth had called on him for service. *They have chosen wisely*, he thought. His reputation for secrecy was exceeded only by that of his deadliness.

So far, he had served them nobly. He had made his kill and delivered the item to Janus as requested. Now, it was up to Janus to use his power to ensure the item's placement.

The placement . . .

The killer wondered how Janus could possibly handle such a staggering task. The man obviously had connections on the inside. The brotherhood's dominion seemed limitless.

Janus, the killer thought. *A code name, obviously*. Was it a reference, he wondered, to the Roman two-faced god . . . or to the moon of Saturn? Not that it made any difference. Janus wielded unfathomable power. He had proven that beyond a doubt.

As the killer walked, he imagined his ancestors smiling down on him. Today he was fighting *their* battle, he was fighting the same enemy they had fought for ages, as far back as the eleventh century . . . when the enemy's crusading armies had first pillaged his land, raping and killing his people, declaring them unclean, defiling their temples and gods.

His ancestors had formed a small but deadly army to defend themselves. The army became famous across the land as protectors – skilled executioners who wandered the countryside slaughtering any of the enemy they could find. They were renowned not only for their brutal killings, but also for celebrating their slayings by plunging themselves into drug-induced stupors. Their drug of choice was

31

a potent intoxicant they called *hashish*.

As their notoriety spread, these lethal men became known by a single word – *Hassassin* – literally 'the followers of hashish.' The name *Hassassin* became synonymous with death in almost every language on earth. The word was still used today, even in modern English . . . but like the craft of killing, the word had evolved.

It was now pronounced *assassin*.

6

Sixty-four minutes had passed when an incredulous and slightly airsick Robert Langdon stepped down the gangplank onto the sun-drenched runway. A crisp breeze rustled the lapels of his tweed jacket. The open space felt wonderful. He squinted out at the lush green valley rising to snowcapped peaks all around them.

I'm dreaming, he told himself. *Any minute now I'll be waking up.*

'Welcome to Switzerland,' the pilot said, yelling over the roar of the X-33's misted-fuel HEDM engines winding down behind them.

Langdon checked his watch. It read 7.07 a.m.

'You just crossed six time zones,' the pilot offered. 'It's a little past 1 p.m. here.'

Langdon reset his watch.

'How do you feel?'

He rubbed his stomach. 'Like I've been eating Styrofoam.'

The pilot nodded. 'Altitude sickness. We were at

sixty thousand feet. You're thirty per cent lighter up there. Lucky we only did a puddle jump. If we'd gone to Tokyo I'd have taken her all the way up – a hundred miles. Now *that'll* get your insides rolling.'

Langdon gave a wan nod and counted himself lucky. All things considered, the flight had been remarkably ordinary. Aside from a bone-crunching acceleration during take off, the plane's motion had been fairly typical – occasional minor turbulence, a few pressure changes as they'd climbed, but nothing at all to suggest they had been hurtling through space at the mind-numbing speed of 11,000 miles per hour.

A handful of technicians scurried onto the runway to tend to the X-33. The pilot escorted Langdon to a black Peugeot sedan in a parking area beside the control tower. Moments later they were speeding down a paved road that stretched out across the valley floor. A faint cluster of buildings rose in the distance. Outside, the grassy plains tore by in a blur.

Langdon watched in disbelief as the pilot pushed the speedometer up around 170 kilometers an hour – over 100 miles per hour. *What is it with this guy and speed?* he wondered.

'Five kilometers to the lab,' the pilot said. 'I'll have you there in two minutes.'

Langdon searched in vain for a seat belt. *Why not make it three and get us there alive?*

The car raced on.

'Do you like Reba?' the pilot asked, jamming a cassette into the tape deck.

A woman started singing. 'It's just the fear of being alone . . .'

No fear here, Langdon thought absently. His female colleagues often ribbed him that his collection of

33

museum-quality artifacts was nothing more than a transparent attempt to fill an empty home, a home they insisted would benefit greatly from the presence of a woman. Langdon always laughed it off, reminding them he already had three loves in his life – symbology, water polo, and bachelorhood – the latter being a freedom that enabled him to travel the world, sleep as late as he wanted, and enjoy quiet nights at home with a brandy and a good book.

'We're like a small city,' the pilot said, pulling Langdon from his daydream. 'Not just labs. We've got supermarkets, a hospital, even a cinema.'

Langdon nodded blankly and looked out at the sprawling expanse of buildings rising before them.

'In fact,' the pilot added, 'we possess the largest machine on earth.'

'Really?' Langdon scanned the countryside.

'You won't see it out there, sir.' The pilot smiled. 'It's buried six stories below the earth.'

Langdon didn't have time to ask. Without warning the pilot jammed on the brakes. The car skidded to a stop outside a reinforced sentry booth.

Langdon read the sign before them. SECURITE. ARRETEZ. He suddenly felt a wave of panic, realizing where he was. 'My God! I didn't bring my passport!'

'Passports are unnecessary,' the driver assured. 'We have a standing arrangement with the Swiss government.'

Langdon watched dumbfounded as his driver gave the guard an ID. The sentry ran it through an electronic authentication device. The machine flashed green.

'Passenger name?'

'Robert Langdon,' the driver replied.

'Guest of?'

'The director.'

The sentry arched his eyebrows. He turned and checked a computer printout, verifying it against the data on his computer screen. Then he returned to the window. 'Enjoy your stay, Mr Langdon.'

The car shot off again, accelerating another 200 yards around a sweeping rotary that led to the facility's main entrance. Looming before them was a rectangular, ultramodern structure of glass and steel. Langdon was amazed by the building's striking transparent design. He had always had a fond love of architecture.

'The Glass Cathedral,' the escort offered.

'A church?'

'Hell, no. A church is the one thing we *don't* have. Physics is the religion around here. Use the Lord's name in vain all you like,' he laughed, 'just don't slander any quarks or mesons.'

Langdon sat bewildered as the driver swung the car around and brought it to a stop in front of the glass building. *Quarks and mesons? No border control? Mach 15 jets? Who the hell ARE these guys?* The engraved granite slab in front of the building bore the answer:

(CERN)
*Conseil Européen pour la
Recherche Nucléaire*

'Nuclear Research?' Langdon asked, fairly certain his translation was correct.

The driver did not answer. He was leaning forward, busily adjusting the car's cassette player. 'This is your stop. The director will meet you at this entrance.'

Langdon noted a man in a wheelchair exiting the building. He looked to be in his early sixties. Gaunt and totally bald with a sternly set jaw, he wore a white lab coat and dress shoes propped firmly on the wheelchair's footrest. Even at a distance his eyes looked lifeless – like two gray stones.

'Is that him?' Langdon asked.

The driver looked up. 'Well, I'll be.' He turned and gave Langdon an ominous smile. 'Speak of the devil.'

Uncertain what to expect, Langdon stepped from the vehicle.

The man in the wheelchair accelerated toward Langdon and offered a clammy hand. 'Mr Langdon? We spoke on the phone. My name is Maximilian Kohler.'

7

Maximilian Kohler, director general of CERN, was known behind his back as *König* – King. It was a title more of fear than reverence for the figure who ruled over his dominion from a wheelchair throne. Although few knew him personally, the horrific story of how he had been crippled was lore at CERN, and there were few there who blamed him for his bitterness . . . nor for his sworn dedication to pure science.

Langdon had only been in Kohler's presence a few moments and already sensed the director was a man who kept his distance. Langdon found himself practically jogging to keep up with Kohler's electric wheelchair as it sped silently toward the main entrance. The wheelchair was like none Langdon had ever seen – equipped with a bank of electronics including a multiline phone, a paging system, computer screen, even a small, detachable video camera. King Kohler's mobile command center.

Langdon followed through a mechanical door into CERN's voluminous main lobby.

The Glass Cathedral, Langdon mused, gazing upward toward heaven.

Overhead, the bluish glass roof shimmered in the afternoon sun, casting rays of geometric patterns in the air and giving the room a sense of grandeur. Angular shadows fell like veins across the white tiled walls and down to the marble floors. The air smelled clean, sterile. A handful of scientists moved briskly about, their footsteps echoing in the resonant space.

'This way, please, Mr Langdon.' His voice sounded almost computerized. His accent was rigid and precise, like his stern features. Kohler coughed and wiped his mouth on a white handkerchief as he fixed his dead gray eyes on Langdon. 'Please hurry.' His wheelchair seemed to leap across the tiled floor.

Langdon followed past what seemed to be countless hallways branching off the main atrium. Every hallway was alive with activity. The scientists who saw Kohler seemed to stare in surprise, eyeing Langdon as if wondering who he must be to command such company.

'I'm embarrassed to admit,' Langdon ventured, trying to make conversation, 'that I've never heard of CERN.'

'Not surprising,' Kohler replied, his clipped response sounding harshly efficient. 'Most Americans do not see Europe as the world leader in scientific research. They see us as nothing but a quaint shopping district – an odd perception if you consider the nationalities of men like Einstein, Galileo, and Newton.'

Langdon was unsure how to respond. He pulled the fax from his pocket. 'This man in the photograph, can you—'

Kohler cut him off with a wave of his hand. 'Please. Not here. I am taking you to him now.' He held out his hand. 'Perhaps I should take that.'

Langdon handed over the fax and fell silently into step.

Kohler took a sharp left and entered a wide hallway adorned with awards and commendations. A particularly large plaque dominated the entry. Langdon slowed to read the engraved bronze as they passed.

ARS ELECTRONICA AWARD
For Cultural Innovation in the Digital Age
Awarded to Tim Berners Lee and CERN
for the invention of the
WORLDWIDE WEB

Well I'll be damned, Langdon thought, reading the text. *This guy wasn't kidding.* Langdon had always thought of the Web as an American invention. Then again, his knowledge was limited to the site for his own book and the occasional on-line exploration of the Louvre or El Prado on his old Macintosh.

'The Web,' Kohler said, coughing again and wiping his mouth, 'began here as a network of in-house computer sites. It enabled scientists from different departments to share daily findings with one another. Of course, the entire world is under the impression the Web is U.S. technology.'

38

Langdon followed down the hall. 'Why not set the record straight?'

Kohler shrugged, apparently disinterested. 'A petty misconception over a petty technology. CERN is far greater than a global connection of computers. Our scientists produce miracles almost daily.'

Langdon gave Kohler a questioning look. *'Miracles?'* The word 'miracle' was certainly not part of the vocabulary around Harvard's Fairchild Science Building. *Miracles* were left for the School of Divinity.

'You sound skeptical,' Kohler said. 'I thought you were a religious symbologist. Do you not believe in miracles?'

'I'm undecided on miracles,' Langdon said. *Particularly those that take place in science labs.*

'Perhaps miracle is the wrong word. I was simply trying to speak your language.'

'My language?' Langdon was suddenly uncomfortable. 'Not to disappoint you, sir, but I study religious *symbology* – I'm an academic, not a priest.'

Kohler slowed suddenly and turned, his gaze softening a bit. 'Of course. How simple of me. One does not need to have cancer to analyze its symptoms.'

Langdon had never heard it put quite that way.

As they moved down the hallway, Kohler gave an accepting nod. 'I suspect you and I will understand each other perfectly, Mr Langdon.'

Somehow Langdon doubted it.

As the pair hurried on, Langdon began to sense a deep rumbling up ahead. The noise got more and more pronounced with every step, reverberating through the walls. It seemed to be coming from the end of the hallway in front of them.

'What's that?' Langdon finally asked, having to yell. He felt like they were approaching an active volcano.

'Free Fall Tube,' Kohler replied, his hollow voice cutting the air effortlessly. He offered no other explanation.

Langdon didn't ask. He was exhausted, and Maximilian Kohler seemed disinterested in winning any hospitality awards. Langdon reminded himself why he was here. *Illuminati*. He assumed somewhere in this colossal facility was a body . . . a body branded with a symbol he had just flown 3,000 miles to see.

As they approached the end of the hall, the rumble became almost deafening, vibrating up through Langdon's soles. They rounded the bend, and a viewing gallery appeared on the right. Four thick-paned portals were embedded in a curved wall, like windows in a submarine. Langdon stopped and looked through one of the holes.

Professor Robert Langdon had seen some strange things in his life, but this was the strangest. He blinked a few times, wondering if he was hallucinating. He was staring into an enormous circular chamber. Inside the chamber, floating as though weightless, were *people*. Three of them. One waved and did a somersault in midair.

My God, he thought. *I'm in the land of Oz*.

The floor of the room was a mesh grid, like a giant sheet of chicken wire. Visible beneath the grid was the metallic blur of a huge propeller.

'Free fall tube,' Kohler said, stopping to wait for him. 'Indoor skydiving. For stress relief. It's a vertical wind tunnel.'

Langdon looked on in amazement. One of the free fallers, an obese woman, maneuvered toward the

40

window. She was being buffeted by the air currents but grinned and flashed Langdon the thumbs-up sign. Langdon smiled weakly and returned the gesture, wondering if she knew it was the ancient phallic symbol for masculine virility.

The heavyset woman, Langdon noticed, was the only one wearing what appeared to be a miniature parachute. The swathe of fabric billowed over her like a toy. 'What's her little chute for?' Langdon asked Kohler. 'It can't be more than a yard in diameter.'

'Friction,' Kohler said. 'Decreases her aerodynamics so the fan can lift her.' He started down the corridor again. 'One square yard of drag will slow a falling body almost twenty percent.'

Langdon nodded blankly.

He never suspected that later that night, in a country hundreds of miles away, the information would save his life.

8

When Kohler and Langdon emerged from the rear of CERN's main complex into the stark Swiss sunlight, Langdon felt as if he'd been transported home. The scene before him looked like an Ivy League campus.

A grassy slope cascaded downward onto an expansive lowlands where clusters of sugar maples dotted quadrangles bordered by brick dormitories and footpaths. Scholarly looking individuals with stacks of books hustled in and out of buildings. As if to accentuate the collegiate atmosphere, two longhaired hippies hurled a Frisbee back and forth while enjoying Mahler's Fourth Symphony blaring from a dorm window.

'These are our residential dorms,' Kohler explained as he accelerated his wheelchair down the path toward the buildings. 'We have over three thousand physicists here. CERN single-handedly employs more than half of the world's particle physicists – the brightest minds on earth – Germans, Japanese, Italians, Dutch, you name it. Our physicists represent over five hundred universities and sixty nationalities.'

Langdon was amazed. 'How do they all communicate?'

'English, of course. The universal language of science.'

Langdon had always heard *math* was the universal language of science, but he was too tired to argue. He dutifully followed Kohler down the path.

Halfway to the bottom, a young man jogged by. His T-shirt proclaimed the message: NO GUT, NO GLORY!

Langdon looked after him, mystified. 'Gut?'

'General Unified Theory,' Kohler quipped. 'The theory of everything.'

'I see,' Langdon said, not seeing at all.

'Are you familiar with particle physics, Mr Langdon?'

Langdon shrugged. 'I'm familiar with general physics – falling bodies, that sort of thing.' His years of high-diving experience had given him a profound respect for the awesome power of gravitational acceleration. 'Particle physics is the study of atoms, isn't it?'

Kohler shook his head. 'Atoms look like planets compared to what we deal with. Our interests lie with an atom's *nucleus* – a mere ten-thousandth the size of the whole.' He coughed again, sounding sick. 'The men and women of CERN are here to find answers to the same questions man has been asking since the beginning of time. Where did we come from? What are we made of?'

'And these answers are in a physics lab?'

'You sound surprised.'

'I am. The questions seem spiritual.'

'Mr Langdon, all questions were once spiritual. Since the beginning of time, spirituality and religion have been called on to fill in the gaps that science did not understand. The rising and setting of the sun was once attributed to *Helios* and a flaming chariot. Earthquakes and tidal waves were the wrath of Poseidon. Science has now proven those gods to be false idols. Soon *all* Gods will be proven to be false idols. Science has now provided answers to almost every question man can ask. There are only a few questions left, and they are the esoteric ones. Where do we come from? What are we doing here? What is the meaning of life and the universe?'

Langdon was amazed. 'And these are questions CERN is trying to answer?'

'Correction. These are questions we *are* answering.'

Langdon fell silent as the two men wound through the residential quadrangles. As they walked, a Frisbee sailed overhead and skidded to a stop directly in front of them. Kohler ignored it and kept going.

A voice called out from across the quad. *'S'il vous plaît!'*

Langdon looked over. An elderly white-haired man in a COLLEGE PARIS sweatshirt waved to him. Langdon picked up the Frisbee and expertly threw it back. The old man caught it on one finger and bounded it a few times before whipping it over his shoulder to his partner. 'Merci!' he called to Langdon.

'Congratulations,' Kohler said when Langdon finally caught up. 'You just played toss with a Nobel prize-winner, Georges Charpak, inventor of the multi-wire proportional chamber.'

Langdon nodded. *My lucky day.*

It took Langdon and Kohler three more minutes to reach their destination – a large, well-kept dormitory sitting in a grove of aspens. Compared to the other dorms, this structure seemed luxurious. The carved stone sign in front read BUILDING C.

Imaginative title, Langdon thought.

But despite its sterile name, Building C appealed to Langdon's sense of architectural style – conservative and solid. It had a red brick facade, an ornate balustrade, and sat framed by sculpted symmetrical hedges. As the two men ascended the stone path toward the entry, they passed under a gateway formed by a pair of marble columns. Someone had put a sticky-note on one of them.

THIS COLUMN IS IONIC

Physicist graffiti? Langdon mused, eyeing the column and chuckling to himself. 'I'm relieved to see that even brilliant physicists make mistakes.'

Kohler looked over. 'What do you mean?'

'Whoever wrote that note made a mistake. That column isn't Ionic. Ionic columns are uniform in width. That one's tapered. It's Doric – the Greek counterpart. A common mistake.'

Kohler did not smile. 'The author meant it as a joke,

Mr Langdon. *Ionic* means containing ions – electrically charged particles. Most objects contain them.'

Langdon looked back at the column and groaned.

Langdon was still feeling stupid when he stepped from the elevator on the top floor of Building C. He followed Kohler down a well-appointed corridor. The decor was unexpected – traditional colonial French – a cherry divan, porcelain floor vase, and scrolled woodwork.

'We like to keep our tenured scientists comfortable,' Kohler explained.

Evidently, Langdon thought. 'So the man in the fax lived up here? One of your upper-level employees?'

'Quite,' Kohler said. 'He missed a meeting with me this morning and did not answer his page. I came up here to locate him and found him dead in his living room.'

Langdon felt a sudden chill realizing that he was about to see a dead body. His stomach had never been particularly stalwart. It was a weakness he'd discovered as an art student when the teacher informed the class that Leonardo da Vinci had gained his expertise in the human form by exhuming corpses and dissecting their musculature.

Kohler led the way to the far end of the hallway. There was a single door. 'The Penthouse, as you would say,' Kohler announced, dabbing a bead of perspiration from his forehead.

Langdon eyed the lone oak door before them. The name plate read:

LEONARDO VETRA

'Leonardo Vetra,' Kohler said, 'would have been

fifty-eight next week. He was one of the most brilliant scientists of our time. His death is a profound loss for science.'

For an instant Langdon thought he sensed emotion in Kohler's hardened face. But as quickly as it had come, it was gone. Kohler reached in his pocket and began sifting through a large key ring.

An odd thought suddenly occurred to Langdon. The building seemed deserted. 'Where is everyone?' he asked. The lack of activity was hardly what he expected considering they were about to enter a murder scene.

'The residents are in their labs,' Kohler replied, finding the key.

'I mean the *police*,' Langdon clarified. 'Have they left already?'

Kohler paused, his key halfway into the lock. 'Police?'

Langdon's eyes met the director's. 'Police. You sent me a fax of a homicide. You *must* have called the police.'

'I most certainly have not.'

'What?'

Kohler's gray eyes sharpened. 'The situation is complex, Mr Langdon.'

Langdon felt a wave of apprehension. 'But . . . certainly someone else knows about this!'

'Yes. Leonardo's adopted daughter. She is also a physicist here at CERN. She and her father share a lab. They are partners. Ms Vetra has been away this week doing field research. I have notified her of her father's death, and she is returning as we speak.'

'But a man has been murd—'

'A formal investigation,' Kohler said, his voice firm,

46

'will take place. However, it will most certainly involve a search of Vetra's lab, a space he and his daughter hold most private. Therefore, it will wait until Ms Vetra has arrived. I feel I owe her at least that modicum of discretion.'

Kohler turned the key.

As the door swung open, a blast of icy air hissed into the hall and hit Langdon in the face. He fell back in bewilderment. He was gazing across the threshold of an alien world. The flat before him was immersed in a thick, white fog. The mist swirled in smoky vortexes around the furniture and shrouded the room in opaque haze.

'What the . . .?' Langdon stammered.

'Freon cooling system,' Kohler replied. 'I chilled the flat to preserve the body.'

Langdon buttoned his tweed jacket against the cold. *I'm in Oz*, he thought. *And I forgot my magic slippers.*

9

The corpse on the floor before Langdon was hideous. The late Leonardo Vetra lay on his back, stripped naked, his skin bluish-gray. His neck bones were jutting out where they had been broken, and his head was twisted completely backward, pointing the wrong way. His face was out of view, pressed against the floor. The man lay in a frozen puddle of his own urine, the hair around his shriveled genitals spidered with frost.

Fighting a wave of nausea, Langdon let his eyes fall to the victim's chest. Although Langdon had stared at the symmetrical wound a dozen times on the fax, the burn was infinitely more commanding in real life. The raised, broiled flesh was perfectly delineated . . . the symbol flawlessly formed.

Langdon wondered if the intense chill now raking through his body was the air-conditioning or his utter amazement with the significance of what he was now staring at.

His heart pounded as he circled the body, reading the word upside down, reaffirming the genius of the symmetry. The symbol seemed even less conceivable now that he was staring at it.

'Mr Langdon?'

Langdon did not hear. He was in another world . . . his world, his element, a world where history, myth, and fact collided, flooding his senses. The gears turned.

'Mr Langdon?' Kohler's eyes probed expectantly.

Langdon did not look up. His disposition now intensified, his focus total. 'How much do you already know?'

'Only what I had time to read on your website. The word *Illuminati* means "the enlightened ones." It is the name of some sort of ancient brotherhood.'

Langdon nodded. 'Had you heard the name before?'

'Not until I saw it branded on Mr Vetra.'

'So you ran a web search for it?'

'Yes.'

'And the word returned hundreds of references, no doubt.'

'Thousands,' Kohler said. 'Yours, however, contained references to Harvard, Oxford, a reputable publisher, as well as a list of related publications. As a scientist I have come to learn that information is only as valuable as its source. Your credentials seemed authentic.'

Langdon's eyes were still riveted on the body.

Kohler said nothing more. He simply stared, apparently waiting for Langdon to shed some light on the scene before them.

Langdon looked up, glancing around the frozen flat. 'Perhaps we should discuss this in a warmer place?'

'This room is fine.' Kohler seemed oblivious to the cold. 'We'll talk here.'

Langdon frowned. The Illuminati history was by no means a simple one. *I'll freeze to death trying to explain it.* He gazed again at the brand, feeling a renewed sense of awe.

Although accounts of the Illuminati emblem were legendary in modern symbology, no academic had ever actually *seen* it. Ancient documents described the symbol as an *ambigram* – *ambi* meaning 'both' – signifying it was legible *both* ways. And although ambigrams were common in symbology – swastikas, yin yang, Jewish stars, simple crosses – the idea that a *word* could be crafted into an ambigram seemed utterly impossible. Modern symbologists had tried for years to forge the word 'Illuminati' into a perfectly symmetrical style, but they had failed miserably. Most academics had now decided the symbol's existence was a myth.

'So who are the Illuminati?' Kohler demanded.

Yes, Langdon thought, *who indeed*? He began his tale.

'Since the beginning of history,' Langdon explained, 'a deep rift has existed between science and religion. Outspoken scientists like Giordano Bruno—'

'Were murdered,' Kohler interjected. 'Murdered by the church for revealing scientific truths. Religion has always persecuted science.'

'Yes. But in the 1500s, a group of men in Rome fought back against the church. Some of Italy's most enlightened men – physicists, mathematicians, astronomers – began meeting secretly to share their concerns about the church's inaccurate teachings. They feared that the church's monopoly on "truth" threatened academic enlightenment around the world. They founded the world's first scientific think tank, calling themselves "the enlightened ones." '

'The Illuminati.'

'Yes,' Langdon said. 'Europe's most learned minds . . . dedicated to the quest for scientific truth.'

Kohler fell silent.

'Of course, the Illuminati were hunted ruthlessly by the Catholic Church. Only through rites of extreme secrecy did the scientists remain safe. Word spread through the academic underground, and the Illuminati brotherhood grew to include academics from all over Europe. The scientists met regularly in Rome at an ultrasecret lair they called the *Church of Illumination*.'

Kohler coughed and shifted in his chair.

'Many of the Illuminati,' Langdon continued, 'wanted to combat the church's tyranny with acts of violence, but their most revered member persuaded

50

them against it. He was a pacifist, as well as one of history's most famous scientists.'

Langdon was certain Kohler would recognize the name. Even nonscientists were familiar with the ill-fated astronomer who had been arrested and almost executed by the church for proclaiming that the *sun*, not the earth, was the center of the solar system. Although his data were incontrovertible, the astronomer was severely punished for implying that God had placed mankind somewhere other than at the *center* of His universe.

'His name was Galileo Galilei,' Langdon said.

Kohler looked up. 'Galileo?'

'Yes. Galileo was an Illuminatus. And he was also a devout Catholic. He tried to soften the church's position on science by proclaiming that science did not undermine the existence of God, but rather *reinforced* it. He wrote once that when he looked through his telescope at the spinning planets, he could hear God's voice in the music of the spheres. He held that science and religion were not enemies, but rather *allies* – two different languages telling the same story, a story of symmetry and balance . . . heaven and hell, night and day, hot and cold, God and Satan. Both science and religion rejoiced in God's symmetry . . . the end-less contest of light and dark.' Langdon paused, stamping his feet to stay warm.

Kohler simply sat in his wheelchair and stared.

'Unfortunately,' Langdon added, 'the unification of science and religion was not what the church wanted.'

'Of course not,' Kohler interrupted. 'The union would have nullified the church's claim as the *sole* vessel through which man could understand God. So the church tried Galileo as a heretic, found him guilty,

51

and put him under permanent house arrest. I am quite aware of scientific history, Mr Langdon. But this was all centuries ago. What does it have to do with Leonardo Vetra?'

The million dollar question. Langdon cut to the chase. 'Galileo's arrest threw the Illuminati into upheaval. Mistakes were made, and the church discovered the identities of four members, whom they captured and interrogated. But the four scientists revealed nothing . . . even under torture.'

'Torture?'

Langdon nodded. 'They were branded alive. On the chest. With the symbol of a cross.'

Kohler's eyes widened, and he shot an uneasy glance at Vetra's body.

'Then the scientists were brutally murdered, their dead bodies dropped in the streets of Rome as a warning to others thinking of joining the Illuminati. With the church closing in, the remaining Illuminati fled Italy.'

Langdon paused to make his point. He looked directly into Kohler's eyes. 'The Illuminati went deep underground, where they began mixing with other refugee groups fleeing the Catholic purges – mystics, alchemists, occultists, Muslims, Jews. Over the years, the Illuminati began absorbing new members. A new Illuminati emerged. A darker Illuminati. A deeply anti-Christian Illuminati. They grew very powerful, employing mysterious rites, deadly secrecy, vowing someday to rise again and take revenge on the Catholic Church. Their power grew to the point where the church considered them the single most dangerous anti-Christian force on earth. The Vatican denounced the brotherhood as *Shaitan*.'

'*Shaitan?*'

'It's Islamic. It means "adversary" ... *God's* adversary. The church chose Islam for the name because it was a language they considered dirty.' Langdon hesitated. '*Shaitan* is the root of an English word ... *Satan.*'

An uneasiness crossed Kohler's face.

Langdon's voice was grim. 'Mr Kohler, I do not know how this marking appeared on this man's chest ... or why ... but you are looking at the long-lost symbol of the world's oldest and most powerful satanic cult.'

10

The alley was narrow and deserted. The Hassassin strode quickly now, his black eyes filling with anticipation. As he approached his destination, Janus's parting words echoed in his mind. *Phase two begins shortly. Get some rest.*

The Hassassin smirked. He had been awake all night, but sleep was the last thing on his mind. Sleep was for the weak. He was a warrior like his ancestors before him, and his people never slept once a battle had begun. This battle had most definitely begun, and he had been given the honor of spilling first blood. Now he had two hours to celebrate his glory before going back to work.

Sleep? There are far better ways to relax ...

An appetite for hedonistic pleasure was something bred into him by his ancestors. His ascendants had indulged in hashish, but he preferred a different kind of gratification. He took pride in his body – a well-tuned, lethal machine, which, despite his heritage, he refused to pollute with narcotics. He had developed a more nourishing addiction than drugs . . . a far more healthy and satisfying reward.

Feeling a familiar anticipation swelling within him, the Hassassin moved faster down the alley. He arrived at the nondescript door and rang the bell. A view slit in the door opened, and two soft brown eyes studied him appraisingly. Then the door swung open.

'Welcome,' the well-dressed woman said. She ushered him into an impeccably furnished sitting room where the lights were low. The air was laced with expensive perfume and musk. 'Whenever you are ready.' She handed him a book of photographs. 'Ring me when you have made your choice.' Then she disappeared.

The Hassassin smiled.

As he sat on the plush divan and positioned the photo album on his lap, he felt a carnal hunger stir. Although his people did not celebrate Christmas, he imagined that this is what it must feel like to be a Christian child, sitting before a stack of Christmas presents, about to discover the miracles inside. He opened the album and examined the photos. A lifetime of sexual fantasies stared back at him.

Marisa. An Italian goddess. Fiery. A young Sophia Loren.

Sachiko. A Japanese geisha. Lithe. No doubt skilled.

Kanara. A stunning black vision. Muscular. Exotic.

He examined the entire album twice and made his choice. He pressed a button on the table beside him. A minute later the woman who had greeted him reappeared. He indicated his selection. She smiled. 'Follow me.'

After handling the financial arrangements, the woman made a hushed phone call. She waited a few minutes and then led him up a winding marble staircase to a luxurious hallway. 'It's the gold door on the end,' she said. 'You have expensive taste.'

I should, he thought. *I am a connoisseur.*

The Hassassin padded the length of the hallway like a panther anticipating a long overdue meal. When he reached the doorway he smiled to himself. It was already ajar . . . welcoming him in. He pushed, and the door swung noiselessly open.

When he saw his selection, he knew he had chosen well. She was exactly as he had requested . . . nude, lying on her back, her arms tied to the bedposts with thick velvet cords.

He crossed the room and ran a dark finger across her ivory abdomen. *I killed last night*, he thought. *You are my reward.*

11

'Satanic?' Kohler wiped his mouth and shifted uncomfortably. 'This is the symbol of a *satanic* cult?'

Langdon paced the frozen room to keep warm. 'The Illuminati were satanic. But not in the modern sense.'

Langdon quickly explained how most people pictured satanic cults as devil-worshiping fiends, and yet Satanists historically were educated men who stood as adversaries to the church. *Shaitan.* The rumors of satanic black-magic animal sacrifices and the pentagram ritual were nothing but lies spread by the church as a smear campaign against their adversaries. Over time, opponents of the church, wanting to emulate the Illuminati, began believing the lies and acting them out. Thus, modern Satanism was born.

Kohler grunted abruptly. 'This is all ancient history. I want to know how this symbol got *here.*'

Langdon took a deep breath. 'The symbol itself was created by an anonymous sixteenth-century Illuminati artist as a tribute to Galileo's love of symmetry – a kind of sacred Illuminati logo. The brotherhood kept the design secret, allegedly planning to reveal it only when they had amassed enough power to resurface and carry out their final goal.'

Kohler looked unsettled. 'So this symbol means the Illuminati brotherhood is resurfacing?'

Langdon frowned. 'That would be impossible. There is one chapter of Illuminati history that I have not yet explained.'

Kohler's voice intensified. 'Enlighten me.'

Langdon rubbed his palms together, mentally sorting through the hundreds of documents he'd read or written on the Illuminati. 'The Illuminati were survivors,' he explained. 'When they fled Rome, they traveled across Europe looking for a safe place to regroup. They were taken in by another secret society . . . a brotherhood of wealthy Bavarian stone craftsmen called the Freemasons.'

Kohler looked startled. 'The Masons?'

Langdon nodded, not at all surprised that Kohler had heard of the group. The brotherhood of the Masons currently had over five million members worldwide, half of them residing in the United States, and over one million of them in Europe.

'Certainly the Masons are not satanic,' Kohler declared, sounding suddenly skeptical.

'Absolutely not. The Masons fell victim of their own benevolence. After harboring the fleeing scientists in the 1700s, the Masons unknowingly became a front for the Illuminati. The Illuminati grew within their ranks, gradually taking over positions of power within the lodges. They quietly reestablished their scientific brotherhood deep within the Masons – a kind of secret society within a secret society. Then the Illuminati used the worldwide connection of Masonic lodges to spread their influence.'

Langdon drew a cold breath before racing on. 'Obliteration of Catholicism was the Illuminati's central covenant. The brotherhood held that the super-stitious dogma spewed forth by the church was mankind's greatest enemy. They feared that if religion continued to promote pious myth as absolute fact, scientific progress would halt, and mankind would be doomed to an ignorant future of senseless holy wars.'

'Much like we see today.'

Langdon frowned. Kohler was right. Holy wars were still making headlines. *My God is better than your God.* It seemed there was always close correlation between true believers and high body counts.

'Go on,' Kohler said.

Langdon gathered his thoughts and continued. 'The Illuminati grew more powerful in Europe and set their sights on America, a fledgling government many of whose leaders were Masons – George Washington, Ben Franklin – honest, God-fearing men who were unaware of the Illuminati stronghold on the Masons.

The Illuminati took advantage of the infiltration and helped found banks, universities, and industry to finance their ultimate quest.' Langdon paused. 'The creation of a single unified world state – a kind of secular New World Order.'

Kohler did not move.

'A New World Order,' Langdon repeated, 'based on scientific enlightenment. They called it their Luciferian Doctrine. The church claimed Lucifer was a reference to the devil, but the brotherhood insisted Lucifer was intended in its literal Latin meaning – *bringer of light*. Or *Illuminator*.'

Kohler sighed, and his voice grew suddenly solemn. 'Mr Langdon, please sit down.'

Langdon sat tentatively on a frost-covered chair.

Kohler moved his wheelchair closer. 'I am not sure I understand everything you have just told me, but I do understand this. Leonardo Vetra was one of CERN's greatest assets. He was also a friend. I need you to help me locate the Illuminati.'

Langdon didn't know how to respond. 'Locate the Illuminati?' *He's kidding, right?* 'I'm afraid, sir, that will be utterly impossible.'

Kohler's brow creased. 'What do you mean? You won't—'

'Mr Kohler,' Langdon leaned toward his host, uncertain how to make him understand what he was about to say. 'I did not finish my story. Despite appearances, it is extremely unlikely that this brand was put here by the Illuminati. There has been no evidence of their existence for over half a century, and most scholars agree the Illuminati have been defunct for many years.'

The words hit silence. Kohler stared through the fog

with a look somewhere between stupefaction and anger. 'How the hell can you tell me this group is extinct when their name is seared into this man!'

Langdon had been asking himself that question all morning. The appearance of the Illuminati ambigram was astonishing. Symbologists worldwide would be dazzled. And yet, the academic in Langdon understood that the brand's reemergence proved absolutely nothing about the Illuminati.

'Symbols,' Langdon said, 'in no way confirm the presence of their original creators.'

'What is *that* supposed to mean?'

'It means that when organized philosophies like the Illuminati go out of existence, their symbols remain . . . available for adoption by other groups. It's called *transference*. It's very common in symbology. The Nazis took the swastika from the Hindus, the Christians adopted the cruciform from the Egyptians, the—'

'This morning,' Kohler challenged, 'when I typed the word "Illuminati" into the computer, it returned thousands of current references. Apparently a lot of people think this group is still active.'

'Conspiracy buffs,' Langdon replied. He had always been annoyed by the plethora of conspiracy theories that circulated in modern pop culture. The media craved apocalyptic headlines, and self-proclaimed 'cult specialists' were still cashing in on millennium hype with fabricated stories that the Illuminati were alive and well and organizing their New World Order. Recently the *New York Times* had reported the eerie Masonic ties of countless famous men – Sir Arthur Conan Doyle, the Duke of Kent, Peter Sellers, Irving Berlin, Prince Philip, Louis Armstrong, as well as a pantheon of well-known modern-day industrialists and banking magnates.

Kohler pointed angrily at Vetra's body. 'Considering the evidence, I would say perhaps the conspiracy buffs are correct.'

'I realize how it appears,' Langdon said as diplomatically as he could. 'And yet a far more plausible explanation is that some *other* organization has taken control of the Illuminati brand and is using it for their own purposes.'

'What purposes? What does this murder prove?'

Good question, Langdon thought. He was also having trouble imagining where anyone could have turned up the Illuminati brand after 400 years. 'All I can tell you is that even if the Illuminati were still active today, which I am virtually positive they are not, they would never be involved in Leonardo Vetra's death.'

'No?'

'No. The Illuminati may have believed in the abolition of Christianity, but they wielded their power through political and financial means, not through terrorist acts. Furthermore, the Illuminati had a strict code of morality regarding who they saw as enemies. They held men of science in the highest regard. There is no way they would have murdered a fellow scientist like Leonardo Vetra.'

Kohler's eyes turned to ice. 'Perhaps I failed to mention that Leonardo Vetra was anything but an ordinary scientist.'

Langdon exhaled patiently. 'Mr Kohler, I'm sure Leonardo Vetra was brilliant in many ways, but the fact remains—'

Without warning, Kohler spun in his wheelchair and accelerated out of the living room, leaving a wake of swirling mist as he disappeared down a hallway.

For the love of God, Langdon groaned. He followed. Kohler was waiting for him in a small alcove at the end of the hallway.

'This is Leonardo's study,' Kohler said, motioning to the sliding door. 'Perhaps when you see it you'll understand things differently.' With an awkward grunt, Kohler heaved, and the door slid open.

Langdon peered into the study and immediately felt his skin crawl. *Holy mother of Jesus*, he said to himself.

12

In another country, a young guard sat patiently before an expansive bank of video monitors. He watched as images flashed before him – live feeds from hundreds of wireless video cameras that surveyed the sprawling complex. The images went by in an endless procession.

An ornate hallway.

A private office.

An industrial-size kitchen.

As the pictures went by, the guard fought off a daydream. He was nearing the end of his shift, and yet he was still vigilant. Service was an honor. Someday he would be granted his ultimate reward.

As his thoughts drifted, an image before him registered alarm. Suddenly, with a reflexive jerk that startled even himself, his hand shot out and hit a button on the control panel. The picture before him froze.

His nerves tingling, he leaned toward the screen for

a closer look. The reading on the monitor told him the image was being transmitted from camera #86 – a camera that was supposed to be overlooking a hallway.

But the image before him was most definitely *not* a hallway.

13

Langdon stared in bewilderment at the study before him. 'What *is* this place?' Despite the welcome blast of warm air on his face, he stepped through the door with trepidation.

Kohler said nothing as he followed Langdon inside.

Langdon scanned the room, not having the slightest idea what to make of it. It contained the most peculiar mix of artifacts he had ever seen. On the far wall, dominating the decor, was an enormous wooden crucifix, which Langdon placed as fourteenth-century Spanish. Above the cruciform, suspended from the ceiling, was a metallic mobile of the orbiting planets. To the left was an oil painting of the Virgin Mary, and beside that was a laminated periodic table of elements. On the side wall, two additional brass cruciforms flanked a poster of Albert Einstein, his famous quote reading, GOD DOES NOT PLAY DICE WITH THE UNIVERSE.

Langdon moved into the room, looking around in astonishment. A leather-bound Bible sat on Vetra's desk beside a plastic Bohr model of an atom and a miniature replica of Michelangelo's Moses.

Talk about eclectic, Langdon thought. The warmth

felt good, but something about the decor sent a new set of chills through his body. He felt like he was witnessing the clash of two philosophical titans . . . an unsettling blur of opposing forces. He scanned the titles on the bookshelf:

The God Particle
The Tao of Physics
God: The Evidence

One of the bookends was etched with a quote:

> TRUE SCIENCE DISCOVERS GOD
> WAITING BEHIND EVERY DOOR.
> —POPE PIUS XII

'Leonardo was a Catholic priest,' Kohler said.

Langdon turned. 'A priest? I thought you said he was a physicist.'

'He was both. Men of science and religion are not unprecedented in history. Leonardo was one of them. He considered physics "God's natural law". He claimed God's handwriting was visible in the natural order all around us. Through science he hoped to prove God's existence to the doubting masses. He considered himself a theo-physicist.'

Theo-physicist? Langdon thought it sounded impossibly oxymoronic.

'The field of particle physics,' Kohler said, 'has made some shocking discoveries lately – discoveries quite spiritual in implication. Leonardo was responsible for many of them.'

Langdon studied CERN's director, still trying to process the bizarre surroundings. 'Spirituality and physics?' Langdon had spent his career studying religious history, and if there was one recurring theme, it was that science and religion had been oil and water since day one . . . archenemies . . . unmixable.

'Vetra was on the cutting edge of particle physics,' Kohler said. 'He was starting to fuse science and religion . . . showing that they complement each other in most unanticipated ways. He called the field *New Physics*.' Kohler pulled a book from the shelf and handed it to Langdon.

Langdon studied the cover. *God, Miracles, and the New Physics* – by Leonardo Vetra.

'The field is small,' Kohler said, 'but it's bringing fresh answers to some old questions – questions about the origin of the universe and the forces that bind us all. Leonardo believed his research had the potential to convert millions to a more spiritual life. Last year he categorically proved the existence of an energy force that unites us all. He actually demonstrated that we are all physically connected . . . that the molecules in your body are intertwined with the molecules in mine . . . that there is a single force moving within all of us.'

Langdon felt disconcerted. *And the power of God shall unite us all.* 'Mr Vetra actually found a way to *demonstrate* that particles are connected?'

'Conclusive evidence. A recent *Scientific American* article hailed *New Physics* as a surer path to God than religion itself.'

The comment hit home. Langdon suddenly found himself thinking of the antireligious Illuminati. Reluctantly, he forced himself to permit a momentary intellectual foray into the impossible. If the Illuminati were indeed still active, would they have killed Leonardo to stop him from bringing his religious message to the masses? Langdon shook off the thought. *Absurd! The Illuminati are ancient history! All academics know that!*

'Vetra had plenty of enemies in the scientific world,' Kohler went on. 'Many scientific purists despised him. Even here at CERN. They felt that using analytical physics to support religious principles was a treason against science.'

'But aren't scientists today a bit less defensive about the church?'

Kohler grunted in disgust. 'Why *should* we be? The church may not be burning scientists at the stake anymore, but if you think they've released their reign over science, ask yourself why half the schools in your country are not allowed to teach evolution. Ask yourself why the U.S. Christian Coalition is the most influential lobby against scientific progress in the world. The battle between science and religion is still raging, Mr Langdon. It has moved from the battlefields to the boardrooms, but it is still raging.'

Langdon realized Kohler was right. Just last week the Harvard School of Divinity had marched on the Biology Building, protesting the genetic engineering taking place in the graduate program. The chairman of the Bio Department, famed ornithologist Richard Aaronian, defended his curriculum by hanging a huge banner from his office window. The banner depicted the Christian 'fish' modified with four little feet – a tribute, Aaronian claimed, to the African lung-fishes' evolution onto dry land. Beneath the fish, instead of the word 'Jesus', was the proclamation 'DARWIN!'

A sharp beeping sound cut the air, and Langdon looked up. Kohler reached down into the array of electronics on his wheelchair. He slipped a beeper out of its holder and read the incoming message.

'Good. That is Leonardo's daughter. Ms Vetra is arriving at the helipad right now. We will meet her there. I think it best she not come up here and see her father this way.'

Langdon agreed. It would be a shock no child deserved.

'I will ask Ms Vetra to explain the project she and her father have been working on . . . perhaps shedding light on why he was murdered.'

'You think Vetra's *work* is why he was killed?'

'Quite possibly. Leonardo told me he was working on something groundbreaking. That is all he said. He had become very secretive about the project. He had a private lab and demanded seclusion, which I gladly afforded him on account of his brilliance. His work had been consuming huge amounts of electric power lately, but I refrained from questioning him.' Kohler rotated toward the study door. 'There is, however, one more thing you need to know before we leave this flat.'

Langdon was not sure he wanted to hear it.

'An item was stolen from Vetra by his murderer.'

'An item?'

'Follow me.'

The director propelled his wheelchair back into the fog-filled living room. Langdon followed, not knowing what to expect. Kohler maneuvered to within inches of Vetra's body and stopped. He ushered Langdon to join him. Reluctantly, Langdon came close, bile rising in his throat at the smell of the victim's frozen urine.

'Look at his face,' Kohler said.

Look at his face? Langdon frowned. *I thought you said something was stolen.*

66

Hesitantly, Langdon knelt down. He tried to see Vetra's face, but the head was twisted 180 degrees backward, his face pressed into the carpet.

Struggling against his handicap Kohler reached down and carefully twisted Vetra's frozen head. Cracking loudly, the corpse's face rotated into view, contorted in agony. Kohler held it there for a moment.

'Sweet Jesus!' Langdon cried, stumbling back in horror. Vetra's face was covered in blood. A single hazel eye stared lifelessly back at him. The other socket was tattered and empty. 'They stole his *eye*?'

14

Langdon stepped out of Building C into the open air, grateful to be outside Vetra's flat. The sun helped dissolve the image of the empty eye socket emblazoned into his mind.

'This way, please,' Kohler said, veering up a steep path. The electric wheelchair seemed to accelerate effortlessly. 'Ms Vetra will be arriving any moment.'

Langdon hurried to keep up.

'So,' Kohler asked. 'Do you still doubt the Illuminati's involvement?'

Langdon had no idea what to think anymore. Vetra's religious affiliations were definitely troubling, and yet Langdon could not bring himself to abandon every shred of academic evidence he had ever researched. Besides, there was the eye . . .

'I still maintain,' Langdon said, more forcefully than

he intended, 'that the Illuminati are *not* responsible for this murder. The missing eye is proof.'

'What?'

'Random mutilation,' Langdon explained, 'is very . . . *un*-Illuminati. Cult specialists see desultory deface-ment from inexperienced fringe sects – zealots who commit random acts of terrorism – but the Illuminati have always been more deliberate.'

'Deliberate? Surgically removing someone's eyeball is not deliberate?'

'It sends no clear message. It serves no higher purpose.'

Kohler's wheelchair stopped short at the top of the hill. He turned. 'Mr Langdon, believe me, that missing eye does *indeed* serve a higher purpose . . . a much higher purpose.'

As the two men crossed the grassy rise, the beating of helicopter blades became audible to the west. A chopper appeared, arching across the open valley toward them. It banked sharply, then slowed to a hover over a helipad painted on the grass.

Langdon watched, detached, his mind churning circles like the blades, wondering if a full night's sleep would make his current disorientation any clearer. Somehow, he doubted it.

As the skids touched down, a pilot jumped out and started unloading gear. There was a lot of it – duffels, vinyl wet bags, scuba tanks, and crates of what appeared to be high-tech diving equipment.

Langdon was confused. 'Is that Ms Vetra's gear?' he yelled to Kohler over the roar of the engines.

Kohler nodded and yelled back, 'She was doing biological research in the Balearic Sea.'

'I thought you said she was a *physicist*!'

'She is. She's a Bio Entanglement Physicist. She studies the interconnectivity of life systems. Her work ties closely with her father's work in particle physics. Recently she disproved one of Einstein's fundamental theories by using atomically synchronized cameras to observe a school of tuna fish.'

Langdon searched his host's face for any glint of humor. *Einstein and tuna fish?* He was starting to wonder if the X-33 space plane had mistakenly dropped him off on the wrong planet.

A moment later, Vittoria Vetra emerged from the fuselage. Robert Langdon realized today was going to be a day of endless surprises. Descending from the chopper in her khaki shorts and white sleeveless top, Vittoria Vetra looked nothing like the bookish physicist he had expected. Lithe and graceful, she was tall with chestnut skin and long black hair that swirled in the backwind of the rotors. Her face was unmistakably Italian – not overly beautiful, but possessing full, earthy features that even at twenty yards seemed to exude a raw sensuality. As the air currents buffeted her body, her clothes clung, accentuating her slender torso and small breasts.

'Ms Vetra is a woman of tremendous personal strength,' Kohler said, seeming to sense Langdon's captivation. 'She spends months at a time working in dangerous ecological systems. She is a strict vegetarian and CERN's resident guru of Hatha yoga.'

Hatha yoga? Langdon mused. The ancient Buddhist art of meditative stretching seemed an odd proficiency for the physicist daughter of a Catholic priest.

Langdon watched Vittoria approach. She had obviously been crying, her deep sable eyes filled with emotions Langdon could not place. Still, she moved toward them with fire and command. Her limbs were strong and toned, radiating the healthy luminescence of Mediterranean flesh that had enjoyed long hours in the sun.

'Vittoria,' Kohler said as she approached. 'My deepest condolences. It's a terrible loss for science . . . for all of us here at CERN.'

Vittoria nodded gratefully. When she spoke, her voice was smooth – a throaty, accented English. 'Do you know who is responsible yet?'

'We're still working on it.'

She turned to Langdon, holding out a slender hand. 'My name is Vittoria Vetra. You're from Interpol, I assume?'

Langdon took her hand, momentarily spellbound by the depth of her watery gaze. 'Robert Langdon.' He was unsure what else to say.

'Mr Langdon is not with the authorities,' Kohler explained. 'He is a specialist from the U.S. He's here to help us locate who is responsible for this situation.'

Vittoria looked uncertain. 'And the police?'

Kohler exhaled but said nothing.

'Where is his body?' she demanded.

'Being attended to.'

The white lie surprised Langdon.

'I want to see him,' Vittoria said.

'Vittoria,' Kohler urged, 'your father was brutally murdered. You would be better to remember him as he was.'

Vittoria began to speak but was interrupted.

'Hey, Vittoria!' voices called from the distance. 'Welcome home!'

She turned. A group of scientists passing near the helipad waved happily.

'Disprove any more of Einstein's theories?' one shouted.

Another added, 'Your dad must be proud!'

Vittoria gave the men an awkward wave as they passed. Then she turned to Kohler, her face now clouded with confusion. 'Nobody *knows* yet?'

'I decided discretion was paramount.'

'You haven't told the staff my father was *murdered*?' Her mystified tone was now laced with anger.

Kohler's tone hardened instantly. 'Perhaps you forget, Ms Vetra, as soon as I report your father's murder, there will be an investigation of CERN. Including a thorough examination of his lab. I have always tried to respect your father's privacy. Your father has told me only two things about your current project. One, that it has the potential to bring CERN millions of francs in licensing contracts in the next decade. And two, that it is not ready for public disclosure because it is still hazardous technology. Considering these two facts, I would prefer strangers not poke around inside his lab and either steal his work or kill themselves in the process and hold CERN liable. Do I make myself clear?'

Vittoria stared, saying nothing. Langdon sensed in her a reluctant respect and acceptance of Kohler's logic.

'Before we report anything to the authorities,' Kohler said, 'I need to know what you two were working on. I need you to take us to your lab.'

'The lab is irrelevant,' Vittoria said. 'Nobody knew what my father and I were doing. The experiment could not possibly have anything to do with my father's murder.'

Kohler exhaled a raspy, ailing breath. 'Evidence suggests otherwise.'

'Evidence? What evidence?'

Langdon was wondering the same thing.

Kohler was dabbing his mouth again. 'You'll just have to trust me.'

It was clear, from Vittoria's smoldering gaze, that she did not.

15

Langdon strode silently behind Vittoria and Kohler as they moved back into the main atrium where Langdon's bizarre visit had begun. Vittoria's legs drove in fluid efficiency – like an Olympic diver – a potency, Langdon figured, no doubt born from the flexibility and control of yoga. He could hear her breathing slowly and deliberately, as if somehow trying to filter her grief.

Langdon wanted to say something to her, offer his sympathy. He too had once felt the abrupt hollowness of unexpectedly losing a parent. He remembered the funeral mostly, rainy and gray. Two days after his twelfth birthday. The house was filled with gray-suited men from the office, men who squeezed his hand too hard when they shook it. They were all mumbling words like *cardiac* and *stress*. His mother joked through teary eyes that she'd always been able to follow the stock market simply by holding her husband's hand ... his pulse her own private ticker tape.

Once, when his father was alive, Langdon had heard his mom begging his father to 'stop and smell the roses'. That year, Langdon bought his father a tiny blown-glass rose for Christmas. It was the most beautiful thing Langdon had ever seen . . . the way the sun caught it, throwing a rainbow of colours on the wall. 'It's lovely,' his father had said when he opened it, kissing Robert on the forehead. 'Let's find a safe spot for it.' Then his father had carefully placed the rose on a high dusty shelf in the darkest corner of the living room. A few days later, Langdon got a stool, retrieved the rose, and took it back to the store. His father never noticed it was gone.

The ping of an elevator pulled Langdon back to the present. Vittoria and Kohler were in front of him, boarding the lift. Langdon hesitated outside the open doors.

'Is something wrong?' Kohler asked, sounding more impatient than concerned.

'Not at all,' Langdon said, forcing himself toward the cramped carriage. He only used elevators when absolutely necessary. He preferred the more open spaces of stairwells.

'Dr Vetra's lab is subterranean,' Kohler said.

Wonderful, Langdon thought as he stepped across the cleft, feeling an icy wind churn up from the depths of the shaft. The doors closed, and the car began to descend.

'Six stories,' Kohler said blankly, like an analytical engine.

Langdon pictured the darkness of the empty shaft below them. He tried to block it out by staring at the numbered display of changing floors. Oddly, the elevator showed only two stops. GROUND LEVEL and LHC.

'What's LHC stand for?' Langdon asked, trying not to sound nervous.

'Large Hadron Collider,' Kohler said. 'A particle accelerator.'

Particle accelerator? Langdon was vaguely familiar with the term. He had first heard it over dinner with some colleagues at Dunster House in Cambridge. A physicist friend of theirs, Bob Brownell, had arrived for dinner one night in a rage.

'The bastards canceled it!' Brownell cursed.

'Canceled what?' they all asked.

'The SSC!'

'The what?'

'The Superconducting Super Collider!'

Someone shrugged. 'I didn't know Harvard was building one.'

'Not Harvard!' he exclaimed. 'The U.S.! It was going to be the world's most powerful particle accelerator! One of the most important scientific projects of the century! Two *billion* dollars into it and the Senate sacks the project! Damn Bible-Belt lobbyists!'

When Brownell finally calmed down, he explained that a particle accelerator was a large, circular tube through which subatomic particles were accelerated. Magnets in the tube turned on and off in rapid succession to 'push' particles around and around until they reached tremendous velocities. Fully accelerated particles circled the tube at over 180,000 miles per *second*.

'But that's almost the speed of light,' one of the professors exclaimed.

'Damn right,' Brownell said. He went on to say that by accelerating two particles in opposite directions around the tube and then colliding them, scientists could shatter the particles into their constituent parts and get a glimpse of nature's most fundamental components. 'Particle accelerators,' Brownell declared, 'are critical to the future of science. Colliding particles is the key to understanding the building blocks of the universe.'

Harvard's *Poet in Residence*, a quiet man named Charles Pratt, did not look impressed. 'It sounds to me,' he said, 'like a rather Neanderthal approach to science . . . akin to smashing clocks together to discern their internal workings.'

Brownell dropped his fork and stormed out of the room.

So CERN has a particle accelerator? Langdon thought, as the elevator dropped. *A circular tube for smashing particles.* He wondered why they had buried it underground.

When the elevator thumped to a stop, Langdon was relieved to feel terra firma beneath his feet. But when the doors slid open, his relief evaporated. Robert Langdon found himself standing once again in a totally alien world.

The passageway stretched out indefinitely in both directions, left and right. It was a smooth cement tunnel, wide enough to allow passage of an eighteen wheeler. Brightly lit where they stood, the corridor turned pitch black further down. A damp wind rustled out of the darkness – an unsettling reminder that they were now deep in the earth. Langdon could almost sense the weight of the dirt and stone now hanging above his head. For an instant he was nine years old . . . the darkness forcing him back . . . back to the five hours of crushing blackness that haunted him still. Clenching his fists, he fought it off.

Vittoria remained hushed as she exited the elevator

and strode off without hesitation into the darkness without them. Overhead the fluorescents flickered on to light her path. The effect was unsettling, Langdon thought, as if the tunnel were alive . . . anticipating her every move. Langdon and Kohler followed, trailing a distance behind. The lights extinguished automatically behind them.

'This particle accelerator,' Langdon said quietly. 'It's down this tunnel someplace?'

'That's it there.' Kohler motioned to his left where a polished, chrome tube ran along the tunnel's inner wall.

Langdon eyed the tube, confused. *'That's* the accelerator?' The device looked nothing like he had imagined. It was perfectly straight, about three feet in diameter, and extended horizontally the visible length of the tunnel before disappearing into the darkness. *Looks more like a high-tech sewer,* Langdon thought. 'I thought particle accelerators were *circular.'*

'This accelerator *is* a circle,' Kohler said. 'It appears straight, but that is an optical illusion. The circumference of this tunnel is so large that the curve is imperceptible – like that of the earth.'

Langdon was flabbergasted. *This is a circle?* 'But . . . it must be enormous!'

'The LHC is the largest machine in the world.'

Langdon did a double take. He remembered the CERN driver saying something about a huge machine buried in the earth. *But—*

'It is over eight kilometers in diameter . . . and twenty-seven kilometres long.'

Langdon's head whipped around. 'Twenty-seven kilometers?' He stared at the director and then turned and looked into the darkened tunnel before him. 'This tunnel is twenty-seven kilometers long? That's ... that's over sixteen miles!'

Kohler nodded. 'Bored in a perfect circle. It extends all the way into France before curving back here to this spot. Fully accelerated particles will circle the tube more than ten thousand times in a single second before they collide.'

Langdon's legs felt rubbery as he stared down the gaping tunnel. 'You're telling me that CERN dug out millions of tons of earth just to smash tiny particles?'

Kohler shrugged. 'Sometimes to find truth, one must move mountains.'

16

Hundreds of miles from CERN, a voice crackled through a walkie-talkie. 'Okay, I'm in the hallway.'

The technician monitoring the video screens pressed the button on his transmitter. 'You're looking for camera #86. It's supposed to be at the far end.'

There was a long silence on the radio. The waiting technician broke a light sweat. Finally his radio clicked.

'The camera isn't here,' the voice said. 'I can see where it was mounted, though. Somebody must have removed it.'

The technician exhaled heavily. 'Thanks. Hold on a second, will you?'

Sighing, he redirected his attention to the bank of video screens in front of him. Huge portions of the complex were open to the public, and wireless cameras had gone missing before, usually stolen by visiting pranksters looking for souvenirs. But as soon as a camera left the facility and was out of range, the signal was lost, and the screen went blank. Perplexed, the technician gazed up at the monitor. A crystal clear image was still coming from camera #86.

If the camera was stolen, he wondered, *why are we still getting a signal?* He knew, of course, there was only one explanation. The camera was still inside the complex, and someone had simply moved it. *But who? And why?*

He studied the monitor a long moment. Finally he picked up his walkie-talkie. 'Are there any closets in that stairwell? Any cupboards or dark alcoves?'

The voice replying sounded confused. 'No. Why?'

The technician frowned. 'Never mind. Thanks for your help.' He turned off his walkie-talkie and pursed his lips.

Considering the small size of the video camera and the fact that it was wireless, the technician knew that camera #86 could be transmitting from just about *anywhere* within the heavily guarded compound – a densely packed collection of thirty-two separate buildings covering a half-mile radius. The only clue was that the camera seemed to have been placed somewhere dark. Of course, that wasn't much help. The complex contained endless dark locations – maintenance closets, heating ducts, gardening sheds, bedroom wardrobes, even a labyrinth of underground tunnels. Camera #86 could take weeks to locate.

But that's the least of my problems, he thought.

Despite the dilemma posed by the camera's relocation, there was another far more unsettling matter at hand. The technician gazed up at the image the lost camera was transmitting. It was a stationary object. A modern-looking device like nothing the technician had ever seen. He studied the blinking electronic display at its base.

Although the guard had undergone rigorous training preparing him for tense situations, he still sensed his pulse rising. He told himself not to panic. There had to be an explanation. The object appeared too small to be of significant danger. Then again, its presence inside the complex was troubling. *Very* troubling, indeed.

Today of all days, he thought.

Security was always a top priority for his employer, but *today*, more than any other day in the past twelve years, security was of the utmost importance. The technician stared at the object for a long time and sensed the rumblings of a distant gathering storm.

Then, sweating, he dialed his superior.

17

Not many children could say they remembered the day they met their father, but Vittoria Vetra could. She was eight years old, living where she always had, *Orfanotrofio di Siena*, a Catholic orphanage near Florence, deserted by parents she never knew. It was raining that day. The nuns had called for her twice to come to dinner, but as always she pretended not to hear. She lay outside in the courtyard, staring up at the raindrops . . . feeling them hit her body . . . trying to guess where one would land next. The nuns called again, threatening that pneumonia might make an insufferably headstrong child a lot less curious about nature.

I can't hear you, Vittoria thought.

She was soaked to the bone when the young priest came out to get her. She didn't know him. He was new there. Vittoria waited for him to grab her and drag her back inside. But he didn't. Instead, to her wonder, he lay down beside her, soaking his robes in a puddle.

'They say you ask a lot of questions,' the young man said.

Vittoria scowled. 'Are questions bad?'

He laughed. 'Guess they were right.'

'What are you doing out here?'

'Same thing you're doing . . . wondering why raindrops fall.'

'I'm not wondering why they fall! I already know!'

The priest gave her an astonished look. 'You *do*?'

'Sister Francisca says raindrops are angels' tears coming down to wash away our sins.'

'Wow!' he said, sounding amazed. 'So *that* explains it.'

'No it doesn't!' the girl fired back. 'Raindrops fall because *everything* falls! *Everything* falls! Not just rain!'

The priest scratched his head, looking perplexed. 'You know, young lady, you're right. Everything *does* fall. It must be gravity.'

'It must be *what*?'

He gave her an astonished look. 'You haven't heard of *gravity*?'

'No.'

The priest shrugged sadly. 'Too bad. Gravity answers a *lot* of questions.'

Vittoria sat up. 'What's gravity?' she demanded. 'Tell me!'

The priest gave her a wink. 'What do you say I tell you over dinner.'

The young priest was Leonardo Vetra. Although he had been an award-winning physics student while in university, he'd heard another call and gone into the seminary. Leonardo and Vittoria became unlikely best friends in the lonely world of nuns and regulations. Vittoria made Leonardo laugh, and he took her under his wing, teaching her that beautiful things like rainbows and the rivers had many explanations. He told her about light, planets, stars, and all of nature through the eyes of both God and science. Vittoria's innate intellect and curiosity made her a captivating student. Leonardo protected her like a daughter.

Vittoria was happy too. She had never known the joy of having a father. When every other adult answered her questions with a slap on the wrist, Leonardo spent hours showing her books. He even asked what *her* ideas were. Vittoria prayed Leonardo would stay with her forever. Then one day, her worst nightmare came true. Father Leonardo told her he was leaving the orphanage.

'I'm moving to Switzerland,' Leonardo said. 'I have a grant to study physics at the University of Geneva.'

'Physics?' Vittoria cried. 'I thought you loved *God*!'

'I do, very much. Which is why I want to study his divine rules. The laws of physics are the canvas God laid down on which to paint his masterpiece.'

Vittoria was devastated. But Father Leonardo had some other news. He told Vittoria he had spoken to his superiors, and they said it was okay if Father Leonardo adopted her.

'Would you *like* me to adopt you?' Leonardo asked.

'What's *adopt* mean?' Vittoria said.

Father Leonardo told her.

Vittoria hugged him for five minutes, crying tears of joy. 'Oh yes! Yes!'

Leonardo told her he had to leave for a while and get their new home settled in Switzerland, but he promised to send for her in six months. It was the longest wait of Vittoria's life, but Leonardo kept his word. Five days before her ninth birthday, Vittoria moved to Geneva. She attended Geneva International School during the day and learned from her father at night.

Three years later Leonardo Vetra was hired by CERN. Vittoria and Leonardo relocated to a wonderland the likes of which the young Vittoria had never imagined.

Vittoria Vetra's body felt numb as she strode down the LHC tunnel. She saw her muted reflection in the LHC and sensed her father's absence. Normally she existed in a state of deep calm, in harmony with the world around her. But now, very suddenly, nothing made sense. The last three hours had been a blur.

It had been 10 a.m. in the Balearic Islands when Kohler's call came through. *Your father has been murdered. Come home immediately.* Despite the sweltering heat on the deck of the dive boat, the words had chilled her to the bone. Kohler's emotionless tone hurting as much as the news.

Now she had returned home. *But home to what?* CERN, her world since she was twelve, seemed suddenly foreign. Her father, the man who had made it magical, was gone.

82

Deep breaths, she told herself, but she couldn't calm her mind. The questions circled faster and faster. Who killed her father? And why? Who was this American 'specialist'? Why was Kohler insisting on seeing the lab?

Kohler had said there was evidence that her father's murder was related to the current project. *What evidence? Nobody knew what we were working on! And even if someone found out, why would they kill him?*

As she moved down the LHC tunnel toward her father's lab, Vittoria realized she was about to unveil her father's greatest achievement without him there. She had pictured this moment much differently. She had imagined her father calling CERN's top scientists to his lab, showing them his discovery, watching their awestruck faces. Then he would beam with fatherly pride as he explained to them how it had been one of *Vittoria's* ideas that had helped him make the project a reality ... that his *daughter* had been integral in his breakthrough. Vittoria felt a lump in her throat. *My father and I were supposed to share this moment together.* But here she was alone. No colleagues. No happy faces. Just an American stranger and Maximilian Kohler.

Maximilian Kohler. Der König.

Even as a child, Vittoria had disliked the man. Although she eventually came to respect his potent intellect, his icy demeanor always seemed inhuman, the exact antithesis of her father's warmth. Kohler pursued science for its immaculate logic ... her father for its spiritual wonder. And yet oddly there had always seemed to be an unspoken respect between the two men. *Genius*, someone had once explained to her, *accepts genius unconditionally.*

Genius, she thought. *My father ... Dad. Dead.*

The entry to Leonardo Vetra's lab was a long sterile hallway paved entirely in white tile. Langdon felt like he was entering some kind of underground insane asylum. Lining the corridor were dozens of framed, black-and-white images. Although Langdon had made a career of studying images, these were entirely alien to him. They looked like chaotic negatives of random streaks and spirals. *Modern art?* he mused. *Jackson Pollock on amphetamines?*

'Scatter plots,' Vittoria said, apparently noting Langdon's interest. 'Computer representations of particle collisions. That's the Z-particle,' she said, pointing to a faint track that was almost invisible in the confusion. 'My father discovered it five years ago. Pure energy – no mass at all. It may well be the smallest building block in nature. Matter is nothing but trapped energy.'

Matter is energy? Langdon cocked his head. *Sounds pretty Zen.* He gazed at the tiny streak in the photograph and wondered what his buddies in the Harvard physics department would say when he told them he'd spent the weekend hanging out in a Large Hadron Collider admiring Z-particles.

'Vittoria,' Kohler said, as they approached the lab's imposing steel door, 'I should mention that I came down here this morning looking for your father.'

Vittoria flushed slightly. 'You did?'

'Yes. And imagine my surprise when I discovered he had replaced CERN's standard keypad security with something else.' Kohler motioned to an intricate electronic device mounted beside the door.

'I apologize,' she said. 'You know how he was about privacy. He didn't want anyone but the two of us to have access.'

Kohler said, 'Fine. Open the door.'

Vittoria stood for a long moment. Then, pulling a deep breath, she walked to the mechanism on the wall.

Langdon was in no way prepared for what happened next.

Vittoria stepped up to the device and carefully aligned her right eye with a protruding lens that looked like a telescope. Then she pressed a button. Inside the machine, something clicked. A shaft of light oscillated back and forth, scanning her eyeball like a copy machine.

'It's a retina scan,' she said. 'Infallible security. Authorized for two retina patterns only. Mine and my father's.'

Robert Langdon stood in horrified revelation. The image of Leonardo Vetra came back in grisly detail – the bloody face, the solitary hazel eye staring back, and the empty eye socket. He tried to reject the obvious truth, but then he saw it . . . beneath the scanner on the white tile floor . . . faint droplets of crimson. Dried blood.

Vittoria, thankfully, did not notice.

The steel door slid open and she walked through.

Kohler fixed Langdon with an adamant stare. His message was clear: *As I told you . . . the missing eye serves a higher purpose.*

18

The woman's hands were tied, her wrists now purple and swollen from chafing. The mahogany-skinned

Hassassin lay beside her, spent, admiring his naked prize. He wondered if her current slumber was just a deception, a pathetic attempt to avoid further service to him.

He did not care. He had reaped sufficient reward. Sated, he sat up in bed.

In *his* country women were possessions. Weak. Tools of pleasure. Chattel to be traded like livestock. And they understood their place. But *here*, in Europe, women feigned a strength and independence that both amused and excited him. Forcing them into physical submission was a gratification he always enjoyed.

Now, despite the contentment in his loins, the Hassassin sensed another appetite growing within him. He had killed last night, killed and mutilated, and for him killing was like heroin . . . each encounter satisfying only temporarily before increasing his longing for more. The exhilaration had worn off. The craving had returned.

He studied the sleeping woman beside him. Running his palm across her neck, he felt aroused with the knowledge that he could end her life in an instant. What would it matter? She was subhuman, a vehicle only of pleasure and service. His strong fingers encircled her throat, savoring her delicate pulse. Then, fighting desire, he removed his hand. There was work to do. Service to a higher cause than his own desire.

As he got out of bed, he reveled in the honor of the job before him. He still could not fathom the influence of this man named Janus and the ancient brotherhood he commanded. Wondrously, the brotherhood had chosen *him*. Somehow they had learned of his loathing . . . and of his skills. How, he would never know. *Their roots reach wide.*

Now they had bestowed on him the ultimate honor. He would be their hands and their voice. Their assassin and their messenger. The one his people knew as *Malk al-haq* – the Angel of Truth.

19

Vetra's lab was wildly futuristic.

Stark white and bounded on all sides by computers and specialized electronic equipment, it looked like some sort of operating room. Langdon wondered what secrets this place could possibly hold to justify cutting out someone's eye to gain entrance.

Kohler looked uneasy as they entered, his eyes seeming to dart about for signs of an intruder. But the lab was deserted. Vittoria moved slowly too . . . as if the lab felt unknown without her father there.

Langdon's gaze landed immediately in the center of the room, where a series of short pillars rose from the floor. Like a miniature Stonehenge, a dozen or so columns of polished steel stood in a circle in the middle of the room. The pillars were about three feet tall, reminding Langdon of museum displays for valuable gems. These pillars, however, were clearly not for precious stones. Each supported a thick, transparent canister about the size of a tennis ball can. They appeared empty.

Kohler eyed the canisters, looking puzzled. He apparently decided to ignore them for the time being. He turned to Vittoria. 'Has anything been stolen?'

'Stolen? *How?*' she argued. 'The retina scan only allows entry to us.'

'Just look around.'

Vittoria sighed and surveyed the room for a few moments. She shrugged. 'Everything looks as my father always leaves it. Ordered chaos.'

Langdon sensed Kohler weighing his options, as if wondering how far to push Vittoria . . . how much to tell her. Apparently he decided to leave it for the moment. Moving his wheelchair toward the center of the room, he surveyed the mysterious cluster of seemingly empty canisters.

'Secrets,' Kohler finally said, 'are a luxury we can no longer afford.'

Vittoria nodded in acquiescence, looking suddenly emotional, as if being here brought with it a torrent of memories.

Give her a minute, Langdon thought.

As though preparing for what she was about to reveal, Vittoria closed her eyes and breathed. Then she breathed again. And again. And again . . .

Langdon watched her, suddenly concerned. *Is she okay?* He glanced at Kohler, who appeared unfazed, apparently having seen this ritual before. Ten seconds passed before Vittoria opened her eyes.

Langdon could not believe the metamorphosis. Vittoria Vetra had been transformed. Her full lips were lax, her shoulders down, and her eyes soft and assenting. It was as though she had realigned every muscle in her body to accept the situation. The resentful fire and personal anguish had been quelled somehow beneath a deeper, watery cool.

'Where to begin . . .' she said, her accent unruffled.

'At the beginning,' Kohler said. 'Tell us about your father's experiment.'

'Rectifying science with religion has been my father's life dream,' Vittoria said. 'He hoped to prove that science and religion are two totally compatible fields – two different approaches to finding the same truth.' She paused as if unable to believe what she was about to say. 'And recently . . . he conceived of a way to do that.'

Kohler said nothing.

'He devised an experiment, one he hoped would settle one of the most bitter conflicts in the history of science and religion.'

Langdon wondered which conflict she could mean. There were so many.

'Creationism,' Vittoria declared. 'The battle over how the universe came to be.'

Oh, Langdon thought. *THE debate.*

'The Bible, of course, states that God created the universe,' she explained. 'God said, "Let there be light," and everything we see appeared out of a vast emptiness. Unfortunately, one of the fundamental laws of physics states that matter cannot be created out of nothing.'

Langdon had read about this stalemate. The idea that God allegedly created 'something from nothing' was totally contrary to accepted laws of modern physics and therefore, scientists claimed, Genesis was scientifically absurd.

'Mr Langdon,' Vittoria said, turning, 'I assume you are familiar with the Big Bang Theory?'

Langdon shrugged. 'More or less.' The Big Bang, he knew, was *the* scientifically accepted model for the creation of the universe. He didn't really understand it, but according to the theory, a single point of intensely focused energy erupted in a cataclysmic explosion, expanding outward to form the universe. Or something like that.

Vittoria continued. 'When the Catholic Church first proposed the Big Bang Theory in 1927, the—'

'I'm sorry?' Langdon interrupted, before he could stop himself. 'You say the Big Bang was a *Catholic* idea?'

Vittoria looked surprised by his question. 'Of course. Proposed by a Catholic monk, Georges Lemaître in 1927.'

'But, I thought . . .' he hesitated. 'Wasn't the Big Bang proposed by Harvard astronomer Edwin Hubble?'

Kohler glowered. 'Again, American scientific arrogance. Hubble published in 1929, two years *after* Lemaître.'

Langdon scowled. *It's called the Hubble Telescope, sir – I've never heard of any Lemaître Telescope!*

'Mr Kohler is right,' Vittoria said, 'the idea belonged to Lemaître. Hubble only *confirmed* it by gathering the hard evidence that proved the Big Bang was scientifically probable.'

'Oh,' Langdon said, wondering if the Hubble-fanatics in the Harvard Astronomy Department ever mentioned Lemaître in their lectures.

'When Lemaître first proposed the Big Bang Theory,' Vittoria continued, 'scientists claimed it was utterly ridiculous. Matter, science said, could not be created out of nothing. So, when Hubble shocked the world by scientifically proving the Big Bang was accurate, the church claimed victory, heralding this as *proof* that the Bible was scientifically accurate. The divine truth.'

Langdon nodded, focusing intently now.

'Of course scientists did not appreciate having their discoveries used by the church to promote religion, so they immediately mathematicized the Big Bang Theory, removed all religious overtones, and claimed it as their own. Unfortunately for science, however, their equations, even today, have one serious deficiency that the church likes to point out.'

Kohler grunted. 'The *singularity*.' He spoke the word as if it were the bane of his existence.

'Yes, the singularity,' Vittoria said. 'The exact moment of creation. Time zero.' She looked at Langdon. 'Even today, science cannot grasp the initial moment of creation. Our equations explain the *early* universe quite effectively, but as we move back in time, approaching time zero, suddenly our mathematics disintegrates, and everything becomes meaningless.'

'Correct,' Kohler said, his voice edgy, 'and the church holds up this deficiency as proof of God's miraculous involvement. Come to your point.'

Vittoria's expression became distant. 'My point is that my father had always believed in God's involvement in the Big Bang. Even though science was unable to comprehend the divine moment of creation, he believed someday it *would*.' She motioned sadly to a laser-printed memo tacked over her father's work area. 'My dad used to wave that in my face every time I had doubts.'

Langdon read the message:

SCIENCE AND RELIGION ARE NOT AT ODDS.
SCIENCE IS SIMPLY TOO YOUNG TO UNDERSTAND.

'My dad wanted to bring science to a higher level,'

Vittoria said, 'where science supported the concept of God.' She ran a hand through her long hair, looking melancholy. 'He set out to do something no scientist had ever thought to do. Something that no one has ever had the *technology* to do.' She paused, as though uncertain how to speak the next words. 'He designed an experiment to prove Genesis was possible.'

Prove Genesis? Langdon wondered. *Let there be light? Matter from nothing?*

Kohler's dead gaze bore across the room. 'I beg your pardon?'

'My father created a universe . . . from nothing at all.'

Kohler snapped his head around. 'What!'

'Better said, he recreated the Big Bang.'

Kohler looked ready to jump to his feet.

Langdon was officially lost. *Creating a universe? Recreating the Big Bang?*

'It was done on a much smaller scale, of course,' Vittoria said, talking faster now. 'The process was remarkably simple. He accelerated two ultrathin particle beams in opposite directions around the accelerator tube. The two beams collided head-on at enormous speeds, driving into one another and compressing all their energy into a single pinpoint. He achieved extreme energy densities.' She started rattling off a stream of units, and the director's eyes grew wider.

Langdon tried to keep up. *So Leonardo Vetra was simulating the compressed point of energy from which the universe supposedly sprang.*

'The result,' Vittoria said, 'was nothing short of wondrous. When it is published, it will shake the very foundation of modern physics.' She spoke slowly now, as though savoring the immensity of her news. 'Without warning, inside the accelerator tube, at this point of highly focused energy, particles of matter began appearing out of nowhere.'

Kohler made no reaction. He simply stared.

'*Matter*,' Vittoria repeated. 'Blossoming out of nothing. An incredible display of subatomic fireworks. A miniature universe springing to life. He proved not only that matter *can* be created from nothing, but that the Big Bang *and* Genesis can be explained simply by accepting the presence of an enormous source of energy.'

'You mean *God*?' Kohler demanded.

'God, Buddha, The Force, Yahweh, the singularity, the unicity point – call it whatever you like – the result is the same. Science and religion support the same truth – pure *energy* is the father of creation.'

When Kohler finally spoke, his voice was somber. 'Vittoria, you have me at a loss. It sounds like you're telling me your father *created* matter ... out of nothing?'

'Yes.' Vittoria motioned to the canisters. 'And there is the proof. In those canisters are specimens of the matter he created.'

Kohler coughed and moved towards the canisters like a wary animal circling something he instinctively sensed was wrong. 'I've obviously missed something,' he said. 'How do you expect anyone to believe these canisters contain particles of matter your father actually *created*? They could be particles from anywhere at all.'

'Actually,' Vittoria said, sounding confident, 'they couldn't. These particles are unique. They are a type of matter that does not exist anywhere on earth ... hence they *had* to be created.'

Kohler's expression darkened. 'Vittoria, what do you mean a certain *type* of matter? There is only *one* type of matter, and it—' Kohler stopped short.

Vittoria's expression was triumphant. 'You've lectured on it yourself, director. The universe contains *two* kinds of matter. Scientific fact.' Vittoria turned to Langdon. 'Mr Langdon, what does the Bible say about the Creation? What did God create?'

Langdon felt awkward, not sure what this had to do with anything. 'Um, God created . . . light and dark, heaven and hell—'

'Exactly,' Vittoria said. 'He created everything in opposites. Symmetry. Perfect balance.' She turned back to Kohler. 'Director, science claims the same thing as religion, that the Big Bang created everything in the universe with an opposite.'

'Including *matter* itself,' Kohler whispered, as if to himself.

Vittoria nodded. 'And when my father ran his experiment, sure enough, *two* kinds of matter appeared.'

Langdon wondered what this meant. *Leonardo Vetra created matter's opposite?*

Kohler looked angry. 'The substance you're referring to only exists *elsewhere* in the universe. Certainly not on earth. And possibly not even in our galaxy!'

'Exactly,' Vittoria replied, 'which is proof that the particles in these canisters had to be *created*.'

Kohler's face hardened. 'Vittoria, surely you can't be saying those canisters contain actual specimens?'

'I am.' She gazed proudly at the canisters. 'Director, you are looking at the world's first specimens of *antimatter*.'

20

Phase two, the Hassassin thought, striding into the darkened tunnel.

The torch in his hand was overkill. He knew that. But it was for effect. Effect was everything. Fear, he had learned, was his ally. *Fear cripples faster than any implement of war.*

There was no mirror in the passage to admire his disguise, but he could sense from the shadow of his billowing robe that he was perfect. Blending in was part of the plan . . . part of the depravity of the plot. In his wildest dreams he had never imagined playing this part.

Two weeks ago, he would have considered the task awaiting him at the far end of this tunnel impossible. A suicide mission. Walking naked into a lion's lair. But Janus had changed the definition of impossible.

The secrets Janus had shared with the Hassassin in the last two weeks had been numerous . . . this very tunnel being one of them. Ancient, and yet still perfectly passable.

As he drew closer to his enemy, the Hassassin wondered if what awaited him inside would be as easy as Janus had promised. Janus had assured him someone on the inside would make the necessary arrangements. *Someone on the inside. Incredible.* The more he considered it, the more he realized it was child's play.

Wahad . . . tintain . . . thalatha . . . arbaa, he said to himself in Arabic as he neared the end. *One . . . two . . . three . . . four . . .*

21

'I sense you've heard of antimatter, Mr Langdon?' Vittoria was studying him, her dark skin in stark contrast to the white lab.

Langdon looked up. He felt suddenly numb. 'Yes. Well . . . sort of.'

A faint smile crossed her lips. 'You watch *Star Trek*.'

Langdon flushed. 'Well, my students enjoy . . .' He frowned. 'Isn't antimatter what fuels the *U.S.S. Enterprise*?'

She nodded. 'Good science fiction has its roots in good science.'

'So antimatter is *real*?'

'A fact of nature. Everything has an opposite. Protons have electrons. Up-quarks have down-quarks. There is a cosmic symmetry at the subatomic level. Antimatter is *yin* to matter's *yang*. It balances the physical equation.'

Langdon thought of Galileo's belief of duality.

'Scientists have known since 1918,' Vittoria said, 'that *two* kinds of matter were created in the Big Bang. One matter is the kind we see here on earth, making up rocks, trees, people. The other is its inverse – identical to matter in all respects except that the charges of its particles are reversed.'

Kohler spoke as though emerging from a fog. His voice sounded suddenly precarious. 'But there are enormous technological barriers to actually *storing* antimatter. What about neutralization?'

'My father built a reverse polarity vacuum to pull the antimatter positrons out of the accelerator before they could decay.'

Kohler scowled. 'But a vacuum would pull out the *matter* also. There would be no way to separate the particles.'

'He applied a magnetic field. Matter arced right, and antimatter arced left. They are polar opposites.'

At that instant, Kohler's wall of doubt seemed to crack. He looked up at Vittoria in clear astonishment and then without warning was overcome by a fit of coughing. 'Incred ... ible ...' he said, wiping his mouth, 'and yet ...' It seemed his logic was still resisting. 'Yet even if the vacuum *worked*, these canisters are made of matter. Antimatter cannot be stored inside canisters made out of *matter*. The antimatter would instantly react with—'

'The specimen is not touching the canister,' Vittoria said, apparently expecting the question. 'The antimatter is suspended. The canisters are called "antimatter traps" because they literally trap the antimatter in the center of the canister, suspending it at a safe distance from the sides and bottom.'

'Suspended? But ... *how*?'

'Between two intersecting magnetic fields. Here, have a look.'

Vittoria walked across the room and retrieved a large electronic apparatus. The contraption reminded Langdon of some sort of cartoon ray gun – a wide canonlike barrel with a sighting scope on top and a tangle of electronics dangling below. Vittoria aligned the scope with one of the canisters, peered into the eyepiece, and calibrated some knobs. Then she stepped away, offering Kohler a look.

Kohler looked nonplussed. 'You collected *visible* amounts?'

'Five thousand nanograms,' Vittoria said. 'A

liquid plasma containing millions of positrons.'

'Millions? But a few *particles* is all anyone has ever detected . . . *anywhere.*'

'Xenon,' Vittoria said flatly. 'He accelerated the particle beam through a jet of xenon, stripping away the electrons. He insisted on keeping the exact procedure a secret, but it involved simultaneously injecting raw electrons into the accelerator.'

Langdon felt lost, wondering if their conversation was still in English.

Kohler paused, the lines in his brow deepening. Suddenly he drew a short breath. He slumped like he'd been hit with a bullet. 'Technically that would leave . . .'

Vittoria nodded. 'Yes. *Lots* of it.'

Kohler returned his gaze to the canister before him. With a look of uncertainty, he hoisted himself in his chair and placed his eye to the viewer, peering inside. He stared a long time without saying anything. When he finally sat down, his forehead was covered with sweat. The lines on his face had disappeared. His voice was a whisper. 'My God . . . you really did it.'

Vittoria nodded. 'My *father* did it.'

'I . . . I don't know what to say.'

Vittoria turned to Langdon. 'Would you like a look?' She motioned to the viewing device.

Uncertain what to expect, Langdon moved forward. From two feet away, the canister appeared empty. Whatever was inside was infinitesimal. Langdon placed his eye to the viewer. It took a moment for the image before him to come into focus.

Then he saw it.

The object was not on the bottom of the container as he expected, but rather it was floating in the center –

98

suspended in midair – a shimmering globule of mercurylike liquid. Hovering as if by magic, the liquid tumbled in space. Metallic wavelets rippled across the droplet's surface. The suspended fluid reminded Langdon of a video he had once seen of a water droplet in zero G. Although he knew the globule was microscopic, he could see every changing gorge and undulation as the ball of plasma rolled slowly in suspension.

'It's . . . floating,' he said.

'It had better be,' Vittoria replied. 'Antimatter is highly unstable. Energetically speaking, antimatter is the mirror of matter, so the two instantly cancel each other out if they come in contact. Keeping antimatter isolated from matter is a challenge, of course, because *everything* on earth is made of matter. The samples have to be stored without ever touching anything at all – even air.'

Langdon was amazed. *Talk about working in a vacuum.*

'These antimatter traps?' Kohler interrupted, looking amazed as he ran a pallid finger around one's base. 'They are your father's design?'

'Actually,' she said, 'they are mine.'

Kohler looked up.

Vittoria's voice was unassuming. 'My father produced the first particles of antimatter but was stymied by how to store them. I suggested these. Airtight nanocomposite shells with opposing electromagnets at each end.'

'It seems your father's genius has rubbed off.'

'Not really. I borrowed the idea from nature. Portuguese man-o'-wars trap fish between their tentacles using nematocystic charges. Same principle here. Each canister has two electromagnets, one at each end. Their opposing magnetic fields intersect in the center of the canister and hold the antimatter there, suspended in midvacuum.'

Langdon looked again at the canister. Antimatter floating in a vacuum, not touching anything at all. Kohler was right. It was genius.

'Where's the power source for the magnets?' Kohler asked.

Vittoria pointed. 'In the pillar beneath the trap. The canisters are screwed into a docking port that continuously recharges them so the magnets never fail.'

'And if the field fails?'

'The obvious. The antimatter falls out of suspension, hits the bottom of the trap, and we see an annihilation.'

Langdon's ears pricked up. 'Annihilation?' He didn't like the sound of it.

Vittoria looked unconcerned. 'Yes. If antimatter and matter make contact, both are destroyed instantly. Physicists call the process "annihilation".'

Langdon nodded. 'Oh.'

'It is nature's simplest reaction. A particle of matter and a particle of antimatter combine to release two *new* particles – called photons. A photon is effectively a tiny puff of light.'

Langdon had read about photons – light particles – the purest form of energy. He decided to refrain from asking about Captain Kirk's use of photon torpedoes against the Klingons. 'So if the antimatter falls, we see a tiny puff of light?'

Vittoria shrugged. 'Depends what you call tiny. Here, let me demonstrate.' She reached for the canister and started to unscrew it from its charging podium.

Without warning, Kohler let out a cry of terror and lunged forward, knocking her hands away. 'Vittoria! Are you insane!'

22

Kohler, incredibly, was standing for a moment, teetering on two withered legs. His face was white with fear. 'Vittoria! You can't remove that trap!'

Langdon watched, bewildered by the director's sudden panic.

'Five hundred nanograms!' Kohler said. 'If you break the magnetic field—'

'Director,' Vittoria assured, 'it's perfectly safe. Every trap has a failsafe – a back-up battery in case it is removed from its recharger. The specimen remains suspended even if I remove the canister.'

Kohler looked uncertain. Then, hesitantly, he settled back into his chair.

'The batteries activate automatically,' Vittoria said, 'when the trap is moved from the recharger. They work for twenty-four hours. Like a reserve tank of gas.' She turned to Langdon, as if sensing his discomfort. 'Antimatter has some astonishing characteristics, Mr Langdon, which make it quite dangerous. A ten milligram sample – the volume of a grain of sand – is hypothesized to hold as much energy as about two hundred metric tons of conventional rocket fuel.'

Langdon's head was spinning again.

'It is the energy source of tomorrow. A thousand times more powerful than nuclear energy. One hundred percent efficient. No byproducts. No radiation. No pollution. A few grams could power a major city for a week.'

Grams? Langdon stepped uneasily back from the podium.

'Don't worry,' Vittoria said. '*These* samples are minuscule fractions of a gram – *millionths*. Relatively harmless.' She reached for the canister again and twisted it from its docking platform.

Kohler twitched but did not interfere. As the trap came free, there was a sharp bleep, and a small LED display activated near the base of the trap. The red digits blinked, counting down from twenty-four hours.

24:00:00 . . .
23:59:59 . . .
23:59:58 . . .

Langdon studied the descending counter and decided it looked unsettlingly like a bomb.

'The battery,' Vittoria explained, 'will run for the full twenty-four hours before dying. It can be recharged by placing the trap back on the podium. It's designed as a safety measure, but it's also convenient for transport.'

'Transport?' Kohler looked thunderstruck. 'You take this stuff out of the lab?'

'Of course not,' Vittoria said. 'But the mobility allows us to study it.'

Vittoria led Langdon and Kohler to the far end of the room. She pulled a curtain aside to reveal a window, beyond which was a large room. The walls, floors, and ceiling were entirely plated in steel. The room reminded Langdon of the holding tank of an oil freighter he had once taken to Papua New Guinea to study *Hanta* body graffiti.

'It's an annihilation tank,' Vittoria declared.

Kohler looked up. 'You actually *observe* annihilations?'

'My father was fascinated with the physics of the Big Bang – large amounts of energy from minuscule kernels of matter.' Vittoria pulled open a steel drawer beneath the window. She placed the trap inside the drawer and closed it. Then she pulled a lever beside the drawer. A moment later, the trap appeared on the other side of the glass, rolling smoothly in a wide arc across the metal floor until it came to a stop near the center of the room.

Vittoria gave a tight smile. 'You're about to witness your first antimatter-matter annihilation. A few millionths of a gram. A relatively minuscule specimen.'

Langdon looked out at the antimatter trap sitting alone on the floor of the enormous tank. Kohler also turned toward the window, looking uncertain.

'Normally,' Vittoria explained, 'we'd have to wait the full twenty-four hours until the batteries died, but this chamber contains magnets beneath the floor that can override the trap, pulling the antimatter out of suspension. And when the matter and antimatter touch . . .'

'Annihilation,' Kohler whispered.

'One more thing,' Vittoria said. 'Antimatter releases pure energy. A one hundred per cent conversion of mass to photons. So don't look directly at the sample. Shield your eyes.'

Langdon was wary, but he now sensed Vittoria was being overly dramatic. *Don't look directly at the canister?* The device was more than thirty yards away, behind an ultrathick wall of tinted Plexiglas. Moreover, the speck in the canister was invisible, microscopic. *Shield my eyes?* Langdon thought. *How much energy could that speck possibly—*

Vittoria pressed the button.

Instantly, Langdon was blinded. A brilliant point of light shone in the canister and then exploded outward in a shock wave of light that radiated in all directions, erupting against the window before him with thunderous force. He stumbled back as the detonation rocked the vault. The light burned bright for a moment, searing, and then, after an instant, it rushed back inward, absorbing in on itself, and collapsing into a tiny speck that disappeared to nothing. Langdon blinked in pain, slowly recovering his eyesight. He squinted into the smoldering chamber. The canister on the floor had entirely disappeared. Vaporized. Not a trace.

He stared in wonder. 'G . . . God.'

Vittoria nodded sadly. 'That's precisely what my father said.'

23

Kohler was staring into the annihilation chamber with a look of utter amazement at the spectacle he had just seen. Robert Langdon was beside him, looking even more dazed.

'I want to see my father,' Vittoria demanded. 'I showed you the lab. Now I want to see my father.'

Kohler turned slowly, apparently not hearing her. 'Why did you wait so long, Vittoria? You and your father should have told me about this discovery immediately.'

Vittoria stared at him. *How many reasons do you want?* 'Director, we can argue about this later. Right now, I want to see my father.'

'Do you know what this technology implies?'

'Sure,' Vittoria shot back. 'Revenue for CERN. A lot of it. Now I want—'

'Is that why you kept it secret?' Kohler demanded, clearly baiting her. 'Because you feared the board and I would vote to license it out?'

'It *should* be licensed,' Vittoria fired back, feeling herself dragged into the argument. 'Antimatter is important technology. But it's also dangerous. My father and I wanted time to refine the procedures and make it safe.'

'In other words, you didn't trust the board of directors to place prudent science before financial greed.'

Vittoria was surprised by the indifference in Kohler's tone. 'There were other issues as well,' she said. 'My father wanted time to present antimatter in the appropriate light.'

'Meaning?'

What do you think I mean? 'Matter from energy? Something from nothing? It's practically proof that Genesis is a scientific possibility.'

'So he didn't want the religious implications of his discovery lost in an onslaught of commercialism?'

'In a manner of speaking.'

'And you?'

Vittoria's concerns, ironically, were somewhat the opposite. Commercialism was critical for the success of any new energy source. Although antimatter technology had staggering potential as an efficient and nonpolluting energy source – if unveiled prematurely,

105

antimatter ran the risk of being vilified by the politics and PR fiascoes that had killed nuclear and solar power. Nuclear had proliferated before it was safe, and there were accidents. Solar had proliferated before it was efficient, and people lost money. Both technologies got bad reputations and withered on the vine.

'My interests,' Vittoria said, 'were a bit less lofty than uniting science and religion.'

'The environment,' Kohler ventured assuredly.

'Limitless energy. No strip mining. No pollution. No radiation. Antimatter technology could save the planet.'

'Or destroy it,' Kohler quipped. 'Depending on who uses it for what.' Vittoria felt a chill emanating from Kohler's crippled form. 'Who else knew about this?' he asked.

'No one,' Vittoria said. 'I told you that.'

'Then why do you think your father was killed?'

Vittoria's muscles tightened. 'I have no idea. He had enemies here at CERN, you know that, but it couldn't have had anything to do with antimatter. We swore to each other to keep it between us for another few months, until we were ready.'

'And you're certain your father kept his vow of silence?'

Now Vittoria was getting mad. 'My father has kept tougher vows than that!'

'And *you* told no one?'

'Of course not!'

Kohler exhaled. He paused, as though choosing his next words carefully. 'Suppose someone *did* find out. And suppose someone gained access to this lab. What do you imagine they would be after? Did your father have notes down here? Documentation of his processes?'

'Director, I've been patient. I need some answers now. You keep talking about a break-in, but you saw the retina scan. My father has been vigilant about secrecy and security.'

'Humor me,' Kohler snapped, startling her. 'What would be missing?'

'I have no idea.' Vittoria angrily scanned the lab. All the antimatter specimens were accounted for. Her father's work area looked in order. 'Nobody came in here,' she declared. 'Everything up here looks fine.'

Kohler looked surprised. '*Up* here?'

Vittoria had said it instinctively. 'Yes, here in the upper lab.'

'You're using the lower lab too?'

'For storage.'

Kohler rolled towards her, coughing again. 'You're using the Haz-Mat chamber for storage? Storage of *what*?'

Hazardous material, what else! Vittoria was losing her patience. 'Antimatter.'

Kohler lifted himself on the arms of his chair. 'There are *other* specimens? Why the hell didn't you tell me!'

'I just did,' Vittoria fired back. 'And you've barely given me a chance!'

'We need to check those specimens,' Kohler said. 'Now.'

'Specimen,' Vittoria corrected. 'Singular. And it's fine. Nobody could ever—'

'Only one?' Kohler hesitated. 'Why isn't it up here?'

'My father wanted it below the bedrock as a precaution. It's larger than the others.'

The look of alarm that shot between Kohler and Langdon was not lost on Vittoria. Kohler rolled toward her again. 'You created a specimen *larger* than five hundred nanograms?'

'A necessity,' Vittoria defended. 'We had to prove the input/yield threshold could be safely crossed.' The question with new fuel sources, she knew, was always one of input vs. yield – how much money one had to expend to harvest the fuel. Building an oil rig to yield a single barrel of oil was a losing endeavour. However, if that same rig, with minimal added expense, could deliver millions of barrels, then you were in business. Antimatter was the same way. Firing up sixteen miles of electromagnets to create a tiny specimen of anti-matter expended more energy than the resulting antimatter contained. In order to prove antimatter efficient and viable, one had to create specimens of a larger magnitude.

Although Vittoria's father had been hesitant to create a large specimen, Vittoria had pushed him hard. She argued that in order for antimatter to be taken seriously, she and her father had to prove two things. First, that cost-effective amounts could be produced. And second, that the specimens could be safely stored. In the end she had won, and her father had acquiesced against his better judgment. Not, however, without some firm guidelines regarding secrecy and access. The antimatter, her father had insisted, would be stored in Haz-Mat – a small granite hollow, an additional seventy-five feet below ground. The specimen would be their secret. And only the two of them would have access.

'Vittoria?' Kohler insisted, his voice tense. 'How large a specimen did you and your father create?'

Vittoria felt a wry pleasure inside. She knew the amount would stun even the great Maximilian Kohler.

She pictured the antimatter below. An incredible sight. Suspended inside the trap, perfectly visible to the naked eye, danced a tiny sphere of antimatter. This was no microscopic speck. This was a droplet the size of a BB.

Vittoria took a deep breath. 'A full quarter of a gram.'

The blood drained from Kohler's face. 'What!' He broke into a fit of coughing. 'A quarter of a gram? That converts to . . . almost five kilotons!'

Kilotons. Vittoria hated the word. It was one she and her father never used. A kiloton was equal to 1,000 metric tons of TNT. Kilotons were for weaponry. Payload. Destructive power. She and her father spoke in electron volts and joules – constructive energy output.

'That much antimatter could literally liquidate everything in a half-mile radius!' Kohler exclaimed.

'Yes, if annihilated all at once,' Vittoria shot back, 'which nobody would ever do!'

'Except someone who didn't know better. Or if your power source failed!' Kohler was already heading for the elevator.

'Which is why my father kept it in Haz-Mat under a fail-safe power and a redundant security system.'

Kohler turned, looking hopeful. 'You have additional security on Haz-Mat?'

'Yes. A second retina-scan.'

Kohler spoke only two words. 'Downstairs. Now.'

The freight elevator dropped like a rock.

Another seventy-five feet into the earth.

Vittoria was certain she sensed fear in both men as the elevator fell deeper. Kohler's usually emotionless

109

face was taut. *I know,* Vittoria thought, *the sample is enormous, but the precautions we've taken are—*

They reached the bottom.

The elevator opened, and Vittoria led the way down the dimly lit corridor. Up ahead the corridor dead-ended at a huge steel door. HAZ-MAT. The retina device beside the door was identical to the one upstairs. She approached. Carefully, she aligned her eye with the lens.

She pulled back. Something was wrong. The usually spotless lens was splattered . . . smeared with something that looked like . . . *blood*? Confused she turned to the two men, but her gaze met waxen faces. Both Kohler and Langdon were white, their eyes fixed on the floor at her feet.

Vittoria followed their line of sight . . . down.

'No!' Langdon yelled, reaching for her. But it was too late.

Vittoria's vision locked on the object on the floor. It was both utterly foreign and intimately familiar to her.

It took only an instant.

Then, with a reeling horror, she knew. Staring up at her from the floor, discarded like a piece of trash, was an eyeball. She would have recognized that shade of hazel anywhere.

24

The security technician held his breath as his commander leaned over his shoulder, studying the bank of security monitors before them. A minute passed.

The commander's silence was to be expected, the technician told himself. The commander was a man of rigid protocol. He had not risen to command one of the world's most elite security forces by talking first and thinking second.

But what is he thinking?

The object they were pondering on the monitor was a canister of some sort – a canister with transparent sides. That much was easy. It was the rest that was difficult.

Inside the container, as if by some special effect, a small droplet of metallic liquid seemed to be *floating* in midair. The droplet appeared and disappeared in the robotic red blinking of a digital LED descending resolutely, making the technician's skin crawl.

'Can you lighten the contrast?' the commander asked, startling the technician.

The technician heeded the instruction, and the image lightened somewhat. The commander leaned forward, squinting closer at something that had just come visible on the base of the container.

The technician followed his commander's gaze. Ever so faintly, printed next to the LED was an acronym. Four capital letters gleaming in the intermittent spurts of light.

'Stay here,' the commander said. 'Say nothing. I'll handle this.'

25

Haz-Mat. Fifty meters below ground.

Vittoria Vetra stumbled forward, almost falling into

the retina scan. She sensed the American rushing to help her, holding her, supporting her weight. On the floor at her feet, her father's eyeball stared up. She felt the air crushed from her lungs. *They cut out his eye!* Her world twisted. Kohler pressed close behind, speaking. Langdon guided her. As if in a dream, she found herself gazing into the retina scan. The mechanism beeped.

The door slid open.

Even with the terror of her father's eye boring into her soul, Vittoria sensed an additional horror awaited inside. When she leveled her blurry gaze into the room, she confirmed the next chapter of the nightmare. Before her, the solitary recharging podium was empty.

The canister was gone. They had cut out her father's eye to steal it. The implications came too fast for her to fully comprehend. Everything had backfired. The specimen that was supposed to prove antimatter was a safe and viable energy source had been stolen. *But nobody knew this specimen even existed!* The truth, however, was undeniable. Someone had found out. Vittoria could not imagine who. Even Kohler, whom they said knew everything at CERN, clearly had no idea about the project.

Her father was dead. Murdered for his genius.

As the grief strafed her heart, a new emotion surged into Vittoria's conscious. This one was far worse. Crushing. Stabbing at her. The emotion was guilt. Uncontrollable, relentless guilt. Vittoria knew it had been *she* who convinced her father to create the specimen. Against his better judgment. And he had been killed for it.

A quarter of a gram . . .

112

Like any technology – fire, gunpowder, the combustion engine – in the wrong hands, antimatter could be deadly. Very deadly. Antimatter was a lethal weapon. Potent, and unstoppable. Once removed from its recharging platform at CERN, the canister would count down inexorably. A runaway train.

And when time ran out . . .

A blinding light. The roar of thunder. Spontaneous incineration. Just the flash . . . and an empty crater. A *big* empty crater.

The image of her father's quiet genius being used as a tool of destruction was like poison in her blood. Antimatter was the ultimate terrorist weapon. It had no metallic parts to trip metal detectors, no chemical signature for dogs to trace, no fuse to deactivate if the authorities located the canister. The countdown had begun . . .

Langdon didn't know what else to do. He took his handkerchief and laid it on the floor over Leonardo Vetra's eyeball. Vittoria was standing now in the doorway of the empty Haz-Mat chamber, her expression wrought with grief and panic. Langdon moved toward her again, instinctively, but Kohler intervened.

'Mr Langdon?' Kohler's face was expressionless. He motioned Langdon out of earshot. Langdon reluctantly followed, leaving Vittoria to fend for herself. 'You're the specialist,' Kohler said, his whisper intense. 'I want to know what these Illuminati bastards intend to do with this antimatter.'

Langdon tried to focus. Despite the madness around him, his first reaction was logical. Academic rejection. Kohler was still making assumptions. Impossible assumptions. 'The Illuminati are defunct,

Mr Kohler. I stand by that. This crime could be any-thing – maybe even another CERN employee who found out about Mr Vetra's breakthrough and thought the project was too dangerous to continue.'

Kohler looked stunned. 'You think this is a crime of *conscience*, Mr Langdon? Absurd. Whoever killed Leonardo wanted one thing – the antimatter specimen. And no doubt they have plans for it.'

'You mean terrorism.'

'Plainly.'

'But the Illuminati were not terrorists.'

'Tell that to Leonardo Vetra.'

Langdon felt a pang of truth in the statement. Leonardo Vetra had indeed been branded with the Illuminati symbol. Where had it come from? The sacred brand seemed too difficult a hoax for someone trying to cover his tracks by casting suspicion else-where. There had to be another explanation.

Again, Langdon forced himself to consider the implausible. *If the Illuminati were still active, and if they stole the antimatter, what would be their intention? What would be their target?* The answer furnished by his brain was instantaneous. Langdon dismissed it just as fast. True, the Illuminati had an obvious enemy, but a wide-scale terrorist attack against that enemy was inconceivable. It was entirely out of character. Yes, the Illuminati had killed people, but *individuals*, carefully conscripted targets. Mass destruction was somehow heavy-handed. Langdon paused. Then again, he thought, there would be a rather majestic eloquence to it – antimatter, the ultimate scientific achievement, being used to vaporize—

He refused to accept the preposterous thought.

'There is,' he said suddenly, 'a logical explanation other than terrorism.'

Kohler stared, obviously waiting.

Langdon tried to sort out the thought. The Illuminati had always wielded tremendous power through *financial* means. They controlled banks. They owned gold bullion. They were even rumoured to possess the single most valuable gem on earth – the Illuminati Diamond, a flawless diamond of enormous proportions. 'Money,' Langdon said. 'The antimatter could have been stolen for financial gain.'

Kohler looked incredulous. 'Financial gain? Where does one sell a droplet of antimatter?'

'Not the specimen,' Langdon countered. 'The technology. Antimatter technology must be worth a mint. Maybe someone stole the specimen to do analysis and R and D.'

'Industrial espionage? But that canister has twenty-four hours before the batteries die. The researchers would blow themselves up before they learned anything at all.'

'They could recharge it before it explodes. They could build a compatible recharging podium like the ones here at CERN.'

'In twenty-four hours?' Kohler challenged. 'Even if they stole the schematics, a recharger like that would take *months* to engineer, not hours!'

'He's right.' Vittoria's voice was frail.

Both men turned. Vittoria was moving toward them, her gait as tremulous as her words.

'He's right. Nobody could reverse engineer a recharger in time. The interface alone would take weeks. Flux filters, servo-coils, power conditioning alloys, all calibrated to the specific energy grade of the locale.'

Langdon frowned. The point was taken. An anti-matter trap was not something one could simply plug into a wall socket. Once removed from CERN, the canister was on a one-way, twenty-four-hour trip to oblivion.

Which left only one, very disturbing, conclusion.

'We need to call Interpol,' Vittoria said. Even to herself, her voice sounded distant. 'We need to call the proper authorities. Immediately.'

Kohler shook his head. 'Absolutely not.'

The words stunned her. 'No? What do you mean?'

'You and your father have put me in a very difficult position here.'

'Director, we need help. We need to find that trap and get it back here before someone gets hurt. We have a responsibility!'

'We have a responsibility to *think*,' Kohler said, his tone hardening. 'This situation could have very, very serious repercussions for CERN.'

'You're worried about CERN's *reputation*? Do you know what that canister could do to an urban area? It has a blast radius of a half mile! Nine city blocks!'

'Perhaps you and your father should have considered that before you created the specimen.'

Vittoria felt like she'd been stabbed. 'But . . . we took every precaution.'

'Apparently, it was not enough.'

'But nobody *knew* about the antimatter.' She realized, of course, it was an absurd argument. Of course somebody knew. Someone had found out.

Vittoria had told no one. That left only two explanations. Either her father had taken someone into his confidence without telling her, which made no sense because it was her *father* who had sworn them both to secrecy, or she and her father had been monitored. The cell phone maybe? She knew they had spoken a few times while Vittoria was traveling. Had they said too much? It was possible. There was also their E-mail. But they had been discreet, hadn't they? CERN's security system? Had they been monitored somehow without their knowledge? She knew none of that mattered anymore. What was done, was done. *My father is dead.*

The thought spurred her to action. She pulled her cell phone from her shorts pocket.

Kohler accelerated toward her, coughing violently, eyes flashing anger. 'Who . . . are you calling?'

'CERN's switchboard. They can connect us to Interpol.'

'Think!' Kohler choked, screeching to a halt in front of her. 'Are you really so naïve? That canister could be anywhere in the world by now. No intelligence agency on earth could possibly mobilize to find it in time.'

'So we do *nothing*?' Vittoria felt compunction challenging a man in such frail health, but the director was so far out of line she didn't even know him anymore.

'We do what is *smart*,' Kohler said. 'We don't risk CERN's reputation by involving the authorities who cannot help anyway. Not yet. Not without thinking.'

Vittoria knew there was logic somewhere in Kohler's argument, but she also knew that logic, by definition, was bereft of moral responsibility. Her father had *lived* for moral responsibility – careful science, accountability, faith in man's inherent goodness. Vittoria believed in those things too, but she saw them in terms of *karma*. Turning away from Kohler, she snapped open her phone.

'You can't do that,' he said.

'Just try and stop me.'

Kohler did not move.

An instant later, Vittoria realized why. This far underground, her cell phone had no dial tone.

Fuming, she headed for the elevator.

26

The Hassassin stood at the end of the stone tunnel. His torch still burned bright, the smoke mixing with the smell of moss and stale air. Silence surrounded him. The iron door blocking his way looked as old as the tunnel itself, rusted but still holding strong. He waited in the darkness, trusting.

It was almost time.

Janus had promised someone on the inside would open the door. The Hassassin marveled at the betrayal. He would have waited all night at that door to carry out his task, but he sensed it would not be necessary. He was working for determined men.

Minutes later, exactly at the appointed hour, there was a loud clank of heavy keys on the other side of the door. Metal scraped on metal as multiple locks disengaged. One by one, three huge deadbolts ground open. The locks creaked as if they had not been used in centuries. Finally all three were open.

Then there was silence.

The Hassassin waited patiently, five minutes, exactly as he had been told. Then, with electricity in his blood, he pushed. The great door swung open.

27

'Vittoria, I will not allow it!' Kohler's breath was labored and getting worse as the Haz-Mat elevator ascended.

Vittoria blocked him out. She craved sanctuary, something familiar in this place that no longer felt like home. She knew it was not to be. Right now, she had to swallow the pain and act. *Get to a phone.*

Robert Langdon was beside her, silent as usual. Vittoria had given up wondering who the man was. *A specialist?* Could Kohler be any less specific? *Mr Langdon can help us find your father's killer.* Langdon was being no help at all. His warmth and kindness seemed genuine, but he was clearly hiding something. They both were.

Kohler was at her again. 'As director of CERN, I have a responsibility to the future of science. If you amplify this into an international incident and CERN suffers—'

'Future of science?' Vittoria turned on him. 'Do you really plan to escape accountability by never admitting this antimatter came from CERN? Do you plan to ignore the people's lives we've put in danger?'

'Not *we*,' Kohler countered. '*You.* You and your father.'

Vittoria looked away.

'And as far as endangering lives,' Kohler said, '*life* is exactly what this is about. You know antimatter technology has enormous implications for life on this planet. If CERN goes bankrupt, destroyed by scandal, *everybody* loses. Man's future is in the hands of places like CERN, scientists like you and your father, working to solve tomorrow's problems.'

Vittoria had heard Kohler's Science-as-God lecture before, and she never bought it. Science *itself* caused half the problems it was trying to solve. 'Progress' was Mother Earth's ultimate malignancy.

'Scientific advancement carries risk,' Kohler argued. 'It always has. Space programs, genetic research, medicine – they all make mistakes. Science needs to survive its own blunders, at any cost. For *everyone's* sake.'

Vittoria was amazed at Kohler's ability to weigh moral issues with scientific detachment. His intellect seemed to be the product of an icy divorce from his inner spirit. 'You think CERN is so critical to the earth's future that we should be immune from moral responsibility?'

'Do not argue *morals* with me. You crossed a line when you made that specimen, and you have put this entire facility at risk. I'm trying to protect not only the jobs of the three thousand scientists who work here, but also your father's reputation. Think about *him*. A man like your father does not deserve to be remembered as the creator of a weapon of mass destruction.'

Vittoria felt his spear hit home. *I am the one who convinced my father to create that specimen. This is my fault!*

When the door opened, Kohler was still talking. Vittoria stepped out of the elevator, pulled out her phone, and tried again.

Still no dial tone. *Damn!* She headed for the door.

'Vittoria, stop.' The director sounded asthmatic now, as he accelerated after her. 'Slow down. We need to talk.'

'*Basta di parlare!*'

120

'Think of your father,' Kohler urged. 'What would he do?'

She kept going.

'Vittoria, I haven't been totally honest with you.'

Vittoria felt her legs slow.

'I don't know what I was thinking,' Kohler said. 'I was just trying to protect you. Just tell me what you want. We need to work together here.'

Vittoria came to a full stop halfway across the lab, but she did not turn. 'I want to find the antimatter. And I want to know who killed my father.' She waited.

Kohler sighed. 'Vittoria, we already know who killed your father. I'm sorry.'

Now Vittoria turned. 'You what?'

'I didn't know how to tell you. It's a difficult—'

'You *know* who killed my father?'

'We have a very good idea, yes. The killer left somewhat of a calling card. That's the reason I called Mr Langdon. The group claiming responsibility is his specialty.'

'The group? A terrorist group?'

'Vittoria, they stole a quarter *gram* of antimatter.'

Vittoria looked at Robert Langdon standing there across the room. Everything began falling into place. *That explains some of the secrecy.* She was amazed it hadn't occurred to her earlier. Kohler had called the authorities after all. *The* authorities. Now it seemed obvious. Robert Langdon was American, clean-cut, conservative, obviously very sharp. Who else could it be? Vittoria should have guessed from the start. She felt a newfound hope as she turned to him.

'Mr Langdon, I want to know who killed my father. And I want to know if your agency can find the anti-matter.'

Langdon looked flustered. 'My agency?'

'You're with U.S. Intelligence, I assume.'

'Actually . . . no.'

Kohler intervened. 'Mr Langdon is a professor of art history at Harvard University.'

Vittoria felt like she had been doused with ice water. 'An art teacher?'

'He is a specialist in cult symbology.' Kohler sighed. 'Vittoria, we believe your father was killed by a satanic cult.'

Vittoria heard the words in her mind, but she was unable to process them. *A satanic cult.*

'The group claiming responsibility calls themselves the Illuminati.'

Vittoria looked at Kohler and then at Langdon, wondering if this was some kind of perverse joke. 'The Illuminati?' she demanded.'As in the *Bavarian Illuminati?*'

Kohler looked stunned. 'You've *heard* of them?'

Vittoria felt the tears of frustration welling right below the surface. '*Bavarian Illuminati: New World Order.* Steve Jackson computer games. Half the techies here play it on the Internet.' Her voice cracked. 'But I don't understand . . .'

Kohler shot Langdon a confused look.

Langdon nodded. 'Popular game. Ancient brotherhood takes over the world. Semihistorical. I didn't know it was in Europe too.'

Vittoria was bewildered. 'What are you talking about? The Illuminati? It's a computer game!'

'Vittoria,' Kohler said, 'the Illuminati is the group claiming responsibility for your father's death.'

Vittoria mustered every bit of courage she could find to fight the tears. She forced herself to hold on and

122

assess the situation logically. But the harder she focused, the less she understood. Her father had been murdered. CERN had suffered a major breach of security. There was a bomb counting down somewhere that *she* was responsible for. And the director had nominated an art teacher to help them find a mythical fraternity of Satanists.

Vittoria felt suddenly all alone. She turned to go, but Kohler cut her off. He reached for something in his pocket. He produced a crumpled piece of fax paper and handed it to her.

Vittoria swayed in horror as her eyes hit the image.

'They branded him,' Kohler said. 'They branded his goddamn chest.'

28

Secretary Sylvie Baudeloque was now in a panic. She paced outside the director's empty office. *Where the hell is he? What do I do?*

It had been a bizarre day. Of course, any day working for Maximilian Kohler had the potential to be strange, but Kohler had been in rare form today.

'Find me Leonardo Vetra!' he had demanded when Sylvie arrived this morning.

Dutifully, Sylvie paged, phoned, and E-mailed Leonardo Vetra.

Nothing.

So Kohler had left in a huff, apparently to go find Vetra himself. When he rolled back in a few hours later, Kohler looked decidedly not well . . . not that he ever actually looked *well*, but he looked worse than usual. He locked himself in his office, and she could hear him on his modem, his phone, faxing, talking. Then Kohler rolled out again. He hadn't been back since.

Sylvie had decided to ignore the antics as yet another Kohlerian melodrama, but she began to get concerned when Kohler failed to return at the proper time for his daily injections; the director's physical condition required regular treatment, and when he decided to push his luck, the results were never pretty – respiratory shock, coughing fits, and a mad dash by the infirmary personnel. Sometimes Sylvie thought Maximilian Kohler had a death wish.

She considered paging him to remind him, but she'd learned charity was something Kohler's pride despised. Last week, he had become so enraged with a visiting scientist who had shown him undue pity that Kohler clambered to his feet and threw a clipboard at the man's head. King Kohler could be surprisingly agile when he was *pissé*.

At the moment, however, Sylvie's concern for the director's health was taking a back burner . . . replaced by a much more pressing dilemma. The CERN switchboard had phoned five minutes ago in a frenzy to say they had an urgent call for the director.

'He's not available,' Sylvie had said.

Then the CERN operator told her who was calling.

Sylvie half laughed aloud. 'You're kidding, right?' She listened, and her face clouded with disbelief. 'And your caller ID confirms—' Sylvie was frowning. 'I see. Okay. Can you ask what the—' She sighed. 'No. That's fine. Tell him to hold. I'll locate the director right away. Yes, I understand. I'll hurry.'

But Sylvie had not been able to find the director. She had called his cell line three times and each time gotten the same message: 'The mobile customer you are trying to reach is out of range.' *Out of range? How far could he go?* So Sylvie had dialed Kohler's beeper. Twice. No response. Most unlike him. She'd even E-mailed his mobile computer. Nothing. It was like the man had disappeared off the face of the earth.

So what do I do? she now wondered.

Short of searching CERN's entire complex herself, Sylvie knew there was only one other way to get the director's attention. He would not be pleased, but the man on the phone was not someone the director should keep waiting. Nor did it sound like the caller was in any mood to be told the director was unavailable.

Startled with her own boldness, Sylvie made her decision. She walked into Kohler's office and went to the metal box on his wall behind his desk. She opened the cover, stared at the controls, and found the correct button.

Then she took a deep breath and grabbed the microphone.

29

Vittoria did not remember how they had gotten to the main elevator, but they were there. Ascending. Kohler was behind her, his breathing labored now. Langdon's concerned gaze passed through her like a ghost. He had taken the fax from her hand and slipped it in his jacket pocket away from her sight, but the image was still burned into her memory.

As the elevator climbed, Vittoria's world swirled into darkness. *Papa!* In her mind she reached for him. For just a moment, in the oasis of her memory, Vittoria was with him. She was nine years old, rolling down hills of edelweiss flowers, the Swiss sky spinning overhead.

Papa! Papa!

Leonardo Vetra was laughing beside her, beaming. 'What is it, angel?'

'Papa!' she giggled, nuzzling close to him. 'Ask me what's the matter!'

'But you look happy, sweetie. Why would I ask you what's the matter?'

'Just ask me.'

He shrugged. 'What's the matter?'

She immediately started laughing. 'What's the matter? *Everything* is the matter! Rocks! Trees! Atoms! Even anteaters! Everything is the matter!'

He laughed. 'Did you make that up?'

'Pretty smart, huh?'

'My little Einstein.'

She frowned. 'He has stupid hair. I saw his picture.'

'He's got a smart head, though. I told you what he proved, right?'

Her eyes widened with dread. 'Dad! No! You *promised!*'

'$E=MC^2$!' He tickled her playfully. '$E=MC^2$!'

'No *math*! I told you! I hate it!'

'I'm glad you hate it. Because girls aren't even *allowed* to do math.'

Vittoria stopped short. 'They *aren't*?'

'Of course not. Everyone knows that. Girls play with dollies. Boys do math. No math for girls. I'm not even *permitted* to talk to little girls about math.'

'What! But that's not fair!'

'Rules are rules. Absolutely no math for little girls.'

Vittoria looked horrified. 'But dolls are boring!'

'I'm sorry,' her father said. 'I could tell you about math, but if I got caught . . .' He looked nervously around the deserted hills.

Vittoria followed his gaze. 'Okay,' she whispered, 'just tell me quietly.'

The motion of the elevator startled her. Vittoria opened her eyes. He was gone.

Reality rushed in, wrapping a frosty grip around her. She looked to Langdon. The earnest concern in his gaze felt like the warmth of a guardian angel, especially in the aura of Kohler's chill.

A single sentient thought began pounding at Vittoria with unrelenting force.

Where is the antimatter?

The horrifying answer was only a moment away.

30

'Maximilian Kohler. Kindly call your office immediately.'

Blazing sunbeams flooded Langdon's eyes as the elevator doors opened into the main atrium. Before the echo of the announcement on the intercom overhead faded, every electronic device on Kohler's wheelchair started beeping and buzzing simultaneously. His pager. His phone. His E-mail. Kohler glanced down at the blinking lights in apparent bewilderment. The director had resurfaced, and he was back in range.

'Director Kohler. Please call your office.'

The sound of his name on the PA seemed to startle Kohler.

He glanced up, looking angered and then almost immediately concerned. Langdon's eyes met his, and Vittoria's too. The three of them were motionless a moment, as if all the tension between them had been erased and replaced by a single, unifying foreboding.

Kohler took his cell phone from the armrest. He dialed an extension and fought off another coughing fit. Vittoria and Langdon waited.

'This is . . . Director Kohler,' he said, wheezing. 'Yes? I was subterranean, out of range.' He listened, his gray eyes widening. *'Who?* Yes, patch it through.' There was a pause. 'Hello? This is Maximilian Kohler. I am the director of CERN. With whom am I speaking?'

Vittoria and Langdon watched in silence as Kohler listened.

'It would be unwise,' Kohler finally said, 'to speak of this by phone. I will be there immediately.' He was coughing again. 'Meet me . . . at Leonardo da Vinci Airport. Forty minutes.' Kohler's breath seemed to be failing him now. He descended into a fit of coughing and barely managed to choke out the words. 'Locate the canister immediately . . . I am coming.' Then he clicked off his phone.

Vittoria ran to Kohler's side, but Kohler could no longer speak. Langdon watched as Vittoria pulled out her cell phone and paged CERN's infirmary. Langdon felt like a ship on the periphery of a storm . . . tossed but detached.

Meet me at Leonardo da Vinci Airport. Kohler's words echoed.

The uncertain shadows that had fogged Langdon's mind all morning, in a single instant, solidified into a vivid image. As he stood there in the swirl of confusion, he felt a door inside him open . . . as if some mystic threshold had just been breached. *The ambigram. The murdered priest/scientist. The antimatter. And now . . . the target.* Leonardo da Vinci Airport could only mean one thing. In a moment of stark realization, Langdon knew he had just crossed over. He had become a believer.

Five kilotons. Let there be light.

Two paramedics materialized, racing across the atrium in white smocks. They knelt by Kohler, putting an oxygen mask on his face. Scientists in the hall stopped and stood back.

Kohler took two long pulls, pushed the mask aside, and still gasping for air, looked up at Vittoria and Langdon. 'Rome.'

'Rome?' Vittoria demanded. 'The antimatter is in Rome? Who called?'

Kohler's face was twisted, his gray eyes watering. 'The Swiss . . .' He choked on the words, and the paramedics put the mask back over his face. As they prepared to take him away, Kohler reached up and grabbed Langdon's arm.

Langdon nodded. He knew.

'Go . . .' Kohler wheezed beneath his mask. 'Go . . . call me . . .' Then the paramedics were rolling him away.

Vittoria stood riveted to the floor, watching him go. Then she turned to Langdon. 'Rome? But . . . what was that about *the Swiss*?'

Langdon put a hand on her shoulder, barely whispering the words. 'The Swiss Guard,' he said. 'The sworn sentinels of Vatican City.'

31

The X-33 space plane roared into the sky and arched south toward Rome. On board, Langdon sat in silence. The last fifteen minutes had been a blur. Now that he had finished briefing Vittoria on the Illuminati and their covenant against the Vatican, the scope of this situation was starting to sink in.

What the hell am I doing? Langdon wondered. *I should have gone home when I had the chance!* Deep down, though, he knew he'd never had the chance.

Langdon's better judgment had screamed at him to return to Boston. Nonetheless, academic astonishment had somehow vetoed prudence. Everything he had ever believed about the demise of the Illuminati was suddenly looking like a brilliant sham. Part of him craved proof. Confirmation. There was also a question of conscience. With Kohler ailing and Vittoria on her own, Langdon knew that if his knowledge of the Illuminati could assist in any way, he had a moral obligation to be here.

There was more, though. Although Langdon was ashamed to admit it, his initial horror on hearing about the antimatter's location was not only the danger to human life in Vatican City, but for something else as well.

Art.

The world's largest art collection was now sitting on a time bomb. The Vatican Museum housed over 60,000 priceless pieces in 1,407 rooms – Michelangelo, da Vinci, Bernini, Botticelli. Langdon wondered if all of the art could possibly be evacuated if necessary. He knew it was impossible. Many of the pieces were sculptures weighing tons. Not to mention, the greatest treasures were architectural – the Sistine Chapel, St Peter's Basilica, Bramante's famed spiral staircase leading to the *Museo Vaticano* – priceless testaments to man's creative genius. Langdon wondered how much time was left on the canister.

'Thanks for coming,' Vittoria said, her voice quiet.

Langdon emerged from his daydream and looked up. Vittoria was sitting across the aisle. Even in the stark fluorescent light of the cabin, there was an aura of composure about her – an almost magnetic radiance of wholeness. Her breathing seemed deeper now, as if a spark of self-preservation had ignited within her . . . a craving for justice and retribution, fueled by a daughter's love.

Vittoria had not had time to change from her shorts and sleeveless top, and her tawny legs were now goose-bumped in the cold of the plane. Instinctively Langdon removed his jacket and offered it to her.

'American chivalry?' She accepted, her eyes thanking him silently.

The plane jostled across some turbulence, and Langdon felt a surge of danger. The windowless cabin felt cramped again, and he tried to imagine himself in an open field. The notion, he realized, was ironic. He had been in an open field when it had happened. *Crushing darkness.* He pushed the memory from his mind. *Ancient history.*

Vittoria was watching him. 'Do you believe in God, Mr Langdon?'

The question startled him. The earnestness in Vittoria's voice was even more disarming than the inquiry. *Do I believe in God?* He had hoped for a lighter topic of conversation to pass the trip.

A spiritual conundrum, Langdon thought. *That's what my friends call me.* Although he studied religion for years, Langdon was not a religious man. He respected the power of faith, the benevolence of churches, the strength religion gave so many people ... and yet, for him, the intellectual suspension of disbelief that was imperative if one were truly going to 'believe' had always proved too big an obstacle for his academic mind. 'I *want* to believe,' he heard himself say.

Vittoria's reply carried no judgment or challenge. 'So why *don't* you?'

He chuckled. 'Well, it's not that easy. *Having* faith requires *leaps* of faith, cerebral acceptance of miracles – immaculate conceptions and divine interventions. And then there are the codes of conduct. The Bible, the Koran, Buddhist scripture ... they all carry similar requirements – and similar penalties. They claim that if I don't live by a specific code I will go to hell. I can't imagine a God who would rule that way.'

'I hope you don't let your students dodge questions that shamelessly.'

The comment caught him off guard. 'What?'

'Mr Langdon, I did not ask if you believe what *man* says about God. I asked if you believe in God. There is a difference. Holy scripture is stories ... legends and history of man's quest to understand his own need for meaning. I am not asking you to pass judgment on literature. I am asking if you believe in *God*. When you lie out under the stars, do you sense the divine? Do you feel in your gut that you are staring up at the work of God's hand?'

Langdon took a long moment to consider it.

'I'm prying,' Vittoria apologized.

'No, I just . . .'

'Certainly you must debate issues of faith with your classes.'

'Endlessly.'

'And you play devil's advocate, I imagine. Always fueling the debate.'

Langdon smiled. 'You must be a teacher too.'

'No, but I learned from a master. My father could argue two sides of a Möbius Strip.'

Langdon laughed, picturing the artful crafting of a Möbius Strip – a twisted ring of paper, which technically possessed only *one* side. Langdon had first seen the single-sided shape in the artwork of M. C. Escher. 'May I ask you a question, Ms Vetra?'

'Call me Vittoria. Ms Vetra makes me feel old.'

He sighed inwardly, suddenly sensing his own age. 'Vittoria, I'm Robert.'

'You had a question.'

'Yes. As a scientist and the daughter of a Catholic priest, what do *you* think of religion?'

Vittoria paused, brushing a lock of hair from her eyes. 'Religion is like language or dress. We gravitate toward the practices with which we were raised. In the end, though, we are all proclaiming the same thing. That life has meaning. That we are grateful for the power that created us.'

Langdon was intrigued. 'So you're saying that whether you are a Christian or a Muslim simply depends on where you were born?'

'Isn't it obvious? Look at the diffusion of religion around the globe.'

'So faith is random?'

'Hardly. Faith is universal. Our specific methods for understanding it are arbitrary. Some of us pray to Jesus, some of us go to Mecca, some of us study subatomic particles. In the end we are all just searching for truth, that which is greater than ourselves.'

Langdon wished his students could express themselves so clearly. Hell, he wished *he* could express himself so clearly. 'And God?' he asked. 'Do you believe in God?'

Vittoria was silent for a long time. 'Science tells me God must exist. My mind tells me I will never understand God. And my heart tells me I am not meant to.'

How's that for concise, he thought. 'So you believe God is fact, but we will never understand Him.'

'*Her,*' she said with a smile. 'Your Native Americans had it right.'

Langdon chuckled. 'Mother Earth.'

'*Gaea.* The planet is an organism. All of us are cells with different purposes. And yet we are intertwined. Serving each other. Serving the whole.'

Looking at her, Langdon felt something stir within him that he had not felt in a long time. There was a bewitching clarity in her eyes . . . a purity in her voice. He felt drawn.

'Mr Langdon, let me ask you another question.'

'Robert,' he said. *Mr Langdon makes me feel old. I am old!*

'If you don't mind my asking, Robert, how did you get involved with the Illuminati?'

Langdon thought back. 'Actually, it was money.'

Vittoria looked disappointed. 'Money? Consulting, you mean?'

Langdon laughed, realizing how it must have sounded. 'No. Money as in *currency*.' He reached in his pants pocket and pulled out some money. He found a one-dollar bill. 'I became fascinated with the cult when I first learned that U.S. currency is covered with Illuminati symbology.'

Vittoria's eyes narrowed, apparently not knowing whether or not to take him seriously.

Langdon handed her the bill. 'Look at the back. See the Great Seal on the left?'

Vittoria turned the one-dollar bill over. 'You mean the pyramid?'

'The pyramid. Do you know what pyramids have to do with U.S. history?'

Vittoria shrugged.

'Exactly,' Langdon said. 'Absolutely *nothing*.'

Vittoria frowned. 'So why is it the *central* symbol of your Great Seal?'

'An eerie bit of history,' Langdon said. 'The pyramid is an occult symbol representing a convergence upward, toward the ultimate source of Illumination. See what's above it?'

Vittoria studied the bill. 'An eye inside a triangle.'

'It's called the *trinacria*. Have you ever seen that eye in a triangle anywhere else?'

Vittoria was silent a moment. 'Actually, yes, but I'm not sure . . .'

'It's emblazoned on Masonic lodges around the world.'

'The symbol is Masonic?'

'Actually, no. It's Illuminati. They called it their "shining delta". A call for enlightened change. The eye

135

signifies the Illuminati's ability to infiltrate and watch all things. The shining triangle represents enlightenment. And the triangle is also the Greek letter delta, which is the mathematical symbol for—'

'Change. Transition.'

Langdon smiled. 'I forgot I was talking to a scientist.'

'So you're saying the U.S. Great Seal is a call for enlightened, all-seeing change?'

'Some would call it a New World Order.'

Vittoria seemed startled. She glanced down at the bill again. 'The writing under the pyramid says *Novus . . . Ordo . . .*'

'*Novus Ordo Seclorum*,' Langdon said. 'It means New Secular Order.'

'Secular as in *non*religious?'

'Nonreligious. The phrase not only clearly states the Illuminati objective, but it also blatantly contradicts the phrase beside it. In God We Trust.'

Vittoria seemed troubled. 'But how could all this symbology end up on the most powerful currency in the world?'

'Most academics believe it was through Vice President Henry Wallace. He was an upper echelon Mason and certainly had ties to the Illuminati. Whether it was as a member or innocently under their influence, nobody knows. But it was Wallace who sold the design of the Great Seal to the president.'

'How? Why would the president have agreed to—'

'The president was Franklin D. Roosevelt. Wallace simply told him *Novus Ordo Seclorum* meant *New Deal*.'

Vittoria seemed skeptical. 'And Roosevelt didn't have anyone *else* look at the symbol before telling the Treasury to print it?'

'No need. He and Wallace were like brothers.'

'Brothers?'

'Check your history books,' Langdon said with a
smile. 'Franklin D. Roosevelt was a well-known
Mason.'

32

Langdon held his breath as the X-33 spiraled into
Rome's Leonardo da Vinci International Airport.
Vittoria sat across from him, eyes closed as if trying to
will the situation into control. The craft touched down
and taxied to a private hangar.

'Sorry for the slow flight,' the pilot apologized,
emerging from the cockpit. 'Had to trim her back.
Noise regulations over populated areas.'

Langdon checked his watch. They had been airborne thirty-seven minutes.

The pilot popped the outer door. 'Anybody want to
tell me what's going on?'

Neither Vittoria nor Langdon responded.

'Fine,' he said, stretching. 'I'll be in the cockpit with
the air-conditioning and my music. Just me and
Garth.'

The late-afternoon sun blazed outside the hangar.
Langdon carried his tweed jacket over his shoulder.
Vittoria turned her face skyward and inhaled deeply,
as if the sun's rays somehow transferred to her some
mystical replenishing energy.

Mediterraneans, Langdon mused, already sweating.

'Little old for cartoons, aren't you?' Vittoria asked, without opening her eyes.

'I'm sorry?'

'Your wristwatch. I saw it on the plane.'

Langdon flushed slightly. He was accustomed to having to defend his timepiece. The collector's edition Mickey Mouse watch had been a childhood gift from his parents. Despite the contorted foolishness of Mickey's outstretched arms designating the hour, it was the only watch Langdon had ever worn. Waterproof and glow-in-the-dark, it was perfect for swimming laps or walking unlit college paths at night. When Langdon's students questioned his fashion sense, he told them he wore Mickey as a daily reminder to stay young at heart.

'It's six o'clock,' he said.

Vittoria nodded, eyes still closed. 'I think our ride's here.'

Langdon heard the distant whine, looked up, and felt a sinking feeling. Approaching from the north was a helicopter, slicing low across the runway. Langdon had been on a helicopter once in the Andean Palpa Valley looking at the *Nazca* sand drawings and had not enjoyed it one bit. *A flying shoebox.* After a morning of space plane rides, Langdon had hoped the Vatican would send a car.

Apparently not.

The chopper slowed overhead, hovered a moment, and dropped toward the runway in front of them. The craft was white and carried a coat of arms emblazoned on the side – two skeleton keys crossing a shield and papal crown. He knew the symbol well. It was the traditional seal of the Vatican – the sacred symbol of the *Holy See* or 'holy seat' of government, the *seat* being literally the ancient throne of St Peter.

The Holy Chopper, Langdon groaned, watching the craft land. He'd forgotten the Vatican owned one of these things, used for transporting the Pope to the airport, to meetings, or to his summer palace in Gandolfo. Langdon definitely would have preferred a car.

The pilot jumped from the cockpit and strode toward them across the tarmac.

Now it was Vittoria who looked uneasy. '*That's* our pilot?'

Langdon shared her concern. 'To fly, or not to fly. That is the question.'

The pilot looked like he was festooned for a Shakespearean melodrama. His puffy tunic was vertically striped in brilliant blue and gold. He wore matching pantaloons and spats. On his feet were black flats that looked like slippers. On top of it all, he wore a black felt beret.

'Traditional Swiss Guard uniforms,' Langdon explained. 'Designed by Michelangelo himself.' As the man drew closer, Langdon winced. 'I admit, *not* one of Michelangelo's better efforts.'

Despite the man's garish attire, Langdon could tell the pilot meant business. He moved toward them with all the rigidity and dignity of a U.S. Marine. Langdon had read many times about the rigorous requirements for becoming one of the elite Swiss Guard. Recruited from one of Switzerland's four Catholic cantons, applicants had to be Swiss males between nineteen and thirty years old, at least 5 feet 6 inches, trained by the Swiss Army, and unmarried. This imperial corps was envied by world governments as the most allegiant and deadly security force in the world.

'You are from CERN?' the guard asked, arriving before them. His voice was steely.

'Yes, sir,' Langdon replied.

'You made remarkable time,' he said, giving the X-33 a mystified stare. He turned to Vittoria. 'Ma'am, do you have any other clothing?'

'I beg your pardon?'

He motioned to her legs. 'Short pants are not permitted inside Vatican City.'

Langdon glanced down at Vittoria's legs and frowned. He had forgotten. Vatican City had a strict ban on visible legs above the knee – both male and female. The regulation was a way of showing respect for the sanctity of God's city.

'This is all I have,' she said. 'We came in a hurry.'

The guard nodded, clearly displeased. He turned next to Langdon. 'Are you carrying any weapons?'

Weapons? Langdon thought. *I'm not even carrying a change of underwear!* He shook his head.

The officer crouched at Langdon's feet and began patting him down, starting at his socks. *Trusting guy,* Langdon thought. The guard's strong hands moved up Langdon's legs, coming uncomfortably close to his groin. Finally they moved up to his chest and shoulders. Apparently content Langdon was clean, the guard turned to Vittoria. He ran his eyes up her legs and torso.

Vittoria glared. 'Don't even think about it.'

The guard fixed Vittoria with a gaze clearly intended to intimidate. Vittoria did not flinch.

'What's that?' the guard said, pointing to a faint square bulge in the front pocket of her shorts.

Vittoria removed an ultrathin cell phone. The guard took it, clicked it on, waited for a dial tone, and then,

140

apparently satisfied that it was indeed nothing more than a phone, returned it to her. Vittoria slid it back into her pocket.

'Turn around, please,' the guard said.

Vittoria obliged, holding her arms out and rotating a full 360 degrees.

The guard carefully studied her. Langdon had already decided that Vittoria's form-fitting shorts and blouse were not bulging anywhere they shouldn't have been. Apparently the guard came to the same conclusion.

'Thank you. This way please.'

The Swiss Guard chopper churned in neutral as Langdon and Vittoria approached. Vittoria boarded first, like a seasoned pro, barely even stooping as she passed beneath the whirling rotors. Langdon held back a moment.

'No chance of a car?' he yelled, half-joking to the Swiss Guard, who was climbing in the pilot's seat.

The man did not answer.

Langdon knew that with Rome's maniacal drivers, flying was probably safer anyway. He took a deep breath and boarded, stooping cautiously as he passed beneath the spinning rotors.

As the guard fired up the engines, Vittoria called out, 'Have you located the canister?'

The guard glanced over his shoulder, looking confused. 'The what?'

'The canister. You called CERN about a canister?'

The man shrugged. 'No idea what you're talking about. We've been busy today. My commander told me to pick you up. That's all I know.'

Vittoria gave Langdon an unsettled look.

'Buckle up, please,' the pilot said as the engine revved.

Langdon reached for his seat belt and strapped himself in. The tiny fuselage seemed to shrink around him. Then with a roar, the craft shot up and banked sharply north toward Rome.

Rome . . . the *caput mundi*, where Caesar once ruled, where St Peter was crucified. The cradle of modern civilization. And at its core . . . a ticking bomb.

33

Rome from the air is a labyrinth – an indecipherable maze of ancient roadways winding around buildings, fountains, and crumbling ruins.

The Vatican chopper stayed low in the sky as it sliced northwest through the permanent smog layer coughed up by the congestion below. Langdon gazed down at the mopeds, sight-seeing buses, and armies of miniature Fiat sedans buzzing around rotaries in all directions. *Koyaanisqatsi*, he thought, recalling the Hopi term for 'life out of balance.'

Vittoria sat in silent determination in the seat beside him.

The chopper banked hard.

His stomach dropping, Langdon gazed farther into the distance. His eyes found the crumbling ruins of the Roman Coliseum. The Coliseum, Langdon had always thought, was one of history's greatest ironies. Now a dignified symbol for the rise of human culture and civilization, the stadium had been built to host centuries of barbaric events – hungry lions shredding prisoners, armies of slaves battling to the death, gang rapes of exotic women captured from far-off lands, as well as public beheadings and castrations. It was ironic, Langdon thought, or perhaps fitting, that the Coliseum had served as the architectural blueprint for Harvard's Soldier Field – the football stadium where the ancient traditions of savagery were reenacted every fall . . . crazed fans screaming for bloodshed as Harvard battled Yale.

As the chopper headed north, Langdon spied the Roman Forum – the heart of pre-Christian Rome. The decaying columns looked like toppled gravestones in a cemetery that had somehow avoided being swallowed by the metropolis surrounding it.

To the west the wide basin of the Tiber River wound enormous arcs across the city. Even from the air Langdon could tell the water was deep. The churning currents were brown, filled with silt and foam from heavy rains.

'Straight ahead,' the pilot said, climbing higher.

Langdon and Vittoria looked out and saw it. Like a mountain parting the morning fog, the colossal dome rose out of the haze before them: St Peter's Basilica.

'Now *that*,' Langdon said to Vittoria, 'is something Michelangelo got right.'

Langdon had never seen St Peter's from the air. The marble façade blazed like fire in the afternoon sun. Adorned with 140 statues of saints, martyrs, and angels, the Herculean edifice stretched two football fields wide and a staggering *six* long. The cavernous interior of the basilica had room for over 60,000 worshipers . . . over one hundred times the population of Vatican City, the smallest country in the world.

143

Incredibly, though, not even a citadel of this magnitude could dwarf the piazza before it. A sprawling expanse of granite, St Peter's Square was a staggering open space in the congestion of Rome, like a classical Central Park. In front of the basilica, bordering the vast oval common, 284 columns swept outward in four concentric arcs of diminishing size . . . an architectural *trompe l'oeil* used to heighten the piazza's sense of grandeur.

As he stared at the magnificent shrine before him, Langdon wondered what St Peter would think if he were here now. The Saint had died a gruesome death, crucified upside down on this very spot. Now he rested in the most sacred of tombs, buried five stories down, directly beneath the central cupola of the basilica.

'Vatican City,' the pilot said, sounding anything but welcoming.

Langdon looked out at the towering stone bastions that loomed ahead – impenetrable fortifications surrounding the complex . . . a strangely earthly defense for a spiritual world of secrets, power and mystery.

'Look!' Vittoria said suddenly, grabbing Langdon's arm. She motioned frantically downward toward St Peter's Square directly beneath them. Langdon put his face to the window and looked.

'Over there,' she said, pointing.

Langdon looked. The rear of the piazza looked like a parking lot crowded with a dozen or so trailer trucks. Huge satellite dishes pointed skyward from the roof of every truck. The dishes were emblazoned with familiar names:

TELEVISOR EUROPEA
VIDEO ITALIA
BBC
UNITED PRESS INTERNATIONAL

Langdon felt suddenly confused, wondering if the news of the antimatter had already leaked out.

Vittoria seemed suddenly tense. 'Why is the press here? What's going on?'

The pilot turned and gave her an odd look over his shoulder. 'What's going on? You don't know?'

'No,' she fired back, her accent husky and strong.

'*Il Conclave,*' he said. 'It is to be sealed in about an hour. The whole world is watching.'

Il Conclave.

The word rang a long moment in Langdon's ears before dropping like a brick to the pit of his stomach. *Il Conclave. The Vatican Conclave.* How could he have forgotten? It had been in the news recently.

Fifteen days ago, the Pope, after a tremendously popular twelve-year reign, had passed away. Every paper in the world had carried the story about the Pope's fatal stroke while sleeping – a sudden and unexpected death many whispered was suspicious. But now, in keeping with the sacred tradition, fifteen days after the death of a Pope, the Vatican was holding *Il Conclave* – the sacred ceremony in which the 165 cardinals of the world – the most powerful men in Christendom – gathered in Vatican City to elect the new Pope.

Every cardinal on the planet is here today, Langdon thought as the chopper passed over St Peter's Basilica. The expansive inner world of Vatican City spread out beneath him. *The entire power structure of the Roman Catholic Church is sitting on a time bomb.*

34

Cardinal Mortati gazed up at the lavish ceiling of the Sistine Chapel and tried to find a moment of quiet reflection. The frescoed walls echoed with the voices of cardinals from nations around the globe. The men jostled in the candlelit tabernacle, whispering excitedly and consulting with one another in numerous languages, the universal tongues being English, Italian and Spanish.

The light in the chapel was usually sublime – long rays of tinted sun slicing through the darkness like rays from heaven – but not today. As was the custom, all of the chapel's windows had been covered in black velvet in the name of secrecy. This ensured that no one on the inside could send signals or communicate in any way with the outside world. The result was a profound darkness lit only by candles ... a shimmering radiance that seemed to purify everyone it touched, making them all ghostly ... like saints.

What privilege, Mortati thought, *that I am to oversee this sanctified event*. Cardinals over eighty years of age were too old to be eligible for election and did not attend conclave, but at seventy-nine years old, Mortati was the most senior cardinal here and had been appointed to oversee the proceedings.

Following tradition, the cardinals gathered here two hours before conclave to catch up with friends and engage in last-minute discussion. At 7 p.m., the late Pope's chamberlain would arrive, give opening prayer, and then leave. Then the Swiss Guard would seal the doors and lock all the cardinals inside. It was then that the oldest and most secretive political ritual in the world would begin. The cardinals would not be released until they decided who among them would be the next Pope.

Conclave. Even the name was secretive. *'Con clave'* literally meant 'locked with a key.' The cardinals were permitted no contact whatsoever with the outside world. No phone calls. No messages. No whispers through doorways. Conclave was a vacuum, not to be influenced by anything in the outside world. This would ensure that the cardinals kept *Solum Dum prae oculis* . . . only God before their eyes.

Outside the walls of the chapel, of course, the media watched and waited, speculating as to which of the cardinals would become the ruler of one billion Catholics worldwide. Conclaves created an intense, politically charged atmosphere, and over the centuries they had turned deadly; poisonings, fist fights, and even murder had erupted within the sacred walls. *Ancient history*, Mortati thought. *Tonight's conclave will be unified, blissful, and above all . . . brief.*

Or at least that had been his speculation.

Now, however, an unexpected development had emerged. Mystifyingly, four cardinals were absent from the chapel. Mortati knew that all the exits to Vatican City were guarded, and the missing cardinals could not have gone far, but still, with less than an hour before opening prayer, he was feeling disconcerted. After all, the four missing men were no *ordinary* cardinals. They were *the* cardinals.

The chosen four.

As overseer of the conclave, Mortati had already sent word through the proper channels to the Swiss Guard alerting them to the cardinals' absence. He had yet to hear back. Other cardinals had now noticed the puzzling absence. The anxious whispers had begun. Of *all* cardinals, these *four* should be on time! Cardinal Mortati was starting to fear it might be a long evening after all.

He had no idea.

35

The Vatican's helipad, for reasons of safety and noise control, is located in the northwest tip of Vatican City, as far from St Peter's Basilica as possible.

'Terra firma,' the pilot announced as they touched down. He exited and opened the sliding door for Langdon and Vittoria.

Langdon descended from the craft and turned to help Vittoria, but she had already dropped effortlessly to the ground. Every muscle in her body seemed tuned to one objective – finding the antimatter before it left a horrific legacy.

After stretching a reflective sun tarp across the cockpit window, the pilot ushered them to an oversized electric golf cart waiting near the helipad. The cart whisked them silently alongside the country's western border – a fifty-foot-tall cement bulwark thick enough to ward off attacks even by tanks. Lining the interior of the wall, posted at fifty-meter intervals, Swiss Guards stood at attention, surveying the interior of the grounds. The cart turned sharply right onto Via della Osservatorio. Signs pointed in all directions:

PALAZZO GOVERNATORIO
COLLEGIO ETIOPE
BASILICA SAN PIETRO
CAPELLA SISTINA

They accelerated up the manicured road past a squat building marked RADIO VATICANA. This, Langdon realized to his amazement, was the hub of the world's most listened-to radio programming – *Radio Vaticana* – spreading the word of God to millions of listeners around the globe.

'*Attenzione,*' the pilot said, turning sharply into a rotary.

As the cart wound round, Langdon could barely believe the sight now coming into view. *Giardini Vaticani*, he thought. The heart of Vatican City. Directly ahead rose the rear of St Peter's Basilica, a view, Langdon realized, most people never saw. To the right loomed the Palace of the Tribunal, the lush papal residence rivaled only by Versailles in its baroque embellishment. The severe-looking Governatorato building was now behind them, housing Vatican City's administration. And up ahead on the left, the massive rectangular edifice of the Vatican Museum. Langdon knew there would be no time for a museum visit this trip.

'Where is everyone?' Vittoria asked, surveying the deserted lawns and walkways.

The guard checked his black, military-style chronograph – an odd anachronism beneath his puffy sleeve.

149

'The cardinals are convened in the Sistine Chapel. Conclave begins in a little under an hour.'

Langdon nodded, vaguely recalling that before conclave the cardinals spent two hours inside the Sistine Chapel in quiet reflection and visitations with their fellow cardinals from around the globe. The time was meant to renew old friendships among the cardinals and facilitate a less heated election process. 'And the rest of the residents and staff?'

'Banned from the city for secrecy and security until the conclave concludes.'

'And when does it conclude?'

The guard shrugged. 'God only knows.' The words sounded oddly literal.

After parking the cart on the wide lawn directly behind St Peter's Basilica, the guard escorted Langdon and Vittoria up a stone escarpment to a marble plaza off the back of the basilica. Crossing the plaza, they approached the rear wall of the basilica and followed it through a triangular courtyard, across Via Belvedere, and into a series of buildings closely huddled together. Langdon's art history had taught him enough Italian to pick out signs for the Vatican Printing Office, the Tapestry Restoration Lab, Post Office Management, and the Church of St Ann. They crossed another small square and arrived at their destination.

The Office of the Swiss Guard is housed adjacent to Il Corpo di Vigilanza, directly northeast of St Peter's Basilica. The office is a squat, stone building. On either side of the entrance, like two stone statues, stood a pair of guards.

Langdon had to admit, these guards did not look

quite so comical. Although they also wore the blue and gold uniform, each wielded the traditional 'Vatican long sword' – an eight-foot spear with a razor-sharp scythe – rumored to have decapitated countless Muslims while defending the Christian crusaders in the fifteenth century.

As Langdon and Vittoria approached, the two guards stepped forward, crossing their long swords, blocking the entrance. One looked up at the pilot in confusion. '*I pantaloni,*' he said, motioning to Vittoria's shorts.

The pilot waved them off. '*Il comandante vuole vederli subito.*'

The guards frowned. Reluctantly they stepped aside.

Inside, the air was cool. It looked nothing like the administrative security offices Langdon would have imagined. Ornate and impeccably furnished, the hallways contained paintings Langdon was certain any museum worldwide would gladly have featured in its main gallery.

The pilot pointed down a steep set of stairs. 'Down, please.'

Langdon and Vittoria followed the white marble treads as they descended between a gauntlet of nude male sculptures. Each statue wore a fig leaf that was lighter in color than the rest of the body.

The Great Castration, Langdon thought.

It was one of the most horrific tragedies in Renaissance art. In 1857, Pope Pius IX decided that the accurate representation of the male form might incite lust inside the Vatican. So he got a chisel and mallet and hacked off the genitalia of every single male statue inside Vatican City. He defaced works by Michel-angelo, Bramante, and Bernini. Plaster fig leaves were used to patch the damage. Hundreds of sculptures had been emasculated. Langdon had often wondered if there was a huge crate of stone penises someplace.

'Here,' the guard announced.

They reached the bottom of the stairs and dead-ended at a heavy, steel door. The guard typed an entry code, and the door slid open. Langdon and Vittoria entered.

Beyond the threshold was absolute mayhem.

36

The Office of the Swiss Guard.

Langdon stood in the doorway, surveying the collision of centuries before them. *Mixed media*. The room was a lushly adorned Renaissance library com-plete with inlaid bookshelves, oriental carpets, and colorful tapestries ... and yet the room bristled with high-tech gear – banks of computers, faxes, electronic maps of the Vatican complex, and televisions tuned to CNN. Men in colorful pantaloons typed feverishly on computers and listened intently in futuristic head-phones.

'Wait here,' the guard said.

Langdon and Vittoria waited as the guard crossed the room to an exceptionally tall, wiry man in a dark blue military uniform. He was talking on a cellular phone and stood so straight he was almost bent back-ward. The guard said something to him, and the man shot a glance over at Langdon and Vittoria. He nodded, then turned his back on them and continued his phone call.

The guard returned. 'Commander Olivetti will be with you in a moment.'

'Thank you.'

The guard left and headed back up the stairs.

Langdon studied Commander Olivetti across the room, realizing he was actually the Commander in Chief of the armed forces of an entire country. Vittoria and Langdon waited, observing the action before them. Brightly dressed guards bustled about yelling orders in Italian.

'Continua cercando!' one yelled into a telephone.

'Probasti il museo?' another asked.

Langdon did not need fluent Italian to discern that the security center was currently in intense search mode. This was the good news. The bad news was that they obviously had not yet found the antimatter.

'You okay?' Langdon asked Vittoria.

She shrugged, offering a tired smile.

When the commander finally clicked off his phone and approached across the room, he seemed to grow with each step. Langdon was tall himself and not accustomed to looking up at many people, but Commander Olivetti demanded it. Langdon sensed immediately that the commander was a man who had weathered tempests, his face hale and steeled. His dark hair was cropped in a military buzz cut, and his eyes burned with the kind of hardened determination only attainable through years of intense training. He moved with ramrod exactness, the earpiece hidden discreetly behind one ear making him look more like U.S. Secret Service than Swiss Guard.

The commander addressed them in accented English. His voice was startlingly quiet for such a large man, barely a whisper. It bit with a tight, military efficiency. 'Good afternoon,' he said. 'I am Commander Olivetti – *Comandante Principale* of the Swiss Guard. I'm the one who called your director.'

Vittoria gazed upward. 'Thank you for seeing us, sir.'

The commander did not respond. He motioned for them to follow and led them through the tangle of electronics to a door in the side wall of the chamber. 'Enter,' he said, holding the door for them.

Langdon and Vittoria walked through and found themselves in a darkened control room where a wall of video monitors was cycling lazily through a series of black-and-white images of the complex. A young guard sat watching the images intently.

'*Fuori*,' Olivetti said.

The guard packed up and left.

Olivetti walked over to one of the screens and pointed to it. Then he turned toward his guests. 'This image is from a remote camera hidden somewhere inside Vatican City. I'd like an explanation.'

Langdon and Vittoria looked at the screen and inhaled in unison. The image was absolute. No doubt. It was CERN's antimatter canister. Inside, a shimmering droplet of metallic liquid hung ominously in the air, lit by the rhythmic blinking of the LED digital clock. Eerily, the area around the canister was almost entirely dark, as if the antimatter were in a closet or darkened room. At the top of the monitor flashed superimposed text: LIVE FEED – CAMERA #86.

Vittoria looked at the time remaining on the flashing indicator on the canister. 'Under six hours,' she whispered to Langdon, her face tense.

Langdon checked his watch. 'So we have until . . .' He stopped, a knot tightening in his stomach.

'Midnight,' Vittoria said, with a withering look.

Midnight, Langdon thought. *A flair for the dramatic.* Apparently whoever stole the canister last night had timed it perfectly. A stark foreboding set in as he realized he was currently sitting at ground zero.

Olivetti's whisper now sounded more like a hiss. 'Does this object belong to your facility?'

Vittoria nodded. 'Yes, sir. It was stolen from us. It contains an extremely combustible substance called antimatter.'

Olivetti looked unmoved. 'I am quite familiar with incendiaries, Ms Vetra. I have not heard of antimatter.'

'It's new technology. We need to locate it immediately or evacuate Vatican City.'

Olivetti closed his eyes slowly and reopened them, as if refocusing on Vittoria might change what he just heard. 'Evacuate? Are you aware what is going on here this evening?'

'Yes, sir. And the lives of your cardinals are in danger. We have about six hours. Have you made any headway locating the canister?'

Olivetti shook his head. 'We haven't started looking.'

Vittoria choked. 'What? But we expressly heard your guards talking about searching the—'

'Searching, *yes*,' Olivetti said, 'but not for your canister. My men are looking for something else that does not concern you.'

Vittoria's voice cracked. 'You haven't even *begun* looking for this canister?'

Olivetti's pupils seemed to recede into his head. He had the passionless look of an insect. 'Ms Vetra, is it?

Let me explain something to you. The director of your faculty refused to share any details about this object with me over the phone except to say that I needed to find it immediately. We are exceptionally busy, and I do not have the luxury of dedicating manpower to a situation until I get some facts.'

'There is only one relevant fact at this moment, sir,' Vittoria said, 'that being that in six hours that device is going to vaporize this entire complex.'

Olivetti stood motionless. 'Ms Vetra, there is something you need to know.' His tone hinted at patronizing. 'Despite the archaic appearance of Vatican City, every single entrance, both public and private, is equipped with the most advanced sensing equipment known to man. If someone tried to enter with any sort of incendiary device it would be detected instantly. We have radioactive isotope scanners, olfactory filters designed by the American DEA to detect the faintest chemical signatures of combustibles and toxins. We also use the most advanced metal detectors and X-ray scanners available.'

'Very impressive,' Vittoria said, matching Olivetti's cool. 'Unfortunately, antimatter is nonradioactive, its chemical signature is that of pure hydrogen, and the canister is plastic. None of those devices would have detected it.'

'But the device has an energy source,' Olivetti said, motioning to the blinking LED. 'Even the smallest trace of nickel-cadmium would register as—'

'The batteries are also plastic.'

Olivetti's patience was clearly starting to wane. 'Plastic batteries?'

'Polymer gel electrolyte with Teflon.'

Olivetti leaned towards her, as if to accentuate his

height advantage. '*Signorina*, the Vatican is the target of dozens of bomb threats a month. I personally train every Swiss Guard in modern explosive technology. I am well aware that there is no substance on earth powerful enough to do what you are describing unless you are talking about a nuclear warhead with a fuel core the size of a baseball.'

Vittoria framed him with a fervent stare. 'Nature has many mysteries yet to unveil.'

Olivetti leaned closer. 'Might I ask exactly *who* you are? What is your position at CERN?'

'I am a senior member of the research staff and appointed liaison to the Vatican for this crisis.'

'Excuse me for being rude, but if there is indeed a *crisis*, why am I dealing with *you* and not your director? And what disrespect do you intend by coming into Vatican City in short pants?'

Langdon groaned. He couldn't believe that under the circumstances the man was being a stickler for dress code. Then again, he realized, if stone penises could induce lustful thoughts in Vatican residents, Vittoria Vetra in shorts could *certainly* be a threat to national security.

'Commander Olivetti,' Langdon intervened, trying to diffuse what looked like a second bomb about to explode. 'My name is Robert Langdon. I'm a professor of religious studies in the U.S. and unaffiliated with CERN. I have seen an antimatter demonstration and will vouch for Ms Vetra's claim that it is exceptionally dangerous. We have reason to believe it was placed inside your complex by an antireligious cult hoping to disrupt your conclave.'

Olivetti turned, peering down at Langdon. 'I have a woman in shorts telling me that a droplet of liquid is going to blow up Vatican City, and I have an American professor telling me we are being targeted by some antireligious cult. What exactly is it you expect me to do?'

'Find the canister,' Vittoria said. 'Right away.'

'Impossible. That device could be anywhere. Vatican City is enormous.'

'Your cameras don't have GPS locators on them?'

'They are not generally *stolen*. This missing camera will take days to locate.'

'We don't have *days*,' Vittoria said adamantly. 'We have six hours.'

'Six hours until what, Ms Vetra?' Olivetti's voice grew louder suddenly. He pointed to the image on the screen. 'Until these numbers count down? Until Vatican City disappears? Believe me, I do not take kindly to people tampering with my security system. Nor do I like mechanical contraptions appearing mysteriously inside my walls. I *am* concerned. It is my *job* to be concerned. But what you have told me here is unacceptable.'

Langdon spoke before he could stop himself. 'Have you heard of the Illuminati?'

The commander's icy exterior cracked. His eyes went white, like a shark about to attack. 'I am warning you. I do not have time for this.'

'So you *have* heard of the Illuminati?'

Olivetti's eyes stabbed like bayonets. 'I am a sworn defendant of the Catholic Church. *Of course* I have heard of the Illuminati. They have been dead for decades.'

Langdon reached in his pocket and pulled out the fax image of Leonardo Vetra's branded body. He handed it to Olivetti.

'I am an Illuminati scholar,' Langdon said as Olivetti studied the picture. 'I am having a difficult time accepting that the Illuminati are still active, and yet the appearance of this brand combined with the fact that the Illuminati have a well-known covenant against Vatican City has changed my mind.'

'A computer-generated hoax.' Olivetti handed the fax back to Langdon.

Langdon stared, incredulous. 'Hoax? Look at the symmetry! You of all people should realize the authenticity of—'

'Authenticity is precisely what you lack. Perhaps Ms Vetra has not informed you, but CERN scientists have been criticizing Vatican policies for decades. They regularly petition us for retraction of Creationist theory, formal apologies for Galileo and Copernicus, repeal of our criticism against dangerous or immoral research. What scenario seems more likely to you – that a four-hundred-year-old satanic cult has re-surfaced with an advanced weapon of mass destruction, or that some prankster at CERN is trying to disrupt a sacred Vatican event with a well-executed fraud?'

'That photo,' Vittoria said, her voice like boiling lava, 'is of my father. *Murdered*. You think this is my idea of a *joke*?'

'I don't know, Ms Vetra. But I do know until I get some answers that make *sense*, there is no way I will raise any sort of alarm. Vigilance and discretion are my duty . . . such that spiritual matters can take place here with clarity of mind. Today of all days.'

Langdon said, 'At least postpone the event.'

'Postpone?' Olivetti's jaw dropped. 'Such arrogance! A conclave is not some American baseball game you call off on account of rain. This is a sacred event with a strict code and process. Never mind that one billion Catholics in the world are waiting for a leader. Never mind that the world media is outside. The protocols for this event are holy – *not* subject to modification. Since 1179, conclaves have survived earthquakes, famines, and even the plague. Believe me, it is not about to be canceled on account of a murdered scientist and a droplet of God knows what.'

'Take me to the person in charge,' Vittoria demanded.

Olivetti glared. 'You've got him.'

'No,' she said. 'Someone in the *clergy*.'

The veins on Olivetti's brow began to show. 'The clergy has gone. With the exception of the Swiss Guard, the only ones present in Vatican City at this time are the College of Cardinals. And they are inside the Sistine Chapel.'

'How about the *chamberlain*?' Langdon stated flatly.

'Who?'

'The late Pope's *chamberlain*.' Langdon repeated the word self-assuredly, praying his memory served him. He recalled reading once about the curious arrangement of Vatican authority following the death of a Pope. If Langdon was correct, during the interim between Popes, complete autonomous power shifted temporarily to the late Pope's personal assistant – his chamberlain – a secretarial underling who oversaw conclave until the cardinals chose the new Holy Father. 'I believe the *chamberlain* is the man in charge at the moment.'

'*Il camerlengo*?' Olivetti scowled. 'The camerlengo is only a priest here. He is the late Pope's hand servant.'

'But he is here. And you answer to him.'

Olivetti crossed his arms. 'Mr Langdon, it is true that Vatican rule dictates the camerlengo assume chief executive office during conclave, but it is only because his lack of eligibility for the papacy ensures an unbiased election. It is as if your president died, and one of his aides temporarily sat in the oval office. The camerlengo is young, and his understanding of security, or anything else for that matter, is extremely limited. For all intents and purposes, I am in charge here.'

'Take us to him,' Vittoria said.

'Impossible. Conclave begins in forty minutes. The camerlengo is in the Office of the Pope preparing. I have no intention of disturbing him with matters of security.'

Vittoria opened her mouth to respond but was interrupted by a knocking at the door. Olivetti opened it.

A guard in full regalia stood outside, pointing to his watch. '*É l'ora, comandante.*'

Olivetti checked his own watch and nodded. He turned back to Langdon and Vittoria like a judge pondering their fate. 'Follow me.' He led them out of the monitoring room across the security center to a small clear cubicle against the rear wall. 'My office.' Olivetti ushered them inside. The room was unspecial – a cluttered desk, file cabinets, folding chairs, a water cooler. 'I will be back in ten minutes. I suggest you use the time to decide how you would like to proceed.'

Vittoria wheeled. 'You can't just leave! That canister is—'

'I do not have time for this,' Olivetti seethed. 'Perhaps I should detain you until after the conclave when I *do* have time.'

'Signore,' the guard urged, pointing to his watch again. '*Spazzare di cappella.*'

161

Olivetti nodded and started to leave.

'*Spazzare di cappella?*' Vittoria demanded. 'You're leaving to *sweep* the chapel?'

Olivetti turned, his eyes boring through her. 'We sweep for electronic bugs, Miss Vetra – a matter of *discretion.*' He motioned to her legs. 'Not something I would expect you to understand.'

With that he slammed the door, rattling the heavy glass. In one fluid motion he produced a key, inserted it, and twisted. A heavy deadbolt slid into place.

'*Idiòta!*' Vittoria yelled. 'You can't keep us in here!'

Through the glass, Langdon could see Olivetti say something to the guard. The sentinel nodded. As Olivetti strode out of the room, the guard spun and faced them on the other side of the glass, arms crossed, a large sidearm visible on his hip.

Perfect, Langdon thought. *Just bloody perfect.*

37

Vittoria glared at the Swiss Guard standing outside Olivetti's locked door. The sentinel glared back, his colorful costume belying his decidedly ominous air.

Che fiasco, Vittoria thought. *Held hostage by an armed man in pajamas.*

Langdon had fallen silent, and Vittoria hoped he was using that Harvard brain of his to think them out of this. She sensed, however, from the look on his face, that he was more in shock than in thought. She regretted getting him so involved.

Vittoria's first instinct was to pull out her cell phone

and call Kohler, but she knew it was foolish. First, the guard would probably walk in and take her phone. Second, if Kohler's episode ran its usual course, he was probably still incapacitated. Not that it mattered . . . Olivetti seemed unlikely to take anybody's word on anything at the moment.

Remember! she told herself. *Remember the solution to this test!*

Remembrance was a Buddhist philosopher's trick. Rather than asking her mind to search for a solution to a potentially impossible challenge, Vittoria asked her mind simply to remember it. The presupposition that one once *knew* the answer created the mindset that the answer must *exist* . . . thus eliminating the crippling conception of hopelessness. Vittoria often used the process to solve scientific quandaries . . . those that most people thought had no solution.

At the moment, however, her remembrance trick was drawing a major blank. So she measured her options . . . her needs. She needed to warn someone. Someone at the Vatican needed to take her seriously. But who? The camerlengo? How? She was in a glass box with one exit.

Tools, she told herself. *There are always tools. Reevaluate your environment.*

Instinctively she lowered her shoulders, relaxed her eyes, and took three deep breaths into her lungs. She sensed her heart rate slow and her muscles soften. The chaotic panic in her mind dissolved. *Okay*, she thought, *let your mind be free. What makes this situation positive? What are my assets?*

The analytical mind of Vittoria Vetra, once calmed, was a powerful force. Within seconds she realized their incarceration was actually their key to escape.

'I'm making a phone call,' she said suddenly.

Langdon looked up. 'I was about to suggest you call Kohler, but—'

'Not Kohler. Someone else.'

'Who?'

'The camerlengo.'

Langdon looked totally lost. 'You're calling the chamberlain? How?'

'Olivetti said the camerlengo was in the Pope's office.'

'Okay. You know the Pope's private number?'

'No. But I'm not calling on *my* phone.' She nodded to a high-tech phone system on Olivetti's desk. It was riddled with speed dial buttons. 'The head of security *must* have a direct line to the Pope's office.'

'He also has a weight lifter with a gun planted six feet away.'

'And we're locked in.'

'I was actually aware of that.'

'I mean the *guard* is locked out. This is Olivetti's private office. I doubt anyone else has a key.'

Langdon looked out at the guard. 'This is pretty thin glass, and that's a pretty big gun.'

'What's he going to do, shoot me for using the phone?'

'Who the hell knows! This is a pretty strange place, and the way things are going—'

'Either that,' Vittoria said, 'or we can spend the next five hours and forty-eight minutes in Vatican Prison. At least we'll have a front-row seat when the anti-matter goes off.'

Langdon paled. 'But the guard will get Olivetti the second you pick up that phone. Besides, there are twenty buttons on there. And I don't see any identification. You going to try them all and hope to get lucky?'

'Nope,' she said, striding to the phone. 'Just one.' Vittoria picked up the phone and pressed the top button. 'Number *one*. I bet you one of those Illuminati U.S. dollars you have in your pocket that this is the Pope's office. What else would take primary importance for a Swiss Guard commander?'

Langdon did not have time to respond. The guard outside the door started rapping on the glass with the butt of his gun. He motioned for her to set down the phone.

Vittoria winked at him. The guard seemed to inflate with rage.

Langdon moved away from the door and turned back to Vittoria. 'You damn well better be right, 'cause this guy does not look amused!'

'Damn!' she said, listening to the receiver. 'A recording.'

'Recording?' Langdon demanded. 'The Pope has an answering machine?'

'It wasn't the Pope's office,' Vittoria said, hanging up. 'It was the damn weekly menu for the Vatican commissary.'

Langdon offered a weak smile to the guard outside who was now glaring angrily through the glass while he hailed Olivetti on his walkie-talkie.

38

The Vatican switchboard is located in the Ufficio di Communicazione behind the Vatican post office. It is a relatively small room containing an eight-line Corelco 141 switchboard. The office handles over 2,000 calls a day, most routed automatically to the recording information system.

Tonight, the sole communications operator on duty sat quietly sipping a cup of caffeinated tea. He felt proud to be one of only a handful of employees still allowed inside Vatican City tonight. Of course the honor was tainted somewhat by the presence of the Swiss Guards hovering outside his door. *An escort to the bathroom*, the operator thought. *Ah, the indignities we endure in the name of Holy Conclave.*

Fortunately, the calls this evening had been light. Or maybe it was not so *fortunate*, he thought. World interest in Vatican events seemed to have dwindled in the last few years. The number of press calls had thinned, and even the crazies weren't calling as often. The press office had hoped tonight's event would have more of a festive buzz about it. Sadly, though, despite St Peter's Square being filled with press trucks, the vans looked to be mostly standard Italian and Euro press. Only a handful of global cover-all networks were there . . . no doubt having sent their *giornalisti secondarii*.

The operator gripped his mug and wondered how long tonight would last. *Midnight or so*, he guessed. Nowadays, most insiders already knew who was favored to become Pope well before conclave convened, so the process was more of a three- or four-hour ritual than an actual election. Of course, last-minute dissension in the ranks could prolong the ceremony through dawn . . . or beyond. The conclave of 1831 had lasted fifty-four days. *Not tonight*, he told himself; rumor was *this* conclave would be a 'smoke-watch'.

The operator's thoughts evaporated with the buzz

of an inside line on his switchboard. He looked at the blinking red light and scratched his head. *That's odd,* he thought. *The zero-line. Who on the inside would be calling operator information tonight? Who is even inside?*

'*Città del Vaticano, prego?*' he said, picking up the phone.

The voice on the line spoke in rapid Italian. The operator vaguely recognized the accent as that common to Swiss Guards – fluent Italian tainted by the Franco-Swiss influence. This caller, however, was most definitely not Swiss Guard.

On hearing the woman's voice, the operator stood suddenly, almost spilling his tea. He shot a look back down at the line. He had not been mistaken. *An internal extension.* The call was from the inside. *There must be some mistake!* he thought. *A woman inside Vatican City? Tonight?*

The woman was speaking fast and furiously. The operator had spent enough years on the phones to know when he was dealing with a *pazzo.* This woman did not sound crazy. She was urgent but rational. Calm and efficient. He listened to her request, bewildered.

'*Il camerlengo?*' the operator said, still trying to figure out where the hell the call was coming from. 'I cannot possibly connect . . . yes, I am aware he is in the Pope's office but . . . who are you again? . . . and you want to warn him of . . .' He listened, more and more unnerved. *Everyone is in danger? How? And where are you calling from?* 'Perhaps I should contact the Swiss . . .' The operator stopped short. 'You say you're *where? Where?*'

He listened in shock, then made a decision. 'Hold, please,' he said, putting the woman on hold before she could respond. Then he called Commander

Olivetti's direct line. *There is no way that woman is really —*

The line picked up instantly.

'Per l'amore di Dio!' a familiar woman's voice shouted at him. 'Place the damn call!'

The door of the Swiss Guards' security center hissed open. The guards parted as Commander Olivetti entered the room like a rocket. Turning the corner to his office, Olivetti confirmed what his guard on the walkie-talkie had just told him; Vittoria Vetra was standing at his desk talking on the commander's private telephone.

Che coglioni che ha questa! he thought. *The balls on this one!*

Livid, he strode to the door and rammed the key into the lock. He pulled open the door and demanded, 'What are you doing!'

Vittoria ignored him. 'Yes,' she was saying into the phone. 'And I must warn—'

Olivetti ripped the receiver from her hand, and raised it to his ear. 'Who the hell is this!'

For the tiniest of an instant, Olivetti's inelastic posture slumped. 'Yes, camerlengo . . .' he said. 'Correct, signore . . . but questions of security demand . . . of course not . . . I am holding her here for . . . certainly, but . . .' He listened. 'Yes, sir,' he said finally. 'I will bring them up immediately.'

39

The Apostolic Palace is a conglomeration of buildings located near the Sistine Chapel in the northeast corner of Vatican City. With a commanding view of St Peter's Square, the palace houses both the Papal Apartments and the Office of the Pope.

Vittoria and Langdon followed in silence as Commander Olivetti led them down a long rococo corridor, the muscles in his neck pulsing with rage. After climbing three sets of stairs, they entered a wide, dimly lit hallway.

Langdon could not believe the artwork on the walls – mint-condition busts, tapestries, friezes – works worth hundreds of thousands of dollars. Two-thirds of the way down the hall they passed an alabaster fountain. Olivetti turned left into an alcove and strode to one of the largest doors Langdon had ever seen.

'*Ufficio di Papa*,' the commander declared, giving Vittoria an acrimonious scowl. Vittoria didn't flinch. She reached over Olivetti and knocked loudly on the door.

Office of the Pope, Langdon thought, having difficulty fathoming that he was standing outside one of the most sacred rooms in all of world religion.

'*Avanti!*' someone called from within.

When the door opened, Langdon had to shield his eyes. The sunlight was blinding. Slowly, the image before him came into focus.

The Office of the Pope seemed more of a ballroom than an office. Red marble floors sprawled out in all directions to walls adorned with vivid frescoes. A colossal chandelier hung overhead, beyond which a bank of arched windows offered a stunning panorama of the sun-drenched St Peter's Square.

My God, Langdon thought. *This is a room with a view.*

At the far end of the hall, at a carved desk, a man sat writing furiously. '*Avanti*,' he called out again, setting down his pen and waving them over.

Olivetti led the way, his gait military. *'Signore,'* he said apologetically. *'No ho potuto—'*

The man cut him off. He stood and studied his two visitors.

The camerlengo was nothing like the images of frail, beatific old men Langdon usually imagined roaming the Vatican. He wore no rosary beads or pendants. No heavy robes. He was dressed instead in a simple black cassock that seemed to amplify the solidity of his substantial frame. He looked to be in his late-thirties, indeed a child by Vatican standards. He had a surprisingly handsome face, a swirl of coarse brown hair, and almost radiant green eyes that shone as if they were somehow fueled by the mysteries of the universe. As the man drew nearer, though, Langdon saw in his eyes a profound exhaustion – like a soul who had been through the toughest fifteen days of his life.

'I am Carlo Ventresca,' he said, his English perfect. 'The late Pope's camerlengo.' His voice was unpretentious and kind, with only the slightest hint of Italian inflection.

'Vittoria Vetra,' she said, stepping forward and offering her hand. 'Thank you for seeing us.'

Olivetti twitched as the camerlengo shook Vittoria's hand.

'This is Robert Langdon,' Vittoria said. 'A religious historian from Harvard University.'

'Padre,' Langdon said, in his best Italian accent. He bowed his head as he extended his hand.

'No, no,' the camerlengo insisted, lifting Langdon back up. 'His Holiness's office does not make me holy. I am merely a priest – a chamberlain serving in a time of need.'

Langdon stood upright.

'Please,' the camerlengo said, 'everyone sit.' He arranged some chairs around his desk. Langdon and Vittoria sat. Olivetti apparently preferred to stand.

The camerlengo seated himself at the desk, folded his hands, sighed, and eyed his visitors.

'Signore,' Olivetti said. 'The woman's attire is my fault. I—'

'Her attire is *not* what concerns me,' the camerlengo replied, sounding too exhausted to be bothered. 'When the Vatican operator calls me a half hour before I begin conclave to tell me a woman is calling from *your* private office to warn me of some sort of major security threat of which I have not been informed, *that* concerns me.'

Olivetti stood rigid, his back arched like a soldier under intense inspection.

Langdon felt hypnotized by the camerlengo's presence. Young and wearied as he was, the priest had the air of some mythical hero – radiating charisma and authority.

'Signore,' Olivetti said, his tone apologetic but still unyielding. 'You should not concern yourself with matters of security. You have other responsibilities.'

'I am well aware of my other responsibilities. I am also aware that as *direttore intermediario*, I have a responsibility for the safety and wellbeing of everyone at this conclave. What is going on here?'

'I have the situation under control.'

'Apparently not.'

'Father,' Langdon interrupted, taking out the crumpled fax and handing it to the camerlengo, 'please.'

Commander Olivetti stepped forward, trying to intervene. 'Father, please do not trouble your thoughts with—'

171

The camerlengo took the fax, ignoring Olivetti for a long moment. He looked at the image of the murdered Leonardo Vetra and drew a startled breath. 'What is this?'

'That is my father,' Vittoria said, her voice wavering. 'He was a priest and a man of science. He was murdered last night.'

The camerlengo's face softened instantly. He looked up at her. 'My dear child. I'm so sorry.' He crossed himself and looked again at the fax, his eyes seeming to pool with waves of abhorrence. 'Who would . . . and this burn on his . . .' The camerlengo paused, squinting closer at the image.

'It says *Illuminati*,' Langdon said. 'No doubt you are familiar with the name.'

An odd look came across the camerlengo's face. 'I have heard the name, yes, but . . .'

'The Illuminati murdered Leonardo Vetra so they could steal a new technology he was—'

'Signore,' Olivetti interjected. 'This is absurd. The Illuminati? This is clearly some sort of elaborate hoax.'

The camerlengo seemed to ponder Olivetti's words. Then he turned and contemplated Langdon so fully that Langdon felt the air leave his lungs. 'Mr Langdon, I have spent my life in the Catholic Church. I am familiar with the Illuminati lore . . . and the legend of the brandings. And yet I must warn you, I am a man of the present tense. Christianity has enough real enemies without resurrecting ghosts.'

'The symbol is authentic,' Langdon said, a little too defensively he thought. He reached over and rotated the fax for the camerlengo.

The camerlengo fell silent when he saw the symmetry.

'Even modern computers,' Langdon added, 'have been unable to forge a symmetrical ambigram of this word.'

The camerlengo folded his hands and said nothing for a long time. 'The Illuminati are dead,' he finally said. 'Long ago. That is historical fact.'

Langdon nodded. 'Yesterday, I would have agreed with you.'

'Yesterday?'

'Before today's chain of events. I believe the Illuminati have resurfaced to make good on an ancient pact.'

'Forgive me. My history is rusty. What ancient pact is this?'

Langdon took a deep breath. 'The destruction of Vatican City.'

'*Destroy* Vatican City?' The camerlengo looked less frightened than confused. 'But that would be impossible.'

Vittoria shook her head. 'I'm afraid we have some more bad news.'

40

'Is this *true*?' the camerlengo demanded, looking amazed as he turned from Vittoria to Olivetti.

'Signore,' Olivetti assured, 'I'll admit there is some sort of device here. It is visible on one of our security monitors, but as for Ms Vetra's claims as to the power of this substance, I cannot possibly—'

'Wait a minute,' the camerlengo said. 'You can *see* this thing?'

'Yes, signore. On wireless camera #86.'

'Then why haven't you recovered it?' The camerlengo's voice echoed anger now.

'Very difficult, signore.' Olivetti stood straight as he explained the situation.

The camerlengo listened, and Vittoria sensed his growing concern. 'Are you certain it is inside Vatican City?' the camerlengo asked. 'Maybe someone took the camera out and is transmitting from somewhere else.'

'Impossible,' Olivetti said. 'Our external walls are shielded electronically to protect our internal communications. This signal can *only* be coming from the inside or we would not be receiving it.'

'And I assume,' he said, 'that you are now looking for the missing camera with all available resources?'

Olivetti shook his head. 'No, signore. Locating that camera could take hundreds of man hours. We have a number of other security concerns at the moment, and with all due respect to Ms Vetra, this droplet she talks about is very small. It could not possibly be as explosive as she claims.'

Vittoria's patience evaporated. 'That droplet is enough to level Vatican City! Did you even listen to a word I told you?'

'Ma'am,' Olivetti said, his voice like steel, 'my experience with explosives is extensive.'

'Your experience is obsolete,' she fired back, equally tough. 'Despite my attire, which I realize you find troublesome, I am a senior level physicist at the world's most advanced subatomic research facility. I personally designed the antimatter trap that is keeping that sample from annihilating right now. And I am warning you that unless you find that canister in the next six hours, your guards will have nothing to protect for the next century but a big hole in the ground.'

Olivetti wheeled to the camerlengo, his insect eyes flashing rage. 'Signore, I cannot in good conscience allow this to go any further. Your time is being wasted by pranksters. The Illuminati? A droplet that will destroy us all?'

'*Basta*,' the camerlengo declared. He spoke the word quietly and yet it seemed to echo across the chamber. Then there was silence. He continued in a whisper. 'Dangerous or not, Illuminati or no Illuminati, whatever this thing is, it most certainly should not be inside Vatican City . . . no less on the eve of the conclave. I want it found and removed. Organize a search immediately.'

Olivetti persisted. 'Signore, even if we used all the guards to search the complex, it could take days to find this camera. Also, after speaking to Ms Vetra, I had one of my guards consult our most advanced ballistics guide for any mention of this substance called antimatter. I found no mention of it anywhere. Nothing.'

Pompous ass, Vittoria thought. *A ballistics guide? Did you try an encyclopedia? Under A!*

Olivetti was still talking. 'Signore, if you are suggesting we make a naked-eye search of the entirety of Vatican City then I must object.'

'Commander.' The camerlengo's voice simmered with rage. 'May I remind you that when you address me, you are addressing this office. I realize you do not take my position seriously – nonetheless, by law, I am in charge. If I am not mistaken, the cardinals are now safely within the Sistine Chapel, and your security concerns are at a minimum until the conclave breaks. I do not understand why you are hesitant to look for this device. If I did not know better it would appear that you are causing this conclave intentional danger.'

Olivetti looked scornful. 'How dare you! I have served your Pope for twelve years! And the Pope before that for fourteen years! Since 1438 the Swiss Guard have—'

The walkie-talkie on Olivetti's belt squawked loudly, cutting him off. '*Comandante?*'

Olivetti snatched it up and pressed the transmitter. '*Sono occupato! Cosa voi!!*'

'*Scusi,*' the Swiss Guard on the radio said. 'Communications here. I thought you would want to be informed that we have received a bomb threat.'

Olivetti could not have looked less interested. 'So handle it! Run the usual trace, and write it up.'

'We did, sir, but the caller . . .' The guard paused. 'I would not trouble you, commander, except that he mentioned the substance you just asked me to research. *Antimatter.*'

Everyone in the room exchanged stunned looks.

'He mentioned *what*?' Olivetti stammered.

'Antimatter, sir. While we were trying to run a trace, I did some additional research on his claim. The information on antimatter is . . . well, frankly, it's quite troubling.'

'I thought you said the ballistics guide showed no mention of it.'

'I found it on-line.'

Alleluia, Vittoria thought.

'The substance appears to be quite explosive,' the guard said. 'It's hard to imagine this information is accurate but it says here that pound for pound antimatter carries about a hundred times more

176

payload than a nuclear warhead.'

Olivetti slumped. It was like watching a mountain crumble. Vittoria's feeling of triumph was erased by the look of horror on the camerlengo's face.

'Did you trace the call?' Olivetti stammered.

'No luck. Cellular with heavy encryption. The SAT lines are interfused, so triangulation is out. The IF signature suggests he's somewhere in Rome, but there's really no way to trace him.'

'Did he make demands?' Olivetti said, his voice quiet.

'No sir. Just warned us that there is antimatter hidden inside the complex. He seemed surprised I didn't know. Asked me if I'd *seen* it yet. You'd asked me about antimatter, so I decided to advise you.'

'You did the right thing,' Olivetti said. 'I'll be down in a minute. Alert me immediately if he calls back.'

There was a moment of silence on the walkie-talkie. 'The caller is still on the line, sir.'

Olivetti looked like he'd just been electrocuted. 'The line is open?'

'Yes, sir. We've been trying to trace him for ten minutes, getting nothing but splayed ferreting. He must know we can't touch him because he refuses to hang up until he speaks to the camerlengo.'

'Patch him through,' the camerlengo commanded. 'Now!'

Olivetti wheeled. 'Father, no. A trained Swiss Guard negotiator is much better suited to handle this.'

'*Now!*'

Olivetti gave the order.

A moment later, the phone on Camerlengo Ventresca's desk began to ring. The camerlengo rammed his fingers down on the speaker-phone button. 'Who in the name of God do you think you are?'

41

The voice emanating from the camerlengo's speaker phone was metallic and cold, laced with arrogance. Everyone in the room listened.

Langdon tried to place the accent. *Middle Eastern, perhaps?*

'I am a messenger of an ancient brotherhood,' the voice announced in an alien cadence. 'A brotherhood you have wronged for centuries. I am a messenger of the Illuminati.'

Langdon felt his muscles tighten, the last shreds of doubt withering away. For an instant he felt the familiar collision of thrill, privilege, and dead fear that he had experienced when he first saw the ambigram this morning.

'What do you want?' the camerlengo demanded.

'I represent men of science. Men who like yourselves are searching for the answers. Answers to man's destiny, his purpose, his creator.'

'Whoever you are,' the camerlengo said, 'I—'

'*Silenzio.* You will do better to listen. For two millennia your church has dominated the quest for truth. You have crushed your opposition with lies and prohesies of doom. You have manipulated the truth to serve your needs, murdering those whose discoveries did not serve your politics. Are you surprised you are the target of enlightened men from around the globe?'

'Enlightened men do not resort to blackmail to further their causes.'

'Blackmail?' The caller laughed. 'This is not blackmail. We have no demands. The abolition of the Vatican is nonnegotiable. We have waited four

178

hundred years for this day. At midnight, your city will be destroyed. There is nothing you can do.'

Olivetti stormed toward the speaker phone. 'Access to this city is impossible! You could not possibly have planted explosives in here!'

'You speak with the ignorant devotion of a Swiss Guard. Perhaps even an officer? Surely you are aware that for centuries the Illuminati have infiltrated elitist organizations across the globe. Do you really believe the Vatican is immune?'

Jesus, Langdon thought, *they've got someone on the inside*. It was no secret that infiltration was the Illuminati trademark of power. They had infiltrated the Masons, major banking networks, government bodies. In fact, Churchill had once told reporters that if English spies had infiltrated the Nazis to the degree the Illuminati had infiltrated English Parliament, the war would have been over in one month.

'A transparent bluff,' Olivetti snapped. 'Your influence cannot possibly extend so far.'

'Why? Because your Swiss Guards are vigilant? Because they watch every corner of your private world? How about the Swiss Guards themselves? Are they not men? Do you truly believe they stake their lives on a fable about a man who walks on water? Ask yourself how else the canister could have entered your city. Or how four of your most precious assets could have disappeared this afternoon.'

'Our assets?' Olivetti scowled. 'What do you mean?'

'One, two, three, four. You haven't missed them by now?'

'What the hell are you talk—' Olivetti stopped short, his eyes rocketing wide as though he'd just been punched in the gut.

'Light dawns,' the caller said. 'Shall I read their names?'

'What's going on?' the camerlengo said, looking bewildered.

The caller laughed. 'Your officer has not yet informed you? How sinful. No surprise. Such pride. I imagine the disgrace of telling you the truth . . . that four cardinals he had sworn to protect seem to have disappeared . . .'

Olivetti erupted. 'Where did you get this information!'

'Camerlengo,' the caller gloated, 'ask your commander if *all* your cardinals are present in the Sistine Chapel.'

The camerlengo turned to Olivetti, his green eyes demanding an explanation.

'Signore,' Olivetti whispered in the camerlengo's ear, 'it is true that four of our cardinals have not yet reported to the Sistine Chapel, but there is no need for alarm. Every one of them checked into the residence hall this morning, so we know they are safely inside Vatican City. You yourself had tea with them only hours ago. They are simply late for the fellowship preceding conclave. We are searching, but I'm sure they just lost track of time and are still out enjoying the grounds.'

'Enjoying the grounds?' The calm departed from the camerlengo's voice. 'They were due in the chapel over an hour ago!'

Langdon shot Vittoria a look of amazement. *Missing cardinals? So that's what they were looking for downstairs?*

'Our inventory,' the caller said, 'you will find quite convincing. There is Cardinal Lamassé from Paris, Cardinal Guidera from Barcelona, Cardinal Ebner from Frankfurt . . .'

Olivetti seemed to shrink smaller and smaller after each name was read.

The caller paused, as though taking special pleasure in the final name. 'And from Italy . . . Cardinal Baggia.'

The camerlengo loosened like a tall ship that had just run sheets first into a dead calm. His frock billowed, and he collapsed in his chair. '*I preferiti*,' he whispered. 'The four favorites . . . including Baggia . . . the most likely successor as Supreme Pontiff . . . how is it possible?'

Langdon had read enough about modern papal elections to understand the look of desperation on the camerlengo's face. Although technically *any* cardinal under eighty years old could become Pope, only a very few had the respect necessary to command a two-thirds majority in the ferociously partisan balloting procedure. They were known as the *preferiti*. And they were all gone.

Sweat dripped from the camerlengo's brow. 'What do you intend with these men?'

'What do you think I intend? I am a descendant of the Hassassin.'

Langdon felt a shiver. He knew the name well. The church had made some deadly enemies through the years – the Hassassin, the Knights Templar, armies that had been either hunted by the Vatican or betrayed by them.

'Let the cardinals go,' the camerlengo said. 'Isn't threatening to destroy the City of God enough?'

'Forget your four cardinals. They are lost to you. Be assured their deaths will be remembered though . . . by millions. Every martyr's dream. I will make them media luminaries. One by one. By midnight the Illuminati will have everyone's attention. Why change the world if the world is not watching? Public killings have an intoxicating horror about them, don't they? You proved that long ago ... the inquisition, the torture of the Knights Templar, the Crusades.' He paused. 'And of course, *la purga*.'

The camerlengo was silent.

'Do you not recall *la purga*?' the caller asked. 'Of course not, you are a child. Priests are poor historians, anyway. Perhaps because their history shames them?'

'*La purga*,' Langdon heard himself say. 'Sixteen sixty-eight. The church branded four Illuminati scientists with the symbol of the cross. To purge their sins.'

'Who is speaking?' the voice demanded, sounding more intrigued than concerned. 'Who else is there?'

Langdon felt shaky. 'My name is not important,' he said, trying to keep his voice from wavering. Speaking to a living Illuminatus was disorienting for him . . . like speaking to George Washington. 'I am an academic who has studied the history of your brotherhood.'

'Superb,' the voice replied. 'I am pleased there are still those alive who remember the crimes against us.'

'Most of us think you are dead.'

'A misconception the brotherhood has worked hard to promote. What else do you know of *la purga*?'

Langdon hesitated. *What else do I know? That this whole situation is insanity, that's what I know!* 'After the brandings, the scientists were murdered, and their bodies were dropped in public locations around Rome as a warning to other scientists not to join the Illuminati.'

'Yes. So we shall do the same. *Quid pro quo*. Consider it symbolic retribution for our slain bothers. Your four cardinals will die, one every hour starting at eight. By

182

midnight the whole world will be enthralled.'

Langdon moved toward the phone. 'You actually intend to *brand* and kill these four men?'

'History repeats itself, does it not? Of course, we will be more elegant and bold than the church was. They killed privately, dropping bodies when no one was looking. It seems so cowardly.'

'What are you saying?' Langdon asked. 'That you are going to brand and kill these men in *public*?'

'Very good. Although it depends what you consider public. I realize not many people go to church anymore.'

Langdon did a double take. 'You're going to kill them in *churches*?'

'A gesture of kindness. Enabling God to commend their souls to heaven more expeditiously. It seems only right. Of course the press will enjoy it too, I imagine.'

'You're bluffing,' Olivetti said, the cool back in his voice. 'You cannot kill a man in a church and expect to get away with it.'

'Bluffing? We move among your Swiss Guard like ghosts, remove four of your cardinals from within your walls, plant a deadly explosive at the heart of your most sacred shrine, and you think this is a bluff? As the killings occur and the victims are found, the media will swarm. By midnight the world will know the Illuminati cause.'

'And if we stake guards in every church?' Olivetti said.

The caller laughed. 'I fear the prolific nature of your religion will make that a trying task. Have you not counted lately? There are over four hundred Catholic churches in Rome. Cathedrals, chapels, tabernacles, abbeys, monasteries, convents, parochial schools . . .'

Olivetti's face remained hard.

'In ninety minutes it begins,' the caller said with a note of finality. 'One an hour. A mathematical progression of death. Now I must go.'

'Wait!' Langdon demanded. 'Tell me about the brands you intend to use on these men.'

The killer sounded amused. 'I suspect you know what the brands will be already. Or perhaps you are a skeptic? You will see them soon enough. Proof the ancient legends are true.'

Langdon felt light-headed. He knew exactly what the man was claiming. Langdon pictured the brand on Leonardo Vetra's chest. Illuminati folklore spoke of five brands in all. *Four brands are left*, Langdon thought, *and four missing cardinals.*

'I am sworn,' the camerlengo said, 'to bring a new Pope tonight. Sworn by God.'

'Camerlengo,' the caller said, 'the world does not need a new Pope. After midnight he will have nothing to rule over but a pile of rubble. The Catholic Church is finished. Your run on earth is done.'

Silence hung.

The camerlengo looked sincerely sad. 'You are misguided. A church is more than mortar and stone. You cannot simply erase two thousand years of faith . . . *any* faith. You cannot crush faith simply by removing its earthly manifestations. The Catholic Church will continue with or without Vatican City.'

'A noble lie. But a lie all the same. We both know the truth. Tell me, why is Vatican City a walled citadel?'

'Men of God live in a dangerous world,' the camerlengo said.

'How young *are* you? The Vatican is a fortress

184

because the Catholic Church holds half of its equity *inside* its walls – rare paintings, sculpture, devalued jewels, priceless books ... then there is the gold bullion and the real estate deeds inside the Vatican Bank vaults. Inside estimates put the raw value of Vatican City at 48.5 billion dollars. Quite a nest egg you're sitting on. Tomorrow it will be ash. Liquidated assets as it were. You will be bankrupt. Not even men of cloth can work for nothing.'

The accuracy of the statement seemed to be reflected in Olivetti's and the camerlengo's shell-shocked looks. Langdon wasn't sure what was more amazing, that the Catholic Church had that kind of money, or that the Illuminati somehow knew about it.

The camerlengo sighed heavily. 'Faith, not money, is the backbone of this church.'

'More lies,' the caller said. 'Last year you spent 183 million dollars trying to support your struggling dioceses worldwide. Church attendance is at an all-time low – down forty-six per cent in the last decade. Donations are half what they were only seven years ago. Fewer and fewer men are entering the seminary. Although you will not admit it, your church is dying. Consider this a chance to go out with a bang.'

Olivetti stepped forward. He seemed less combative now, as if he now sensed the reality facing him. He looked like a man searching for an out. Any out. 'And what if some of that bullion went to fund *your* cause?'

'Do not insult us both.'

'We have money.'

'As do we. More than you can fathom.'

Langdon flashed on the alleged Illuminati fortunes, the ancient wealth of the Bavarian stone masons, the

Rothschilds, the Bilderbergers, the legendary Illuminati Diamond.

'*I preferiti,*' the camerlengo said, changing the subject. His voice was pleading. 'Spare them. They are old. They—'

'They are virgin sacrifices.' The caller laughed. 'Tell me, do you think they are *really* virgins? Will the little lambs squeal when they die? *Sacrifici vergini nell' altare di scienza.*'

The camerlengo was silent for a long time. 'They are men of faith,' he finally said. 'They do not fear death.'

The caller sneered. 'Leonardo Vetra was a man of faith, and yet I saw fear in his eyes last night. A fear I removed.'

Vittoria, who had been silent, was suddenly airborne, her body taut with hatred. '*Asino!* He was my father!'

A cackle echoed from the speaker. 'Your father? What is this? Vetra has a daughter? You should know your father whimpered like a child at the end. Pitiful really. A pathetic man.'

Vittoria reeled as if knocked backward by the words. Langdon reached for her, but she regained her balance and fixed her dark eyes on the phone. 'I swear on my life, before this night is over, I will find you.' Her voice sharpened like a laser. 'And when I do . . .'

The caller laughed coarsely. 'A woman of spirit. I am aroused. Perhaps before this night is over, I will find *you*. And when I do . . .'

The words hung like a blade. Then he was gone.

42

Cardinal Mortati was sweating now in his black robe. Not only was the Sistine Chapel starting to feel like a sauna, but conclave was scheduled to begin in twenty minutes, and there was still no word on the four missing cardinals. In their absence, the initial whispers of confusion among the other cardinals had turned to outspoken anxiety..

Mortati could not imagine where the truant men could be. *With the camerlengo perhaps?* He knew the camerlengo had held the traditional private tea for the four *preferiti* earlier that afternoon, but that had been hours ago. *Were they ill? Something they ate?* Mortati doubted it. Even on the verge of death the *preferiti* would be here. It was once in a lifetime, usually *never*, that a cardinal had the chance to be elected Supreme Pontiff, and by Vatican Law the cardinal had to be *inside* the Sistine Chapel when the vote took place. Otherwise, he was ineligible.

Although there were four *preferiti*, few cardinals had any doubt who the next Pope would be. The past fifteen days had seen a blizzard of faxes and phone calls discussing potential candidates. As was the custom, four names had been chosen as *preferiti*, each of them fulfilling the unspoken requisites for becoming Pope.

Multilingual in Italian, Spanish, and English.

No skeletons in his closet.

Between sixty-five and eighty years old.

As usual, one of the *preferiti* had risen above the others as the man the college proposed to elect. Tonight that man was Cardinal Aldo Baggia from

Milan. Baggia's untainted record of service, combined with unparalleled language skills and the ability to communicate the essence of spirituality, had made him the clear favorite.

So where the devil is he? Mortati wondered.

Mortati was particularly unnerved by the missing cardinals because the task of supervising this conclave had fallen to him. A week ago, the College of Cardinals had unanimously chosen Mortati for the office known as *The Great Elector* – the conclave's internal master of ceremonies. Even though the camerlengo was the church's ranking official, the camerlengo was only a priest and had little familiarity with the complex election process, so one cardinal was selected to oversee the ceremony from within the Sistine Chapel.

Cardinals often joked that being appointed The Great Elector was the cruelest honor in Christendom. The appointment made one *ineligible* as a candidate during the election, and it also required one spend many days prior to conclave poring over the pages of the *Universi Dominici Gregis* reviewing the subtleties of conclave's arcane rituals to ensure the election was properly administered.

Mortati held no grudge, though. He knew he was the logical choice. Not only was he the senior cardinal, but he had also been a confidant of the late Pope, a fact that elevated his esteem. Although Mortati was technically still within the legal age window for election, he was getting a bit old to be a serious candidate. At seventy-nine years old he had crossed the unspoken threshold beyond which the college no longer trusted one's health to withstand the rigorous schedule of the papacy. A Pope usually worked fourteen-hour days, seven days a week, and died of exhaustion in an average of 6.3 years. The inside joke was that accepting the papacy was a cardinal's 'fastest route to heaven'.

Mortati, many believed, could have been Pope in his younger days had he not been so broad-minded. When it came to pursuing the papacy, there was a Holy Trinity–Conservative. Conservative. Conservative.

Mortati had always found it pleasantly ironic that the late Pope, God rest his soul, had revealed himself as surprisingly liberal once he had taken office. Perhaps sensing the modern world progressing away from the church, the Pope had made overtures, softening the church's position on the sciences, even donating money to selective scientific causes. Sadly, it had been political suicide. Conservative Catholics declared the Pope 'senile', while scientific purists accused him of trying to spread the church's influence where it did not belong.

'So where are they?'

Mortati turned.

One of the cardinals was tapping him nervously on the shoulder. 'You know where they are, don't you?'

Mortati tried not to show too much concern. 'Perhaps still with the camerlengo.'

'At this hour? That would be highly unorthodox!' The cardinal frowned mistrustingly. 'Perhaps the camerlengo lost track of time?'

Mortati sincerely doubted it, but he said nothing. He was well aware that most cardinals did not much care for the camerlengo, feeling he was too young to serve the Pope so closely. Mortati suspected much of the cardinals' dislike was jealousy, and Mortati actually admired the young man, secretly applauding the late Pope's selection for chamberlain. Mortati saw only conviction when he looked in the camerlengo's eyes, and unlike many of the cardinals, the camerlengo put church and faith before petty politics. He was truly a man of God.

Throughout his tenure, the camerlengo's steadfast devotion had become legendary. Many attributed it to the miraculous event in his childhood . . . an event that would have left a permanent impression on any man's heart. *The miracle and wonder of it*, Mortati thought, often wishing his own childhood had presented an event that fostered that kind of doubtless faith.

Unfortunately for the church, Mortati knew, the camerlengo would never become Pope in his elder years. Attaining the papacy required a certain amount of political ambition, something the young camerlengo apparently lacked; he had refused his Pope's offers for higher clerical stations many times, saying he preferred to serve the church as a simple man.

'What next?' The cardinal tapped Mortati, waiting.

Mortati looked up. 'I'm sorry?'

'They're late! What shall we do!'

'What *can* we do?' Mortati replied. 'We wait. And have faith.'

Looking entirely unsatisfied with Mortati's response, the cardinal shrunk back into the shadows.

Mortati stood a moment, dabbing his temples and trying to clear his mind. *Indeed, what shall we do?* He gazed past the altar up to Michelangelo's renowned fresco, 'The Last Judgment'. The painting did nothing to soothe his anxiety. It was a horrifying, fifty-foot-tall depiction of Jesus Christ separating mankind into the righteous and sinners, casting the sinners into hell. There was flayed flesh, burning bodies, and even one of Michelangelo's rivals sitting in hell wearing ass's ears. Guy de Maupassant had once written that the painting looked like something painted for a carnival wrestling booth by an ignorant coal heaver.

Cardinal Mortati had to agree.

43

Langdon stood motionless at the Pope's bulletproof window and gazed down at the bustle of media trailers in St Peter's Square. The eerie phone conversation had left him feeling turgid ... distended somehow. Not himself.

The Illuminati, like a serpent from the forgotten depths of history, had risen and wrapped themselves around an ancient foe. No demands. No negotiation. Just retribution. Demonically simple. Squeezing. A revenge 400 years in the making. It seemed that after centuries of persecution, science had bitten back.

The camerlengo stood at his desk, staring blankly at the phone. Olivetti was the first to break the silence. 'Carlo,' he said, using the camerlengo's first name and sounding more like a weary friend than an officer. 'For twenty-six years, I have sworn my life to the protection of this office. It seems tonight I am dishonored.'

The camerlengo shook his head. 'You and I serve God in different capacities, but service always brings honor.'

'These events ... I can't imagine how ... this situation ...' Olivetti looked overwhelmed.

'You realize we have only one possible course of action. I have a responsibility for the safety of the College of Cardinals.'

'I fear that responsibility was mine, signore.'

'Then your men will oversee the immediate evacuation.'

'Signore?'

'Other options can be exercised later – a search for this device, a manhunt for the missing cardinals and their captors. But first the cardinals must be taken to safety. The sanctity of human life weighs above all. Those men are the foundation of this church.'

'You suggest we cancel conclave right now?'

'Do I have a choice?'

'What about your charge to bring a new Pope?'

The young chamberlain sighed and turned to the window, his eyes drifting out onto the sprawl of Rome below. 'His Holiness once told me that a Pope is a man torn between two worlds ... the real world and the divine. He warned that any church that ignored reality would not survive to enjoy the divine.' His voice sounded suddenly wise for its years. 'The real world is upon us tonight. We would be vain to ignore it. Pride and precedent cannot overshadow reason.'

Olivetti nodded, looking impressed. 'I have under-estimated you, signore.'

The camerlengo did not seem to hear. His gaze was distant on the window.

'I will speak openly, signore. The real world is *my* world. I immerse myself in its ugliness every day such that others are unencumbered to seek something more pure. Let me advise you on the present situation. It is what I am trained for. Your instincts, though worthy ... could be disastrous.'

The camerlengo turned.

Olivetti sighed. 'The evacuation of the College of

Cardinals from the Sistine Chapel is the worst possible thing you could do right now.'

The camerlengo did not look indignant, only at a loss. 'What do you suggest?'

'Say nothing to the cardinals. Seal conclave. It will buy us time to try other options.'

The camerlengo looked troubled. 'Are you suggesting I lock the entire College of Cardinals on top of a time bomb?'

'Yes, signore. For now. Later, if need be, we can arrange evacuation.'

The camerlengo shook his head. 'Postponing the ceremony *before* it starts is grounds alone for an inquiry, but after the doors are sealed nothing intervenes. Conclave procedure obligates—'

'*Real* world, signore. You're in it tonight. Listen closely.' Olivetti spoke now with the efficient rattle of a field officer. 'Marching one hundred sixty-five cardinals unprepared and unprotected into Rome would be reckless. It would cause confusion and panic in some very old men, and frankly, one fatal stroke this month is enough.'

One fatal stroke. The commander's words recalled the headlines Langdon had read over dinner with some students in the Harvard Commons: POPE SUFFERS STROKE. DIES IN SLEEP.

'In addition,' Olivetti said, 'the Sistine Chapel is a fortress. Although we don't advertise the fact, the structure is heavily reinforced and can repel any attack short of missiles. As preparation we searched every inch of the chapel this afternoon, scanning for bugs and other surveillance equipment. The chapel is clean, a safe haven, and I am confident the antimatter is not inside. There is no safer place those men can be right now. We can always discuss emergency evacuation later if it comes to that.'

Langdon was impressed. Olivetti's cold, smart logic reminded him of Kohler.

'Commander,' Vittoria said, her voice tense, 'there are other concerns. Nobody has ever created this much antimatter. The blast radius, I can only estimate. Some of surrounding Rome may be in danger. If the canister is in one of your central buildings or underground, the effect outside these walls may be minimal, but if the canister is near the perimeter . . . in *this* building for example . . .' She glanced warily out the window at the crowd in St Peter's Square.

'I am well aware of my responsibilities to the outside world,' Olivetti replied, 'and it makes this situation no more grave. The protection of this sanctuary has been my sole charge for over two decades. I have no intention of allowing this weapon to detonate.'

Camerlengo Ventresca looked up. 'You think you can *find* it?'

'Let me discuss our options with some of my surveillance specialists. There is a possibility, if we kill power to Vatican City, that we can eliminate the background RF and create a clean enough environment to get a reading on that canister's magnetic field.'

Vittoria looked surprised, and then impressed. 'You want to *black out* Vatican City?'

'Possibly. I don't yet know if it's possible, but it is one option I want to explore.'

'The cardinals would certainly wonder what happened,' Vittoria remarked.

Olivetti shook his head. 'Conclaves are held by candlelight. The cardinals would never know. After

194

conclave is sealed, I could pull all except a few of my perimeter guards and begin a search. A hundred men could cover a lot of ground in five hours.'

'*Four* hours,' Vittoria corrected. 'I need to fly the canister back to CERN. Detonation is unavoidable without recharging the batteries.'

'There's no way to recharge here?'

Vittoria shook her head. 'The interface is complex. I'd have brought it if I could.'

'*Four* hours then,' Olivetti said, frowning. 'Still time enough. Panic serves no one. Signore, you have ten minutes. Go to the chapel, seal conclave. Give my men some time to do their job. As we get closer to the critical hour, we will make the critical decisions.'

Langdon wondered how close to 'the critical hour' Olivetti would let things get.

The camerlengo looked troubled. 'But the college will ask about the *preferiti* . . . especially about Baggia . . . where they are.'

'Then you will have to think of something, signore. Tell them you served the four cardinals something at tea that disagreed with them.'

The camerlengo looked riled. 'Stand on the altar of the Sistine Chapel and lie to the College of Cardinals?'

'For their own safety. *Una bugia veniale.* A white lie. Your job will be to keep the peace.' Olivetti headed for the door. 'Now if you will excuse me, I need to get started.'

'Commandante,' the camerlengo urged, 'we cannot simply turn our backs on missing cardinals.'

Olivetti stopped in the doorway. 'Baggia and the others are currently outside our sphere of influence. We must let them go . . . for the good of the whole. The military calls it *triage*.'

'Don't you mean *abandonment*?'

His voice hardened. 'If there were *any* way, signore . . . any way in heaven to locate those four cardinals, I would lay down my life to do it. And yet . . .' He pointed across the room at the window where the early evening sun glinted off an endless sea of Roman rooftops. 'Searching a city of five million is not within my power. I will not waste precious time to appease my conscience in a futile exercise. I'm sorry.'

Vittoria spoke suddenly. 'But if we *caught* the killer, couldn't you make him talk?'

Olivetti frowned at her. 'Soldiers cannot afford to be saints, Ms Vetra. Believe me, I empathize with your personal incentive to catch this man.'

'It's not only personal,' she said. 'The *killer* knows where the antimatter is . . . *and* the missing cardinals. If we could somehow find him . . .'

'Play into their hands?' Olivetti said. 'Believe me, removing all protection from Vatican City in order to stake out hundreds of churches is what the Illuminati *hope* we will do . . . wasting precious time and manpower when we should be searching . . . or worse yet, leaving the Vatican Bank totally unprotected. Not to mention the remaining cardinals.'

The point hit home.

'How about the Roman Police?' the camerlengo asked. 'We could alert citywide enforcement of the crisis. Enlist their help in finding the cardinals' captor.'

'Another mistake,' Olivetti said. 'You know how the Roman *Carabinieri* feel about us. We'd get a half-hearted effort of a few men in exchange for their selling our crisis to the global media. Exactly what our enemies want. We'll have to deal with the media soon enough as it is.'

I will make your cardinals media luminaries, Langdon

thought, recalling the killer's words. *The first cardinal's body appears at eight o'clock. Then one every hour. The press will love it.*

The camerlengo was talking again, a trace of anger in his voice. 'Commander, we cannot in good conscience do *nothing* about the missing cardinals!'

Olivetti looked the camerlengo dead in the eye. 'The prayer of St Francis, signore. Do you recall it?'

The young priest spoke the single line with pain in his voice. 'God, grant me strength to accept those things I cannot change.'

'Trust me,' Olivetti said. '*This* is one of those things.' Then he was gone.

44

The central office of the British Broadcasting Corporation (BBC) is in London just west of Piccadilly Circus. The switchboard phone rang, and a junior content editor picked up.

'BBC,' she said, stubbing out her Dunhill cigarette.

The voice on the line was raspy, with a Mid-East accent. 'I have a breaking story your network might be interested in.'

The editor took out a pen and a standard Lead Sheet. 'Regarding?'

'The papal election.'

She frowned wearily. The BBC had run a preliminary story yesterday to mediocre response. The public, it seemed, had little interest in Vatican City. 'What's the angle?'

'Do you have a TV reporter in Rome covering the election?'

'I believe so.'

'I need to speak to him directly.'

'I'm sorry, but I cannot give you that number without some idea—'

'There is a threat to the conclave. That is all I can tell you.'

The editor took notes. 'Your name?'

'My name is immaterial.'

The editor was not surprised. 'And you have proof of this claim?'

'I do.'

'I would be happy to take the information, but it is not our policy to give out our reporters' numbers unless—'

'I understand. I will call another network. Thank you for your time. Good-b—'

'Just a moment,' she said. 'Can you hold?'

The editor put the caller on hold and stretched her neck. The art of screening out potential crank calls was by no means a perfect science, but this caller had just passed the BBC's two tacit tests for authenticity of a phone source. He had refused to give his name, and he was eager to get off the phone. Hacks and glory hounds usually whined and pleaded.

Fortunately for her, reporters lived in eternal fear of missing the big story, so they seldom chastised her for passing along the occasional delusional psychotic. Wasting five minutes of a reporter's time was forgivable. Missing a headline was not.

Yawning, she looked at her computer and typed in the keywords 'Vatican City'. When she saw the name of the field reporter covering the papal election, she chuckled to herself. He was a new guy the BBC had just brought up from some trashy London tabloid to handle some of the BBC's more mundane coverage. Editorial had obviously started him at the bottom rung.

He was probably bored out of his mind, waiting all night to record his ten-second video spot. He would most likely be grateful for a break in the monotony.

The BBC content editor copied down the reporter's satellite extension in Vatican City. Then, lighting another cigarette, she gave the anonymous caller the reporter's number.

45

'It won't work,' Vittoria said, pacing the Pope's office. She looked up at the camerlengo. 'Even if a Swiss Guard team can filter electronic interference, they will have to be practically *on top* of the canister before they detect any signal. And that's if the canister is even accessible . . . unenclosed by other barriers. What if it's buried in a metal box somewhere on your grounds? Or up in a metal ventilating duct. There's no way they'll trace it. And what if the Swiss Guards *have* been infiltrated? Who's to say the search will be clean?'

The camerlengo looked drained. 'What are you proposing, Ms Vetra?'

Vittoria felt flustered. *Isn't it obvious!* 'I am proposing, sir, that you take other precautions *immediately*. We can hope against all hope that the commander's search is successful. At the same time, look out the window. Do you see those people? Those buildings across the piazza? Those media vans? The tourists? They are quite possibly within range of the blast. You need to act *now*.'

The camerlengo nodded vacantly.

Vittoria felt frustrated. Olivetti had convinced everyone there was plenty of time. But Vittoria knew if news of the Vatican predicament leaked out, the entire area could fill with onlookers in a matter of minutes. She had seen it once outside the Swiss Parliament building. During a hostage situation involving a bomb, thousands had congregated outside the building to witness the outcome. Despite police warnings that they were in danger, the crowd packed in closer and closer. Nothing captured human interest like human tragedy.

'Signore,' Vittoria urged, 'the man who killed my father is out there somewhere. Every cell in this body wants to run from here and hunt him down. But I am standing in your office . . . because I have a responsibility to you. To you and others. Lives are in danger, signore. Do you hear me?'

The camerlengo did not answer.

Vittoria could hear her own heart racing. *Why couldn't the Swiss Guard trace that damn caller? The Illuminati assassin is the key! He knows where the anti-matter is . . . hell, he knows where the cardinals are! Catch the killer, and everything is solved.*

Vittoria sensed she was starting to come unhinged, an alien distress she recalled only faintly from childhood, the orphanage years, frustration with no tools to handle it. *You have tools*, she told herself, *you always have tools.* But it was no use. Her thoughts intruded, strangling her. She was a researcher and problem

200

solver. But this was a problem with no solution. *What data do you require? What do you want?* She told herself to breathe deeply, but for the first time in her life, she could not. She was suffocating.

Langdon's head ached, and he felt like he was skirting the edges of rationality. He watched Vittoria and the camerlengo, but his vision was blurred by hideous images: explosions, press swarming, cameras rolling, four branded humans.

Shaitan . . . Lucifer . . . Bringer of light . . . Satan . . .

He shook the fiendish images from his mind. *Calculated terrorism*, he reminded himself, grasping at reality. *Planned chaos*. He thought back to a Radcliffe seminar he had once audited while researching praetorian symbolism. He had never seen terrorists the same way since.

'Terrorism,' the professor had lectured, 'has a singular goal. What is it?'

'Killing innocent people?' a student ventured.

'Incorrect. Death is only a *byproduct* of terrorism.'

'A show of strength?'

'No. A weaker persuasion does not exist.'

'To cause terror?'

'Concisely put. Quite simply, the goal of terrorism is to create terror and fear. Fear undermines faith in the establishment. It weakens the enemy from within . . . causing unrest in the masses. Write this down. Terrorism is *not* an expression of rage. Terrorism is a political weapon. Remove a government's façade of infallibility, and you remove its people's faith.'

Loss of faith . . .

Is that what this was all about? Langdon wondered how Christians of the world would react to cardinals being laid out like mutilated dogs. If the faith of a priest did not protect him from the evils of Satan, what hope was there for the rest of us? Langdon's head was pounding louder now ... tiny voices playing tug of war.

Faith does not protect you. Medicine and airbags ... those are things that protect you. God does not protect you. Intelligence protects you. Enlightenment. Put your faith in something with tangible results. How long has it been since someone walked on water? Modern miracles belong to science ... computers, vaccines, space stations ... even the divine miracle of creation. Matter from nothing ... in a lab. Who needs God? No! Science is God.

The killer's voice resonated in Langdon's mind. *Midnight ... mathematical progression of death ... sacrifici vergini nell' altare di scienza.*

Then suddenly, like a crowd dispersed by a single gunshot, the voices were gone.

Robert Langdon bolted to his feet. His chair fell backward and crashed on the marble floor.

Vittoria and the camerlengo jumped.

'I missed it,' Langdon whispered, spellbound. 'It was right in front of me ...'

'Missed what?' Vittoria demanded.

Langdon turned to the priest. 'Father, for three years I have petitioned this office for access to the Vatican Archives. I have been denied seven times.'

'Mr Langdon, I am sorry, but this hardly seems the moment to raise such complaints.'

'I need access immediately. The four missing cardinals. I may be able to figure out where they're going to be killed.'

Vittoria stared, looking certain she had misunderstood.

The camerlengo looked troubled, as if he were the brunt of a cruel joke. 'You expect me to believe this information is in our *archives*?'

'I can't promise I can locate it in time, but if you let me in . . .'

'Mr Langdon, I am due in the Sistine Chapel in four minutes. The archives are across Vatican City.'

'You're serious aren't you?' Vittoria interrupted, staring deep into Langdon's eyes, seeming to sense his earnestness.

'Hardly a joking time,' Langdon said.

'Father,' Vittoria said, turning to the camerlengo, 'if there's a chance . . . any at all of finding where these killings are going to happen, we could stake out the locations and—'

'But the archives?' the camerlengo insisted. 'How could they possibly contain any clue?'

'Explaining it,' Langdon, 'will take longer than you've got. But if I'm right, we can use the information to catch the Hassassin.'

The camerlengo looked as though he wanted to believe but somehow could not. 'Christianity's most sacred codices are in that archive. Treasures I myself am not privileged enough to see.'

'I am aware of that.'

'Access is permitted only by written decree of the curator and the Board of Vatican Librarians.'

'*Or*,' Langdon declared, 'by *papal* mandate. It says so in every rejection letter your curator ever sent me.'

The camerlengo nodded.

'Not to be rude,' Langdon urged, 'but if I'm not mistaken a papal mandate comes from *this* office. As far as I can tell, tonight you hold the trust of his station. Considering the circumstances . . .'

The camerlengo pulled a pocket watch from his cassock and looked at it. 'Mr Langdon, I am prepared to give my life tonight, quite literally, to save this church.'

Langdon sensed nothing but truth in the man's eyes.

'This document,' the camerlengo said, 'do you truly believe it is here? And that it can help us locate these four churches?'

'I would not have made countless solicitations for access if I were not convinced. Italy is a bit far to come on a lark when you make a teacher's salary. The document you have is an ancient—'

'Please,' the camerlengo interrupted. 'Forgive me. My mind cannot process any more details at the moment. Do you know where the secret archives are located?'

Langdon felt a rush of excitement. 'Just behind the Santa Ana Gate.'

'Impressive. Most scholars believe it is through the secret door behind St Peter's Throne.'

'No. That would be the Archivio della Reverenda di Fabbrica di S. Pietro. A common misconception.'

'A librarian docent accompanies every entrant at all times. Tonight, the docents are gone. What you are requesting is carte blanche access. Not even our cardinals enter alone.'

'I will treat your treasures with the utmost respect and care. Your librarians will find not a trace that I was there.'

Overhead the bells of St Peter's began to toll. The camerlengo checked his pocket watch. 'I must go.' He paused a taut moment and looked up at Langdon. 'I will have a Swiss Guard meet you at the archives. I am giving you my trust, Mr Langdon. Go now.'

Langdon was speechless.

The young priest now seemed to possess an eerie poise. Reaching over, he squeezed Langdon's shoulder with surprising strength. 'I want you to find what you are looking for. And find it quickly.'

46

The Secret Vatican Archives are located at the far end of the Belvedere Courtyard directly up a hill from the Gate of Santa Ana. They contain over 20,000 volumes and are rumored to hold such treasures as Leonardo da Vinci's missing diaries and even unpublished books of the Holy Bible.

Langdon strode powerfully up the deserted Via della Fondamenta toward the archives, his mind barely able to accept that he was about to be granted access. Vittoria was at his side, keeping pace effortlessly. Her almond-scented hair tossed lightly in the breeze, and Langdon breathed it in. He felt his thoughts straying and reeled himself back.

Vittoria said, 'You going to tell me what we're looking for?'

'A little book written by a guy named Galileo.'

She sounded surprised. 'You don't mess around. What's in it?'

'It is supposed to contain something called *il segno*.'

'The sign?'

'Sign, clue, signal . . . depends on your translation.'

'Sign to *what*?'

Langdon picked up the pace. 'A secret location.

Galileo's Illuminati needed to protect themselves from the Vatican, so they founded an ultrasecret Illuminati meeting place here in Rome. They called it The Church of Illumination.'

'Pretty bold calling a satanic lair a *church*.'

Langdon shook his head. 'Galileo's Illuminati were not the least bit satanic. They were scientists who revered enlightenment. Their meeting place was simply where they could safely congregate and discuss topics forbidden by the Vatican. Although we know the secret lair existed, to this day nobody has ever located it.'

'Sounds like the Illuminati know how to keep a secret.'

'Absolutely. In fact, they never revealed the location of their hideaway to anyone outside the brotherhood. This secrecy protected them, but it also posed a problem when it came to recruiting new members.'

'They couldn't grow if they couldn't advertise,' Vittoria said, her legs and mind keeping perfect pace.

'Exactly. Word of Galileo's brotherhood started to spread in the 1630s, and scientists from around the world made secret pilgrimages to Rome hoping to join the Illuminati ... eager for a chance to look through Galileo's telescope and hear the master's ideas. Unfortunately, though, because of the Illuminati's secrecy, scientists arriving in Rome never knew where to go for the meetings or to whom they could safely speak. The Illuminati wanted new blood, but they could not afford to risk their secrecy by making their whereabouts known.'

Vittoria frowned. 'Sounds like a *situazione senza soluzione*.'

'Exactly. A catch-22, as we would say.'

'So what did they do?'

'They were scientists. They examined the problem and found a solution. A brilliant one, actually. The Illuminati created a kind of ingenious *map* directing scientists to their sanctuary.'

Vittoria looked suddenly skeptical and slowed. 'A map? Sounds careless. If a copy fell into the wrong hands . . .'

'It couldn't,' Langdon said. 'No copies existed anywhere. It was not the kind of map that fit on paper. It was enormous. A blazed trail of sorts across the city.'

Vittoria slowed even further. 'Arrows painted on sidewalks?'

'In a sense, yes, but much more subtle. The map consisted of a series of carefully concealed symbolic markers placed in public locations around the city. One marker led to the next . . . and the next . . . a trail . . . eventually leading to the Illuminati lair.'

Vittoria eyed him askance. 'Sounds like a treasure hunt.'

Langdon chuckled. 'In a manner of speaking, it is. The Illuminati called their string of markers "The Path of Illumination", and anyone who wanted to join the brotherhood had to follow it all the way to the end. A kind of test.'

'But if the Vatican wanted to find the Illuminati,' Vittoria argued, 'couldn't *they* simply follow the markers?'

'No. The path was hidden. A puzzle, constructed in such a way that only certain people would have the ability to track the markers and figure out where the Illuminati church was hidden. The Illuminati intended it as a kind of initiation, functioning not only as a security measure but also as a screening process to

207

ensure that only the brightest scientists arrived at their door.'

'I don't buy it. In the 1600s the clergy were some of the most educated men in the world. If these markers were in public locations, certainly there existed members of the Vatican who could have figured it out.'

'Sure,' Langdon said, 'if they had *known* about the markers. But they didn't. And they never noticed them because the Illuminati designed them in such a way that clerics would never suspect what they were. They used a method known in symbology as *dissimulation*.'

'Camouflage.'

Langdon was impressed. 'You know the term.'

'*Dissimulazione*,' she said. 'Nature's best defense. Try spotting a trumpet fish floating vertically in seagrass.'

'Okay,' Langdon said. 'The Illuminati used the same concept. They created markers that faded into the backdrop of ancient Rome. They couldn't use ambigrams or scientific symbology because it would be far too conspicuous, so they called on an Illuminati artist – the same anonymous prodigy who had created their ambigrammatic symbol "Illuminati" – and they commissioned him to carve four sculptures.'

'Illuminati *sculptures*?'

'Yes, sculptures with two strict guidelines. First, the sculptures had to look like the rest of the artwork in Rome . . . artwork that the Vatican would *never* suspect belonged to the Illuminati.'

'*Religious* art.'

Langdon nodded, feeling a tinge of excitement, talking faster now. 'And the *second* guideline was that the four sculptures had to have very specific themes. Each piece needed to be a subtle tribute to one of the four elements of science.'

'*Four* elements?' Vittoria said. 'There are over a hundred.'

'Not in the 1600s,' Langdon reminded her. 'Early alchemists believed the entire universe was made up of only four substances: Earth, Air, Fire and Water.'

The early cross, Langdon knew, was the most common symbol of the four elements – four arms representing Earth, Air, Fire and Water. Beyond that, though, there existed literally *dozens* of symbolic occurrences of Earth, Air, Fire and Water throughout history – the Pythagorean cycles of life, the Chinese *Hong-Fan*, the Jungian male and female rudiments, the quadrants of the Zodiac, even the Muslims revered the four ancient elements . . . although in Islam they were known as 'squares, clouds, lightning, and waves.' For Langdon, though, it was a more modern usage that always gave him chills – the Mason's four mystic grades of Absolute Initiation: Earth, Air, Fire, and Water.

Vittoria seemed mystified. 'So this Illuminati artist created four pieces of art that *looked* religious, but were actually tributes to Earth, Air, Fire, and Water?'

'Exactly,' Langdon said, quickly turning up Via Sentinel toward the archives. 'The pieces blended into the sea of religious artwork all over Rome. By donating the artwork anonymously to specific churches and then using their political influence, the brotherhood facilitated placement of these four pieces in carefully chosen churches in Rome. Each piece of course was a marker . . . subtly pointing to the next church . . . where the next marker awaited. It functioned as a trail of clues disguised as religious art. If an Illuminati candidate could find the first church and the marker for Earth, he could follow it to Air . . . and then to Fire . . .

and then to Water ... and finally to the Church of Illumination.'

Vittoria was looking less and less clear. 'And this has something to do with catching the Illuminati assassin?'

Langdon smiled as he played his ace. 'Oh, yes. The Illuminati called these four churches by a very special name. *The Altars of Science.*'

Vittoria frowned. 'I'm sorry, that means noth—' She stopped short. '*L'altare di scienza?*' she exclaimed. 'The Illuminati assassin. He warned that the cardinals would be virgin sacrifices on the altars of science!'

Langdon gave her a smile. 'Four cardinals. Four churches. The four altars of science.'

She looked stunned. 'You're saying the four churches where the cardinals will be sacrificed are the *same* four churches that mark the ancient Path of Illumination?'

'I believe so, yes.'

'But why would the killer have given us that clue?'

'Why not?' Langdon replied. 'Very few historians know about those sculptures. Even fewer believe they exist. And their locations have remained secret for four hundred years. No doubt the Illuminati trusted the secret for another five hours. Besides, the Illuminati don't *need* their Path of Illumination anymore. Their secret lair is probably long gone anyway. They live in the modern world. They meet in bank boardrooms, eating clubs, private golf courses. Tonight they *want* to make their secrets public. This is their moment. Their grand unveiling.'

Langdon feared the Illuminati unveiling would have a special symmetry to it that he had not yet mentioned. *The four brands.* The killer had sworn each cardinal would be branded with a different symbol. *Proof the ancient legends are true,* the killer had said. The legend of the four ambigrammatic brands was as old as the Illuminati itself: earth, air, fire, water – four words crafted in perfect symmetry. Just like the word Illuminati. Each cardinal was to be branded with one of the ancient elements of science. The rumor that the four brands were in *English* rather than Italian remained a point of debate among historians. English seemed a random deviation from their natural tongue . . . and the Illuminati did nothing randomly.

Langdon turned up the brick pathway before the archive building. Ghastly images thrashed in his mind. The overall Illuminati plot was starting to reveal its patient grandeur. The brotherhood had vowed to stay silent as long as it took, amassing enough influence and power that they could resurface without fear, make their stand, fight their cause in broad daylight. The Illuminati were no longer about hiding. They were about flaunting their power, confirming the conspiratorial myths as fact. Tonight was a global publicity stunt.

Vittoria said, 'Here comes our escort.' Langdon looked up to see a Swiss Guard hurrying across an adjacent lawn toward the front door.

When the guard saw them, he stopped in his tracks. He stared at them, as though he thought he was hallucinating. Without a word he turned away and pulled out his walkie-talkie. Apparently incredulous at what he was being asked to do, the guard spoke urgently to the person on the other end. The angry bark coming back was indecipherable to Langdon, but its message was clear. The guard slumped, put away the walkie-talkie, and turned to them with a look of discontent.

Not a word was spoken as the guard guided them into the building. They passed through four steel doors, two passkey entries, down a long stairwell, and into a foyer with two combination keypads. Passing through a high-tech series of electronic gates, they arrived at the end of a long hallway outside a set of wide oak double doors. The guard stopped, looked them over again and, mumbling under his breath, walked to a metal box on the wall. He unlocked it, reached inside, and pressed a code. The doors before them buzzed, and the deadbolt fell open.

The guard turned, speaking to them for the first time. 'The archives are beyond that door. I have been instructed to escort you this far and return for briefing on another matter.'

'You're leaving?' Vittoria demanded.

'Swiss Guards are not cleared for access to the Secret Archives. You are here only because my commander received a direct order from the camerlengo.'

'But how do we get *out*?'

'Monodirectional security. You will have no difficulties.' That being the entirety of the conversation, the guard spun on his heel and marched off down the hall.

Vittoria made some comment, but Langdon did not hear. His mind was fixed on the double doors before him, wondering what mysteries lay beyond.

47

Although he knew time was short, Camerlengo Carlo Ventresca walked slowly. He needed the time alone to gather his thoughts before facing opening prayer. So much was happening. As he moved in dim solitude down the Northern Wing, the challenge of the past fifteen days weighed heavy in his bones.

He had followed his holy duties to the letter.

As was Vatican tradition, following the Pope's death the camerlengo had personally confirmed expiration by placing his fingers on the Pope's carotid artery, listening for breath, and then calling the Pope's name three times. By law there was no autopsy. Then he had sealed the Pope's bedroom, destroyed the papal fisherman's ring, shattered the die used to make lead seals, and arranged for the funeral. That done, he began preparations for the conclave.

Conclave, he thought. *The final hurdle.* It was one of the oldest traditions in Christendom. Nowadays, because the outcome of conclave was usually known before it began, the process was criticized as obsolete – more of a burlesque than an election. The camerlengo knew, however, this was only a lack of understanding. Conclave was not an election. It was an ancient, mystic transference of power. The tradition was timeless . . . the secrecy, the folded slips of paper, the burning of the ballots, the mixing of ancient chemicals, the smoke signals.

As the camerlengo approached through the Loggias of Gregory XIII, he wondered if Cardinal Mortati was in a panic yet. Certainly Mortati had noticed the *preferiti* were missing. Without them the voting would go on all night. Mortati's appointment as the Great Elector, the camerlengo assured himself, was a good one. The man was a free-thinker and could speak his mind. The conclave would need a leader tonight more than ever.

As the camerlengo arrived at the top of the Royal Staircase, he felt as though he were standing on the precipice of his life. Even from up here he could hear the rumble of activity in the Sistine Chapel below – the uneasy chatter of 165 cardinals.

One hundred sixty-one cardinals, he corrected.

For an instant the camerlengo was falling, plummeting toward hell, people screaming, flames engulfing him, stones and blood raining from the sky.

And then silence.

When the child awoke, he was in heaven. Everything around him was white. The light was blinding and pure. Although some would say a ten year old could not possibly understand heaven, the young Carlo Ventresca understood heaven very well. He was in heaven right now. Where else would he be? Even in his short decade on earth Carlo had felt the majesty of God – the thundering pipe organs, the towering domes, the voices raised in song, the stained glass, shimmering bronze and gold. Carlo's mother, Maria, brought him to Mass every day. The church was Carlo's home.

'Why do we come to Mass every single day?' Carlo asked, not that he minded at all.

'Because I promised God I would,' she replied. 'And a promise to God is the most important promise of all. Never break a promise to God.'

Carlo promised her he would never break a promise to God. He loved his mother more than anything in the world. She was his holy angel. Sometimes he called her *Maria benedetta* – the Blessed Mary – although she did not like that at all. He knelt with her as she prayed, smelling the sweet scent of her flesh and listening to the murmur of her voice as she counted the rosary. *Hail Mary, Mother of God . . . pray for us sinners . . . now and at the hour of our death.*

'Where is my father?' Carlo asked, already knowing his father had died before he was born.

'God is your father, now,' she would always reply. 'You are a child of the church.'

Carlo loved that.

'Whenever you feel frightened,' she said, 'remember that God is your father now. He will watch over you and protect you forever. God has *big plans* for you, Carlo.' The boy knew she was right. He could already feel God in his blood.

Blood . . .

Blood raining from the sky!

Silence. Then heaven.

His heaven, Carlo learned as the blinding lights were turned off, was actually the Intensive Care Unit in *Santa Clara Hospital* outside of Palermo. Carlo had been the sole survivor of a terrorist bombing that had collapsed a chapel where he and his mother had been attending Mass while on vacation. Thirty-seven people had died, including Carlo's mother. The papers called Carlo's survival *The Miracle of St Francis.* Carlo had, for some unknown reason, only moments before the blast, left his mother's side and ventured into a protected alcove to ponder a tapestry depicting the story of St Francis.

God called me there, he decided. *He wanted to save me.*

Carlo was delirious with pain. He could still see his mother, kneeling at the pew, blowing him a kiss, and then with a concussive roar, her sweet-smelling flesh was torn apart. He could still taste man's *evil.* Blood showered down. His mother's blood! The blessed Maria!

God will watch over you and protect you forever, his mother had told him.

But where was God now!

Then, like a worldly manifestation of his mother's truth, a clergyman had come to the hospital. He was not any clergyman. He was a bishop. He prayed over Carlo. The Miracle of St Francis. When Carlo recovered, the bishop arranged for him to live in a small monastery attached to the cathedral over which the bishop presided. Carlo lived and tutored with the monks. He even became an altar boy for his new protector. The bishop suggested Carlo entered public school, but Carlo refused. He could not have been more happy with his new home. He now truly lived in the house of God.

Every night Carlo prayed for his mother.

God saved me for a reason, he thought. *What is the reason?*

When Carlo turned sixteen, he was obliged by Italian law to serve two years of reserve military training. The bishop told Carlo that if he entered seminary he would be exempt from this duty. Carlo told the priest that he planned to enter seminary but that first he needed to understand *evil*.

The bishop did not understand.

Carlo told him that if he was going to spend his life in the church fighting evil, first he had to understand it. He could not think of any better place to understand evil than in the army. The army used guns and bombs. *A bomb killed my Blessed mother!*

The bishop tried to dissuade him, but Carlo's mind was made up.

'Be careful, my son,' the bishop had said. 'And remember the church awaits you when you return.'

216

Carlo's two years of military service had been dreadful. Carlo's youth had been one of silence and reflection. But in the army there was no quiet for reflection. Endless noise. Huge machines everywhere. Not a moment of peace. Although the soldiers went to Mass once a week at the barracks, Carlo did not sense God's presence in any of his fellow soldiers. Their minds were too filled with chaos to see God.

Carlo hated his new life and wanted to go home. But he was determined to stick it out. He had yet to understand evil. He refused to fire a gun, so the military taught him how to fly a medical helicopter. Carlo hated the noise and the smell, but at least it let him fly up in the sky and be closer to his mother in heaven. When he was informed his pilot's training included learning how to parachute, Carlo was terrified. Still, he had no choice.

God will protect me, he told himself.

Carlo's first parachute jump was the most exhilarating physical experience of his life. It was like flying with God. Carlo could not get enough . . . the silence . . . the floating . . . seeing his mother's face in the billowing white clouds as he soared to earth. *God has plans for you, Carlo.* When he returned from the military, Carlo entered the seminary.

That had been twenty-three years ago.

Now, as Camerlengo Carlo Ventresca descended the Royal Staircase, he tried to comprehend the chain of events that had delivered him to this extraordinary crossroads.

Abandon all fear, he told himself, *and give this night over to God.*

He could see the great bronze door of the Sistine

Chapel now, dutifully protected by four Swiss Guards. The guards unbolted the door and pulled it open. Inside, every head turned. The camerlengo gazed out at the black robes and red sashes before him. He understood what God's plans for him were. The fate of the church had been placed in his hands.

The camerlengo crossed himself and stepped over the threshold.

48

BBC journalist Gunther Glick sat sweating in the BBC network van parked on the eastern edge of St Peter's Square and cursed his assignment editor. Although Glick's first monthly review had come back filled with superlatives – resourceful, sharp, dependable – here he was in Vatican City on 'Pope-Watch'. He reminded himself that reporting for the BBC carried a hell of a lot more credibility than fabricating fodder for the *British Tatler*, but still, this was *not* his idea of reporting.

Glick's assignment was simple. Insultingly simple. He was to sit here waiting for a bunch of old farts to elect their next chief old fart, then he was to step outside and record a fifteen-second 'live' spot with the Vatican as a backdrop.

Brilliant.

Glick couldn't believe the BBC still sent reporters into the field to cover this schlock. *You don't see the American networks here tonight. Hell no!* That was because the big boys did it right. They watched CNN, synopsized it, and then filmed their 'live' report in front of a blue screen, superimposing stock video for a realistic backdrop. MSNBC even used in-studio wind and rain machines to give that on-the-scene authenticity. Viewers didn't want truth anymore; they wanted entertainment.

Glick gazed out through the windshield and felt more and more depressed by the minute. The imperial mountain of Vatican City rose before him as a dismal reminder of what men could accomplish when they put their minds to it.

'What have I accomplished in my life?' he wondered aloud. 'Nothing.'

'So give up,' a woman's voice said from behind him.

Glick jumped. He had almost forgotten he was not alone. He turned to the back seat, where his camerawoman, Chinita Macri, sat silently polishing her glasses. She was always polishing her glasses. Chinita was black, although she preferred African American, a little heavy and smart as hell. She wouldn't let you forget it either. She was an odd bird, but Glick liked her. And Glick could sure as hell use the company.

'What's the problem, Gunth?' Chinita asked.

'What are we doing here?'

She kept polishing. 'Witnessing an exciting event.'

'Old men locked in the dark is exciting?'

'You *do* know you're going to hell, don't you?'

'Already there.'

'Talk to me.' She sounded like his mother.

'I just feel like I want to leave my mark.'

'You wrote for the *British Tatler*.'

'Yeah, but nothing with any resonance.'

'Oh, come on, I heard you did a groundbreaking article on the queen's secret sex life with aliens.'

'Thanks.'

219

'Hey, things are looking up. Tonight you make your first fifteen seconds of TV history.'

Glick groaned. He could hear the news anchor already. 'Thanks Gunther, great report.' Then the anchor would roll his eyes and move on to the weather. 'I should have tried for an anchor spot.'

Macri laughed. 'With no experience? And *that* beard? Forget it.'

Glick ran his hands through the reddish gob of hair on his chin. 'I think it makes me look clever.'

The van's cell phone rang, mercifully interrupting yet another one of Glick's failures. 'Maybe that's editorial,' he said, suddenly hopeful. 'You think they want a live update?'

'On *this* story?' Macri laughed. 'You keep dreaming.'

Glick answered the phone in his best anchorman voice. 'Gunther Glick, BBC, Live in Vatican City.'

The man on the line had a thick Arabic accent. 'Listen carefully,' he said. 'I am about to change your life.'

49

Langdon and Vittoria stood alone now outside the double doors that led to the inner sanctum of the Secret Archives. The decor in the colonnade was an incongruous mix of wall-to-wall carpets over marble floors and wireless security cameras gazing down from beside carved cherubs in the ceiling. Langdon dubbed it *Sterile Renaissance*. Beside the arched ingress hung a small bronze plaque.

Curatore, Padre Jaqui Tomaso

Father Jaqui Tomaso. Langdon recognized the curator's name from the rejection letters at home in his desk. *Dear Mr Langdon, It is with regret that I am writing to deny* . . .

Regret. *Bullshit*. Since Jaqui Tomaso's reign had begun, Langdon had never met a single non-Catholic American scholar who had been given access to the Secret Vatican Archives. *Il guardiano*, historians called him. Jaqui Tomaso was the toughest librarian on earth.

As Langdon pushed the doors open and stepped through the vaulted portal into the inner sanctum, he half expected to see Father Jaqui in full military fatigues and helmet standing guard with a bazooka. The space, however, was deserted.

Silence. Soft lighting.

Archivio Vaticano. One of his life dreams.

As Langdon's eyes took in the sacred chamber, his first reaction was one of embarrassment. He realized what a callow romantic he was. The images he had held for so many years of this room could not have been more inaccurate. He had imagined dusty book-shelves piled high with tattered volumes, priests cataloging by the light of candles and stained-glass windows, monks poring over scrolls . . .

Not even close.

At first glance the room appeared to be a darkened airline hangar in which someone had built a dozen free-standing racquetball courts. Langdon knew of course what the glass-walled enclosures were. He was not surprised to see them; humidity and heat eroded ancient vellums and parchments, and proper preservation required hermitic vaults like these – airtight cubicles that kept out humidity and natural acids in the air. Langdon had been inside hermetic vaults many times, but it was always an unsettling experience ... something about entering an airtight container where the oxygen was regulated by a reference librarian.

The vaults were dark, ghostly even, faintly outlined by tiny dome lights at the end of each stack. In the blackness of each cell, Langdon sensed the phantom giants, row upon row of towering stacks, laden with history. This was one hell of a collection.

Vittoria also seemed dazzled. She stood beside him staring mutely at the giant transparent cubes.

Time was short, and Langdon wasted none of it scanning the dimly lit room for a book catalog – a bound encyclopedia that cataloged the library's collection. All he saw was the glow of a handful of computer terminals dotting the room. 'Looks like they've got a Biblion. Their index is computerized.'

Vittoria looked hopeful. 'That should speed things up.'

Langdon wished he shared her enthusiasm, but he sensed this was bad news. He walked to a terminal and began typing. His fears were instantly confirmed. 'The old-fashioned method would have been better.'

'Why?'

He stepped back from the monitor. 'Because *real* books don't have password protection. I don't suppose physicists are natural born hackers?'

Vittoria shook her head. 'I can open oysters, that's about it.'

Langdon took a deep breath and turned to face the eerie collection of diaphanous vaults. He walked to the nearest one and squinted into the dim interior. Inside the glass were amorphous shapes Langdon recognized as the usual bookshelves, parchment bins, and examination tables. He looked up at the indicator tabs glowing at the end of each stack. As in all libraries, the tabs indicated the contents of that row. He read the headings as he moved down the transparent barrier.

PIETRO L'EREMITA ... LE CROCIATE ... URBANO II ... LEVANT ...

'They're labeled,' he said, still walking. 'But it's not alpha-author.' He wasn't surprised. Ancient archives were almost never cataloged alphabetically because so many of the authors were unknown. Titles didn't work either because many historical documents were untitled letters or parchment fragments. Most cataloging was done chronologically. Disconcertingly, however, *this* arrangement did not appear to be chronological.

Langdon felt precious time already slipping away. 'Looks like the Vatican has its own system.'

'What a surprise.'

He examined the labels again. The documents spanned centuries, but all the keywords, he realized, were interrelated. 'I think it's a thematic classification.'

'Thematic?' Vittoria said, sounding like a disapproving scientist. 'Sounds inefficient.'

Actually ... Langdon thought, considering it more closely. *This may be the shrewdest cataloging I've ever seen.* He had always urged his students to understand the overall tones and motifs of an artistic period rather than getting lost in the minutia of dates and specific works. The Vatican Archives, it seemed, were cataloged on a similar philosophy. *Broad strokes* ...

'Everything in this vault,' Langdon said, feeling

223

more confident now, 'centuries of material, has to do with the Crusades. That's this vault's theme.' It was all here, he realized. *Historical accounts, letters, artwork, socio-political data, modern analyses. All in one place . . . encouraging a deeper understanding of a topic. Brilliant.*

Vittoria frowned. 'But data can relate to *multiple* themes simultaneously.'

'Which is why they cross-reference with proxy markers.' Langdon pointed through the glass to the colourful plastic tabs inserted among the documents. 'Those indicate secondary documents located elsewhere with their primary themes.'

'Sure,' she said, apparently letting it go. She put her hands on her hips and surveyed the enormous space. Then she looked at Langdon. 'So, Professor, what's the name of this Galileo thing we're looking for?'

Langdon couldn't help but smile. He still couldn't fathom that he was standing in this room. *It's in here,* he thought. *Somewhere in the dark, it's waiting.*

'Follow me,' Langdon said. He started briskly down the first aisle, examining the indicator tabs of each vault. 'Remember how I told you about the Path of Illumination? How the Illuminati recruited new members using an elaborate test?'

'The treasure hunt,' Vittoria said, following closely.

'The challenge the Illuminati had was that after they placed the markers, they needed some way to tell the scientific community the path existed.'

'Logical,' Vittoria said. 'Otherwise nobody would know to look for it.'

'Yes, and even if they *knew* the path existed, scientists would have no way of knowing where the path began. Rome is huge.'

'Okay.'

Langdon proceeded down the next aisle, scanning the tabs as he talked. 'About fifteen years ago, some historians at the Sorbonne and I uncovered a series of Illuminati letters filled with references to the *segno*.'

'The sign. The announcement about the path and where it began.'

'Yes. And since then, plenty of Illuminati academics, myself included, have uncovered other references to the *segno*. It is accepted theory now that the clue exists and that Galileo mass distributed it to the scientific community without the Vatican ever knowing.'

'How?'

'We're not sure, but most likely printed publications. He published many books and newsletters over the years.'

'That the Vatican no doubt saw. Sounds dangerous.'

'True. Nonetheless the *segno* was distributed.'

'But nobody has ever actually found it?'

'No. Oddly though, wherever allusions to the *segno* appear – Masonic diaries, ancient scientific journals, Illuminati letters – it is often referred to by a number.'

'666?'

Langdon smiled. 'Actually it's 503.'

'Meaning?'

'None of us could ever figure it out. I became fascinated with 503, trying everything to find meaning in the number – numerology, map references, latitudes.' Langdon reached the end of the aisle, turned the corner, and hurried to scan the next row of tabs as he spoke. 'For many years the only clue seemed to be that 503 began with the number five . . . one of the sacred Illuminati digits.' He paused.

'Something tells me you recently figured it out, and that's why we're here.'

'Correct,' Langdon said, allowing himself a rare moment of pride in his work. 'Are you familiar with a book by Galileo called *Diàlogo*?'

'Of course. Famous among scientists as the ultimate scientific sellout.'

Sellout wasn't quite the word Langdon would have used, but he knew what Vittoria meant. In the early 1630s, Galileo had wanted to publish a book endorsing the Copernican heliocentric model of the solar system, but the Vatican would not permit the book's release unless Galileo included equally persuasive evidence for the church's *geo*centric model – a model Galileo knew to be dead wrong. Galileo had no choice but to acquiesce to the church's demands and publish a book giving equal time to both the accurate and inaccurate models.

'As you probably know,' Langdon said, 'despite Galileo's compromise, *Diàlogo* was still seen as heretical, and the Vatican placed him under house arrest.'

'No good deed goes unpunished.'

Langdon smiled. 'So true. And yet Galileo was persistent. While under house arrest, he secretly wrote a lesser-known manuscript that scholars often confuse with *Diàlogo*. That book is called *Discorsi*.'

Vittoria nodded. 'I've heard of it. *Discourses on the Tides.*'

Langdon stopped short, amazed she had heard of the obscure publication abut planetary motion and its effect on the tides.

'Hey,' she said, 'you're talking to an Italian marine physicist whose father worshiped Galileo.'

Langdon laughed. *Discorsi* however was not what they were looking for. Langdon explained that *Discorsi* had not been Galileo's only work while under house

226

arrest. Historians believed he had also written an obscure booklet called *Diagramma*.

'*Diagramma della Verità*,' Langdon said. '*Diagram of Truth*.'

'Never heard of it.'

'I'm not surprised. *Diagramma* was Galileo's most secretive work – supposedly some sort of treatise on scientific facts he held to be true but was not allowed to share. Like some of Galileo's previous manuscripts, *Diagramma* was smuggled out of Rome by a friend and quietly published in Holland. The booklet became wildly popular in the European scientific underground. Then the Vatican caught wind of it and went on a book-burning campaign.'

Vittoria now looked intrigued. 'And you think *Diagramma* contained the clue? The *segno*. The information about the Path of Illumination.'

'*Diagramma* is how Galileo got the word out. That I'm sure of.' Langdon entered the third row of vaults and continued surveying the indicator tabs. 'Archivists have been looking for a copy of *Diagramma* for years. But between the Vatican burnings and the booklet's low permanence rating, the booklet has disappeared off the face of the earth.'

'Permanence rating?'

'Durability. Archivists rate documents one through ten for their structural integrity. *Diagramma* was printed on sedge papyrus. It's like tissue paper. Life span of no more than a century.'

'Why not something stronger?'

'Galileo's behest. To protect his followers. This way any scientists caught with a copy could simply drop it in water and the booklet would dissolve. It was great for destruction of evidence, but terrible for archivists.

It is believed that only *one* copy of *Diagramma* survived beyond the eighteenth century.'

'One?' Vittoria looked momentarily starstruck as she glanced around the room. 'And it's *here*?'

'Confiscated from the Netherlands by the Vatican shortly after Galileo's death. I've been petitioning to see it for years now. Ever since I realized what was in it.'

As if reading Langdon's mind, Vittoria moved across the aisle and began scanning the adjacent bay of vaults, doubling their pace.

'Thanks,' he said. 'Look for reference tabs that have anything to do with Galileo, science, scientists. You'll know it when you see it.'

'Okay, but you still haven't told me how you figured out *Diagramma* contained the clue. It had something to do with the number you kept seeing in Illuminati letters? 503?'

Langdon smiled. 'Yes. It took some time, but I finally figured out that 503 is a simple code. It clearly points to *Diagramma*.'

For an instant Langdon relived his moment of unexpected revelation: August 16. Two years ago. He was standing lakeside at the wedding of the son of a colleague. Bagpipes droned on the water as the wedding party made their unique entrance . . . across the lake on a barge. The craft was festooned with flowers and wreaths. It carried a Roman numeral painted proudly on the hull – DCII.

Puzzled by the marking Langdon asked the father of the bride, 'What's with 602?'

'602?'

Langdon pointed to the barge. 'DCII is the Roman numeral for 602.'

The man laughed. 'That's not a Roman numeral.

228

That's the name of the barge.'

'The DCII?'

The man nodded. '*The Dick and Connie II.*'

Langdon felt sheepish. Dick and Connie were the wedding couple. The barge obviously had been named in their honor. 'What happened to the *DCI*?'

The man groaned. 'It sank yesterday during the rehearsal luncheon.'

Langdon laughed. 'Sorry to hear that.' He looked back out at the barge. *The DCII*, he thought. *Like a miniature QEII.* A second later, it had hit him.

Now Langdon turned to Vittoria. '503,' he said, 'as I mentioned, is a code. It's an Illuminati trick for concealing what was actually intended as a Roman numeral. The number 503 in Roman numerals is—'

'DIII.'

Langdon glanced up. 'That was fast. Please don't tell me you're an Illuminata.'

She laughed. 'I use Roman numerals to codify pelagic strata.'

Of course, Langdon thought. *Don't we all.*

Vittoria looked over. 'So what is the meaning of DIII?'

'DI and DII and DIII are very odd abbreviations. The were used by ancient scientists to distinguish between the three Galilean documents most commonly confused.'

Vittoria drew a quick breath. '*Diàlogo . . . Discorsi . . . Diagramma.*'

'D-one. D-two. D-three. All scientific. All controversial. 503 is DIII. *Diagramma.* The third of his books.'

Vittoria looked troubled. 'But one thing still doesn't make sense. If this *segno*, this clue, this advertisement about the Path of Illumination was really in Galileo's

Diagramma, why didn't the Vatican see it when they repossessed all the copies?'

'They may have seen it and not noticed. Remember the Illuminati markers? Hiding things in plain view? Dissimulation? The *segno* apparently was hidden the same way – in plain view. Invisible to those who were not looking for it. And also invisible to those who didn't *understand* it.'

'Meaning?'

'Meaning Galileo hid it well. According to historic record, the *segno* was revealed in a mode the Illuminati called *lingua pura*.'

'The pure language?'

'Yes.'

'Mathematics?'

'That's my guess. Seems pretty obvious. Galileo was a scientist after all, and he was writing *for* scientists. Math would be a logical language in which to lay out the clue. The booklet is called *Diagramma*, so mathematical diagrams may also be part of the code.'

Vittoria sounded only slightly more hopeful. 'I suppose Galileo could have created some sort of mathematical code that went unnoticed by the clergy.'

'You don't sound sold,' Langdon said, moving down the row.

'I'm not. Mainly because *you* aren't. If you were so sure about DIII, why didn't you publish? Then someone who *did* have access to the Vatican Archives could have come in here and checked out *Diagramma* a long time ago.'

'I didn't *want* to publish,' Langdon said. 'I had worked hard to find the information and—' He stopped himself, embarrassed.

'You wanted the *glory*.'

Langdon felt himself flush. 'In a manner of speaking. It's just that—'

'Don't look so embarrassed. You're talking to a scientist. Publish or perish. At CERN we call it "Substantiate or suffocate."'

'It wasn't only wanting to be the first. I was also concerned that if the wrong people found out about the information in *Diagramma*, it might disappear.'

'The wrong people being the Vatican?'

'Not that they are wrong, per se, but the church has always downplayed the Illuminati threat. In the early 1900s the Vatican went so far as to say the Illuminati were a figment of overactive imaginations. The clergy felt, and perhaps rightly so, that the last thing Christians needed to know was that there was a very powerful anti-Christian movement infiltrating their banks, politics and universities.' *Present tense, Robert,* he reminded himself. *There IS a powerful anti-Christian force infiltrating their banks, politics, and universities.*

'So you think the Vatican would have buried any evidence corroborating the Illuminati threat?'

'Quite possibly. Any threat, real or imagined, weakens faith in the church's power.'

'One more question.' Vittoria stopped short and looked at him like he was an alien. 'Are you *serious*?'

Langdon stopped. 'What do you mean?'

'I mean is this *really* your plan to save the day?'

Langdon wasn't sure whether he saw amused pity or sheer terror in her eyes. 'You mean finding *Diagramma*?'

'No, I mean finding *Diagramma*, locating a four-hundred-year-old *segno*, deciphering some mathematical code, and following an ancient trail of art that only the most brilliant scientists in history have ever been able to follow . . all in the next four hours.'

Langdon shrugged. 'I'm open to other suggestions.'

50

Robert Langdon stood outside Archive Vault 9 and read the labels on the stacks.

BRAHE . . . CLAVIUS . . . COPERNICUS . . . KEPLER . . . NEWTON . . .

As he read the names again, he felt a sudden uneasiness. *Here are the scientists . . but where is Galileo?*

He turned to Vittoria, who was checking the contents of a nearby vault. 'I found the right theme, but Galileo's missing.'

'No he isn't,' she said, frowning as she motioned to the next vault. 'He's over here. But I hope you brought your reading glasses, because this *entire* vault is his.'

Langdon ran over. Vittoria was right. Every indicator tab in Vault 10 carried the same keyword.

IL PROCESSO GALILEANO

Langdon let out a low whistle, now realizing why Galileo had his own vault. 'The Galileo Affair,' he marveled, peering through the glass at the dark outlines of the stacks. 'The longest and most expensive legal proceedings in Vatican history. Fourteen years and six hundred million lire. It's all here.'

'Have a few legal documents.'

'I guess lawyers haven't evolved much over the centuries.'

'Neither have sharks.'

Langdon strode to a large yellow button on the side of the vault. He pressed it, and a bank of overhead lights hummed on inside. The lights were deep red, turning the cube into a glowing crimson cell . . . a maze of towering shelves.

'My God,' Vittoria said, looking spooked. 'Are we tanning or working?'

'Parchment and vellum fades, so vault lighting is always done with dark lights.'

'You could go mad in here.'

Or worse, Langdon thought, moving toward the vault's sole entrance. 'A quick word of warning. Oxygen is an oxidant, so hermetic vaults contain very little of it. It's a partial vacuum inside. Your breathing will feel strained.'

'Hey, if old cardinals can survive it.'

True, Langdon thought. *May we be as lucky.*

The vault entrance was a single electronic revolving door. Langdon noted the common arrangement of four access buttons on the door's inner shaft, one accessible from each compartment. When a button was pressed, the motorized door would kick into gear and make the conventional half rotation before grinding to a halt – a standard procedure to preserve the integrity of the inner atmosphere.

'After I'm in,' Langdon said, 'just press the button and follow me through. There's only eight per cent humidity inside, so be prepared to feel some dry mouth.'

Langdon stepped into the rotating compartment and pressed the button. The door buzzed loudly and began to rotate. As he followed its motion, Langdon prepared his body for the physical shock that always accompanied the first few seconds in a hermetic vault. Entering a sealed archive was like going from sea level to 20,000 feet in an instant. Nausea and light-headedness were not uncommon. *Double vision, double over*, he reminded himself, quoting the archivist's mantra. Langdon felt his ears pop. There was a hiss of air, and the door spun to a stop.

He was in.

Langdon's first realization was that the air inside was thinner than he had anticipated. The Vatican, it seemed, took their archives a bit more seriously than most. Langdon fought the gag reflex and relaxed his chest while his pulmonary capillaries dilated. The tightness passed quickly. *Enter the Dolphin*, he mused, gratified his fifty laps a day were good for something. Breathing more normally now, he looked around the vault. Despite the transparent outer walls, he felt a familiar anxiety. *I'm in a box*, he thought. *A blood red box.*

The door buzzed behind him, and Langdon turned to watch Vittoria enter. When she arrived inside, her eyes immediately began watering, and she started breathing heavily.

'Give it a minute,' Langdon said. 'If you get light-headed, bend over.'

'I . . . feel . . .' Vittoria choked, 'like I'm . . . scuba diving . . . with the wrong . . . mixture.'

Langdon waited for her to acclimatize. He knew she would be fine. Vittoria Vetra was obviously in terrific shape, nothing like the doddering ancient Radcliffe alumnae Langdon had once squired through Widener Library's hermetic vault. The tour had ended with

Langdon giving mouth-to-mouth to an old woman who'd almost aspirated her false teeth.

'Feeling better?' he asked.

Vittoria nodded.

'I rode your damn space plane, so I thought I owed you.'

This brought a smile. '*Touché.*'

Langdon reached into the box beside the door and extracted some white cotton gloves.

'Formal affair?' Vittoria asked.

'Finger acid. We can't handle the documents without them. You'll need a pair.'

Vittoria donned some gloves. 'How long do we have?'

Langdon checked his Mickey Mouse watch. 'It's just past seven.'

'We have to find this thing within the hour.'

'Actually,' Langdon said, 'we don't have that kind of time.' He pointed overhead to a filtered cut. 'Normally the curator would turn on a reoxygenation system when someone is inside the vault. Not today. Twenty minutes, we'll both be sucking wind.'

Vittoria blanched noticeably in the reddish glow.

Langdon smiled and smoothed his gloves. 'Substantiate or suffocate, Ms Vetra. Mickey's ticking.'

51

BBC reporter Gunther Glick stared at the cell phone in his hand for ten seconds before he finally hung up.

Chinita Macri studied him from the back of the van. 'What happened? Who was that?'

Glick turned, feeling like a child who had just received a Christmas gift he feared was not really for him. 'I just got a tip. Something's going on inside the Vatican.'

'It's called conclave,' Chinita said. 'Helluva tip.'

'No, something else.' *Something big.* He wondered if the story the caller had just told him could possibly be true. Glick felt ashamed when he realized he was praying it was. 'What if I told you four cardinals have been kidnapped and are going to be murdered at different churches tonight.'

'I'd say you're being hazed by someone at the office with a sick sense of humor.'

'What if I told you we were going to be given the exact location of the first murder?'

'I'd want to know who the hell you just talked to.'

'He didn't say.'

'Perhaps because he's full of shit?'

Glick had come to expect Macri's cynicism, but what she was forgetting was that liars and lunatics had been Glick's business for almost a decade at the *British Tatler*. This caller had been neither. This man had been coldly sane. Logical. *I will call you just before eight*, the man had said, *and tell you where the first killing will occur. The images you record will make you famous.* When Glick had demanded why the caller was giving him this information, the answer had been as icy as the man's Mideastern accent. *The media is the right arm of anarchy.*

'He told me something else too,' Glick said.

'What? That Elvis Presley was just elected Pope?'

'Dial into the BBC database, will you?' Glick's

236

adrenaline was pumping now. 'I want to see what other stories we've run on these guys.'

'What guys?'

'Indulge me.'

Macri sighed and pulled up the connection to the BBC database. 'This'll take a minute.'

Glick's mind was swimming. 'The caller was very intent to know if I had a cameraman.'

'Videographer.'

'And if we could transmit live.'

'One point five three seven megahertz. What is this about?' The database beeped. 'Okay, we're in. Who is it you're looking for?'

Glick gave her the keyword.

Macri turned and stared. 'I sure as hell hope you're kidding.'

52

The internal organization of Archival Vault 10 was not as intuitive as Langdon had hoped, and the *Diagramma* manuscript did not appear to be located with other similar Galilean publications. Without access to the computerized Biblion and a reference locator, Langdon and Vittoria were stuck.

'You're sure *Diagramma* is in here?' Vittoria asked.

'Positive. It's a confirmed listing in both the *Uficcio della Propaganda delle Fede*—'

'Fine. As long as you're sure.' She headed left, while he went right.

Langdon began his manual search. He needed every

bit of self-restraint not to stop and read every treasure he passed. The collection was staggering. *The Assayer* ... *The Starry Messenger* ... *The Sunspot Letters* ... *Letter to the Grand Duchess Christina* ... *Apologia pro Galileo* ... On and on.

It was Vittoria who finally struck gold near the back of the vault. Her throaty voice called out, '*Diagramma della Verità!*'

Langdon dashed through the crimson haze to join her. 'Where?'

Vittoria pointed, and Langdon immediately realized why they had not found it earlier. The manuscript was in a folio bin, not on the shelves. Folio bins were a common means of storing unbound pages. The label on the front of the container left no doubt about the contents.

DIAGRAMMA DELLA VERITA
Galileo Galilei, 1639

Langdon dropped to his knees, his heart pounding, '*Diagramma*.' He gave her a grin. 'Nice work. Help me pull out this bin.'

Vittoria knelt beside him, and they heaved. The metal tray on which the bin was sitting rolled toward them on castors, revealing the top of the container.

'No lock?' Vittoria said, sounding surprised at the simple latch.

'Never. Documents sometimes need to be evacuated quickly. Floods and fires.'

'So open it.'

Langdon didn't need any encouragement. With his academic life's dream right in front of him and the thinning air in the chamber, he was in no mood to dawdle. He unsnapped the latch and lifted the lid. Inside, flat on the floor of the bin, lay a black, duck-cloth pouch. The cloth's breathability was critical to the preservation of its contents. Reaching in with both hands and keeping the pouch horizontal, Langdon lifted it out of the bin.

'I expected a treasure chest,' Vittoria said. 'Looks more like a pillowcase.'

'Follow me,' he said. Holding the bag before him like a sacred offering, Langdon walked to the center of the vault where he found the customary glass-topped archival exam table. Although the central location was intended to minimize in-vault travel of documents, researchers appreciated the privacy the surrounding stacks afforded. Career-making discoveries were uncovered in the top vaults of the world, and most academics did not like rivals peering through the glass as they worked.

Langdon laid the pouch on the table and un-buttoned the opening. Vittoria stood by. Rummaging through a tray of archivist tools, Langdon found the felt-pad pincers archivists called *finger cymbals* – over-sized tweezers with flattened disks on each arm. As his excitement mounted, Langdon feared at any moment he might awake back in Cambridge with a pile of test papers to grade. Inhaling deeply, he opened the bag. Fingers trembling in their cotton gloves, he reached in with his tongs.

'Relax,' Vittoria said. 'It's paper, not plutonium.'

Langdon slid the tongs around the stack of docu-ments inside and was careful to apply even pressure. Then, rather than pulling out the documents, he held them in place while he slid off the bag – an archivist's procedure for minimizing torque on the artifact. Not until the bag was removed and Langdon had turned on the exam darklight beneath the table did he begin breathing again.

Vittoria looked like a specter now, lit from below by the lamp beneath the glass. 'Small sheets,' she said, her voice reverent.

Langdon nodded. The stack of folios before them looked like loose pages from a small paperback novel. Langdon could see that the top sheet was an ornate pen and ink cover sheet with the title, the date, and Galileo's name in his own hand.

In that instant, Langdon forgot the cramped quarters, forgot his exhaustion, forgot the horrifying situation that had brought him here. He simply stared in wonder. Close encounters with history always left Langdon numbed with reverence . . . like seeing the brushstrokes on the Mona Lisa.

The muted, yellow papyrus left no doubt in Langdon's mind as to its age and authenticity, but excluding the inevitable fading, the document was in superb condition. *Slight bleaching of the pigment. Minor sundering and cohesion of the papyrus. But all in all . . . in damn fine condition.* He studied the ornate hand etching of the cover, his vision blurring in the lack of humidity. Vittoria was silent.

'Hand me a spatula, please.' Langdon motioned beside Vittoria to a tray filled with stainless-steel archival tools. She handed it to him. Langdon took the tool in his hand. It was a good one. He ran his fingers across the face to remove any static charge and then, ever so carefully, slid the blade beneath the cover. Then, lifting the spatula, he turned over the cover sheet.

The first page was written in longhand, the tiny,

stylized calligraphy almost impossible to read. Langdon immediately noticed that there were no diagrams or numbers on the page. It was an essay.

'Heliocentricity,' Vittoria said, translating the heading on folio one. She scanned the text. 'Looks like Galileo renouncing the geocentric model once and for all. Ancient Italian, though, so no promises on the translation.'

'Forget it,' Langdon said. 'We're looking for math. The pure language.' He used the spatula tool to flip the next page. Another essay. No math or diagrams. Langdon's hands began to sweat inside his gloves.

'Movement of the Planets,' Vittoria said, translating the title.

Langdon frowned. On any other day, he would have been fascinated to read it; incredibly NASA's current model of planetary orbits, observed through high-powered telescopes, was supposedly almost identical to Galileo's original predictions.

'No math,' Vittoria said. 'He's talking about retrograde motions and elliptical orbits or something.'

Elliptical orbits. Langdon recalled that much of Galileo's legal trouble had begun when he described planetary motion as *elliptical*. The Vatican exalted the perfection of the *circle* and insisted heavenly motion must be only circular. Galileo's Illuminati, however, saw perfection in the ellipse as well, revering the mathematical duality of its twin foci. The Illuminati's ellipse was prominent even today in modern Masonic tracing boards and footing inlays.

'Next,' Vittoria said.

Langdon flipped.

'Lunar phases and tidal moon,' she said. 'No numbers. No diagrams.'

241

Langdon flipped again. Nothing. He kept flipping through a dozen or so pages. Nothing. Nothing. Nothing.

'I thought this guy was a mathematician,' Vittoria said. 'This is all text.'

Langdon felt the air in his lungs beginning to thin. His hopes were thinning too. The pile was waning.

'Nothing here,' Vittoria said. 'No math. A few dates, a few standard figures, but nothing that looks like it could be a clue.'

Langdon flipped over the last folio and sighed. It, too, was an essay.

'Short book,' Vittoria said, frowning.

Langdon nodded.

'*Merda*, as we say in Rome.'

Shit is right, Langdon thought. His reflection in the glass seemed mocking, like the image staring back at him this morning from his bay window. *An aging ghost.* 'There's *got* to be something,' he said, the hoarse desperation in his voice surprising him. 'The *segno* is here somewhere. I know it!'

'Maybe you were wrong about DIII?'

Langdon turned and stared at her.

'Okay,' she agreed, 'DIII makes perfect sense. But maybe the clue isn't mathematical?'

'*Lingua pura*. What else would it be?'

'Art?'

'Except there are no diagrams or pictures in the book.'

'All I know is that *lingua pura* refers to something other than Italian. Math just seems logical.'

'I agree.'

Langdon refused to accept defeat so quickly. 'The numbers must be written longhand. The math must be in words rather than equations.'

'It'll take some time to read all the pages.'

'Time's something we don't have. We'll have to split the work.' Langdon flipped the stack back over to the beginning. 'I know enough Italian to spot numbers.' Using his spatula, he cut the stack like a deck of cards and laid the first half-dozen pages in front of Vittoria. 'It's in here somewhere. I'm sure.'

Vittoria reached down and flipped her first page by hand.

'Spatula!' Langdon said, grabbing her an extra tool from the tray. 'Use the spatula.'

'I'm wearing gloves,' she grumbled. 'How much damage could I cause?'

'Just use it.'

Vittoria picked up the spatula. 'You feeling what I'm feeling?'

'Tense?'

'No. Short of breath.'

Langdon was definitely starting to feel it too. The air was thinning faster than he had imagined. He knew they had to hurry. Archival conundrums were nothing new for him, but usually he had more than a few minutes to work them out. Without another word, Langdon bowed his head and began translating the first page in his stack.

Show yourself, damn it! Show yourself!

53

Somewhere beneath Rome the dark figure prowled down a stone ramp into the underground tunnel. The ancient passageway was lit only by torches, making the air hot and thick. Up ahead the frightened voices of grown men called out in vain, echoing in the cramped spaces.

As he rounded the corner he saw them, exactly as he had left them – four old men, terrified, sealed behind rusted iron bars in a stone cubicle.

'*Qui êtes-vous?*' one of the men demanded in French. 'What do you want with us?'

'*Hilfe!*' another said in German. 'Let us go!'

'Are you aware who we are?' one asked in English, his accent Spanish.

'Silence,' the raspy voice commanded. There was a finality about the word.

The fourth prisoner, an Italian, quiet and thoughtful, looked into the inky void of his captor's eyes and swore he saw hell itself. *God help us,* he thought.

The killer checked his watch and then returned his gaze to the prisoners. 'Now then,' he said. 'Who will be first?'

54

Inside Archive Vault 10 Robert Langdon recited Italian numbers as he scanned the calligraphy before him. *Mille . . . centi . . . uno, duo, tre . . . cinquanta. I need a numerical reference! Anything, damnit!*

When he reached the end of his current folio, he lifted the spatula to flip the page. As he aligned the blade with the next page, he fumbled, having difficulty holding the tool steady. Minutes later, he looked down and realized he had abandoned his spatula and was turning pages by hand. *Oops,* he thought, feeling vaguely criminal. The lack of oxygen was affecting his inhibitions. *Looks like I'll burn in archivist's hell.*

'About damn time,' Vittoria choked when she saw Langdon turning pages by hand. She dropped her spatula and followed suit.

'Any luck?'

Vittoria shook her head. 'Nothing that looks purely mathematical. I'm skimming . . . but none of this reads like a clue.'

Langdon continued translating his folios with increasing difficulty. His Italian skills were rocky at best, and the tiny penmanship and archaic language were making it slow going. Vittoria reached the end of her stack before Langdon and looked disheartened as she flipped the pages over. She hunkered down for another more intense inspection.

When Langdon finished his final page, he cursed under his breath and looked over at Vittoria. She was scowling, squinting at something on one of her folios. 'What is it?' he asked.

Vittoria did not look up. 'Did you have any foot-notes on your pages?'

'Not that I noticed. Why?'

'This page has a footnote. It's obscured in a crease.'

Langdon tried to see what she was looking at, but all he could make out was the page number in the upper right-hand corner of the sheet. Folio 5. It took a moment for the coincidence to register, and even when it did the connection seemed vague. *Folio Five. Five, Pythagoras, pentagrams, Illuminati.* Langdon wondered if the Illuminati would have chosen page five on which to hide their clue. Through the reddish fog surrounding them, Langdon sensed a tiny ray of hope. 'Is the footnote mathematical?'

Vittoria shook her head. 'Text. One line. Very small printing. Almost illegible.'

His hopes faded. 'It's supposed to be math. *Lingua pura.*'

'Yeah, I know.' She hesitated. 'I think you'll want to hear this, though.' Langdon sensed excitement in her voice.

'Go ahead.'

Squinting at the folio, Vittoria read the line. 'The path of light is laid, the sacred test.'

The words were nothing like what Langdon had imagined. 'I'm sorry?'

Vittoria repeated the line. 'The path of light is laid, the sacred test.'

'Path of light?' Langdon felt his posture straightening.

'That's what it says. Path of light.'

As the words sank in, Langdon felt his delirium pierced by an instant of clarity. *The path of light is laid, the sacred test.* He had no idea how it helped them, but the line was as direct a reference to the Path of Illumination as he could imagine. *Path of light. Sacred test.* His head felt like an engine revving on bad fuel. 'Are you sure of the translation?'

Vittoria hesitated. 'Actually . . .' She glanced over at him with a strange look. 'It's not technically a translation. The line is written in *English.*'

For an instant, Langdon thought the acoustics in the chamber had affected his hearing. '*English?*'

Vittoria pushed the document over to him, and Langdon read the minuscule printing at the bottom of the page. '*The path of light is laid, the sacred test.* English? What is *English* doing in an Italian book?'

Vittoria shrugged. She too was looking tipsy. 'Maybe English is what they meant by the *lingua pura*? It's considered the international language of science. It's all we speak at CERN.'

'But this was in the 1600s,' Langdon argued. 'Nobody spoke English in Italy, not even—' He stopped short, realizing what he was about to say. 'Not even . . . the *clergy*.' Langdon's academic mind hummed in high gear. 'In the 1600s,' he said, talking faster now, '*English* was one language the Vatican had not yet embraced. They dealt in Italian, Latin, German, even Spanish and French, but English was totally foreign inside the Vatican. They considered English a polluted, free-thinkers language for profane men like Chaucer and Shakespeare.' Langdon flashed suddenly on the Illuminati brands of Earth, Air, Fire, Water. The legend that the brands were in *English* now made a bizarre kind of sense.

'So you're saying maybe Galileo considered English *la lingua pura* because it was the one language the Vatican did not control?'

'Yes. Or maybe by putting the clue in English, Galileo was subtly restricting the readership away from the Vatican.'

'But it's not even a clue,' Vittoria argued. '*The path of light is laid, the sacred test?* What the hell does that mean?'

She's right, Langdon thought. The line didn't help in any way. But as he spoke the phrase again in his mind, a strange fact hit him. *Now that's odd*, he thought. *What are the chances of that?*

'We need to get out of here,' Vittoria said, sounding hoarse.

Langdon wasn't listening. *The path of light is laid, the*

sacred test. 'It's a damn line of iambic pentameter,' he said suddenly, counting the syllables again. 'Five couplets of alternating stressed and unstressed syllables.'

Vittoria looked lost. 'Iambic who?'

For an instant Langdon was back at Phillips Exeter Academy sitting in a Saturday morning English class. *Hell on earth.* The school baseball star, Peter Greer, was having trouble remembering the number of couplets necessary for a line of Shakespearean iambic pentameter. Their professor, an animated schoolmaster named Bissell, leapt onto the table and bellowed, 'Penta-meter, Greer! Think of home plate! A pentagon! Five sides! Penta! Penta! Penta! Jeeeesh!'

Five couplets, Langdon thought. Each couplet, by definition, having *two* syllables. He could not believe in his entire career he had never made the connection. Iambic pentameter was a symmetrical meter based on the sacred Illuminati numbers of 5 and 2!

You're reaching! Langdon told himself, trying to push it from his mind. *A meaningless coincidence!* But the thought stuck. *Five . . . for Pythagoras and the pentagram. Two . . . for the duality of all things.*

A moment later, another realization sent a numbing sensation down his legs. Iambic pentameter, on account of its simplicity, was often called 'pure verse' or 'pure meter'. *La lingua pura?* Could this have been the pure language the Illuminati had been referring to? *The path of light is laid, the sacred test . . .*

'Uh oh,' Vittoria said.

Langdon wheeled to see her rotating the folio upside down. He felt a knot in his gut. *Not again.* 'There's no way that line is an ambigram!'

'No, it's not an ambigram ... but it's ...' She

248

kept turning the document, 90 degrees at every turn.

'It's what?'

Vittoria looked up. 'It's not the *only* line.'

'There's another?'

'There's a different line on every margin. Top, bottom, left, and right. I think it's a poem.'

'Four lines?' Langdon bristled with excitement. *Galileo was a poet?* 'Let me see!'

Vittoria did not relinquish the page. She kept turning the page in quarter turns. 'I didn't see the lines before because they're on the edges.' She cocked her head over the last line. 'Huh. You know what? Galileo didn't even write this.'

'What!'

'The poem is signed John Milton.'

'John *Milton*?' The influential English poet who wrote *Paradise Lost* was a contemporary of Galileo's and a savant who conspiracy buffs put at the top of their list of Illuminati suspects. Milton's alleged affiliation with Galileo's Illuminati was one legend Langdon suspected was true. Not only had Milton made a well-documented 1638 pilgrimage to Rome to 'commune with enlightened men,' but he had held meetings with Galileo during the scientist's house arrest, meetings portrayed in many Renaissance paintings, including Annibale Gatti's famous *Galileo and Milton*, which hung even now in the IMSS Museum in Florence.

'Milton knew Galileo, didn't he?' Vittoria said, finally pushing the folio over to Langdon. 'Maybe he wrote the poem as a favor?'

Langdon clenched his teeth as he took the sheathed document. Leaving it flat on the table, he read the line at the top. Then he rotated the page 90 degrees, reading the line in the right margin. Another twist, and he read the bottom. Another twist, the left. A final twist completed the circle. There were four lines in all. The first line Vittoria had found was actually the third line of the poem. Utterly agape, he read the four lines again, clockwise in sequence: top, right, bottom, left. When he was done, he exhaled. There was no doubt in his mind. 'You found it, Ms Vetra.'

She smiled tightly. 'Good, now can we get the hell out of here?'

'I have to copy these lines down. I need to find a pencil and paper.'

Vittoria shook her head. 'Forget it, professor. No time to play scribe. Mickey's ticking.' She took the page from him and headed for the door.

Langdon stood up. 'You can't take that outside! It's a—'

But Vittoria was already gone.

55

Langdon and Vittoria exploded onto the courtyard outside the Secret Archives. The fresh air felt like a drug as it flowed into Langdon's lungs. The purple spots in his vision quickly faded. The guilt, however, did not. He had just been accomplice to stealing a priceless relic from the world's most private vault. The camerlengo had said, *I am giving you my trust.*

'Hurry,' Vittoria said, still holding the folio in her hand and striding at a half-jog across *Via Belvedere* in the direction of Olivetti's office.

'If any water gets on that papyrus—'

'Calm down. When we decipher this thing, we can return their sacred Folio 5.'

Langdon accelerated to keep up. Beyond feeling like a criminal, he was still dazed over the document's spellbinding implications. *John Milton was an Illuminatus. He composed the poem for Galileo to publish in Folio 5 . . . far from the eyes of the Vatican.*

As they left the courtyard, Vittoria held out the folio for Langdon. 'You think you can decipher this thing? Or did we just kill all those brain cells for kicks?'

Langdon took the document carefully in his hands. Without hesitation he slipped it into one of the breast pockets of his tweed jacket, out of the sunlight and dangers of moisture. 'I deciphered it already.'

Vittoria stopped short. 'You *what*?'

Langdon kept moving.

Vittoria hustled to catch up. 'You read it *once*! I thought it was supposed to be hard!'

Langdon knew she was right, and yet he had deciphered the *segno* in a single reading. A perfect stanza of iambic pentameter, and the first altar of science had revealed itself in pristine clarity. Admittedly, the ease with which he had accomplished the task left him with a nagging disquietude. He was a child of the Puritan work ethic. He could still hear his father speaking the old New England aphorism: *If it wasn't painfully difficult, you did it wrong.* Langdon hoped the saying was false. 'I deciphered it,' he said, moving faster now. 'I know where the first killing is going to happen. We need to warn Olivetti.'

Vittoria closed in on him. 'How could you already know? Let me see that thing again.' With the sleight of a boxer, she slipped a lissome hand into his pocket and pulled out the folio again.

'Careful!' Langdon said. 'You can't—'

Vittoria ignored him. Folio in hand, she floated beside him, holding the document up to the evening light, examining the margins. As she began reading aloud, Langdon moved to retrieve the folio but instead found himself bewitched by Vittoria's accented alto speaking the syllables in perfect rhythm with her gait.

For a moment, hearing the verse aloud, Langdon felt transported in time . . . as though he were one of Galileo's contemporaries, listening to the poem for the first time . . . knowing it was a test, a map, a clue unveiling the four altars of science . . . the four markers that blazed a secret path across Rome. The verse flowed from Vittoria's lips like a song.

> *From Santi's earthly tomb with demon's hole,*
> *'Cross Rome the mystic elements unfold.*
> *The path of light is laid, the sacred test,*
> *Let angels guide you on your lofty quest.*

Vittoria read it twice and then fell silent, as if letting the ancient words resonate on their own.

From Santi's earthly tomb, Langdon repeated in his mind. The poem was crystal clear about that. The Path of Illumination began at Santi's tomb. From there, across Rome, the markers blazed the trail.

> *From Santi's earthly tomb with demon's hole,*
> *'Cross Rome the mystic elements unfold.*

Mystic elements. Also clear. *Earth, Air, Fire, Water.*

Elements of science, the four Illuminati markers disguised as religious sculpture.

'The first marker,' Vittoria said, 'sounds like it's at Santi's tomb.'

Langdon smiled. 'I told you it wasn't that tough.'

'So who is Santi?' she asked, sounding suddenly excited. 'And where's his tomb?'

Langdon chuckled to himself. He was amazed how few people knew *Santi*, the last name of one of the most famous Renaissance artists ever to live. His first name was world renowned . . . the child prodigy who at the age of twenty-five was already doing commissions for Pope Julius II, and when he died at only thirty-eight, left behind the greatest collection of frescoes the world had ever seen. Santi was a behemoth in the art world, and being known solely by one's first name was a level of fame achieved only by an elite few . . . people like Napoleon, Galileo, and Jesus . . . and, of course, the demigods Langdon now heard blaring from Harvard dormitories – Sting, Madonna, Jewel, and the artist formerly known as Prince, who had changed his name to the symbol ⚥, causing Langdon to dub him 'The Tau Cross With Intersecting Hermaphroditic Ankh.'

'Santi,' Langdon said, 'is the last name of the great Renaissance master, Raphael.'

Vittoria looked surprised. 'Raphael? As in *the* Raphael?'

'The one and only.' Langdon pushed on toward the Office of the Swiss Guard.

'So the path starts at Raphael's tomb?'

'It actually makes perfect sense,' Langdon said as they rushed on. 'The Illuminati often considered great artists and sculptors honorary brothers in enlightenment. The Illuminati could have chosen Raphael's tomb as a kind of tribute.' Langdon also knew that Raphael, like many other religious artists, was a suspected closet atheist.

Vittoria slipped the folio carefully back in Langdon's pocket. 'So where is he buried?'

Langdon took a deep breath. 'Believe it or not, Raphael's buried in the Pantheon.'

Vittoria looked skeptical. '*The* Pantheon?'

'*The* Raphael at *the* Pantheon.' Langdon had to admit, the Pantheon was not what he had expected for the placement of the first marker. He would have guessed the first altar of science to be at some quiet, out of the way church, something subtle. Even in the 1600s, the Pantheon, with its tremendous, holed dome, was one of the best known sites in Rome.

'Is the Pantheon even a *church*?' Vittoria asked.

'Oldest Catholic church in Rome.'

Vittoria shook her head. 'But do you really think the first cardinal could be killed at the Pantheon? That's got to be one of the busiest tourist spots in Rome.'

Langdon shrugged. 'The Illuminati said they wanted the whole world watching. Killing a cardinal at the Pantheon would certainly open some eyes.'

'But how does this guy expect to kill someone at the Pantheon and get away unnoticed? It would be impossible.'

'As impossible as kidnapping four cardinals from Vatican City? The poem is precise.'

'And you're *certain* Raphael is buried inside the Pantheon?'

'I've seen his tomb many times.'

Vittoria nodded, still looking troubled. 'What time is it?'

Langdon checked. 'Seven-thirty.'

'Is the Pantheon far?'

'A mile maybe. We've got time.'

'The poem said Santi's *earthly* tomb. Does that mean anything to you?'

Langdon hastened diagonally across the Courtyard of the Sentinel. 'Earthly? Actually, there's probably no more earthly place in Rome than the Pantheon. It got its name from the original religion practiced there – Pantheism – the worship of all gods, specifically the pagan gods of Mother Earth.'

As a student of architecture, Langdon had been amazed to learn that the dimensions of the Pantheon's main chamber were a tribute to Gaea – the goddess of the Earth. The proportions were so exact that a giant spherical globe could fit perfectly inside the building with less than a millimeter to spare.

'Okay,' Vittoria said, sounding more convinced. 'And demon's hole? *From Santi's earthly tomb with demon's hole?*'

Langdon was not quite as sure about this. '*Demon's hole* must mean the *oculus*,' he said, making a logical guess. 'The famous circular opening in the Pantheon's roof.'

'But it's a *church*,' Vittoria said, moving effortlessly beside him. 'Why would they call the opening a *demon's* hole?'

Langdon had actually been wondering that himself. He had never heard the term 'demon's hole', but he did recall a famous sixth-century critique of the Pantheon whose words seemed oddly appropriate now. The Venerable Bede had once written that the hole in the Pantheon's roof had been bored by demons trying to escape the building when it

255

was consecrated by Boniface IV.

'And why,' Vittoria added as they entered a smaller courtyard, 'would the Illuminati use the name Santi if he was really known as *Raphael*?'

'You ask a lot of questions.'

'My dad used to say that.'

'Two possible reasons. One, the word *Raphael* has too many syllables. It would have destroyed the poem's iambic pentameter.'

'Sounds like a stretch.'

Langdon agreed. 'Okay, then maybe using "Santi" was to make the clue more obscure, so only very enlightened men would recognize the reference to Raphael.'

Vittoria didn't appear to buy this either. 'I'm sure Raphael's last name was very well known when he was alive.'

'Surprisingly not. Single name recognition was a status symbol. Raphael shunned his last name much like pop stars do today. Take Madonna, for example. She never uses her surname, Ciccone.'

Victoria looked amused. 'You know Madonna's last name?'

Langdon regretted the example. It was amazing the kind of garbage a mind picked up living with 10,000 adolescents.

As he and Vittoria passed the final gate towards the Office of the Swiss Guard, their progress was halted without warning.

'*Para!*' a voice bellowed behind them.

Langdon and Vittoria wheeled to find themselves looking into the barrel of a rifle.

'*Attento!*' Vittoria exclaimed, jumping back. 'Watch it with—'

'*Non sportarti!*' the guard snapped, cocking the weapon.

'*Soldato!*' a voice commanded from across the courtyard. Olivetti was emerging from the security center. 'Let them go!'

The guard looked bewildered. '*Ma, signore, è una donna—*'

'Inside!' he yelled at the guard.

'Signore, *non posso—*'

'Now! You have new orders. Captain Rocher will be briefing the corps in two minutes. We will be organizing a search.'

Looking bewildered, the guard hurried into the security center. Olivetti marched toward Langdon, rigid and steaming. 'Our most secret archives? I'll want an explanation.'

'We have good news,' Langdon said.

Olivetti's eyes narrowed. 'It better be *damn* good.'

56

The four unmarked Alfa Romeo 155 T-Sparks roared down Via dei Coronari like fighter jets off a runway. The vehicles carried twelve plainclothed Swiss Guards armed with Cherchi-Pardini semiautomatics, local-radius nerve gas canisters, and long-range stun guns. The three sharpshooters carried laser-sighted rifles.

Sitting in the passenger seat of the lead car, Olivetti turned backward toward Langdon and Vittoria. His eyes were filled with rage. 'You assured me a sound explanation, and *this* is what I get?'

Langdon felt cramped in the small car. 'I understand your—'

'No, you don't understand!' Olivetti never raised his voice, but his intensity tripled. 'I have just removed a dozen of my best men from Vatican City on the eve of conclave. And I have done this to stake out the Pantheon based on the testimony of some American I have never met who has just interpreted a four-hundred-year-old poem. I have also just left the search for this antimatter weapon in the hands of secondary officers.'

Langdon resisted the urge to pull Folio 5 from his pocket and wave it in Olivetti's face. 'All I know is that the information we found refers to Raphael's tomb, and Raphael's tomb is inside the Pantheon.'

The officer behind the wheel nodded. 'He's right, commander. My wife and I—'

'Drive,' Olivetti snapped. He turned back to Langdon. 'How could a killer accomplish an assassination in such a crowded place and escape unseen?'

'I don't know,' Langdon said. 'But the Illuminati are obviously highly resourceful. They've broken into both CERN and Vatican City. It's only by luck we know where the first kill zone is. The Pantheon is your one chance to catch this guy.'

'More contradictions,' Olivetti said. '*One* chance? I thought you said there was some sort of pathway. A series of markers. If the Pantheon is the right spot, we can follow the pathway to the other markers. We will have *four* chances to catch this guy.'

'I had hoped so,' Langdon said. 'And we *would* have . . . a century ago.'

Langdon's realization that the Pantheon was the first altar of science had been a bittersweet moment.

History had a way of playing cruel tricks on those who chased it. It was a long shot that the Path of Illumination would be intact after all of these years, with all of its statues in place, but part of Langdon had fantasized about following the path all the way to the end and coming face to face with the sacred Illuminati lair. Alas, he realized, it was not to be. 'The Vatican had all the statues in the Pantheon removed and destroyed in the late 1600s.'

Vittoria looked shocked. 'Why?'

'The statues were pagan Olympian Gods. Unfortunately, that means the first marker is gone . . . and with it—'

'Any hope,' Vittoria said, 'of finding the Path of Illumination and additional markers?'

Langdon shook his head. 'We have *one* shot. The Pantheon. After that, the path disappears.'

Olivetti stared at them both a long moment and then turned and faced front. 'Pull over,' he barked to the driver.

The driver swerved the car toward the curb and put on the brakes. Three other Alfa Romeos skidded in behind them. The Swiss Guard convey screeched to a halt.

'What are you doing!' Vittoria demanded.

'My job,' Olivetti said, turning in his seat, his voice like stone. 'Mr Langdon, when you told me you would explain the situation en route, I assumed I would be approaching the Pantheon with a clear idea of why my men are here. That is not the case. Because I am abandoning critical duties by being here, and because I have found very little that makes sense in this theory of yours about virgin sacrifices and ancient poetry, I cannot in good conscience continue. I am recalling this

259

mission immediately.' He pulled out his walkie-talkie and clicked it on.

Vittoria reached across the seat and grabbed his arm. 'You can't!'

Olivetti slammed down the walkie-talkie and fixed her with a red-hot stare. 'Have you been to the Pantheon, Ms Vetra?'

'No, but I—'

'Let me tell you something about it. The Pantheon is a single room. A circular cell made of stone and cement. It has *one* entrance. No windows. One *narrow* entrance. That entrance is flanked at all times by no less than four armed Roman policemen who protect this shrine from art defacers, anti-Christian terrorists, and gypsy tourist scams.'

'Your point?' she said coolly.

'My point?' Olivetti's knuckles gripped the seat. 'My point is that what you have just told me is going to happen is utterly impossible! Can you give me one plausible scenario of how someone could kill a cardinal *inside* the Pantheon? How does one even get a hostage past the guards *into* the Pantheon in the first place? Much less actually kill him and get away?' Olivetti leaned over the seat, his coffee breath now in Langdon's face. 'How, Mr Langdon? *One* plausible scenario.'

Langdon felt the tiny car shrink around him. *I have no idea! I'm not an assassin! I don't know how he will do it! I only know—*

'*One* scenario?' Vittoria quipped, her voice unruffled. 'How about this? The killer flies over in a helicopter and drops a screaming, branded cardinal down through the hole in the roof. The cardinal hits the marble floor and dies.'

Everyone in the car turned and stared at Vittoria. Langdon didn't know what to think. *You've got one sick imagination, lady, but you are quick.*

Olivetti frowned. 'Possible, I admit . . . but hardly—'

'Or the killer drugs the cardinal,' Vittoria said, 'brings him to the Pantheon in a wheelchair like some old tourist. He wheels him inside, quietly slits his throat, and then walks out.'

This seemed to wake up Olivetti a bit.

Not bad! Langdon thought.

'Or,' she said, 'the killer could—'

'I heard you,' Olivetti said. 'Enough.' He took a deep breath and blew it out. Someone rapped sharply on the window, and everyone jumped. It was a soldier from one of the other cars. Olivetti rolled down the window.

'Everything all right, commander?' The soldier was dressed in street clothes. He pulled back the sleeve of his denim shirt to reveal a black chronograph military watch. 'Seven-forty, commander. We'll need time to get in position.'

Olivetti nodded vaguely but said nothing for many moments. He ran a finger back and forth across the dash, making a line in the dust. He studied Langdon in the side-view mirror, and Langdon felt himself being measured and weighed. Finally Olivetti turned back to the guard. There was reluctance in his voice. 'I'll want separate approaches. Cars to Piazza della Rotunda, Via degli Orfani, Piazza Sant'Ignacio, and Sant'Eustachio. No closer than two blocks. Once you're parked, gear up and await my orders. Three minutes.'

'Very good, sir.' The soldier returned to his car.

Langdon gave Vittoria an impressed nod. She

smiled back, and for an instant Langdon felt an un-expected connection ... a thread of magnetism between them.

The commander turned in his seat and locked eyes with Langdon. 'Mr Langdon, this had better not blow up in our faces.'

Langdon smiled uneasily. *How could it?*

57

The director of CERN, Maximilian Kohler, opened his eyes to the cool rush of cromolyn and leukotriene in his body, dilating his bronchial tubes and pulmonary capillaries. He was breathing normally again. He found himself lying in a private room in the CERN infirmary, his wheelchair beside the bed.

He took stock, examining the paper robe they had put him in. His clothing was folded on the chair beside the bed. Outside he could hear a nurse making the rounds. He lay there a long minute listening. Then, as quietly as possible, he pulled himself to the edge of the bed and retrieved his clothing. Struggling with his dead legs, he dressed himself. Then he dragged his body onto his wheelchair.

Muffling a cough, he wheeled himself to the door. He moved manually, careful not to engage the motor. When he arrived at the door he peered out. The hall was empty.

Silently, Maximilian Kohler slipped out of the infirmary.

58

'Seven-forty six and thirty . . . *mark.*' Even speaking into his walkie-talkie, Olivetti's voice never seemed to rise above a whisper.

Langdon felt himself sweating now in his Harris tweed in the backseat of the Alfa Romeo, which was idling in Piazza de la Concorde, three blocks from the Pantheon. Vittoria sat beside him, looking engrossed by Olivetti, who was transmitting his final orders.

'Deployment will be an eight-point hem,' the commander said. 'Full perimeter with a bias on the entry. Target may know you visually, so you will be *pasvisible.* Nonmortal force only. We'll need someone to spot the roof. Target is primary. Asset secondary.'

Jesus, Langdon thought, chilled by the efficiency with which Olivetti had just told his men the cardinal was expendable. *Asset secondary.*

'I repeat. Nonmortal procurement. We need the target alive. Go.' Olivetti snapped off his walkie-talkie.

Vittoria looked stunned, almost angry. 'Commander, isn't anyone going *inside*?'

Olivetti turned. 'Inside?'

'Inside the Pantheon! Where this is supposed to happen?'

'*Attento,*' Olivetti said, his eyes fossilizing. 'If my ranks have been infiltrated, my men may be known by sight. Your colleague has just finished warning me that *this* will be our sole chance to catch the target. I have no intention of scaring anyone off by marching my men inside.'

'But what if the killer is *already* inside?'

Olivetti checked his watch. 'The target was specific.

Eight o'clock. We have fifteen minutes.'

'He said he would *kill* the cardinal at eight o'clock. But he may already have gotten the victim inside somehow. What if your men see the target come out but don't know who he is? Someone needs to make sure the inside is clean.'

'Too risky at this point.'

'Not if the person going in was unrecognizable.'

'Disguising operatives is time consuming and—'

'I meant *me*,' Vittoria said.

Langdon turned and stared at her.

Olivetti shook his head. 'Absolutely not.'

'He killed my father.'

'Exactly, so he may know who you are.'

'You heard him on the phone. He had no idea Leonardo Vetra even *had* a daughter. He sure as hell doesn't know what I look like. I could walk in like a tourist. If I see anything suspicious, I could walk into the square and signal your men to move in.'

'I'm sorry, I cannot allow that.'

'*Comandante?*' Olivetti's receiver crackled. 'We've got a situation from the north point. The fountain is blocking our line of sight. We can't see the entrance unless we move into plain view on the piazza. What's your call? Do you want us blind or vulnerable?'

Vittoria apparently had endured enough. 'That's it. I'm going.' She opened her door and got out.

Olivetti dropped his walkie-talkie and jumped out of the car, circling in front of Vittoria.

Langdon got out too. *What the hell is she doing!*

Olivetti blocked Vittoria's way. 'Ms Vetra, your instincts are good, but I cannot let a civilian interfere.'

'Interfere? You're flying blind. Let me help.'

'I would love to have a recon point inside, but . . .'

'But what?' Vittoria demanded. 'But I'm a *woman*?'

Olivetti said nothing.

'That had better not be what you were going to say, Commander, because you know damn well this is a good idea, and if you let some archaic *macho* bullshit—'

'Let us do our job.'

'Let me help.'

'Too dangerous. We would have no lines of communication with you. I can't let you carry a walkie-talkie, it would give you away.'

Vittoria reached in her shirt pocket and produced her cell phone. 'Plenty of tourists carry phones.'

Olivetti frowned.

Vittoria unsnapped the phone and mimicked a call. 'Hi, honey, I'm standing in the Pantheon. You should see this place!' She snapped the phone shut and glared at Olivetti. 'Who the hell is going to know? It is a no-risk situation. Let me be your eyes!' She motioned to the cell phone on Olivetti's belt. 'What's your number?'

Olivetti did not reply.

The driver had been looking on and seemed to have some thoughts of his own. He got out of the car and took the commander aside. They spoke in hushed tones for ten seconds. Finally Olivetti nodded and returned. 'Program this number.' He began dictating digits.

Vittoria programmed her phone.

'Now call the number.'

Vittoria pressed the auto dial. The phone on Olivetti's belt began ringing. He picked it up and spoke into the receiver. 'Go into the building, Ms Vetra, look around, exit the building, then call and tell me what you see.'

Vittoria snapped the phone shut. 'Thank you, sir.'

Langdon felt a sudden, unexpected surge of protective instinct. 'Wait a minute,' he said to Olivetti. 'You're sending her in there *alone*.'

Vittoria scowled at him. 'Robert, I'll be fine.'

The Swiss Guard driver was talking to Olivetti again.

'It's dangerous,' Langdon said to Vittoria.

'He's right,' Olivetti said. 'Even my best men don't work alone. My lieutenant has just pointed out that the masquerade will be more convincing with both of you anyway.'

Both of us? Langdon hesitated. *Actually, what I meant—*

'Both of you entering together,' Olivetti said, 'will look like a couple on holiday. You can also back each other up. I'm more comfortable with that.'

Vittoria shrugged. 'Fine, but we'll need to go fast.'

Langdon groaned. *Nice move, cowboy.*

Olivetti pointed down the street. 'First street you hit will be Via degli Orfani. Go left. It takes you directly to the Pantheon. Two-minute walk, tops. I'll be here, directing my men and waiting for your call. I'd like you to have protection.' He pulled out his pistol. 'Do either of you know how to use a gun?'

Langdon's heart skipped. *We don't need a gun!*

Vittoria held her hand out. 'I can tag a breaching porpoise from forty meters off the bow of a rocking ship.'

'Good.' Olivetti handed the gun to her. 'You'll have to conceal it.'

Vittoria glanced down at her shorts. Then she looked at Langdon.

Oh no you don't! Langdon thought, but Vittoria was

266

too fast. She opened his jacket, and inserted the weapon into one of his breast pockets. It felt like a rock dropping into his coat, his only consolation being that *Diagramma* was in the other pocket.

'We look harmless,' Vittoria said. 'We're leaving.' She took Langdon's arm and headed down the street.

The driver called out, 'Arm in arm is good. Remember, you're tourists. *Newlyweds* even. Perhaps if you held hands?'

As they turned the corner Langdon could have sworn he saw on Vittoria's face the hint of a smile.

59

The Swiss Guard 'staging room' is located adjacent to the Corpo di Vigilanza barracks and is used primarily for planning the security surrounding papal appearances and public Vatican events. Today, however, it was being used for something else.

The man addressing the assembled task force was the second-in-command of the Swiss Guard, Captain Elias Rocher. Rocher was a barrel-chested man with soft, puttylike features. He wore the traditional blue captain's uniform with his own personal flair – a red beret cocked sideways on his head. His voice was surprisingly crystalline for such a large man, and when he spoke, his tone had the clarity of a musical instrument. Despite the precision of his inflection, Rocher's eyes were cloudy like those of some nocturnal mammal. His men called him 'orso' – grizzly bear. They sometimes joked that Rocher was 'the bear who walked in the viper's shadow'. Commander Olivetti was the viper. Rocher was just as deadly as the viper, but at least you could see him coming.

Rocher's men stood at sharp attention, nobody moving a muscle, although the information they had just received had increased their aggregate blood pressure by a few thousand points.

Rookie Lieutenant Chartrand stood in the back of the room wishing he had been among the 99 per cent of applicants who had *not* qualified to be here. At twenty years old, Chartrand was the youngest guard on the force. He had been in Vatican City only three months. Like every man there, Chartrand was Swiss Army trained and had endured two years of additional *Ausbildung* in Bern before qualifying for the grueling Vatican *pròva* held in a secret barracks outside of Rome. Nothing in his training, however, had prepared him for a crisis like this.

At first Chartrand thought the briefing was some sort of bizarre training exercise. *Futuristic weapons? Ancient cults? Kidnapped cardinals?* Then Rocher had shown them the live video feed of the weapon in question. Apparently this was no exercise.

'We will be killing power in selected areas,' Rocher was saying, 'to eradicate extraneous magnetic inter-ference. We will move in teams of four. We will wear infrared goggles for vision. Reconnaissance will be done with traditional bug sweepers, recalibrated for sub-three-ohm flux fields. Any questions?'

None.

Chartrand's mind was on overload. 'What if we don't find it in time?' he asked, immediately wishing he had not.

The grizzly bear gazed out at him from beneath his

red beret. Then he dismissed the group with a somber salute. 'Godspeed, men.'

60

Two blocks from the Pantheon, Langdon and Vittoria approached on foot past a line of taxis, their drivers sleeping in the front seats. Nap time was eternal in the Eternal City – the ubiquitous public dozing a perfected extension of the afternoon siestas born of ancient Spain.

Langdon fought to focus his thoughts, but the situation was too bizarre to grasp rationally. Six hours ago he had been sound asleep in Cambridge. Now he was in Europe, caught up in a surreal battle of ancient titans, packing a semiautomatic in his Harris tweed, and holding hands with a woman he had only just met.

He looked at Vittoria. She was focused straight ahead. There was a strength in her grasp – that of an independent and determined woman. Her fingers wrapped around his with the comfort of innate acceptance. No hesitation. Langdon felt a growing attraction. *Get real*, he told himself.

Vittoria seemed to sense his uneasiness. 'Relax,' she said, without turning her head. 'We're supposed to look like newlyweds.'

'I'm relaxed.'

'You're crushing my hand.'

Langdon flushed and loosened up.

'Breathe through your eyes,' she said.

269

'I'm sorry?'

'It relaxes the muscles. It's called *pranayama*.'

'Piranha?'

'Not the fish. *Pranayama*. Never mind.'

As they rounded the corner into Piazza della Rotunda, the Pantheon rose before them. Langdon admired it, as always, with awe. *The Pantheon. Temple to all gods. Pagan gods. Gods of Nature and Earth.* The structure seemed boxier from the outside than he remembered. The vertical pillars and triangular *pronaus* all but obscured the circular dome behind it. Still, the bold and immodest inscription over the entrance assured him they were in the right spot. M AGRIPPA L F COS TERTIUM FECIT. Langdon translated it, as always, with amusement. *Marcus Agrippa, Consul for the third time, built this.*

So much for humility, he thought, turning his eyes to the surrounding area. A scattering of tourists with video cameras wandered the area. Others sat enjoying Rome's best iced coffee at *La Tazza di Oro*'s outdoor café. Outside the entrance to the Pantheon, four armed Roman policemen stood at attention just as Olivetti had predicted.

'Looks pretty quiet,' Vittoria said.

Langdon nodded, but he felt troubled. Now that he was standing here in person, the whole scenario seemed surreal. Despite Vittoria's apparent faith that he was right, Langdon realized he had put everyone on the line here. The Illuminati poem lingered. *From Santi's earthly tomb with demon's hole. YES*, he told himself. This was the spot. Santi's tomb. He had been here many times beneath the Pantheon's *oculus* and stood before the grave of the great Raphael.

'What time is it?' Vittoria asked.

Langdon checked his watch. 'Seven-fifty. Ten minutes till show time.'

'Hope these guys are good,' Vittoria said, eyeing the scattered tourists entering the Pantheon. 'If anything happens inside that dome, we'll all be in the crossfire.'

Langdon exhaled heavily as they moved toward the entrance. The gun felt heavy in his pocket. He wondered what would happen if the policemen frisked him and found the weapon, but the officers did not give them a second look. Apparently the disguise was convincing.

Langdon whispered to Vittoria. 'Ever fire anything other than a tranquilizer gun?'

'Don't you trust me?'

'Trust you? I barely know you.'

Vittoria frowned. 'And here I thought we were newlyweds.'

61

The air inside the Pantheon was cool and damp, heavy with history. The sprawling ceiling hovered overhead as though weightless – the 141-foot unsupported span larger even than the cupola at St Peter's. As always, Langdon felt a chill as he entered the cavernous room. It was a remarkable fusion of engineering and art. Above them the famous circular hole in the roof glowed with a narrow shaft of evening sun. *The oculus*, Langdon thought. *The demon's hole.*

They had arrived.

Langdon's eyes traced the arch of the ceiling sloping

outward to the columned walls and finally down to the polished marble floor beneath their feet. The faint echo of footfalls and tourist murmurs reverberated around the dome. Langdon scanned the dozens or so tourists wandering aimlessly in the shadows. *Are you here?*

'Looks pretty quiet,' Vittoria said, still holding his hand.

Langdon nodded.

'Where's Raphael's tomb?'

Langdon thought for a moment, trying to get his bearings. He surveyed the circumference of the room. Tombs. Altars. Pillars. Niches. He motioned to a particularly ornate funerary across the dome and to the left. 'I think that's Raphael's over there.'

Vittoria scanned the rest of the room. 'I don't see anyone who looks like an assassin about to kill a cardinal. Shall we look around?'

Langdon nodded. 'There's only one spot in here where anyone could be hiding. We better check the *rientranze*.'

'The recesses?'

'Yes.' Langdon pointed. 'The recesses in the wall.'

Around the perimeter, interspersed with the tombs, a series of semicircular niches were hewn in the wall. The niches, although not enormous, were big enough to hide someone in the shadows. Sadly, Langdon knew they once contained statues of the Olympian gods, but the pagan sculptures had been destroyed when the Vatican converted the Pantheon to a Christian church. He felt a pang of frustration to know he was standing at the first altar of science, and the marker was gone. He wondered which statue it had been, and where it had pointed. Langdon could imagine no greater thrill

272

than finding an Illuminati marker – a statue that surreptitiously pointed the way down the Path of Illumination. Again he wondered *who* the anonymous Illuminati sculptor had been.

'I'll take the left arc,' Vittoria said, indicating the left half of the circumference. 'You go right. See you in a hundred and eighty degrees.'

Langdon smiled grimly.

As Vittoria moved off, Langdon felt the eerie horror of the situation seeping back into his mind. As he turned and made his way to the right, the killer's voice seemed to whisper in the dead space around him. *Eight o'clock. Virgin sacrifices on the altars of science. A mathematical progression of death. Eight, nine, ten, eleven . . . and at midnight.* Langdon checked his watch: 7.52. Eight minutes.

As Langdon moved toward the first recess, he passed the tomb of one of Italy's Catholic kings. The sarcophagus, like many in Rome, was askew with the wall, positioned awkwardly. A group of visitors seemed confused by this. Langdon did not stop to explain. Formal Christian tombs were often misaligned with the architecture so they could lie facing *east*. It was an ancient superstition that Langdon's Symbology 212 class had discussed just last month.

'That's totally incongruous!' a female student in the front had blurted when Langdon explained the reason for east-facing tombs. 'Why would Christians want their tombs to face the rising *sun*? We're talking about Christianity . . . not *sun* worship!'

Langdon smiled, pacing before the blackboard, chewing an apple. 'Mr Hitzrot!' he shouted.

A young man dozing in back sat up with a start. 'What! Me?'

Langdon pointed to a Renaissance art poster on the wall. 'Who is that man kneeling before God?'

'Um . . . some saint?'

'Brilliant. And how do you *know* he's a saint?'

'He's got a halo?'

'Excellent, and does that golden halo remind you of anything?'

Hitzrot broke into a smile. 'Yeah! Those Egyptian things we studied last term. Those . . . um . . . *sun disks!*'

'Thank you, Hitzrot. Go back to sleep.' Langdon turned back to the class. 'Halos, like much of Christian symbology, were borrowed from the ancient Egyptian religion of *sun* worship. Christianity is filled with examples of sun worship.'

'Excuse me?' the girl in front said. 'I go to church all the time, and I don't see much sun worshiping going on!'

'Really? What do you celebrate on December twenty-fifth?'

'Christmas. The birth of Jesus Christ.'

'And yet according to the Bible, Christ was born in March, so what are we doing celebrating in late December?'

Silence.

Langdon smiled. 'December twenty-fifth, my friends, is the ancient pagan holiday of *sol invictus* – Unconquered Sun – coinciding with the winter solstice. It's that wonderful time of year when the sun returns, and the days start getting longer.'

Langdon took another bite of apple.

'Conquering religions,' he continued, 'often adopt existing holidays to make conversion less shocking. It's called *transmutation*. It helps people acclimatize to

274

the new faith. Worshipers keep the same holy dates, pray in the same sacred locations, use a similar symbology ... and they simply substitute a different god.'

Now the girl in front looked furious. 'You're implying Christianity is just some kind of ... repackaged *sun worship!*'

'Not at all. Christianity did not borrow *only* from sun worship. The ritual of Christian canonization is taken from the ancient "god-making" rite of Euhemerus. The practice of "god-eating" – that is, Holy Communion – was borrowed from the Aztecs. Even the concept of Christ dying for our sins is arguably not exclusively Christian; the self-sacrifice of a young man to absolve the sins of his people appears in the earliest tradition of the Quetzalcoatl.'

The girl glared. 'So, is *anything* in Christianity original?'

'Very little in *any* organized faith is truly original. Religions are not born from scratch. They grow from one another. Modern religion is a collage ... an assimilated historical record of man's quest to understand the divine.'

'Um ... hold on,' Hitzrot ventured, sounding awake now. 'I know something Christian that's original. How about our *image* of God? Christian art never portrays God as the hawk sun god, or as an Aztec, or as anything weird. It always shows God as an old man with a white beard. So our *image* of God is original, right?'

Langdon smiled. 'When the early Christian converts abandoned their former deities – pagan gods, Roman gods, Greek, sun, Mithraic, whatever – they asked the church what their new Christian God looked like.

Wisely, the church chose the most feared, powerful . . . and familiar face in all of recorded history.'

Hitzrot looked skeptical. 'An old man with a white, flowing beard?'

Langdon pointed to a hierarchy of ancient gods on the wall. At the top sat an old man with a white, flowing beard. 'Does Zeus look familiar?'

The class ended right on cue.

'Good evening,' a man's voice said.

Langdon jumped. He was back in the Pantheon. He turned to face an elderly man in a blue cape with a red cross on the chest. The man gave him a gray-toothed smile.

'You're English, right?' The man's accent was thick Tuscan.

Langdon blinked, confused. 'Actually, no. I'm American.'

The man looked embarrassed. 'Oh heavens, forgive me. You were so nicely dressed, I just figured . . . my apologies.'

'Can I help you?' Langdon asked, his heart beating wildly.

'Actually I thought perhaps I could help *you*. I am the *cicerone* here.' The man pointed proudly to his city-issued badge. 'It is my job to make your visit to Rome more interesting.'

More interesting? Langdon was certain this particular visit to Rome was *plenty* interesting.

'You look like a man of distinction,' the guide fawned, 'no doubt more interested in culture than most. Perhaps I can give you some history on this fascinating building.'

Langdon smiled politely. 'Kind of you, but I'm

276

actually an art historian myself, and—'

'Superb!' The man's eyes lit up like he'd hit the jackpot. 'Then you will no doubt find this delightful!'

'I think I'd prefer to—'

'The Pantheon,' the man declared, launching into his memorized spiel, 'was built by Marcus Agrippa in 27 B.C.'

'Yes,' Langdon interjected, 'and rebuilt by Hadrian in 119 A.D.'

'It was the world's largest free-standing dome until 1960 when it was eclipsed by the Superdome in New Orleans!'

Langdon groaned. The man was unstoppable.

'And a fifth-century theologian once called the Pantheon the *House of the Devil*, warning that the hole in the roof was an entrance for demons!'

Langdon blocked him out. His eyes climbed skyward to the oculus, and the memory of Vittoria's suggested plot flashed a bone-numbing image in his mind . . . a branded cardinal falling through the hole and hitting the marble floor. *Now* that *would be a media event*. Langdon found himself scanning the Pantheon for reporters. None. He inhaled deeply. It was an absurd idea. The logistics of pulling off a stunt like that would be ridiculous.

As Langdon moved off to continue his inspection, the babbling docent followed like a love-starved puppy. *Remind me*, Langdon thought to himself, *there's nothing worse than a gung ho art historian*.

Across the room, Vittoria was immersed in her own search. Standing all alone for the first time since she had heard the news of her father, she felt the stark reality of the last eight hours closing in around her.

Her father had been murdered – cruelly and abruptly. Almost equally painful was that her father's creation had been corrupted – now a tool of terrorists. Vittoria was plagued with guilt to think that it was *her* invention that had enabled the antimatter to be transported . . . *her* canister that was now counting down inside the Vatican. In an effort to serve her father's quest for the simplicity of truth . . . she had become a conspirator of chaos.

Oddly, the only thing that felt right in her life at the moment was the presence of a total stranger. Robert Langdon. She found an inexplicable refuge in his eyes . . . like the harmony of the oceans she had left behind early that morning. She was glad he was there. Not only had he been a source of strength and hope for her, Langdon had used his quick mind to render this one chance to catch her father's killer.

Vittoria breathed deeply as she continued her search, moving around the perimeter. She was overwhelmed by the unexpected images of personal revenge that had dominated her thoughts all day. Even as a sworn lover of all life . . . she wanted this executioner *dead*. No amount of good *karma* could make her turn the other cheek today. Alarmed and electrified, she sensed something coursing through her Italian blood that she had never felt before . . . the whispers of Sicilian ancestors defending family honor with brutal justice. *Vendetta*, Vittoria thought, and for the first time in her life understood.

Visions of reprisal spurred her on. She approached the tomb of Raphael Santi. Even from a distance she could tell this guy was special. His casket, unlike the others, was protected by a Plexiglas shield and recessed into the wall. Through the barrier she could see the front of the sarcophagus.

278

Vittoria studied the grave and then read the one-sentence description plaque beside Raphael's tomb.

Then she read it again.

Then . . . she read it again.

A moment later, she was dashing in horror across the floor. 'Robert! *Robert!*'

62

Langdon's progress around his side of the Pantheon was being hampered somewhat by the guide on his heels, now continuing his tireless narration as Langdon prepared to check the final alcove.

'You certainly seem to be enjoying those niches!' the docent said, looking delighted. 'Were you aware that the tapering thickness of the walls is the reason the dome appears weightless?'

Langdon nodded, not hearing a word as he prepared to examine another niche. Suddenly someone grabbed him from behind. It was Vittoria. She was breathless and tugging at his arm. From the look of terror on her face, Langdon could only imagine one thing. *She found a body.* He felt an upswelling of dread.

'Ah, your wife!' the docent exclaimed, clearly thrilled to have another guest. He motioned to her short pants and hiking boots. 'Now *you* I can tell are American!'

Vittoria's eyes narrowed. 'I'm Italian.'

The guide's smile dimmed. 'Oh, dear.'

'Robert,' Vittoria whispered, trying to turn her back on the guide. 'Galileo's *Diagramma*. I need to see it.'

'*Diagramma?*' the docent said, wheedling back in. 'My! You two certainly know your history! Unfortunately that document is not viewable. It is under secret preservation in the Vatican Arc—'

'Could you excuse us?' Langdon said. He was confused by Vittoria's panic. He took her aside and reached in his pocket, carefully extracting the *Diagramma* folio. 'What's going on?'

'What's the date on this thing?' Vittoria demanded, scanning the sheet.

The docent was on them again, staring at the folio, mouth agape. 'That's not . . . really . . .'

'Tourist reproduction,' Langdon quipped. 'Thank you for your help. Please, my wife and I would like a moment alone.'

The docent backed off, eyes never leaving the paper.

'Date,' Vittoria repeated to Langdon. 'When did Galileo publish . . .'

Langdon pointed to the Roman numeral in the lower line. 'That's the pub date. What's going on?'

Vittoria deciphered the number. '1639?'

'Yes. What's wrong?'

Vittoria's eyes filled with foreboding. 'We're in trouble, Robert. Big trouble. The dates don't match.'

'What dates don't match?'

'Raphael's tomb. He wasn't buried here until 1759. A century *after Diagramma* was published.'

Langdon stared at her, trying to make sense of the words. 'No,' he replied. 'Raphael died in 1520, long *before Diagramma*.'

'Yes, but he wasn't buried *here* until much later.'

Langdon was lost. 'What are you talking about?'

'I just read it. Raphael's body was relocated to the Pantheon in 1758. It was part of some historic tribute to eminent Italians.

As the words settled in, Langdon felt like a rug had just been yanked out from under him.

'When that poem was written,' Vittoria declared, 'Raphael's tomb was somewhere *else*. Back then, the Pantheon had nothing at all to do with Raphael!'

Langdon could not breathe. 'But that . . . means . . .'

'Yes! It means we're in the wrong place!'

Langdon felt himself sway. *Impossible . . . I was certain . . .*

Vittoria ran over and grabbed the docent, pulling him back. 'Signore, excuse us. Where was Raphael's body in the 1600s?'

'Urb . . . Urbino,' he stammered, now looking bewildered. 'His birthplace.'

'Impossible!' Langdon cursed to himself. 'The Illuminati altars of science were here in Rome. I'm certain of it!'

'Illuminati?' The docent gasped, looking again at the document in Langdon's hand. 'Who *are* you people?'

Vittoria took charge. 'We're looking for something called Santi's earthly tomb. In Rome. Can you tell us what that might be?'

The docent looked unsettled. 'This was Raphael's only tomb in Rome.'

Langdon tried to think, but his mind refused to engage. If Raphael's tomb wasn't in Rome in 1655, then what was the poem referring to? *Santi's earthly tomb with demon's hole? What the hell is it? Think!*

'Was there another artist called Santi?' Vittoria asked.

281

The docent shrugged. 'Not that I know of.'

'How about *anyone* famous at all? Maybe a scientist or a poet or an astronomer named Santi?'

The docent now looked like he wanted to leave. 'No, ma'am. The only Santi I've heard of is Raphael the architect.'

'Architect?' Vittoria said. 'I thought he was a painter!'

'He was both, of course. They all were. Michelangelo, da Vinci, Raphael.'

Langdon didn't know whether it was the docent's words or the ornate tombs around him that brought the revelation to mind, but it didn't matter. The thought occurred. *Santi was an architect.* From there the progression of thoughts fell like dominoes. Renaissance architects lived for only two reasons – to glorify God with big churches, and to glorify dignitaries with lavish tombs. *Santi's tomb. Could it be?* The images came faster now . . .

da Vinci's *Mona Lisa*.

Monet's *Water Lilies*.

Michelangelo's *David*.

Santi's *earthly tomb* . . .

'Santi *designed* the tomb,' Langdon said.

Vittoria turned. 'What?'

'It's not a reference to where Raphael is buried, it's referring to a tomb he *designed*.'

'What are you talking about?'

'I misunderstood the clue. It's not Raphael's burial site we're looking for, it's a tomb Raphael designed for someone *else*. I can't believe I missed it. Half of the sculpting done in Renaissance and Baroque Rome was for the funeraries.' Langdon smiled with the revelation. 'Raphael must have designed hundreds of tombs!'

Vittoria did not look happy. 'Hundreds?'

Langdon's smile faded. 'Oh.'

'Any of them *earthly*, professor?'

Langdon felt suddenly inadequate. He knew embarrassingly little about Raphael's work. Michelangelo he could have helped with, but Raphael's work had never captivated him. Langdon could only name a couple of Raphael's more famous tombs, but he wasn't sure what they looked like.

Apparently sensing Langdon's stymie, Vittoria turned to the docent, who was now inching away. She grabbed his arm and reeled him in. 'I need a tomb. Designed by Raphael. A tomb that could be considered *earthly*.'

The docent now looked distressed. 'A tomb of Raphael's? I don't know. He designed so many. And you probably would mean a *chapel* by Raphael, not a tomb. Architects always designed the chapels in conjunction with the tomb.'

Langdon realized the man was right.

'Are any of Raphael's tombs or chapels considered *earthly*?'

The man shrugged. 'I'm sorry. I don't know what you mean. *Earthly* really doesn't describe anything I know of. I should be going.'

Vittoria held his arm and read from the top line of the folio. 'From Santi's earthly tomb with demon's hole. Does that mean anything to you?'

'Not a thing.'

Langdon looked up suddenly. He had momentarily forgotten the second part of the line. *Demon's hole?* 'Yes!' he said to the docent. 'That's it! Do any of Raphael's chapels have an oculus in them?'

The docent shook his head. 'To my knowledge

the Pantheon is unique.' He paused. 'But . . .'

'But what!' Vittoria and Langdon said in unison.

Now the docent cocked his head, stepping toward them again. 'A demon's hole?' He muttered to himself and picked at his teeth. 'Demon's hole . . . that is . . . *buco diàvolo*?'

Vittoria nodded. 'Literally, yes.'

The docent smiled faintly. 'Now there's a term I have not heard in a while. If I'm not mistaken, a *buco diàvolo* refers to an undercroft.'

'An undercroft?' Langdon asked. 'As in a *crypt*?'

'Yes, but a specific kind of crypt. I believe a demon's hole is an ancient term for a massive burial cavity located in a chapel . . . underneath another tomb.'

'An ossuary annex?' Langdon demanded, immediately recognizing what the man was describing.

The docent looked impressed. 'Yes! That is the term I was looking for!'

Langdon considered it. Ossuary annexes were a cheap ecclesiastic fix to an awkward dilemma. When churches honored their most distinguished members with ornate tombs inside the sanctuary, surviving family members often demanded the family be buried together . . . thus ensuring they too would have a coveted burial spot inside the church. However, if the church did not have space or funds to create tombs for an entire family, they sometimes dug an ossuary annex – a hole in the floor near the tomb where they buried the less worthy family members. The hole was then covered with the Renaissance equivalent of a manhole cover. Although convenient, the ossuary annex went out of style quickly because of the stench that often wafted up into the cathedral. *Demon's hole*, Langdon thought. He had never heard the term. It seemed eerily fitting.

Langdon's heart was now pounding fiercely. *From Santi's earthly tomb with demon's hole.* There seemed to be only one question left to ask. 'Did Raphael design any tombs that had one of these demon's holes?'

The docent scratched his head. 'Actually, I'm sorry . . . I can only think of one.'

Only one? Langdon could not have dreamed of a better response.

'Where!' Vittoria almost shouted.

The docent eyed them strangely. 'It's called the Chigi Chapel. Tomb of Agostino Chigi and his brother, wealthy patrons of the arts and sciences.'

'*Sciences?*' Langdon said, exchanging looks with Vittoria.

'Where?' Vittoria asked again.

The docent ignored the question, seeming enthusiastic again to be of service. 'As for whether or not the tomb is *earthly*, I don't know, but certainly it is . . . shall we say *differénte.*'

'Different?' Langdon said. 'How?'

'Incoherent with the architecture. Raphael was only the architect. Some other sculptor did the interior adornments. I can't remember who.'

Langdon was now all ears. *The anonymous Illuminati master, perhaps?*

'Whoever did the interior monuments lacked taste,' the docent said. '*Dio mio! Atrocità!* Who would want to be buried beneath *pirámides?*'

Langdon could scarcely believe his ears. 'Pyramids? The chapel contains pyramids?'

'I know,' the docent scoffed. 'Terrible, isn't it?'

Vittoria grabbed the docent's arm. 'Signore, *where* is this Chigi Chapel?'

'About a mile north. In the church of Santa Maria del Popolo.'

Vittoria exhaled. 'Thank you. Let's—'

'Hey,' the docent said, 'I just thought of something. What a fool I am.'

Vittoria stopped short. 'Please don't tell me you made a mistake.'

He shook his head. 'No, but it should have dawned on me earlier. The Chigi Chapel was not always known as the Chigi. It used to be called Capella della Terra.'

'Chapel of the Land?' Langdon asked.

'No,' Vittoria said, heading for the door. 'Chapel of the *Earth*.'

Vittoria Vetra whipped out her cell phone as she dashed into Piazza della Rotunda. 'Commander Olivetti,' she said. 'This is the wrong place!'

Olivetti sounded bewildered. 'Wrong? What do you mean?'

'The first altar of science is at the Chigi Chapel!'

'Where?' Now Olivetti sounded angry. 'But Mr Langdon said—'

'Santa Maria del Popolo! One mile north. Get your men over there now! We've got four minutes!'

'But my men are in position *here*! I can't possibly—'

'Move!' Vittoria snapped the phone shut.

Behind her, Langdon emerged from the Panteon, dazed.

She grabbed his hand and pulled him toward the queue of seemingly driverless taxis waiting by the curb. She pounded on the hood of the first car in line. The sleeping driver bolted upright with a startled yelp. Vittoria yanked open the rear door and pushed

Langdon inside. Then she jumped in behind him.

'Santa Maria del Popolo,' she ordered. '*Presto!*'

Looking delirious and half terrified, the driver hit the accelerator, peeling out down the street.

63

Gunther Glick had assumed control of the computer from Chinita Macri, who now stood hunched in the back of the cramped BBC van staring in confusion over Glick's shoulder.

'I told you,' Glick said, typing some more keys. 'The *British Tatler* isn't the only paper that runs stories on these guys.'

Macri peered closer. Glick was right. The BBC database showed their distinguished network as having picked up and run six stories in the past ten years on the brotherhood called the Illuminati. *Well, paint me purple*, she thought. 'Who are the journalists who ran the stories,' Macri asked.'Schlock jocks?'

'BBC doesn't hire schlock jocks.'

'They hired *you*.'

Glick scowled. 'I don't know why you're such a skeptic. The Illuminati are well documented throughout history.'

'So are witches, UFOs, and the Loch Ness Monster.'

Glick read the list of stories. 'You ever heard of a guy called Winston Churchill?'

'Rings a bell.'

'BBC did a historical a while back on Churchill's life. Staunch Catholic by the way. Did you know that in

1920 Churchill published a statement condemning the Illuminati and warning Brits of a worldwide conspiracy against morality?'

Macri was dubious. 'Where did it run? In the *British Tatler*?'

Glick smiled. '*London Herald*. February 8, 1920.'

'No way.'

'Feast your eyes.'

Macri looked closer at the clip. *London Herald, Feb. 8, 1920. I had no idea.* 'Well, Churchill was a paranoid.'

'He wasn't alone,' Glick said, reading further. 'Looks like Woodrow Wilson gave three radio broadcasts in 1921 warning of growing Illuminati control over the U.S. banking system. You want a direct quote from the radio transcript?'

'Not really.'

Glick gave her one anyway. 'He said, "There is a power so organized, so subtle, so complete, so pervasive, that none had better speak above their breath when they speak in condemnation of it."'

'I've never heard anything about this.'

'Maybe because in 1921 you were just a kid.'

'Charming.' Macri took the jab in stride. She knew her years were showing. At forty-three, her bushy black curls were streaked with gray. She was too proud for dye. Her mom, a Southern Baptist, had taught Chinita contentedness and self-respect. *When you're a black woman*, her mother said, *ain't no hiding what you are. Day you try, is the day you die. Stand tall, smile bright, and let 'em wonder what secret's making you laugh.*

'Ever heard of Cecil Rhodes?' Glick asked.

Macri looked up. 'The British financier?'

'Yeah. Founded the Rhodes Scholarships.'

'Don't tell me—'

'Illuminatus.'

'BS.'

'BBC, actually. November 16, 1984.'

'*We* wrote that Cecil Rhodes was Illuminati?'

'Sure did. And according to our network, the Rhodes Scholarships were funds set up centuries ago to recruit the world's brightest young minds into the Illuminati.'

'That's ridiculous! My uncle was a Rhodes Scholar!'

Glick winked. 'So was Bill Clinton.'

Macri was getting mad now. She had never had tolerance for shoddy, alarmist reporting. Still, she knew enough about the BBC to know that every story they ran was carefully researched and confirmed.

'Here's one you'll remember,' Glick said. 'BBC, March 5, 1998. Parliament Committee Chair, Chris Mullin, required all members of British Parliament who were Masons to declare their affiliation.'

Macri remembered it. The decree had eventually extended to include policemen and judges as well. 'Why was it again?'

Glick read. '. . . concern that secret factions within the Masons exerted considerable control over political and financial systems.'

'That's right.'

'Caused quite a bustle. The Masons in parliament were furious. Had a right to be. The vast majority turned out to be innocent men who joined the Masons for networking and charity work. They had no clue about the brotherhood's past affiliations.'

'Alleged affiliations.'

'Whatever.' Glick scanned the articles. 'Look at this stuff. Accounts tracing the Illuminati back to Galileo, the *Guerenets* of France, the *Alumbrados* of Spain. Even Karl Marx and the Russian Revolution.'

'History has a way of rewriting itself.'

'Fine, you want something current? Have a look at this. Here's an Illuminati reference from a recent *Wall Street Journal*.'

This caught Macri's ear. 'The *Journal*?'

'Guess what the most popular Internet computer game in America is right now?'

'Pin the tail on Pamela Anderson.'

'Close. It's called, *Illuminati: New World Order*.'

Macri looked over his shoulder at the blurb. *'Steve Jackson Games has a runaway hit . . . a quasi-historical adventure in which an ancient satanic brotherhood from Bavaria sets out to take over the world. You can find them on-line at . . .'* Macri looked up, feeling ill. 'What do these Illuminati guys have against Christianity?'

'Not just Christianity,' Glick said. 'Religion in general.' Glick cocked his head and grinned. 'Although from the phone call we just got, it appears they *do* have a special spot in their hearts for the Vatican.'

'Oh, come on. You don't *really* think that guy who called is who he claims to be, do you?'

'A messenger of the Illuminati? Preparing to kill four cardinals?' Glick smiled. 'I sure hope so.'

64

Langdon and Vittoria's taxi completed the one-mile sprint up the wide Via della Scrofa in just over a minute. They skidded to a stop on the south side of the

Piazza del Popolo just before eight. Not having any lire, Langdon overpaid the driver in U.S. dollars. He and Vittoria jumped out. The piazza was quiet except for the laughter of a handful of locals seated outside the popular Rosati Café – a hot spot of the Italian literati. The breeze smelled of espresso and pastry.

Langdon was still in shock over his mistake at the Pantheon. With a cursory glance at this square, however, his sixth sense was already tingling. The piazza seemed subtly filled with Illuminati significance. Not only was it laid out in a perfectly *elliptical* shape, but dead center stood a towering Egyptian obelisk – a square pillar of stone with a distinctively pyramidal tip. Spoils of Rome's imperial plundering, obelisks were scattered across Rome and referred to by symbologists as 'Lofty Pyramids' – skyward extensions of the sacred pyramidal form.

As Langdon's eyes moved up the monolith, though, his sight was suddenly drawn to something else in the background. Something even more remarkable.

'We're in the right place,' he said quietly, feeling a sudden exposed wariness. 'Have a look at that.' Langdon pointed to the imposing Porta del Popolo – the high stone archway at the far end of the piazza. The vaulted structure had been overlooking the piazza for centuries. Dead center of the archway's highest point was a symbolic engraving. 'Look familiar?'

Vittoria looked up at the huge carving. 'A shining star over a triangular pile of stones?'

Langdon shook his head. 'A source of Illumination over a pyramid.'

Vittoria turned, her eyes suddenly wide. 'Like . . . the Great Seal of the United States.'

'Exactly. The Masonic symbol on the one-dollar bill.'

Vittoria took a deep breath and scanned the piazza. 'So where's this damn church?'

The Church of Santa Maria del Popolo stood out like a misplaced battleship, askew at the base of a hill on the southeast corner of the piazza. The eleventh-century stone aerie was made even more clumsy by the tower of scaffolding covering the façade.

Langdon's thoughts were a blur as they raced toward the edifice. He stared up at the church in wonder. Could a murder really be about to take place inside? He wished Olivetti would hurry. The gun felt awkward in his pocket.

The church's front stairs were *ventaglio* – a welcoming, curved fan – ironic in this case because they were blocked with scaffolding, construction equipment, and a sign warning: COSTRUZIONE. NON ENTRARE.

Langdon realized that a church closed for renovation meant total privacy for a killer. Not like the Pantheon. No fancy tricks needed here. Only to find a way in.

Vittoria slipped without hesitation between the sawhorses and headed up the staircase.

'Vittoria,' Langdon cautioned. 'If he's still in there . . .'

Vittoria did not seem to hear. She ascended the main portico to the church's sole wooden door. Langdon hurried up the stairs behind her. Before he could say a word she had grasped the handle and pulled. Langdon held his breath. The door did not budge.

'There must be another entrance,' Vittoria said.

'Probably,' Langdon said, exhaling, 'but Olivetti will be here in a minute. It's too dangerous to go in. We should cover the church from out here until—'

Vittoria turned, here eyes blazing. 'If there's another way *in*, there's another way *out*. If this guy disappears, we're *fungito*.'

Langdon knew enough Italian to know she was right.

The alley on the right side of the church was pinched and dark, with high walls on both sides. It smelled of urine – a common aroma in a city where bars outnumbered public rest rooms twenty to one.

Langdon and Vittoria hurried into the fetid dimness. They had gone about fifteen yards down when Vittoria tugged Langdon's arm and pointed.

Langdon saw it too. Up ahead was an unassuming wooden door with heavy hinges. Langdon recognized it as the standard *porta sacra* – a private entrance for clergy. Most of these entrances had gone out of use years ago as encroaching buildings and limited real estate relegated side entrances to inconvenient alleyways.

Vittoria hurried to the door. She arrived and stared down at the doorknob, apparently perplexed. Langdon arrived behind her and eyed the peculiar donut-shaped hoop hanging where the doorknob should have been.

'An annulus,' he whispered. Langdon reached out and quietly lifted the ring in his hand. He pulled the ring toward him. The fixture clicked. Vittoria shifted, looking suddenly uneasy. Quietly, Langdon twisted the ring clockwise. It spun loosely 360 degrees, not engaging. Langdon frowned and tried the other direction with the same result.

Vittoria looked down the remainder of the alley. 'You think there's another entrance?'

Langdon doubted it. Most Renaissance cathedrals

were designed as makeshift fortresses in the event a city was stormed. They had as few entrances as possible. 'If there *is* another way in,' he said, 'it's probably recessed in the rear bastion – more of an escape route than an entrance.'

Vittoria was already on the move.

Langdon followed deeper into the alley. The walls shot skyward on both sides of him. Somewhere a bell began ringing eight o'clock . . .

Robert Langdon did not hear Vittoria the first time she called to him. He had slowed at a stained-glass window covered with bars and was trying to peer inside the church.

'Robert!' Her voice was a loud whisper.

Langdon looked up. Vittoria was at the end of the alley. She was pointing around the back of the church and waving to him. Langdon jogged reluctantly toward her. At the base of the rear wall, a stone bulwark jutted out concealing a narrow grotto – a kind of compressed passageway cutting directly into the foundation of the church.

'An entrance?' Vittoria asked.

Langdon nodded. *Actually an exit, but we won't get technical.*

Vittoria knelt and peered into the tunnel. 'Let's check the door. See if it's open.'

Langdon opened his mouth to object, but Vittoria took his hand and pulled him into the opening.

'Wait,' Langdon said.

She turned impatiently toward him.

Langdon sighed. 'I'll go first.'

Vittoria looked surprised. 'More chivalry?'

'Age before beauty.'

'Was that a compliment?'

Langdon smiled and moved past her into the dark. 'Careful on the stairs.'

He inched slowly into the darkness, keeping one hand on the wall. The stone felt sharp on his fingertips. For an instant Langdon recalled the ancient myth of Daedelus, how the boy kept one hand on the wall as he moved through the Minotaur's labyrinth, knowing he was guaranteed to find the end if he never broke contact with the wall. Langdon moved forward, not entirely certain he wanted to find the end.

The tunnel narrowed slightly, and Langdon slowed his pace. He sensed Vittoria close behind him. As the wall curved left, the tunnel opened into a semicircular alcove. Oddly, there was faint light here. In the dimness Langdon saw the outline of a heavy wooden door.

'Oh oh,' he said.

'Locked?'

'It *was.*'

'*Was?*' Vittoria arrived at his side.

Langdon pointed. Lit by a shaft of light coming from within, the door hung ajar . . . its hinges splintered by a wrecking bar still lodged in the wood.

They stood a moment in silence. Then, in the dark, Langdon felt Vittoria's hands on his chest, groping, sliding beneath his jacket.

'Relax, professor,' she said. 'I'm just getting the gun.'

At that moment, inside the Vatican Museums, a task force of Swiss Guards spread out in all directions. The museum was dark, and the guards wore U.S. Marine issue infrared goggles. The goggles made everything appear an eerie shade of green. Every guard wore headphones connected to an antennalike detector that he waved rhythmically in front of him – the same devices they used twice a week to sweep for electronic bugs inside the Vatican. They moved methodically, checking behind statues, inside niches, closets, under furniture. The antennae would sound if they detected even the tiniest magnetic field.

Tonight, however, they were getting no readings at all.

65

The interior of Santa Maria del Popolo was a murky cave in the dimming light. It looked more like a half-finished subway station than a cathedral. The main sanctuary was an obstacle course of torn-up flooring, brick pallets, mounds of dirt, wheelbarrows, and even a rusty backhoe. Mammoth columns rose through the floor, supporting a vaulted roof. In the air, silt drifted lazily in the muted glow of the stained glass. Langdon stood with Vittoria beneath a sprawling Pinturicchio fresco and scanned the gutted shrine.

Nothing moved. Dead silence.

Vittoria held the gun out in front of her with both hands. Langdon checked his watch: 8.04 p.m. *We're crazy to be in here*, he thought. *It's too dangerous*. Still he knew if the killer were inside, the man could leave through any door he wanted, making a one-gun outside stakeout totally fruitless. Catching him inside was the only way ... that was, if he was even still here. Langdon felt guilt-ridden over the blunder that had cost everyone their chance at the Pantheon. He was in no position to insist on precaution now; *he* was the one who had backed them into this corner.

Vittoria looked harrowed as she scanned the church. 'So,' she whispered. 'Where is this Chigi Chapel?'

Langdon gazed through the dusky ghostliness toward the back of the cathedral and studied the outer walls. Contrary to common perception, Renaissance cathedrals invariably contained *multiple* chapels, huge cathedrals like Notre Dame having dozens. Chapels were less *rooms* than they were *hollows* – semi-circular niches holding tombs around a church's perimeter wall.

Bad news, Langdon thought, seeing the four recesses on each side wall. There were eight chapels in all. Although eight was not a particularly overwhelming number, all eight openings were covered with huge sheets of clear polyurethane due to the construction, the translucent curtains apparently intended to keep dust off the tombs inside the alcoves.

'It could be any of those draped recesses,' Langdon said. 'No way to know which is the Chigi without looking inside every one. Could be a good reason to wait for Oliv—'

'Which is the secondary left apse?' she asked.

Langdon studied her, surprised by her command of architectural terminology. 'Secondary left apse?'

Vittoria pointed at the wall behind him. A decorative tile was embedded in the stone. It was engraved with the same symbol they had seen outside – a pyramid beneath a shining star. The grime-covered plaque beside it read:

COAT OF ARMS OF ALEXANDER CHIGI
WHOSE TOMB IS LOCATED IN THE
SECONDARY LEFT APSE OF THIS CATHEDRAL

Langdon nodded. *Chigi's coat of arms was a pyramid and star?* He suddenly found himself wondering if the wealthy patron Chigi had been an Illuminatus. He nodded to Vittoria. 'Nice work, Nancy Drew.'

'What?'

'Never mind. I—'

A piece of metal clattered to the floor only yards away. The clang echoed through the entire church. Langdon pulled Vittoria behind a pillar as she whipped the gun toward the sound and held it there. Silence. They waited. Again there was a sound, this time a rustling. Langdon held his breath. *I never should have let us come in here!* The sound moved closer, an intermittent scuffling, like a man with a limp. Suddenly around the base of the pillar, an object came into view.

'Figlio di puttana!' Vittoria cursed under her breath, jumping back. Langdon fell back with her.

Beside the pillar, dragging a half-eaten sandwich in paper, was an enormous rat. The creature paused when it saw them, staring a long moment down the barrel of Vittoria's weapon, and then, apparently unmoved, continued dragging its prize off to the recesses of the church.

'Son of a . . .' Langdon gasped, his heart racing.

Vittoria lowered the gun, quickly regaining her composure. Langdon peered around the side of the column to see a workman's lunchbox splayed on the floor, apparently knocked off a sawhorse by the resourceful rodent.

298

Langdon scanned the basilica for movement and whispered, 'If this guy's here, he sure as hell heard *that*. You sure you don't want to wait for Olivetti?'

'Secondary left apse,' Vittoria repeated. 'Where is it?'

Reluctantly Langdon turned and tried to get his bearings, Cathedral terminology was like stage directions – totally counterintuitive. He faced the main altar. *Stage center.* Then he pointed with his thumb backward over his shoulder.

They both turned and looked where he was pointing.

It seemed the Chigi Chapel was located in the third of four recessed alcoves to their right. The good news was that Langdon and Vittoria were on the correct *side* of the church. The bad news was that they were at the wrong *end.* They would have to traverse the length of the cathedral, passing three other chapels, each of them, like the Chigi Chapel, covered with translucent plastic shrouds.

'Wait,' Langdon said. 'I'll go first.'

'Forget it.'

'I'm the one who screwed up at the Pantheon.'

She turned. 'But I'm the one with the gun.'

In her eyes Langdon could see what she was really thinking . . . *I'm the one who lost my father. I'm the one who helped build a weapon of mass destruction. This guy's kneecaps are mine . . .*

Langdon sensed the futility and let her go. He moved beside her, cautiously, down the east side of the basilica. As they passed the first shrouded alcove, Langdon felt taut, like a contestant on some surreal game show. *I'll take curtain number three,* he thought.

The church was quiet, the thick stone walls blocking

out all hints of the outside world. As they hurried past one chapel after the other, pale humanoid forms wavered like ghosts behind the rustling plastic. *Carved marble,* Langdon told himself, hoping he was right. It was 8.06 p.m. Had the killer been punctual and slipped out before Langdon and Vittoria had entered? Or was he still here? Langdon was unsure which scenario he preferred.

They passed the second apse, ominous in the slowly darkening cathedral. Night seemed to be falling quickly now, accentuated by the musty tint of the stained-glass windows. As they pressed on, the plastic curtain beside them billowed suddenly, as if caught in a draft. Langdon wondered if someone somewhere had opened a door.

Vittoria slowed as the third niche loomed before them. She held the gun before her, motioning with her head to the stele beside the apse. Carved in the granite block were two words:

CAPELLA CHIGI

Langdon nodded. Without a sound they moved to the corner of the opening, positioning themselves behind a wide pillar. Vittoria leveled the gun around a corner at the plastic. Then she signaled for Langdon to pull back the shroud.

A good time to start praying, he thought. Reluctantly, he reached over her shoulder. As carefully as possible, he began to pull the plastic aside. It moved an inch and then crinkled loudly. They both froze. Silence. After a moment, moving in slow motion, Vittoria leaned forward and peered through the narrow slit. Langdon looked over her shoulder.

300

For a moment, neither one of them breathed.

'Empty,' Vittoria finally said, lowering the gun. 'We're too late.'

Langdon did not hear. He was in awe, transported for an instant to another world. In his life, he had never imagined a chapel that looked like this. Finished entirely in chestnut marble, the Chigi Chapel was breathtaking. Langdon's trained eye devoured it in gulps. It was as *earthly* a chapel as Langdon could fathom, almost as if Galileo and the Illuminati had designed it themselves.

Overhead, the domed cupola shone with a field of illuminated stars and the seven astronomical planets. Below that the twelve signs of the zodiac – pagan, earthly symbols rooted in astronomy. The zodiac was also tied directly to Earth, Air, Fire, Water ... the quadrants representing power, intellect, ardor, emotion. *Earth is for power*, Langdon recalled.

Farther down the wall, Langdon saw tributes to the Earth's four temporal seasons – *primavera, estate, autunno, invérno*. But far more incredible than any of this were the two huge structures dominating the room. Langdon stared at them in silent wonder. *It can't be*, he thought. *It just can't be!* But it was. On either side of the chapel, in perfect symmetry, were two ten-foot-high marble pyramids.

'I don't see a cardinal,' Vittoria whispered. 'Or an assassin.' She pulled aside the plastic and stepped in.

Langdon's eyes were transfixed on the pyramids. *What are pyramids doing inside a Christian chapel?* And incredibly, there was more. Dead center of each pyramid, embedded in their anterior façades, were gold medallions ... medallions like few Langdon had ever seen ... perfect *ellipses*. The burnished disks glimmered in the setting sun as it sifted through the cupola. *Galileo's ellipses? Pyramids? A cupola of stars?* The room had more Illuminati significance than any room Langdon could have fabricated in his mind.

'Robert,' Vittoria blurted, her voice cracking. 'Look!'

Langdon wheeled, reality returning as his eyes dropped to where she was pointing. 'Bloody hell!' he shouted, jumping backward.

Sneering up at them from the floor was the image of a skeleton – an intricately detailed, marble mosaic depicting 'death in flight'. The skeleton was carrying a tablet portraying the same pyramid and stars they had seen outside. It was not the image, however, that had turned Langdon's blood cold. It was the fact that the mosaic was mounted on a circular stone – a *cupermento* – that had been lifted out of the floor like a manhole cover and was now sitting off to one side of a dark opening in the floor.

'Demon's hole,' Langdon gasped. He had been so taken with the ceiling he had not even seen it. Tentatively he moved toward the pit. The stench coming up was overwhelming.

Vittoria put a hand over her mouth. '*Che puzza.*'

'Effluvium,' Langdon said. 'Vapors from decaying bone.' He breathed through his sleeve as he leaned out over the hole, peering down. Blackness. 'I can't see a thing.'

'You think anybody's down there?'

'No way to know.'

Vittoria motioned to the far side of the hole where a rotting, wooden ladder descended into the depths.

Langdon shook his head. 'Like hell.'

'Maybe there's a flashlight outside in those tools.'

She sounded eager for an excuse to escape the smell. 'I'll look.'

'Careful!' Langdon warned. 'We don't know for sure that the Hassassin—'

But Vittoria was already gone.

One strong-willed woman, Langdon thought.

As he turned back to the pit, he felt light-headed from the fumes. Holding his breath, he dropped his head below the rim and peered deep into the darkness. Slowly, as his eyes adjusted, he began to see faint shapes below. The pit appeared to open into a small chamber. *Demon's hole.* He wondered how many generations of Chigis had been unceremoniously dumped in. Langdon closed his eyes and waited, forcing his pupils to dilate so he could see better in the dark. When he opened his eyes again, a pale muted figure hovered below in the darkness. Langdon shivered but fought instinct to pull out. *Am I seeing things? Is that a body?* The figure faded. Langdon closed his eyes again and waited, longer this time, so his eyes would pick up the faintest light.

Dizziness started to set in, and his thoughts wandered in the blackness. *Just a few more seconds.* He wasn't sure if it was breathing the fumes or holding his head at a low inclination, but Langdon was definitely starting to feel squeamish. When he finally opened his eyes again, the image before him was totally inexplicable.

He was now staring at a crypt bathed in an eerie bluish light. A faint hissing sound reverberated in his ears. Light flickered on the steep walls of the shaft. Suddenly, a long shadow materialized over him. Startled, Langdon scrambled up.

'Look out!' someone exclaimed behind him.

Before Langdon could turn, he felt a sharp pain on the back of his neck. He spun to see Vittoria twisting a lit blowtorch away from him, the hissing flame throwing blue light around the chapel.

Langdon grabbed his neck. 'What the hell are you doing?'

'I was giving you some light,' she said. 'You backed right into me.'

Langdon glared at the portable blowtorch in her hand.

'Best I could do,' she said. 'No flashlights.'

Langdon rubbed his neck. 'I didn't hear you come in.'

Vittoria handed him the torch, wincing again at the stench of the crypt. 'You think those fumes are combustible?'

'Let's hope not.'

He took the torch and moved slowly toward the hole. Cautiously, he advanced to the rim and pointed the flame down into the hole, lighting the side wall. As he directed the light, his eyes traced the outline of the wall downward. The crypt was circular and about twenty feet across. Thirty feet down, the glow found the floor. The ground was dark and mottled. Earthy. Then Langdon saw the body.

His instinct was to recoil. 'He's here,' Langdon said, forcing himself not to turn away. The figure was a pallid outline against the earthen floor. 'I think he's been stripped naked.' Langdon flashed on the nude corpse.

'Is it one of the cardinals?'

Langdon had no idea, but he couldn't imagine who the hell else it would be. He stared down at the pale blob. Unmoving. Lifeless. *And yet* ... Langdon hesitated. There was something very strange about the way the figure was positioned. He seemed to be . . .

Langdon called out. 'Hello?'

'You think he's alive?'

There was no response from below.

'He's not moving,' Langdon said. 'But he looks . . .' *No, impossible.*

'He looks *what*?' Vittoria was peering over the edge now too.

Langdon squinted into the darkness. 'He looks like he's standing up.'

Vittoria held her breath and lowered her face over the edge for a better look. After a moment, she pulled back. 'You're right. He's standing up! Maybe he's alive and needs help!' She called into the hole. 'Hello?! *Mi puó sentire?*'

There was no echo off the mossy interior. Only silence.

Vittoria headed for the rickety ladder. 'I'm going down.'

Langdon caught her arm. 'No. It's dangerous. I'll go.'

This time Vittoria didn't argue.

66

Chinita Macri was mad. She sat in the passenger's seat of the BBC van as it idled at a corner on Via Tomacelli. Gunther Glick was checking his map of Rome, apparently lost. As she had feared, his mystery caller had phoned back, this time with information.

'Piazza del Popolo,' Glick insisted. 'That's what we're looking for. There's a church there. And inside is proof.'

'Proof.' Chinita stopped polishing the lens in her hand and turned to him. 'Proof that a cardinal has been murdered?'

'That's what he said.'

'You believe everything you hear?' Chinita wished, as she often did, that *she* was the one in charge. Videographers, however, were at the whim of the crazy reporters for whom they shot footage. If Gunther Glick wanted to follow a feeble phone tip, Macri was his dog on a leash.

She looked at him, sitting there in the driver's seat, his jaw set intently. The man's parents, she decided, must have been frustrated comedians to have given him a name like Gunther Glick. No wonder the guy felt like he had something to prove. Nonetheless, despite his unfortunate appellative and annoying eagerness to make a mark, Glick was sweet . . . charming in a pasty, *Briddish*, unstrung sort of way. Like Hugh Grant on lithium.

'Shouldn't we be back at St Peter's?' Macri said as patiently as possible. 'We can check this mystery church out later. Conclave started an hour ago. What if the cardinals come to a decision while we're gone?'

Glick did not seem to hear. 'I think we go to the right, here.' He tilted the map and studied it again. 'Yes, if I take a right . . . and then an immediate left.' He began to pull out onto the narrow street before them.

'Look out!' Macri yelled. She was a video technician, and her eyes were sharp. Fortunately, Glick was pretty fast too. He slammed on the brakes and

306

avoided entering the intersection just as a line of four Alfa Romeos appeared out of nowhere and tore by in a blur. Once past, the cars skidded, decelerating, and cut sharply left one block ahead, taking the exact route Glick had intended to take.

'Maniacs!' Macri shouted.

Glick looked shaken. 'Did you see that?'

'Yeah, I saw that! They almost killed us!'

'No, I mean the cars,' Glick said, his voice suddenly excited. 'They were all the same.'

'So they were maniacs with no imagination.'

'The cars were also full.'

'So what?'

'Four identical cars, *all* with four passengers?'

'You ever heard of carpooling?'

'In Italy?' Glick checked the intersection. 'They haven't even heard of unleaded gas.' He hit the accelerator and peeled out after the cars.

Macri was thrown back in her seat. 'What the hell are you doing?'

Glick accelerated down the street and hung a left after the Alfa Romeos. 'Something tells me you and I are not the only ones going to church right now.'

67

The descent was slow.

Langdon dropped rung by rung down the creaking ladder . . . deeper and deeper beneath the floor of the Chigi Chapel. *Into the Demon's hole*, he thought. He was facing the side wall, his back to the chamber, and he

307

wondered how many more dark, cramped spaces one day could provide. The ladder groaned with every step, and the pungent smell of rotting flesh and dampness was almost asphyxiating. Langdon wondered where the hell Olivetti was.

Vittoria's outline was still visible above, holding the blowtorch inside the hole, lighting Langdon's way. As he lowered himself deeper into the darkness, the bluish glow from above got fainter. The only thing that got stronger was the stench.

Twelve rungs down, it happened. Langdon's foot hit a spot that was slippery with decay, and he faltered. Lunging forward, he caught the ladder with his forearms to avoid plummeting to the bottom. Cursing the bruises now throbbing on his arms, he dragged his body back onto the ladder and began his descent again.

Three rungs deeper, he almost fell again, but this time it was not a rung that caused the mishap. It was a bolt of fear. He had descended past a hollowed niche in the wall before him and suddenly found himself face to face with a collection of skulls. As he caught his breath and looked around him, he realized the wall at this level was honeycombed with shelflike openings – burial niches – all filled with skeletons. In the phosphorescent light, it made for an eerie collection of empty sockets and decaying rib cages flickering around him.

Skeletons by firelight, he grimaced wryly, realizing he had quite coincidentally endured a similar evening just last month. *An evening of bones and flames.* The New York Museum of Archeology's candlelight benefit dinner – salmon flambé in the shadow of a brontosaurus skeleton. He had attended at the invitation of Rebecca Strauss – one-time fashion model now art critic from the *Times*, a whirlwind of black velvet, cigarettes, and not-so-subtly enhanced breasts. She'd called him twice since. Langdon had not returned her calls. *Most ungentlemanly*, he chided, wondering how long Rebecca Strauss would last in a stink-pit like this.

Langdon was relieved to feel the final rung give way to the spongy earth at the bottom. The ground beneath his shoes felt damp. Assuring himself the walls were not going to close in on him, he turned into the crypt. It was circular, about twenty feet across. Breathing through his sleeve again, Langdon turned his eyes to the body. In the gloom, the image was hazy. A white, fleshy outline. Facing the other direction. Motionless. Silent.

Advancing through the murkiness of the crypt, Langdon tried to make sense of what he was looking at. The man had his back to Langdon, and Langdon could not see his face, but he *did* indeed seem to be standing.

'Hello?' Langdon choked through his sleeve. Nothing. As he drew nearer, he realized the man was very short. *Too short . . .*

'What's happening?' Vittoria called from above, shifting the light.

Langdon did not answer. He was now close enough to see it all. With a tremor of repulsion, he understood. The chamber seemed to contract around him. Emerging like a demon from the earthen floor was an old man . . . or at least half of him. He was buried up to his waist in the earth. Standing upright with half of him below ground. Stripped naked. His hands tied behind his back with a red cardinal's sash. He was

309

propped limply upward, spine arched backward like some sort of hideous punching bag. The man's head lay backward, eyes toward the heavens as if pleading for help from God himself.

'Is he dead?' Vittoria called.

Langdon moved toward the body. *I hope so, for his sake.* As he drew to within a few feet, he looked down at the upturned eyes. They bulged outward, blue and bloodshot. Langdon leaned down to listen for breath but immediately recoiled. 'For Christ's sake!'

'What!'

Langdon almost gagged. 'He's dead all right. I just saw the cause of death.' The sight was gruesome. The man's mouth had been jammed open and packed solid with dirt. 'Somebody stuffed a fistful of dirt down his throat. He suffocated.'

'Dirt?' Vittoria said. 'As in . . . *earth*?'

Langdon did a double take. *Earth.* He had almost forgotten. *The brands. Earth, Air, Fire, Water.* The killer had threatened to brand each victim with one of the ancient elements of science. The first element was *Earth. From Santi's earthly tomb.* Dizzy from the fumes, Langdon circled to the front of the body. As he did, the symbologist within him loudly reasserted the artistic challenge of creating the mythical ambigram. *Earth? How?* And yet, an instant later, it was before him. Centuries of Illuminati legend whirled in his mind. The marking on the cardinal's chest was charred and oozing. The flesh was seared black. *La lingua pura . . .*

Langdon stared at the brand as the room began to spin.

'Earth,' he whispered, tilting his head to see the symbol upside down. 'Earth.'

Then, in a wave of horror, he had one final cognition. *There are three more.*

68

Despite the soft glow of candlelight in the Sistine Chapel, Cardinal Mortati was on edge. Conclave had officially begun. And it had begun in a most inauspicious fashion.

Half an hour ago, at the appointed hour, Camerlengo Carlo Ventresca had entered the chapel. He walked to the front altar and gave opening prayer. Then, he unfolded his hands and spoke to them in a tone as direct as anything Mortati had ever heard from the altar of the Sistine.

'You are well aware,' the camerlengo said, 'that our four *preferiti* are not present in conclave at this moment. I ask, in the name of his late Holiness, that you proceed as you must . . . with faith and purpose. May you have only God before your eyes.' Then he turned to go.

'But,' one cardinal blurted out, 'where *are* they?'

The camerlengo paused. 'That I cannot honestly say.'

'When will they return?'

'That I cannot honestly say.'

'Are they okay?'

'That I cannot honestly say.'

'*Will* they return?'

There was a long pause.

'Have faith,' the camerlengo said. Then he walked out of the room.

The doors to the Sistine Chapel had been sealed, as was the custom, with two heavy chains on the outside. Four Swiss Guards stood watch in the hallway beyond. Mortati knew the only way the doors could be opened now, prior to electing a Pope, was if someone inside fell deathly ill, or if the *preferiti* arrived. Mortati prayed it would be the latter, although from the knot in his stomach he was not so sure.

Proceed as we must, Mortati decided, taking his lead from the resolve in the camerlengo's voice. So he had called for a vote. What else could he do?

It had taken thirty minutes to complete the preparatory rituals leading up to this first vote. Mortati had waited patiently at the main altar as each cardinal, in order of seniority, had approached and performed the specific balloting procedure.

Now, at last, the final cardinal had arrived at the altar and was kneeling before him.

'I call as my witness,' the cardinal declared, exactly as those before him, 'Christ the Lord, who will be my judge that my vote is given to the one who before God I think should be elected.'

The cardinal stood up. He held his ballot high over his head for everyone to see. Then he lowered the ballot to the altar, where a plate sat atop a large chalice. He placed the ballot on the plate. Next he picked up the plate and used it to drop the ballot into the chalice. Use of the plate was to ensure no one secretly dropped multiple ballots.

After he had submitted his ballot, he replaced the plate over the chalice, bowed to the cross, and returned to his seat.

The final ballot had been cast.

Now it was time for Mortati to go to work.

Leaving the plate on top of the chalice, Mortati shook the ballots to mix them. Then he removed the plate and extracted a ballot at random. He unfolded it. The ballot was exactly two inches wide. He read aloud for everyone to hear.

'*Eligo in summum pontificem* . . .' he declared, reading the text that was embossed at the top of every ballot. *I elect as Supreme Pontiff* . . . Then he announced the nominee's name that had been written beneath it. After he read the name, he raised a threaded needle and pierced the ballot through the word *Eligo*, carefully sliding the ballot onto the thread. Then he made note of the vote in a logbook.

Next, he repeated the entire procedure. He chose a ballot from the chalice, read it aloud, threaded it onto the line, and made note in his log. Almost immediately, Mortati sensed this first vote would be failed. No consensus. After only seven ballots, already seven different cardinals had been named. As was normal, the handwriting on each ballot was disguised by block printing or flamboyant script. The concealment was ironic in this case because the cardinals were obviously submitting votes for themselves. This apparent conceit, Mortati knew, had nothing to do with self-centered ambition. It was a holding pattern. A defensive maneuver. A stall tactic to ensure no cardinal received enough votes to win ... and another vote would be forced.

The cardinals were waiting for their *preferiti* ...

When the last of the ballots had been tallied, Mortati declared the vote 'failed'.

He took the thread carrying all the ballots and tied the ends together to create a ring. Then he laid the ring of ballots on a silver tray. He added the proper chemicals and carried the tray to a small chimney behind him. Here he lit the ballots. As the ballots burned, the chemicals he'd added created black smoke. The smoke flowed up a pipe to a hole in the roof where it rose above the chapel for all to see. Cardinal Mortati had just sent his first communication to the outside world.

One balloting. No Pope.

69

Nearly asphyxiated by fumes, Langdon struggled up the ladder toward the light at the top of the pit. Above him he heard voices, but nothing making sense. His head was spinning with images of the branded cardinal.

Earth ... Earth ...

As he pushed upward, his vision narrowed and he

feared consciousness would slip away. Two rungs from the top, his balance faltered. He lunged upward trying to find the lip, but it was too far. He lost his grip on the ladder and almost tumbled backward into the dark. There was a sharp pain under his arms, and suddenly Langdon was airborne, legs swinging wildly out over the chasm.

The strong hands of two Swiss Guards hooked him under the armpits and dragged him skyward. A moment later Langdon's head emerged from the Demon's hole, choking and gasping for air. The guards dragged him over the lip of the opening, across the floor, and laid him down, back against the cold marble floor.

For a moment, Langdon was unsure where he was. Overhead he saw stars .. orbiting planets. Hazy figures raced past him. People were shouting. He tried to sit up. He was lying at the base of a stone pyramid. The familiar bite of an angry tongue echoed inside the chapel, and then Langdon knew.

Olivetti was screaming at Vittoria. 'Why the hell didn't you figure that out in the first place?'

Vittoria was trying the explain the situation.

Olivetti cut her off midsentence and turned to bark orders to his men. 'Get that body out of there! Search the rest of the building!'

Langdon tried to sit up. The Chigi Chapel was packed with Swiss Guards. The plastic curtain over the chapel opening had been torn off the entryway, and fresh air filled Langdon's lungs. As his senses slowly returned, Langdon saw Vittoria coming toward him. She knelt down, her face like an angel.

'You okay?' Vittoria took his arm and felt his pulse. Her hands were tender on his skin.

'Thanks.' Langdon sat up fully. 'Olivetti's mad.'

Vittoria nodded. 'He has a right to be. We blew it.'

'You mean *I* blew it.'

'So redeem yourself. Get him next time.'

Next time? Langdon thought it was a cruel comment. *There is no next time! We missed our shot!*

Vittoria checked Langdon's watch. 'Mickey says we've got forty minutes. Get your head together and help me find the next marker.'

'I told you, Vittoria, the sculptures are gone. The Path of Illumination is—' Langdon halted.

Vittoria smiled softly.

Suddenly Langdon was staggering to his feet. He turned dizzying circles, staring at the artwork around him. *Pyramids, stars, planets, ellipses.* Suddenly everything came back. *This is the first altar of science! Not the Pantheon!* It dawned on him now how perfectly Illuminati the chapel was, far more subtle and selective than the world famous Pantheon. The Chigi was an out of the way alcove, a literal hole-in-the-wall, a tribute to a great patron of science, decorated with earthly symbology. *Perfect.*

Langdon steadied himself against the wall and gazed up at the enormous pyramid sculptures. Vittoria was dead right. If *this* chapel was the first altar of science, it might still contain the Illuminati sculpture that served as the first marker. Langdon felt an electrifying rush of hope to realize there was still a chance. If the marker were indeed here, and they could follow it to the next altar of science, they might have another chance to catch the killer.

Vittoria moved closer. 'I found out who the unknown Illuminati sculptor was.'

Langdon's head whipped around. 'You *what*?'

'Now we just need to figure out which sculpture in here is the—'

'Wait a minute! You *know* who the Illuminati sculptor was?' He had spent years trying to find that information.

Vittoria smiled. 'It was Bernini.' She paused. '*The* Bernini.'

Langdon immediately knew she was mistaken. Bernini was an impossibility. Gianlorenzo Bernini was the second most famous sculptor of all time, his fame eclipsed only by Michelangelo himself. During the 1600s Bernini created more sculptures than any other artist. Unfortunately, the man they were looking for was supposedly an unknown, a nobody.

Vittoria frowned. 'You don't look excited.'

'Bernini is impossible.'

'Why? Bernini was a contemporary of Galileo. He was a brilliant sculptor.'

'He was a very famous man and a Catholic.'

'Yes,' Vittoria said. 'Exactly like Galileo.'

'No,' Langdon argued. '*Nothing* like Galileo. Galileo was a thorn in the Vatican's side. Bernini was the Vatican's wonder boy. The church *loved* Bernini. He was elected the Vatican's overall artistic authority. He practically lived inside Vatican City his entire life!'

'A perfect cover. Illuminati infiltration.'

Langdon felt flustered. 'Vittoria, the Illuminati members referred to their secret artist as *il maestro ignoto* – the unknown master.'

'Yes, unknown to *them*. Think of the secrecy of the Masons – only the upper-echelon members knew the whole truth. Galileo could have kept Bernini's true identity secret from most members . . . for Bernini's own safety. That way, the Vatican would never find out.'

Langdon was unconvinced but had to admit Vittoria's logic made strange sense. The Illuminati were famous for keeping secret information compartmentalized, only revealing the truth to upper-level members. It was the cornerstone of their ability to stay secret . . . very few knew the whole story.

'And Bernini's affiliation with the Illuminati,' Vittoria added with a smile, 'explains why he designed those two pyramids.'

Langdon turned to the huge sculpted pyramids and shook his head. 'Bernini was a *religious* sculptor. There's no way he carved those pyramids.'

Vittoria shrugged. 'Tell that to the sign behind you.'

Langdon turned to the plaque:

ART OF THE CHIGI CHAPEL
While the architecture is Raphael's,
all interior adornments are those of Gianlorenzo Bernini.

Langdon read the plaque twice, and still he was not convinced. Gianlorenzo Bernini was celebrated for his intricate, holy sculptures of the Virgin Mary, angels, prophets, Popes. What was he doing carving *pyramids*?

Langdon looked up at the towering monuments and felt totally disoriented. Two pyramids, each with a shining, elliptical medallion. They were about as un-Christian as sculpture could get. The pyramids, the stars above, the signs of the Zodiac. *All interior adornments are those of Gianlorenzo Bernini.* If that were true, Langdon realized, it meant Vittoria *had* to be right. By default, Bernini was the Illuminati's unknown master; nobody else had contributed artwork to this chapel! The implications came almost too fast for Langdon to process.

Bernini was an Illuminatus.
Bernini designed the Illuminati ambigrams.
Bernini laid out the path of Illumination.

Langdon could barely speak. Could it be that here in this tiny Chigi Chapel, the world-renowned Bernini had placed a sculpture that pointed across Rome toward the next altar of science?

'Bernini,' he said. 'I never would have guessed.'

'Who other than a famous Vatican artist would have had the clout to put his artwork in specific Catholic chapels around Rome and create the Path of Illumination? Certainly not an unknown.'

Langdon considered it. He looked at the pyramids, wondering if one of them could somehow be the marker. *Maybe both of them?* 'The pyramids face opposite directions,' Langdon said, not sure what to make of them. 'They are also identical, so I don't know which . . .'

'I don't think the pyramids are what we're looking for.'

'But they're the only sculptures here.'

Vittoria cut him off by pointing toward Olivetti and some of his guards who were gathered near the demon's hole.

Langdon followed the line of her hand to the far wall. At first he saw nothing. Then someone moved and he caught a glimpse. White marble. An arm. A torso. And then a sculpted face. Partially hidden in its niche. Two life-size human figures intertwined. Langdon's pulse accelerated. He had been so taken with the pyramids and demon's hole, he had not even seen this sculpture. He moved across the room, through the crowd. As he drew near, Langdon recognized the work was pure Bernini – the intensity of the artistic composition, the intricate faces and flowing clothing, all from the purest white marble Vatican money could buy. It was not until he was almost directly in front of it that Langdon recognized the sculpture itself. He stared up at the two faces and gasped.

'Who are they?' Vittoria urged, arriving behind him.

Langdon stood astonished. '*Habakkuk and the Angel*,' he said, his voice almost inaudible. The piece was a fairly well-known Bernini work that was included in some art history texts. Langdon had forgotten it was here.

'Habakkuk?'

'Yes. The prophet who predicted the annihilation of the earth.'

Vittoria looked uneasy. 'You think this is the marker?'

Langdon nodded in amazement. Never in his life had he been so sure of anything. This was the first Illuminati marker. No doubt. Although Langdon had fully expected the sculpture to somehow 'point' to the next altar of science, he did not expect it to be *literal*. Both the angel and Habakkuk had their arms outstretched and were pointing into the distance.

Langdon found himself suddenly smiling. 'Not too subtle, is it?'

Vittoria looked excited but confused. 'I see them pointing, but they are contradicting each other. The angel is pointing one way, and the prophet the other.'

Langdon chuckled. It was true. Although both figures were pointing into the distance, they were pointing in totally opposite directions. Langdon, however, had already solved that problem. With a burst of energy he headed for the door.

'Where are you going?' Vittoria called.

'Outside the building!' Langdon's legs felt light again as he ran toward the door. 'I need to see what direction that sculpture is pointing!'

'Wait! How do you know *which* finger to follow?'

'The poem,' he called over his shoulder. 'The last line!'

' "Let angels guide you on your lofty quest?" ' She gazed upward at the outstretched finger of the angel. Her eyes misted unexpectedly. 'Well I'll be damned!'

70

Gunther Glick and Chinita Macri sat parked in the BBC van in the shadows at the far end of Piazza del Popolo. They had arrived shortly after the four Alfa Romeos, just in time to witness an inconceivable chain of events. Chinita still had no idea what it all meant, but she'd made sure the camera was rolling.

As soon as they'd arrived, Chinita and Glick had seen a veritable army of young men pour out of the Alfa Romeos and surround the church. Some had weapons drawn. One of them, a stiff older man, led a team up the front steps of the church. The soldiers drew guns and blew the locks off the front doors. Macri heard nothing and figured they must have had silencers. Then the soldiers entered.

Chinita had recommended they sit tight and film from the shadows. After all, guns were guns, and they had a clear view of the action from the van. Glick had not argued. Now, across the piazza, men moved in and out of the church. They yelled to each other. Chinita adjusted her camera to follow a team as they searched the surrounding area. All of them, though dressed in civilian clothes, seemed to move with military precision. 'Who do you think they are?' she asked.

'Hell if I know.' Glick looked riveted. 'You getting all this?'

'Every frame.'

Glick sounded smug. 'Still think we should go back to Pope-Watch?'

Chinita wasn't sure what to say. There was obviously something going on here, but she had been in journalism long enough to know that there was often a very dull explanation for interesting events. 'This could be nothing,' she said. 'These guys could have gotten the same tip you got and are just checking it out. Could be a false alarm.'

Glick grabbed her arm. 'Over there! Focus.' He pointed back to the church.

Chinita swung the camera back to the top of the stairs. 'Hello there,' she said, training on the man now emerging from the church.

'Who's the dapper?'

Chinita moved in for a close-up. 'Haven't seen him before.' She tightened in on the man's face and smiled. 'But I wouldn't mind seeing him again.'

Robert Langdon dashed down the stairs outside the church and into the middle of the piazza. It was getting dark now, the springtime sun setting late in southern Rome. The sun had dropped below the surrounding buildings, and shadows streaked the square.

'Okay, Bernini,' he said aloud to himself. 'Where the hell is your angel pointing?'

He turned and examined the orientation of the church from which he had just come. He pictured the Chigi Chapel inside, and the sculpture of the angel inside that. Without hesitation he turned due west, into the glow of the impending sunset. Time was evaporating.

'Southwest,' he said, scowling at the shops and apartments blocking his view. 'The next marker is out there.'

Racking his brain, Langdon pictured page after page of Italian art history. Although very familiar with Bernini's work, Langdon knew the sculptor had been far too prolific for any nonspecialist to know all of it. Still, considering the relative fame of the first marker – *Habakkuk and the Angel* – Langdon hoped the second marker was a work he might know from memory.

Earth, Air, Fire, Water, he thought. *Earth* they had found – inside the Chapel of the Earth – Habakkuk, the prophet who predicted the earth's annihilation.

Air is next. Langdon urged himself to think. *A Bernini sculpture that has something to do with Air!* He was drawing a total blank. Still he felt energized. *I'm on the path of Illumination! It is still intact!*

Looking southwest, Langdon strained to see a spire or cathedral tower jutting up over the obstacles. He saw nothing. He needed a map. If they could figure out what churches were southwest of here, maybe one of them would spark Langdon's memory. *Air,* he pressed. *Air. Bernini. Sculpture. Air. Think!*

Langdon turned and headed back up the cathedral stairs. He was met beneath the scaffolding by Vittoria and Olivetti.

'Southwest,' Langdon said, panting. 'The next church is southwest of here.'

Olivetti's whisper was cold. 'You sure this time?'

Langdon didn't bite. 'We need a map. One that shows all the churches in Rome.'

The commander studied him a moment, his expression never changing.

Langdon checked his watch. 'We only have half an hour.'

Olivetti moved past Langdon down the stairs toward his car, parked directly in front of the cathedral. Langdon hoped he was going for a map.

Vittoria looked excited. 'So the angel's pointing southwest? No idea which churches are southwest?'

'I can't see past the damn buildings.' Langdon turned and faced the square again. 'And I don't know Rome's churches well enou—' He stopped.

Vittoria looked startled. 'What?'

Langdon looked out at the piazza again. Having ascended the church stairs, he was now higher, and his view was better. He still couldn't see anything, but he realized he was moving in the right direction. His eyes climbed the tower of rickety scaffolding above him. It rose six stories, almost to the top of the church's rose window, far higher than the other buildings in the square. He knew in an instant where he was headed.

Across the square, Chinita Macri and Gunther Glick sat glued to the windshield of the BBC van.

'You getting this?' Gunther asked.

Macri tightened her shot on the man now climbing the scaffolding. 'He's a little well dressed to be playing Spiderman if you ask me.'

'And who's Ms Spidey?'

Chinita glanced at the attractive woman beneath the scaffolding. 'Bet you'd like to find out.'

'Think I should call editorial?'

'Not yet. Let's watch. Better to have something in the can before we admit we abandoned conclave.'

'You think somebody really killed one of the old farts in there?'

Chinita clucked. 'You're *definitely* going to hell.'

'And I'll be taking the Pulitzer with me.'

71

The scaffolding seemed less stable the higher Langdon climbed. His view of Rome, however, got better with every step. He continued upward.

He was breathing harder than he expected when he reached the upper tier. He pulled himself onto the last platform, brushed off the plaster, and stood up. The height did not bother him at all. In fact, it was invigorating.

The view was staggering. Like an ocean on fire, the red-tiled rooftops of Rome spread out before him, glowing in the scarlet sunset. From that spot, for the first time in his life, Langdon saw beyond the pollution and traffic of Rome to its ancient roots – *Città di Dio* – The city of God.

Squinting into the sunset, Langdon scanned the rooftops for a church steeple or bell tower. But as he looked farther and farther toward the horizon, he saw nothing. *There are hundreds of churches in Rome*, he thought. *There must be one southwest of here! If the church is even visible*, he reminded himself. *Hell, if the church is even still standing!*

Forcing his eyes to trace the line slowly, he attempted the search again. He knew, of course, that not all churches would have visible spires, especially smaller, out-of-the-way sanctuaries. Not to mention, Rome had changed dramatically since the 1600s when churches were by law the tallest buildings allowed. Now, as Langdon looked out, he saw apartment buildings, high-rises, TV towers.

For the second time, Langdon's eye reached the horizon without seeing anything. Not one single spire. In the distance, on the very edge of Rome, Michelangelo's massive dome blotted the setting sun. St Peter's Basilica. Vatican City. Langdon found himself wondering how the cardinals were faring, and if the Swiss Guards' search had turned up the antimatter. Something told him it hadn't . . . and wouldn't.

The poem was rattling through his head again. He considered it, carefully, line by line. *From Santi's earthly tomb with demon's hole*. They had found Santi's tomb. *'Cross Rome the mystic elements unfold*. The mystic elements were Earth, Air, Fire, Water. *The path of light is laid, the sacred test*. The path of Illumination formed by Bernini's sculptures. *Let angels guide you on your lofty quest*.

The angel was pointing southwest . . .

'Front stairs!' Glick exclaimed, pointing wildly through the windshield of the BBC van. 'Something's going on!'

Macri dropped her shot back down to the main entrance. Something was definitely going on. At the bottom of the stairs, the military-looking man had pulled one of the Alfa Romeos close to the stairs and opened the trunk. Now he was scanning the square as if checking for onlookers. For a moment, Macri thought the man had spotted them, but his eyes kept moving. Apparently satisfied, he pulled out a walkie-talkie and spoke into it.

Almost instantly, it seemed an army emerged from the church. Like an American football team breaking from a huddle, the soldiers formed a straight line across the top of the stairs. Moving like a human wall, they began to descend. Behind them, almost entirely hidden by the wall, four soldiers seemed to be carrying something. Something heavy. Awkward.

Glick leaned forward on the dashboard. 'Are they stealing something from the church?'

Chinita tightened her shot even more, using the telephoto to probe the wall of men, looking for an opening. *One split second*, she willed. *A single frame. That's all I need.* But the men moved as one. *Come on!* Macri stayed with them, and it paid off. When the soldiers tried to lift the object into the trunk, Macri found her opening. Ironically, it was the older man who faltered. Only for an instant, but long enough. Macri had her frame. Actually, it was more like ten frames.

'Call editorial,' Chinita said. 'We've got a dead body.'

Far away, at CERN, Maximilian Kohler maneuvered his wheelchair into Leonardo Vetra's study. With mechanical efficiency, he began sifting through Vetra's files. Not finding what he was after, Kohler moved to Vetra's bedroom. The top drawer of his bedside table was locked. Kohler pried it open with a knife from the kitchen.

Inside Kohler found exactly what he was looking for.

72

Langdon swung off the scaffolding and dropped back to the ground. He brushed the plaster dust from his clothes. Vittoria was there to greet him.

'No luck?' she said.

He shook his head.

'They put the cardinal in the trunk.'

Langdon looked over to the parked car where Olivetti and a group of soldiers now had a map spread out on the hood. 'Are they looking southwest?'

She nodded. 'No churches. From here the first one you hit is St Peter's.'

Langdon grunted. At least they were in agreement. He moved toward Olivetti. The soldiers parted to let him through.

Olivetti looked up. 'Nothing. But this doesn't show every last church. Just the big ones. About fifty of them.'

'Where are we?' Langdon asked.

Olivetti pointed to Piazza del Popolo and traced a straight line exactly southwest. The line missed, by a substantial margin, the cluster of black squares indicating Rome's major churches. Unfortunately, Rome's major churches were also Rome's older churches ... those that would have been around in the 1600s.

'I've got some decisions to make,' Olivetti said. 'Are you *certain* of the direction?'

Langdon pictured the angel's outstretched finger, the urgency rising in him again. 'Yes, sir. Positive.'

Olivetti shrugged and traced the straight line again. The path intersected the Queen Margherita Bridge, Via Cola di Riezo, and passed through Piazza del Risorgimento, hitting no churches at all until it dead-ended abruptly at the center of St Peter's Square.

'What's wrong with St Peter's?' one of the soldiers said. He had a deep scar under his left eye. 'It's a church.'

Langdon shook his head. 'Needs to be a public place. Hardly seems public at the moment.'

'But the line goes through St Peter's *Square*,' Vittoria added, looking over Langdon's shoulder. 'The square is public.'

Langdon had already considered it. 'No statues, though.'

'Isn't there a monolith in the middle?'

She was right. There was an Egyptian monolith in St Peter's Square. Langdon looked out at the monolith in the piazza in front of them. *The lofty pyramid.* An odd coincidence, he thought. He shook it off. 'The Vatican's monolith is not by Bernini. It was brought in by Caligula. And it has nothing to do with *Air*.' There was another problem as well. 'Besides, the poem says the elements are spread across *Rome*. St Peter's Square is in Vatican City. Not Rome.'

'Depends who you ask,' a guard interjected.

Langdon looked up. 'What?'

'Always a bone of contention. Most maps show St Peter's Square as part of Vatican City, but because it's *outside* the walled city, Roman officials for centuries have claimed it as part of Rome.'

'You're kidding,' Langdon said. He had never known that.

'I only mention it,' the guard continued, 'because Commander Olivetti and Ms Vetra were asking about a sculpture that had to do with Air.'

Langdon was wide-eyed. 'And you know of one in St Peter's Square?'

'Not exactly. It's not really a sculpture. Probably not relevant.'

'Let's hear it,' Olivetti pressed.

The guard shrugged. 'The only reason I know about it is because I'm usually on piazza duty. I know every corner of St Peter's Square.'

'The sculpture,' Langdon urged. 'What does it look like?' Langdon was starting to wonder if the Illuminati could really have been gutsy enough to position their second marker right outside St Peter's Church.

'I patrol past it every day,' the guard said. 'It's in the center, directly where that line is pointing. That's what made me think of it. As I said, it's not really a sculpture. It's more of a . . . block.'

Olivetti looked mad. 'A block?'

'Yes, sir. A marble block embedded in the square. At the base of the monolith. But the block is not a rectangle. It's an ellipse. And the block is carved with the image of a billowing gust of wind.' He paused. '*Air*, I suppose, if you wanted to get scientific about it.'

Langdon stared at the young soldier in amazement. 'A relief!' he exclaimed suddenly.

Everyone looked at him.

'*Relief*,' Langdon said, 'is the other half of sculpture!' *Sculpture is the art of shaping figures in the round and also in relief.* He had written the definition on chalkboards for years. Reliefs were essentially two-dimensional sculptures, like Abraham Lincoln's profile on the penny. Bernini's Chigi Chapel medallions were another perfect example.

'*Bassorelievo?*' the guard asked, using the Italian art term.

'Yes! *Bas-relief!*' Langdon rapped his knuckles on the hood. 'I wasn't thinking in those terms! That tile you're talking about in St Peter's Square is called the *West Ponente* – the West Wind. It's also known as *Respiro di Dio.*'

'Breath of God?'

'Yes! *Air!* And it was carved and put there by the original architect!'

Vittoria looked confused. 'But I thought Michelangelo designed St Peter's.'

'Yes, the *basilica*!' Langdon exclaimed, triumph in his voice. 'But St Peter's *Square* was designed by Bernini!'

As the caravan of Alfa Romeos tore out of Piazza del Popolo, everyone was in too much of a hurry to notice the BBC van pulling out behind them.

73

Gunther Glick floored the BBC van's accelerator and swerved through traffic as he tailed the four speeding Alfa Romeos across the Tiber River on Ponte Margherita. Normally Glick would have made an effort to maintain an inconspicuous distance, but today he could barely keep up. These guys were flying.

Macri sat in her work area in the back of the van finishing a phone call with London. She hung up and yelled to Glick over the sound of the traffic. 'You want the good news or bad news?'

Glick frowned. Nothing was ever simple when dealing with the home office. 'Bad news.'

'Editorial is burned we abandoned our post.'

'Surprise.'

'They also think your tipster is a fraud.'

'Of course.'

'And the boss just warned me that you're a few crumpets short of a proper tea.'

Glick scowled. 'Great. And the good news?'

'They agreed to look at the footage we just shot.'

Glick felt his scowl soften into a grin. *I guess we'll see who's short a few crumpets.* 'So fire it off.'

'Can't transmit until we stop and get a fixed cell read.'

Glick gunned the van onto Via Cola di Rienzo. 'Can't stop now.' He tailed the Alfa Romeos through a hard left swerve around Piazza Risorgimento.

Macri held on to her computer gear in back as everything slid. 'Break my transmitter,' she warned, 'and we'll have to *walk* this footage to London.'

'Sit tight, love. Something tells me we're almost there.'

Macri looked up. 'Where?'

Glick gazed out at the familiar dome now looming directly in front of them. He smiled. 'Right back where we started.'

The four Alfa Romeos slipped deftly into traffic surrounding St Peter's Square. They split up and spread out along the piazza perimeter, quietly unloading men at select points. The debarking guards moved into the throng of tourists and media vans on the edge of the square and instantly became invisible. Some of the guards entered the forest of pillars encompassing the colonnade. They too seemed to evaporate into the surroundings. As Langdon watched through the windshield, he sensed a noose tightening around St Peter's.

332

In addition to the men Olivetti had just dispatched, the commander had radioed ahead to the Vatican and sent additional undercover guards to the center where Bernini's *West Ponente* was located. As Langdon looked out at the wide-open spaces of St Peter's Square, a familiar question nagged. *How does the Illuminati assassin plan to get away with this? How will he get a cardinal through all these people and kill him in plain view?* Langdon checked his Mickey Mouse watch. It was 8.54 P.M. Six minutes.

In the front seat, Olivetti turned and faced Langdon and Vittoria. 'I want you two right on top of this Bernini brick or block or whatever the hell it is. Same drill. You're tourists. Use the phone if you see anything.'

Before Langdon could respond, Vittoria had his hand and was pulling him out of the car.

The springtime sun was setting behind St Peter's Basilica, and a massive shadow spread, engulfing the piazza. Langdon felt an ominous chill as he and Vittoria moved into the cool, black umbra. Snaking through the crowd, Langdon found himself searching every face they passed, wondering if the killer was among them. Vittoria's hand felt warm.

As they crossed the open expanse of St Peter's Square, Langdon sensed Bernini's sprawling piazza having the exact effect the artist had been commissioned to create – that of 'humbling all those who entered.' Langdon certainly felt humbled at the moment. *Humbled and hungry*, he realized, surprised such a mundane thought could enter his head at a moment like this.

'To the obelisk?' Vittoria asked.

Langdon nodded, arching left across the piazza.

'Time?' Vittoria asked, walking briskly, but casually.
'Five of.'

Vittoria said nothing, but Langdon felt her grip tighten. He was still carrying the gun. He hoped Vittoria would not decide she needed it. He could not imagine her whipping out a weapon in St Peter's Square and blowing away the kneecaps of some killer while the global media looked on. Then again, an incident like that would be nothing compared to the branding and murder of a cardinal out here.

Air, Langdon thought. *The second element of science.* He tried to picture the brand. The method of murder. Again he scanned the sprawling expanse of granite beneath his feet – St Peter's Square – an open desert surrounded by Swiss Guard. If the Hassassin really dared attempt this, Langdon could not imagine how he would escape.

In the center of the piazza rose Caligula's 350-ton Egyptian obelisk. It stretched eighty-one feet skyward to the pyramidal apex onto which was affixed a hollow iron cross. Sufficiently high to catch the last of the evening sun, the cross shone as if magic ... purportedly containing relics of the cross on which Christ was crucified.

Two fountains flanked the obelisk in perfect symmetry. Art historians knew the fountains marked the exact geometric focal points of Bernini's elliptical piazza, but it was an architectural oddity Langdon had never really considered until today. It seemed Rome was suddenly filled with ellipses, pyramids, and startling geometry.

As they neared the obelisk, Vittoria slowed. She exhaled heavily, as if coaxing Langdon to relax along with her. Langdon made the effort, lowering his shoulders and loosening his clenched jaw

Somewhere around the obelisk, boldly positioned outside the largest church in the world, was the second altar of science – Bernini's *West Ponente* – an elliptical block in St Peter's Square.

Gunther Glick watched from the shadows of the pillars surrounding St Peter's Square. On any other day the man in the tweed jacket and the woman in khaki shorts would not have interested him in the least. They appeared to be nothing but tourists enjoying the square. But today was not any other day. Today had been a day of phone tips, corpses, unmarked cars racing through Rome, and men in tweed jackets climbing scaffolding in search of God only knew what. Glick would stay with them.

He looked out across the square and saw Macri. She was exactly where he had told her to go, on the far side of the couple, hovering on their flank. Macri carried her video camera casually, but despite her imitation of a bored member of the press, she stood out more than Glick would have liked. No other reporters were in this far corner of the square, and the acronym 'BBC' stenciled on her camera was drawing some looks from tourists.

The tape Macri had shot earlier of the naked body dumped in the trunk was playing at this very moment on the VCR transmitter back in the van. Glick knew the images were sailing over his head right now en route to London. He wondered what editorial would say.

He wished he and Macri had reached the body sooner, before the army of plainclothed soldiers had intervened. The same army, he knew, had now fanned out and surrounded this piazza. Something big was about to happen.

The media is the right arm of anarchy, the killer had said. Glick wondered if he had missed his chance for a big scoop. He looked out at the other media vans in the distance and watched Macri tailing the mysterious couple across the piazza. Something told Glick he was still in the game . . .

74

Langdon saw what he was looking for a good ten yards before they reached it. Through the scattered tourists, the white marble ellipse of Bernini's *West Ponente* stood out against the gray granite cubes that made up the rest of the piazza. Vittoria apparently saw it too. Her hand tensed.

'Relax,' Langdon whispered. 'Do your piranha thing.'

Vittoria loosened her grip.

As they drew nearer, everything seemed for-biddingly normal. Tourists wandered, nuns chatted along the perimeter of the piazza, a girl fed pigeons at the base of the obelisk.

Langdon refrained from checking his watch. He knew it was almost time.

The elliptical stone arrived beneath their feet, and Langdon and Vittoria slowed to a stop – not over-eagerly – just two tourists pausing dutifully at a point of mild interest.

'*West Ponente,*' Vittoria said, reading the inscription on the stone.

Langdon gazed down at the marble relief and felt suddenly naïve. Not in his art books, not in his numerous trips to Rome, not *ever* had *West Ponente's* significance jumped out at him.

Not until now.

The relief was elliptical, about three feet long, and carved with a rudimentary face – a depiction of the West Wind as an angel-like countenance. Gusting from the angel's mouth, Bernini had drawn a powerful breath of air blowing outward away from the Vatican . . . *the breath of God*. This was Bernini's tribute to the second element . . . Air . . . an ethereal zephyr blown from angel's lips. As Langdon stared, he realized the significance of the relief went deeper still. Bernini had carved the air in *five* distinct gusts. . . . five! What was more, flanking the medallion were *two* shining stars. Langdon thought of Galileo. *Two stars, five gusts, ellipses, symmetry* . . . He felt hollow. His head hurt.

Vittoria began walking again almost immediately, leading Langdon away from the relief. 'I think someone's following us,' she said.

Langdon looked up. 'Where?'

Vittoria moved a good thirty yards before speaking. She pointed up at the Vatican as if showing Langdon something on the dome. 'The same person has been behind us all the way across the square.' Casually, Vittoria glanced over her shoulder. 'Still on us. Keep moving.'

'You think it's the Hassassin?'

Vittoria shook her head. 'Not unless the Illuminati hires women with BBC cameras.'

When the bells of St Peter's began their deafening clamor, both Langdon and Vittoria jumped. It was time. They had circled away from *West Ponente* in an attempt to lose the reporter but were now moving back toward the relief

Despite the clanging bells, the area seemed perfectly calm. Tourists wandered. A homeless drunk dozed awkwardly at the base of the obelisk. A little girl fed pigeons. Langdon wondered if the reporter had scared the killer off. *Doubtful,* he decided, recalling the killer's promise. *I will make your cardinals media luminaries.*

As the echo of the ninth bell faded away, a peaceful silence descended across the square.

Then . . . the little girl began to scream.

75

Langdon was the first to reach the screaming girl.

The terrified youngster stood frozen, pointing at the base of the obelisk where a shabby, decrepit drunk sat slumped on the stairs. The man was a miserable sight . . . apparently one of Rome's homeless. His gray hair hung in greasy strands in front of his face, and his entire body was wrapped in some sort of dirty cloth. The girl kept screaming as she scampered off into the crowd.

Langdon felt an upsurge of dread as he dashed toward the invalid. There was a dark, widening stain spreading across the man's rags. Fresh, flowing blood.

Then, it was as if everything happened at once.

The old man seemed to crumple in the middle, tottering forward. Langdon lunged, but he was too late. The man pitched forward, toppled off the stairs, and hit the pavement face down. Motionless.

Langdon dropped to his knees. Vittoria arrived beside him. A crowd was gathering.

Vittoria put her fingers on the man's throat from behind. 'There's a pulse,' she declared. 'Roll him.'

Langdon was already in motion. Grasping the man's shoulders, he rolled the body. As he did, the loose rags seemed to slough away like dead flesh. The man flopped limp onto his back. Dead center of his naked chest was a wide area of charred flesh.

Vittoria gasped and pulled back.

Langdon felt paralyzed, pinned somewhere between nausea and awe. The symbol had a terrifying simplicity to it.

'Air,' Vittoria choked. 'It's . . . him.'

Swiss Guards appeared from out of nowhere, shouting orders, racing after an unseen assassin.

Nearby, a tourist explained that only minutes ago, a dark-skinned man had been kind enough to help this poor, wheezing, homeless man across the square . . . even sitting a moment on the stairs with the invalid before disappearing back into the crowd.

Vittoria ripped the rest of the rags off the man's abdomen. He had two deep puncture wounds, one on either side of the brand, just below his rib cage. She cocked the man's head back and began to administer mouth to mouth. Langdon was not prepared for what happened next. As Vittoria blew, the wounds on either side of the man's midsection hissed and sprayed blood into the air like blowholes on a whale. The salty liquid hit Langdon in the face.

Vittoria stopped short, looking horrified. 'His lungs . . .' she stammered. 'They're . . . punctured.'

Langdon wiped his eyes as he looked down at the two perforations. The holes gurgled. The cardinal's lungs were destroyed. He was gone.

Vittoria covered the body as the Swiss Guards moved in.

Langdon stood, disoriented. As he did, he saw her. The woman who had been following them earlier was crouched nearby. Her BBC video camera was shouldered, aimed, and running. She and Langdon locked eyes, and he knew she'd gotten it all. Then, like a cat, she bolted.

76

Chinita Macri was on the run. She had the story of her life.

Her video camera felt like an anchor as she lumbered across St Peter's Square, pushing through the gathering crowd. Everyone seemed to be moving in the opposite direction than her . . . *toward* the commotion. Macri was trying to get as far away as possible. The man in the tweed jacket had seen her, and now she sensed others were after her, men she could not see, closing in from all sides.

Macri was still aghast from the images she had just

recorded. She wondered if the dead man was really who she feared he was. Glick's mysterious phone contact suddenly seemed a little less crazy.

As she hurried in the direction of the BBC van, a young man with a decidedly militaristic air emerged from the crowd before her. Their eyes met, and they both stopped. Like lightning, he raised a walkie-talkie and spoke into it. Then he moved toward her. Macri wheeled and doubled back into the crowd, her heart pounding.

As she stumbled through the mass of arms and legs, she removed the spent video cassette from her camera. *Cellulose gold,* she thought, tucking the tape under her belt flush to her backside and letting her coat tails cover it. For once she was glad she carried some extra weight. *Glick, where the hell are you!*

Another soldier appeared to her left, closing in. Macri knew she had little time. She banked into the crowd again. Yanking a blank cartridge from her case, she slapped it into the camera. Then she prayed.

She was thirty yards from the BBC van when the two men materialized directly in front of her, arms folded. She was going nowhere.

'Film,' one snapped. 'Now'

Macri recoiled, wrapping her arms protectively around her camera. 'No chance.'

One of the men pulled aside his jacket, revealing a sidearm.

'So shoot me,' Macri said, amazed by the boldness of her voice.

'Film,' the first one repeated.

Where the devil is Glick? Macri stamped her foot and yelled as loudly as possible, 'I am a professional video-grapher with the BBC! By Article 12 of the Free Press

341

Act, this film is property of the British Broadcasting Corporation!'

The men did not flinch. The one with the gun took a step toward her. 'I am a lieutenant with the Swiss Guard, and by the Holy Doctrine governing the property on which you are now standing, you are subject to search and seizure.'

A crowd had started to gather now around them.

Macri yelled, 'I will not under any circumstances give you the film in this camera without speaking to my editor in London. I suggest you—'

The guards ended it. One yanked the camera out of her hands. The other forcibly grabbed her by the arm and twisted her in the direction of the Vatican. '*Grazie,*' he said, leading her through a jostling crowd.

Macri prayed they would not search her and find the tape. If she could somehow protect the film long enough to—

Suddenly, the unthinkable happened. Someone in the crowd was groping under her coat. Macri felt the video yanked away from her. She wheeled, but swallowed her words. Behind her, a breathless Gunther Glick gave her a wink and dissolved back into the crowd.

77

Robert Langdon staggered into the private bathroom adjoining the Office of the Pope. He dabbed the blood from his face and lips. The blood was not his own. It was that of Cardinal Lamassé, who had just died horribly in the crowded square outside the Vatican. *Virgin sacrifices on the altars of science.* So far, the Hassassin had made good on his threat.

Langdon felt powerless as he gazed into the mirror. His eyes were drawn, and stubble had begun to darken his cheeks. The room around him was immaculate and lavish – black marble with gold fixtures, cotton towels, and scented hand soaps.

Langdon tried to rid his mind of the bloody brand he had just seen. Air. The image stuck. He had witnessed three ambigrams since waking up this morning . . . and he knew there were two more coming.

Outside the door, it sounded as if Olivetti, the camerlengo, and Captain Rocher were debating what to do next. Apparently, the antimatter search had turned up nothing so far. Either the guards had missed the canister, or the intruder had gotten deeper inside the Vatican than Commander Olivetti had been willing to entertain.

Langdon dried his hands and face. Then he turned and looked for a urinal. No urinal. Just a bowl. He lifted the lid.

As he stood there, tension ebbing from his body, a giddy wave of exhaustion shuddered through his core. The emotions knotting his chest were so many, so incongruous. He was fatigued, running on no food or sleep, walking the Path of Illumination, traumatized by two brutal murders. Langdon felt a deepening horror over the possible outcome of this drama.

Think, he told himself. His mind was blank.

As he flushed, an unexpected realization hit him.

This is the Pope's toilet, he thought. *I just took a leak in the Pope's toilet*. He had to chuckle. *The Holy Throne.*

78

In London, a BBC technician ejected a video cassette from a satellite receiver unit and dashed across the control room floor. She burst into the office of the editor-in-chief, slammed the video into his VCR, and pressed play.

As the tape rolled, she told him about the conversation she had just had with Gunther Glick in Vatican City. In addition, BBC photo archives had just given her a positive ID on the victim in St Peter's Square.

When the editor-in-chief emerged from his office, he was ringing a cowbell. Everything in editorial stopped.

'Live in five!' the man boomed. 'On-air talent to prep! Media coordinators, I want your contacts on line! We've got a story we're selling! And we've got film!'

The market coordinators grabbed their Rolodexes.

'Film specs!' one of them yelled.

'Thirty-second trim,' the chief replied.

'Content?'

'Live homicide.'

The coordinators looked encouraged. 'Usage and licensing price?'

'A million U.S. per.'

Heads shot up. 'What!'

'You heard me! I want top of the food chain. CNN,

MSNBC, then the big three! Offer a dial-in preview. Give them five minutes to piggyback before BBC runs it.'

'What the hell happened?' someone demanded. 'The prime minister get skinned alive?'

The chief shook his head. 'Better.'

At that exact instant, somewhere in Rome, the Hassassin enjoyed a fleeting moment of repose in a comfortable chair. He admired the legendary chamber around him. *I am sitting in the Church of Illumination*, he thought. *The Illuminati lair*. He could not believe it was still here after all of these centuries.

Dutifully, he dialed the BBC reporter to whom he had spoken earlier. It was time. The world had yet to hear the most shocking news of all.

79

Vittoria Vetra sipped a glass of water and nibbled absently at some tea scones just set out by one of the Swiss Guards. She knew she should eat, but she had no appetite. The Office of the Pope was bustling now, echoing with tense conversations. Captain Rocher, Commander Olivetti, and half a dozen guards assessed the damage and debated the next move.

Robert Langdon stood nearby staring out at St Peter's Square. He looked dejected. Vittoria walked over. 'Ideas?'

He shook his head.

'Scone?'

His mood seemed to brighten at the sight of food. 'Hell yes. Thanks.' He ate voraciously.

The conversation behind them went quiet suddenly when two Swiss Guards escorted Camerlengo Ventresca through the door. If the chamberlain had looked drained before, Vittoria thought, now he looked empty.

'What happened?' the camerlengo said to Olivetti. From the look on the camerlengo's face, he appeared to have already been told the worst of it.

Olivetti's official update sounded like a battlefield casualty report. He gave the facts with flat efficacy. 'Cardinal Ebner was found dead in the church of Santa Maria del Popolo just after eight o'clock. He had been suffocated and branded with the ambigrammatic word "Earth." Cardinal Lamassé was murdered in St Peter's Square ten minutes ago. He died of perforations to the chest. He was branded with the word "Air", also ambigrammatic. The killer escaped in both instances.'

The camerlengo crossed the room and sat heavily behind the Pope's desk. He bowed his head.

'Cardinals Guidera and Baggia, however, are still alive.'

The camerlengo's head shot up, his expression pained. 'This is our consolation? Two cardinals have been murdered, commander. And the other two will obviously not be alive much longer unless you find them.'

'We will find them,' Olivetti assured. 'I am encouraged.'

'Encouraged? We've had nothing but failure.'

'Untrue. We've lost two battles, signore, but we're winning the war. The Illuminati had intended to turn

346

this evening into a media circus. So far we have thwarted their plan. Both cardinals' bodies have been recovered without incident. In addition,' Olivetti continued, 'Captain Rocher tells me he is making excellent headway on the antimatter search.'

Captain Rocher stepped forward in his red beret. Vittoria thought he looked more human somehow than the other guards – stern but not so rigid. Rocher's voice was emotional and crystalline, like a violin. 'I am hopeful we will have the canister for you within an hour, signore.'

'Captain,' the camerlengo said, 'excuse me if I seem less than hopeful, but I was under the impression that a search of Vatican City would take far more time than we have.'

'A *full* search, yes. However, after assessing the situation, I am confident the antimatter canister is located in one of our white zones – those Vatican sectors accessible to public tours – the museums and St Peter's Basilica, for example. We have already killed power in those zones and are conducting our scan.'

'You intend to search only a small *percentage* of Vatican City?'

'Yes, signore. It is highly unlikely that an intruder gained access to the inner zones of Vatican City. The fact that the missing security camera was stolen from a public access area – a stairwell in one of the museums – clearly implies that the intruder had limited access. Therefore he would only have been able to *relocate* the camera and antimatter in another public access area. It is these areas on which we are focusing our search.'

'But the intruder kidnapped four cardinals. That certainly implies deeper infiltration than we thought.'

'Not necessarily. We must remember that the

cardinals spent much of today in the Vatican museums and St Peter's Basilica, enjoying those areas without the crowds. It is probable that the missing cardinals were taken in one of these areas.'

'But how were they removed from our walls?'

'We are still assessing that.'

'I see.' The camerlengo exhaled and stood up. He walked over to Olivetti. 'Commander, I would like to hear your contingency plan for evacuation.'

'We are still formalizing that, signore. In the meantime, I am faithful Captain Rocher will find the canister.'

Rocher clicked his boots as if in appreciation of the vote of confidence. 'My men have already scanned two-thirds of the white zones. Confidence is high.'

The camerlengo did not appear to share that confidence.

At that moment the guard with a scar beneath one eye came through the door carrying a clipboard and a map. He strode toward Langdon. 'Mr Langdon? I have the information you requested on the *West Ponente*.'

Langdon swallowed his scone. 'Good. Let's have a look.'

The others kept talking while Vittoria joined Robert and the guard as they spread out the map on the Pope's desk.

The soldier pointed to St Peter's Square. 'This is where we are. The central line of *West Ponente's* breath points due east, directly away from Vatican City.' The guard traced a line with his finger from St Peter's Square across the Tiber River and up into the heart of old Rome. 'As you can see, the line passes through almost all of Rome. There are about twenty Catholic churches that fall near this line.'

Langdon slumped. *'Twenty?'*

'Maybe more.'

'Do any of the churches fall *directly* on the line?'

'Some look closer than others,' the guard said, 'but translating the exact bearing of the *West Ponente* onto a map leaves margin for error.'

Langdon looked out at St Peter's Square a moment. Then he scowled, stroking his chin. 'How about *fire*? Any of them have Bernini artwork that has to do with fire?'

Silence.

'How about obelisks?' he demanded. 'Are any of the churches located near obelisks?'

The guard began checking the map.

Vittoria saw a glimmer of hope in Langdon's eyes and realized what he was thinking. *He's right!* The first two markers had been located on or near piazzas that contained obelisks! Maybe obelisks were a theme? Soaring pyramids marking the Illuminati path? The more Vittoria thought about it, the more perfect it seemed . . . four towering beacons rising over Rome to mark the altars of science.

'It's a long shot,' Langdon said, 'but I know that many of Rome's obelisks were erected or moved during Bernini's reign. He was no doubt involved in their placement.'

'Or,' Vittoria added, 'Bernini could have placed his markers *near* existing obelisks.'

Langdon nodded. 'True.'

'Bad news,' the guard said. 'No obelisks on the line.' He traced his finger across the map. 'None even remotely close. Nothing.'

Langdon sighed.

Vittoria's shoulders slumped. She'd thought it was a

promising idea. Apparently, this was not going to be as easy as they'd hoped. She tried to stay positive. 'Robert, think. You must know of a Bernini statue relating to *fire*. Anything at all.'

'Believe me, I've been thinking. Bernini was incredibly prolific. Hundreds of works. I was hoping *West Ponente* would point to a single church. Something that would ring a bell.'

'*Fuòco*,' she pressed. '*Fire*. No Bernini titles jump out?'

Langdon shrugged. 'There's his famous sketches of *Fireworks*, but they're not sculpture, and they're in Leipzig, Germany.'

Vittoria frowned. 'And you're sure the *breath* is what indicates the direction?'

'You saw the relief, Vittoria. The design was totally symmetrical. The only indication of bearing was the breath.'

Vittoria knew he was right.

'Not to mention,' he added, 'because the *West Ponente* signifies *Air*, following the *breath* seems symbolically appropriate.'

Vittoria nodded. *So we follow the breath. But where?*

Olivetti came over. 'What have you got?'

'Too many churches,' the soldier said. 'Two dozen or so. I suppose we could put four men on each church—'

'Forget it,' Olivetti said. 'We missed this guy twice when we knew exactly where he was going to be. A mass stakeout means leaving Vatican City unprotected and canceling the search.'

'We need a reference book,' Vittoria said. 'An index of Bernini's work. If we can scan titles, maybe something will jump out.'

'I don't know,' Langdon said. 'If it's a work Bernini created specifically for the Illuminati, it may be very obscure. It probably won't be listed in a book.'

Vittoria refused to believe it. 'The other two sculptures were fairly well-known. You'd heard of them both.'

Langdon shrugged. 'Yeah.'

'If we scan titles for references to the word "fire", maybe we'll find a statue that's listed as being in the right direction.'

Langdon seemed convinced it was worth a shot. He turned to Olivetti. 'I need a list of all Bernini's work. You guys probably don't have a coffee-table Bernini book around here, do you?'

'Coffee-table book?' Olivetti seemed unfamiliar with the term.

'Never mind. Any list. How about the Vatican Museum? They must have Bernini references.'

The guard with the scar frowned. 'Power in the museum is out, and the records room is enormous. Without the staff there to help—'

'The Bernini work in question,' Olivetti interrupted. 'Would it have been created while Bernini was employed here at the Vatican?'

'Almost definitely,' Langdon said. 'He was here almost his entire career. And certainly during the time period of the Galileo conflict.'

Olivetti nodded. 'Then there's another reference.'

Vittoria felt a flicker of optimism. 'Where?'

The commander did not reply. He took his guard aside and spoke in hushed tones. The guard seemed uncertain but nodded obediently. When Olivetti was finished talking, the guard turned to Langdon.

'This way please, Mr Langdon. It's nine-fifteen. We'll have to hurry.'

Langdon and the guard headed for the door.

Vittoria started after them. 'I'll help.'

Olivetti caught her by the arm. 'No, Ms Vetra. I need a word with you.' His grasp was authoritative.

Langdon and the guard left. Olivetti's face was wooden as he took Vittoria aside. But whatever it was Olivetti had intended to say to her, he never got the chance. His walkie-talkie crackled loudly. 'Comandante?'

Everyone in the room turned.

The voice on the transmitter was grim. 'I think you better turn on the television.'

80

When Langdon had left the Vatican Secret Archives only two hours ago, he had never imagined he would see them again. Now, winded from having jogged the entire way with his Swiss Guard escort, Langdon found himself back at the archives once again.

His escort, the guard with the scar, now led Langdon through the rows of translucent cubicles. The silence of the archives felt somehow more forbidding now, and Langdon was thankful when the guard broke it.

'Over here, I think,' he said, escorting Langdon to the back of the chamber where a series of smaller vaults lined the wall. The guard scanned the titles on the vaults and motioned to one of them. 'Yes, here it is. Right where the commander said it would be.'

Langdon read the title. ATTIVI VATICANI. Vatican assets? He scanned the list of contents. Real estate ... currency ... Vatican Bank ... antiquities ... The list went on.

'Paperwork of all Vatican assets,' the guard said.

Langdon looked at the cubicle. *Jesus*. Even in the dark, he could tell it was packed.

'My commander said that whatever Bernini created while under Vatican patronage would be listed here as an asset.'

Langdon nodded, realizing the commander's instincts just might pay off. In Bernini's day, everything an artist created while under the patronage of the Pope became, by law, property of the Vatican. It was more like feudalism than patronage, but top artists lived well and seldom complained. 'Including works placed in churches *outside* Vatican City?'

The soldier gave him an odd look. 'Of course. All Catholic churches in Rome are property of the Vatican.'

Langdon looked at the list in his hand. It contained the names of the twenty or so churches that were located on a direct line with *West Ponente's* breath. The third altar of science was one of them, and Langdon hoped he had time to figure out which it was. Under other circumstances, he would gladly have explored each church in person. Today, however, he had about twenty minutes to find what he was looking for – the one church containing a Bernini tribute to *fire*.

Langdon walked to the vault's electronic revolving door. The guard did not follow. Langdon sensed an uncertain hesitation. He smiled. 'The air's fine. Thin, but breathable.'

'My orders are to escort you here and then return immediately to the security center.'

'You're *leaving*?'

'Yes. The Swiss Guard are not allowed inside the archives. I am breaching protocol by escorting you this far. The commander reminded me of that.'

'Breaching protocol?' *Do you have any idea what is going on here tonight?* 'Whose side is your damn commander on!'

All friendliness disappeared from the guard's face. The scar under his eye twitched. The guard stared, looking suddenly a lot like Olivetti himself.

'I apologize,' Langdon said, regretting the comment. 'It's just . . . I could use some help.'

The guard did not blink. 'I am trained to follow orders. Not debate them. When you find what you are looking for, contact the commander immediately.'

Langdon was flustered. 'But where will he be?'

The guard removed his walkie-talkie and set it on a nearby table. 'Channel one.' Then he disappeared into the dark.

81

The television in the Office of the Pope was an oversized Hitachi hidden in a recessed cabinet opposite his desk. The doors to the cabinet were now open, and everyone gathered around. Vittoria moved in close. As the screen warmed up, a young female reporter came into view. She was a doe-eyed brunette.

'For MSNBC news,' she announced, 'this is Kelly

354

Horan-Jones, live from Vatican City.' The image behind her was a night shot of St Peter's Basilica with all its lights blazing.

'You're not *live*,' Rocher snapped. 'That's stock footage! The lights in the basilica are *out*.'

Olivetti silenced him with a hiss.

The reporter continued, sounding tense. 'Shocking developments in the Vatican elections this evening. We have reports that two members of the College of Cardinals have been brutally murdered in Rome.'

Olivetti swore under his breath.

As the reporter continued, a guard appeared at the door, breathless. 'Commander, the central switchboard reports every line lit. They're requesting our official position on—'

'Disconnect it,' Olivetti said, never taking his eyes from the TV.

The guard looked uncertain. 'But, commander—'

'Go!'

The guard ran off.

Vittoria sensed the camerlengo had wanted to say something but had stopped himself. Instead, the man stared long and hard at Olivetti before turning back to the television.

MSNBC was now running tape. The Swiss Guards carried the body of Cardinal Ebner down the stairs outside Santa Maria del Popolo and lifted him into an Alfa Romeo. The tape froze and zoomed in as the cardinal's naked body became visible just before they deposited him in the trunk of the car.

'Who the hell shot this footage?' Olivetti demanded.

The MSNBC reporter kept talking. 'This is believed to be the body of Cardinal Ebner of Frankfurt, Germany. The men removing his body from the church are believed to be Vatican Swiss Guard.' The reporter looked like she was making every effort to appear appropriately moved. They closed in on her face, and she became even more somber. 'At this time, MSNBC would like to issue our viewers a discretionary warning. The images we are about to show are exceptionally vivid and may not be suitable for all audiences.'

Vittoria grunted at the station's feigned concern for viewer sensibility, recognizing the warning as exactly what it was – the ultimate media 'teaser line'. Nobody ever changed channels after a promise like that.

The reporter drove it home. 'Again, this footage may be shocking to some viewers.'

'What footage?' Olivetti demanded. 'You just showed—'

The shot that filled the screen was of a couple in St Peter's Square, moving through the crowd. Vittoria instantly recognized the two people as Robert and herself. In the corner of the screen was a text overlay: COURTESY OF THE BBC. A bell was tolling.

'Oh, no,' Vittoria said aloud. 'Oh . . . no.'

The camerlengo looked confused. He turned to Olivetti. 'I thought you said you confiscated this tape!'

Suddenly, on television, a child was screaming. The image panned to find a little girl pointing at what appeared to be a bloody homeless man. Robert Langdon entered abruptly into the frame, trying to help the little girl. The shot tightened.

Everyone in the Pope's office stared in horrified silence as the drama unfolded before them. The cardinal's body fell face first onto the pavement. Vittoria appeared and called orders. There was blood. A brand. A ghastly, failed attempt to administer CPR.

'This astonishing footage,' the reporter was saying, 'was shot only minutes ago outside the Vatican. Our sources tell us this is the body of Cardinal Lamassé from France. How he came to be dressed this way and why he was not in conclave remain a mystery. So far, the Vatican has refused to comment.' The tape began to roll again.

'Refused comment?' Rocher said. 'Give us a damn minute!'

The reporter was still talking, her eyebrows furrowing with intensity. 'Although MSNBC has yet to confirm a motive for the attack, our sources tell us that responsibility for the murders has been claimed by a group calling themselves the Illuminati.'

Olivetti exploded. *'What!'*

'. . . find out more about the Illuminati by visiting our website at—'

'Non è possibile!' Olivetti declared. He switched channels.

This station had a Hispanic male reporter. '—a satanic cult known as the Illuminati, who some historians believe—'

Olivetti began pressing the remote wildly. Every channel was in the middle of a live update. Most were in English.

'—Swiss Guards removing a body from a church earlier this evening. The body is believed to be that of Cardinal—'

'—lights in the basilica and museums are extinguished leaving speculation—'

'—will be speaking with conspiracy theorist Tyler Tingley, about this shocking resurgence—'

'—rumors of two more assassinations planned for later this evening—'

'—questioning now whether papal hopeful Cardinal Baggia is among the missing—'

Vittoria turned away. Everything was happening so fast. Outside the window, in the settling dark, the raw magnetism of human tragedy seemed to be sucking people toward Vatican City. The crowd in the square thickened almost by the instant. Pedestrians streamed toward them while a new batch of media personnel unloaded vans and staked their claim in St Peter's Square.

Olivetti set down the remote control and turned to the camerlengo. 'Signore, I cannot imagine how this could happen. We took the tape that was in that camera!'

The camerlengo looked momentarily too stunned to speak.

Nobody said a word. The Swiss Guards stood rigid at attention.

'It appears,' the camerlengo said finally, sounding too devastated to be angry, 'that we have not contained this crisis as well as I was led to believe.' He looked out the window at the gathering masses. 'I need to make an address.'

Olivetti shook his head. 'No, signore. That is exactly what the Illuminati want you to do – confirm them, empower them. We must remain silent.'

'And these people?' The camerlengo pointed out the window. 'There will be tens of thousands shortly. Then hundreds of thousands. Continuing this charade only puts them in danger. I need to warn them. Then we need to evacuate our College of Cardinals.'

'There is still time. Let Captain Rocher find the antimatter.'

The camerlengo turned. 'Are you attempting to give me an order?'

'No, I am giving you advice. If you are concerned about the people outside, we can announce a gas leak and clear the area, but admitting we are hostage is dangerous.'

'Commander, I will only say this once. I will not use this office as a pulpit to lie to the world. If I announce anything at all, it will be the truth.'

'The truth? That Vatican City is threatened to be destroyed by satanic terrorists? It only weakens our position.'

The camerlengo glared. 'How much weaker could our position be?'

Rocher shouted suddenly, grabbing the remote and increasing the volume on the television. Everyone turned.

On air, the woman from MSNBC now looked genuinely unnerved. Superimposed beside her was a photo of the late Pope. '. . . breaking information. This just in from the BBC . . .' She glanced off camera as if to confirm she was really supposed to make this announcement. Apparently getting confirmation, she turned and grimly faced the viewers. 'The Illuminati have just claimed responsibility for . . .' She hesitated. 'They have claimed responsibility for the death of the Pope fifteen days ago.'

The camerlengo's jaw fell.

Rocher dropped the remote control.

Vittoria could barely process the information.

'By Vatican law,' the woman continued, 'no formal autopsy is ever performed on a Pope, so the Illuminati claim of murder cannot be confirmed. Nonetheless, the Illuminati hold that the cause of the late Pope's death was not a *stroke* as the Vatican reported, but *poisoning*.'

The room went totally silent again.

Olivetti erupted. 'Madness! A bold-faced lie!'

Rocher began flipping channels again. The bulletin seemed to spread like a plague from station to station. Everyone had the same story. Headlines competed for optimal sensationalism.

> MURDER AT THE VATICAN
> POPE POISONED
> SATAN TOUCHES HOUSE OF GOD

The camerlengo looked away. 'God help us.'

As Rocher flipped, he passed a BBC station. '—tipped me off about the killing at Santa Maria de Popolo—'

'Wait!' the camerlengo said. 'Back.'

Rocher went back. On screen, a prim-looking man sat at a BBC news desk. Superimposed over his shoulder was a still snapshot of an odd-looking man with a red beard. Underneath his photo, it said: GUNTHER GLICK – LIVE IN VATICAN CITY. Reporter Glick was apparently reporting by phone, the connection scratchy '. . . my videographer got the footage of the cardinal being removed from the Chigi Chapel.'

'Let me reiterate for our viewers,' the anchorman in London was saying, 'BBC reporter Gunther Glick is the man who first broke this story. He has been in phone contact twice now with the alleged Illuminati assassin. Gunther, you say the assassin phoned only moments ago to pass along a message from the Illuminati?'

'He did.'

'And their message was that the Illuminati were somehow *responsible* for the Pope's death?' The anchorman sounded incredulous.

'Correct. The caller told me that the Pope's death was *not* a stroke, as the Vatican had thought, but rather that the Pope had been poisoned by the Illuminati.'

Everyone in the Pope's office froze.

'Poisoned?' the anchorman demanded. 'But . . . but *how*!'

'They gave no specifics,' Glick replied, 'except to say that they killed him with a drug known as . . .' – there was a rustling of papers on the line – 'something known as Heparin.'

The camerlengo, Olivetti, and Rocher all exchanged confused looks.

'Heparin?' Rocher demanded, looking unnerved. 'But isn't that . . .?'

The camerlengo blanched. 'The Pope's medication.'

Vittoria was stunned. 'The Pope was on Heparin?'

'He had thrombophlebitis,' the camerlengo said. 'He took an injection once a day.'

Rocher looked flabbergasted. 'But Heparin isn't a *poison*. Why would the Illuminati claim—'

'Heparin is lethal in the wrong dosages,' Vittoria offered. 'It's a powerful anticoagulant. An overdose would cause massive internal bleeding and brain hemorrhages.'

Olivetti eyed her suspiciously. 'How would you know that?'

'Marine biologists use it on sea mammals in captivity to prevent blood clotting from decreased activity. Animals have died from improper administration of the drug.' She paused. 'A Heparin overdose in a human would cause symptoms easily mistaken for a stroke . . . especially in the absence of a proper autopsy.'

The camerlengo now looked deeply troubled.

'Signore,' Olivetti said, 'this is obviously an Illuminati ploy for publicity. Someone overdosing the Pope would be impossible. Nobody had access. And even if we take the bait and try to refute their claim, how could we? Papal law prohibits autopsy. Even *with* an autopsy, we would learn nothing. We would find traces of Heparin in his body from his daily injections.'

'True.' The camerlengo's voice sharpened. 'And yet something else troubles me. No one on the outside *knew* His Holiness was taking this medication.'

There was a silence.

'If he overdosed with Heparin,' Vittoria said, 'his body would show signs.'

Olivetti spun toward her. 'Ms Vetra, in case you didn't hear me, papal autopsies are prohibited by Vatican Law. We are not about to defile His Holiness's body by cutting him open just because an enemy makes a taunting claim!'

Vittoria felt shamed. 'I was not implying . . .' She had not meant to seem disrespectful. 'I certainly was not suggesting you exhume the Pope . . .' She hesitated, though. Something Robert told her in the Chigi passed like a ghost through her mind. He had mentioned that papal sarcophagi were above ground and never cemented shut, a throwback to the days of the pharaohs when sealing and burying a casket was believed to trap the deceased's soul inside. *Gravity* had become the mortar of choice, with coffin lids often weighing hundreds of pounds. *Technically*, she realized, *it would be possible to—*

'What *sort* of signs?' the camerlengo said suddenly.

Vittoria felt her heart flutter with fear. 'Overdoses can cause bleeding of the oral mucosa.'

'Oral what?'

'The victim's gums would bleed. Post mortem, the blood congeals and turns the inside of the mouth black.' Vittoria had once seen a photo taken at an aquarium in London where a pair of killer whales had been mistakenly overdosed by their trainer. The whales floated lifeless in the tank, their mouths hanging open and their tongues black as soot.

The camerlengo made no reply. He turned and stared out the window.

Rocher's voice had lost its optimism. 'Signore, if this claim about poisoning is true . . .'

'It's not true,' Olivetti declared. 'Access to the Pope by an outsider is utterly impossible.'

'*If* this claim is true,' Rocher repeated, 'and our Holy Father *was* poisoned, then that has profound implications for our antimatter search. The alleged assassination implies a much deeper infiltration of Vatican City than we had imagined. Searching the white zones may be inadequate. If we are compromised to such a deep extent, we may not find the canister in time.'

Olivetti leveled his captain with a cold stare. 'Captain, I will tell you what is going to happen.'

'No,' the camerlengo said, turning suddenly. 'I will tell *you* what is going to happen.' He looked directly at Olivetti. 'This has gone far enough. In twenty minutes I will be making a decision whether or not to cancel conclave and evacuate Vatican City. My decision will be final. Is that clear?'

Olivetti did not blink. Nor did he respond.

The camerlengo spoke forcefully now, as though tapping a hidden reserve of power. 'Captain Rocher, you will complete your search of the white zones and report directly to me when you are finished.'

Rocher nodded, throwing Olivetti an uneasy glance.

The camerlengo then singled out two guards. 'I want the BBC reporter, Mr Glick, in this office immediately. If the Illuminati have been communicating with him, he may be able to help us. Go.'

The two soldiers disappeared.

Now the camerlengo turned and addressed the remaining guards. 'Gentlemen, I will not permit any more loss of life this evening. By ten o'clock you will locate the remaining two cardinals and capture the monster responsible for these murders. Do I make myself understood?'

'But, signore,' Olivetti argued, 'we have no idea where—'

'Mr Langdon is working on that. He seems capable. I have faith.'

With that, the camerlengo strode for the door, a new determination in his step. On his way out, he pointed to three guards. 'You three, come with me. Now.'

The guards followed.

In the doorway, the camerlengo stopped. He turned to Vittoria. 'Ms Vetra. You too. Please come with me.'

Vittoria hesitated. 'Where are we going?'

He headed out the door. 'To see an old friend.'

82

At CERN, secretary Sylvie Baudeloque was hungry, wishing she could go home. To her dismay, Kohler had apparently survived his trip to the infirmary; he had phoned and demanded – not asked, *demanded* – that Sylvie stay late this evening. No explanation.

Over the years, Sylvie had programmed herself to ignore Kohler's bizarre mood swings and eccentricities – his silent treatments, his unnerving propensity to secretly film meetings with his wheelchair's porta-video. She secretly hoped one day he would shoot himself during his weekly visit to CERN's recreational pistol range, but apparently he was a pretty good shot.

Now, sitting alone at her desk, Sylvie heard her stomach growling. Kohler had not yet returned, nor had he given her any additional work for the evening. *To hell with sitting here bored and starving*, she decided. She left Kohler a note and headed for the staff dining commons to grab a quick bite.

She never made it.

As she passed CERN's recreational '*suites de loisir*' – a long hallway of lounges with televisions – she noticed the rooms were overflowing with employees who had apparently abandoned dinner to watch the news. Something big was going on. Sylvie entered the first suite. It was packed with byte-heads – wild young computer programmers. When she saw the headlines on the TV, she gasped.

TERROR AT THE VATICAN

Sylvie listened to the report, unable to believe her ears. Some ancient brotherhood killing cardinals? What did that prove? Their hatred? Their dominance? Their ignorance?

And yet, incredibly, the mood in this suite seemed anything but somber.

Two young techies ran by waving T-shirts that bore

a picture of Bill Gates and the message: AND THE GEEK
SHALL INHERIT THE EARTH!

'Illuminati!' one shouted. 'I told you these guys
were real!'

'Incredible! I thought it was just a game!'

'They killed the Pope, man! The *Pope!*'

'Jeez! I wonder how many points you get for *that*?'

They ran off laughing.

Sylvie stood in stunned amazement. As a Catholic
working among scientists, she occasionally endured
the antireligious whisperings, but the party these kids
seemed to be having was all-out euphoria over the
church's loss. How could they be so callous? Why the
hatred?

For Sylvie, the church had always been an innocu-
ous entity . . . a place of fellowship and introspection
. . . sometimes just a place to sing out loud without
people staring at her. The church recorded the bench-
marks of her life – funerals, weddings, baptisms,
holidays – and it asked for nothing in return. Even the
monetary dues were voluntary. Her children emerged
from Sunday School every week uplifted, filled with
ideas about helping others and being kinder. What
could possibly be wrong with *that*?

It never ceased to amaze her that so many of
CERN's so-called 'brilliant minds' failed to comprehend the importance of the church. Did they really
believe quarks and mesons inspired the average
human being? Or that *equations* could replace someone's need for faith in the divine?

Dazed, Sylvie moved down the hallway past the
other lounges. All the TV rooms were packed. She
began wondering now about the call Kohler had
gotten from the Vatican earlier. Coincidence? Perhaps.

The Vatican called CERN from time to time as a 'courtesy' before issuing scathing statements condemning CERN's research – most recently for CERN's breakthroughs in nanotechnology, a field the church denounced because of its implications for genetic engineering. CERN never cared. Invariably, within minutes after a Vatican salvo, Kohler's phone would ring off the hook with tech-investment companies wanting to license the new discovery. 'No such thing as bad press,' Kohler would always say.

Sylvie wondered if she should page Kohler, wherever the hell he was, and tell him to turn on the news. Did he care? Had he heard? Of course, he'd heard. He was probably videotaping the entire report with his freaky little camcorder, smiling for the first time in a year.

As Sylvie continued down the hall, she finally found a lounge where the mood was subdued ... almost melancholy. Here the scientists watching the report were some of CERN's oldest and most respected. They did not even look up as Sylvie slipped in and took a seat.

On the other side of CERN, in Leonardo Vetra's frigid apartment, Maximilian Kohler had finished reading the leather-bound journal he'd taken from Vetra's bedside table. Now he was watching the television reports. After a few minutes, he replaced Vetra's journal, turned off the television, and left the apartment.

Far away, in Vatican City, Cardinal Mortati carried another tray of ballots to the Sistine Chapel chimney. He burned them, and the smoke was black.

Two ballotings. No Pope.

83

Flashlights were no match for the voluminous blackness of St Peter's Basilica. The void overhead pressed down like a starless night, and Vittoria felt the emptiness spread out around her like a desolate ocean. She stayed close as the Swiss Guards and the camerlengo pushed on. High above, a dove cooed and fluttered away.

As if sensing her discomfort, the camerlengo dropped back and laid a hand on her shoulder. A tangible strength transferred in the touch, as if the man were magically infusing her with the calm she needed to do what they were about to do.

What are we about to do? she thought. *This is madness!*

And yet, Vittoria knew, for all its impiety and inevitable horror, the task at hand was inescapable. The grave decisions facing the camerlengo required information . . . information entombed in a sarcophagus in the Vatican Grottoes. She wondered what they would find. *Did the Illuminati murder the Pope? Did their power really reach so far? Am I really about to perform the first papal autopsy?*

Vittoria found it ironic that she felt more apprehensive in this unlit church than she would swimming at night with barracuda. Nature was her refuge. She understood nature. But it was matters of man and spirit that left her mystified. Killer fish gathering in the dark conjured images of the press gathering outside. TV footage of branded bodies reminded her of her father's corpse . . . and the killer's harsh laugh. The killer was out there somewhere. Vittoria felt the anger drowning her fear.

As they circled past a pillar – thicker in girth than any redwood she could imagine – Vittoria saw an orange glow up ahead. The light seemed to emanate from beneath the floor in the center of the basilica. As they came closer, she realized what she was seeing. It was the famous sunken sanctuary beneath the main altar – the sumptuous underground chamber that held the Vatican's most sacred relics. As they drew even with the gate surrounding the hollow, Vittoria gazed down at the golden coffer surrounded by scores of glowing oil lamps.

'St Peter's bones?' she asked, knowing full well that they were. Everyone who came to St Peter's knew what was in the golden casket.

'Actually, no,' the camerlengo said. 'A common misconception. That's not a reliquary. The box holds *palliums* – woven sashes that the Pope gives to newly elected cardinals.'

'But I thought—'

'As does everyone. The guidebooks label this as St Peter's tomb, but his true grave is two stories beneath us, buried in the earth. The Vatican excavated it in the forties. Nobody is allowed down there.'

Vittoria was shocked. As they moved away from the glowing recession into the darkness again, she thought of the stories she'd heard of pilgrims traveling thousands of miles to look at that golden box, thinking they were in the presence of St Peter. 'Shouldn't the Vatican tell people?'

'We all benefit from a sense of contact with divinity . . . even if it is only imagined.'

Vittoria, as a scientist, could not argue the logic. She had read countless studies of the placebo effect – aspirins curing cancer in people who *believed* they were using a miracle drug. What was *faith*, after all?

'Change,' the camerlengo said, 'is not something we do well within Vatican City. Admitting our past faults, modernization, are things we historically eschew. His Holiness was trying to change that.' He paused. 'Reaching to the modern world. Searching for new paths to God.'

Vittoria nodded in the dark. 'Like science?'

'To be honest, science seems irrelevant.'

'Irrelevant?' Vittoria could think of a lot of words to describe science, but in the modern world 'irrelevant' did not seem like one of them.

'Science can heal, or science can kill. It depends on the soul of the man using the science. It is the soul that interests me.'

'When did you hear your call?'

'Before I was born.'

Vittoria looked at him.

'I'm sorry, that always seems like a strange question. What I mean is that I've always known I would serve God. From the moment I could first think. It wasn't until I was a young man, though, in the military, that I truly understood my purpose.'

Vittoria was surprised. 'You were in the military?'

'Two years. I refused to fire a weapon, so they made me fly instead. Medevac helicopters. In fact, I still fly from time to time.'

Vittoria tried to picture the young priest flying a helicopter. Oddly, she could see him perfectly behind the controls. Camerlengo Ventresca possessed a grit that seemed to accentuate his conviction rather than cloud it. 'Did you ever fly the Pope?'

'Heavens no. We left that precious cargo to the professionals. His Holiness let me take the helicopter to our retreat in Gandolfo sometimes.' He paused, looking at her. 'Ms Vetra, thank you for your help here today. I am very sorry about your father. Truly.'

'Thank you.'

'I never knew my father. He died before I was born. I lost my mother when I was ten.'

Vittoria looked up. 'You were orphaned?' She felt a sudden kinship.

'I survived an accident. An accident that took my mother.'

'Who took care of you?'

'God,' the camerlengo said. 'He quite literally sent me another father. A bishop from Palermo appeared at my hospital bed and took me in. At the time I was not surprised. I had sensed God's watchful hand over me even as a boy. The bishop's appearance simply confirmed what I had already suspected, that God had somehow chosen me to serve him.'

'You believed God chose you?'

'I did. And I do.' There was no trace of conceit in the camerlengo's voice, only gratitude. 'I worked under the bishop's tutelage for many years. He eventually became a cardinal. Still, he never forgot me. He is the father I remember.' A beam of a flashlight caught the camerlengo's face, and Vittoria sensed a loneliness in his eyes.

The group arrived beneath a towering pillar, and their lights converged on an opening in the floor. Vittoria looked down at the staircase descending into the void and suddenly wanted to turn back. The guards were already helping the camerlengo onto the stairs. They helped her next.

'What became of him?' she asked, descending, trying to keep her voice steady. 'The cardinal who took you in?'

371

'He left the College of Cardinals for another position.'

Vittoria was surprised.

'And then, I'm sorry to say, he passed on.'

'*Le mie condoglianze,*' Vittoria said. 'Recently?'

The camerlengo turned, shadows accentuating the pain on his face. 'Exactly fifteen days ago. We are going to see him right now.'

84

The dark lights glowed hot inside the archival vault. This vault was much smaller than the previous one Langdon had been in. *Less air. Less time.* He wished he'd asked Olivetti to turn on the recirculating fans.

Langdon quickly located the section of assets containing the ledgers cataloging *Belle Arti.* The section was impossible to miss. It occupied almost eight full stacks. The Catholic church owned millions of individual pieces worldwide.

Langdon scanned the shelves searching for Gianlorenzo Bernini. He began his search about midway down the first stack, at about the spot he thought the *B*'s would begin. After a moment of panic fearing the ledger was missing, he realized, to his greater dismay, that the ledgers were not arranged alphabetically. *Why am I not surprised?*

It was not until Langdon circled back to the beginning of the collection and climbed a rolling ladder to the top shelf that he understood the vault's organization. Perched precariously on the upper stacks he found the fattest ledgers of all – those belonging to the masters of the Renaissance – Michelangelo, Raphael, da Vinci, Botticelli. Langdon now realized, appropriate to a vault called 'Vatican Assets,' the ledgers were arranged by the overall monetary *value* of each artist's collection. Sandwiched between Raphael and Michelangelo, Langdon found the ledger marked Bernini. It was over five inches thick.

Already short of breath and struggling with the cumbersome volume, Langdon descended the ladder. Then, like a kid with a comic book, he spread himself out on the floor and opened the cover.

The book was cloth-bound and very solid. The ledger was handwritten in Italian. Each page cataloged a single work, including a short description, date, location, cost of materials, and sometimes a rough sketch of the piece. Langdon fanned through the pages ... over eight hundred in all. Bernini had been a busy man.

As a young student of art, Langdon had wondered how single artists could create so *much* work in their lifetimes. Later he learned, much to his disappointment, that famous artists actually created very little of their own work. They ran studios where they trained young artists to carry out their designs. Sculptors like Bernini created miniatures in clay and hired others to enlarge them into marble. Langdon knew that if Bernini had been required to *personally* complete all of his commissions, he would still be working today.

'Index,' he said aloud, trying to ward off the mental cobwebs. He flipped to the back of the book, intending to look under the letter F for titles containing the word *fuòco* – fire – but the F's were not together. Langdon swore under his breath. *What the hell do these people have against alphabetizing?*

The entries had apparently been logged chronologically, one by one, as Bernini created each new work. Everything was listed by date. No help at all.

As Langdon stared at the list, another disheartening thought occurred to him. The title of the sculpture he was looking for might not even contain the word *Fire*. The previous two works – *Habakkuk and the Angel* and *West Ponente* – had not contained specific references to *Earth* or *Air*.

He spent a minute or two flipping randomly through the ledger in hopes that an illustration might jump out at him. Nothing did. He saw dozens of obscure works he had never heard of, but he also saw plenty he recognized . . . *Daniel and the Lion, Apollo and Daphne*, as well as a half dozen fountains. When he saw the fountains, his thoughts skipped momentarily ahead. Water. He wondered if the fourth altar of science was a fountain. A fountain seemed a perfect tribute to water. Langdon hoped they could catch the killer before he had to consider *Water* – Bernini had carved dozens of fountains in Rome, most of them in front of churches.

Langdon turned back to the matter at hand. *Fire*. As he looked through the book, Vittoria's words encouraged him. *You were familiar with the first two sculptures . . . you probably know this one too.* As he turned to the index again, he scanned for titles he knew. Some were familiar, but none jumped out. Langdon now realized he would never complete his search before passing out, so he decided, against his better judgment, that he would have to take the book outside the vault. *It's only a ledger*, he told himself. *It's not like I'm removing an*

374

original Galilean folio. Langdon recalled the folio in his breast pocket and reminded himself to return it before leaving.

Hurrying now, he reached down to lift the volume, but as he did, he saw something that gave him pause. Although there were numerous notations throughout the index, the one that had just caught his eye seemed odd.

The note indicated that the famous Bernini sculpture, *The Ecstasy of St Teresa*, shortly after its unveiling, had been moved from its original location inside the Vatican. This in itself was not what had caught Langdon's eye. He was already familiar with the sculpture's checkered past. Though some thought it a masterpiece, Pope Urban VIII had rejected *The Ecstasy of St Teresa* as too sexually explicit for the Vatican. He had banished it to some obscure chapel across town. What had caught Langdon's eye was that the work had apparently been placed in one of the five churches on his list. What was more, the note indicated it had been moved there *per suggerimento del artista.*

By suggestion of the artist? Langdon was confused. It made no sense that Bernini had suggested his masterpiece be hidden in some obscure location. All artists wanted their work displayed prominently, not in some remote—

Langdon hesitated. *Unless . . .*

He was fearful even to entertain the notion. Was it possible? Had Bernini intentionally created a work so explicit that it forced the Vatican to hide it in some out-of-the-way spot? A location perhaps that Bernini himself could suggest? Maybe a remote church on a direct line with *West Ponente's* breath?

As Langdon's excitement mounted, his vague familiarity with the statue intervened, insisting the work had nothing to do with *fire*. The sculpture, as anyone who had seen it could attest, was anything but scientific – *pornographic* maybe, but certainly not scientific. An English critic had once condemned *The Ecstasy of St Teresa* as 'the most unfit ornament ever to be placed in a Christian Church.' Langdon certainly understood the controversy. Though brilliantly rendered, the statue depicted St Teresa on her back in the throes of a toe-curling orgasm. Hardly Vatican fare.

Langdon hurriedly flipped to the ledger's description of the work. When he saw the sketch, he felt an instantaneous and unexpected tingle of hope. In the sketch, St Teresa did indeed appear to be enjoying herself, but there was another figure in the statue who Langdon had forgotten was there.

An angel.

The sordid legend suddenly came back . . .

St Teresa was a nun sainted after she claimed an angel had paid her a blissful visit in her sleep. Critics later decided her encounter had probably been more sexual than spiritual. Scrawled at the bottom of the ledger, Langdon saw a familiar excerpt. St Teresa's own words left little to the imagination:

> . . . his great golden spear . . . filled with fire . . . plunged into me several times . . . penetrated to my entrails . . . a sweetness so extreme that one could not possibly wish it to stop.

Langdon smiled. *If that's not a metaphor for some serious sex, I don't know what is.* He was smiling also because of the ledger's description of the work.

Although the paragraph was in Italian, the word *fuòco* appeared a half dozen times:

... angel's spear tipped with point of *fire* ...
... angel's head emanating rays of *fire* ...
... woman inflamed by passion's *fire* ..

Langdon was not entirely convinced until he glanced up at the sketch again. The angel's fiery spear was raised like a beacon, pointing the way. *Let angels guide you on your lofty quest.* Even the *type* of angel Bernini had selected seemed significant. *It's a seraph,* Langdon realized. *Seraph literally means 'the fiery one.'*

Robert Langdon was not a man who had ever looked for confirmation from above, but when he read the name of the church where the sculpture now resided, he decided he might become a believer after all.

Santa Maria della Vittoria.

Vittoria, he thought, grinning. *Perfect.*

Staggering to his feet, Langdon felt a rush of dizziness. He glanced up the ladder, wondering if he should replace the book. *The hell with it,* he thought. *Father Jaqui can do it.* He closed the book and left it neatly at the bottom of the shelf

As he made his way toward the glowing button on the vault's electronic exit, he was breathing in shallow gasps. Nonetheless, he felt rejuvenated by his good fortune.

His good fortune, however, ran out before he reached the exit.

Without warning, the vault let out a pained sigh. The lights dimmed, and the exit button went dead. Then, like an enormous expiring beast, the archival complex went totally black. Someone had just killed power.

85

The Holy Vatican Grottoes are located beneath the main floor of St Peter's Basilica. They are the burial place of deceased Popes.

Vittoria reached the bottom of the spiral staircase and entered the grotto. The darkened tunnel reminded her of CERN's Large Hadron Collider — black and cold. Lit now only by the flashlights of the Swiss Guards, the tunnel carried a distinctly incorporeal feel. On both sides, hollow niches lined the walls. Recessed in the alcoves, as far as the lights let them see, the hulking shadows of sarcophagi loomed.

An iciness raked her flesh. *It's the cold*, she told herself, knowing that was only partially true. She had the sense they were being watched, not by anyone in the flesh, but by specters in the dark. On top of each tomb, in full papal vestments, lay life-sized semblances of each Pope, shown in death, arms folded across their chests. The prostrate bodies seemed to emerge from within the tombs, pressing upward against the marble lids as if trying to escape their mortal restraints. The flashlight procession moved on, and the papal silhouettes rose and fell against the walls, stretching and vanishing in a macabre shadowbox dance.

A silence had fallen across the group, and Vittoria couldn't tell whether it was one of respect or apprehension. She sensed both. The camerlengo moved with his eyes closed, as if he knew every step by heart. Vittoria suspected he had made this eerie promenade many times since the Pope's death . . . perhaps to pray at his tomb for guidance.

I worked under the cardinal's tutelage for many years,

the camerlengo had said. *He was like a father to me.* Vittoria recalled the camerlengo speaking those words in reference to the cardinal who had 'saved' him from the army. Now, however, Vittoria understood the rest of the story. That very cardinal who had taken the camerlengo under his wing had apparently later risen to the papacy and brought with him his young protégé to serve as chamberlain.

That explains a lot, Vittoria thought. She had always possessed a well-tuned perception for others' inner emotions, and something about the camerlengo had been nagging her all day. Since meeting him, she had sensed an anguish more soulful and private than the overwhelming crisis he now faced. Behind his pious calm, she saw a man tormented by personal demons. Now she knew her instincts had been correct. Not only was he facing the most devastating threat in Vatican history, but he was doing it without his mentor and friend . . . flying solo.

The guards slowed now, as if unsure where exactly in the darkness the most recent Pope was buried. The camerlengo continued assuredly and stopped before a marble tomb that seemed to glisten brighter than the others. Lying atop was a carved figure of the late Pope. When Vittoria recognized his face from television, a shot of fear gripped her. *What are we doing?*

'I realize we do not have much time,' the camerlengo said. 'I still ask we take a moment of prayer.'

The Swiss Guard all bowed their heads where they were standing. Vittoria followed suit, her heart pounding in the silence. The camerlengo knelt before the tomb and prayed in Italian. As Vittoria listened to his words, an unexpected grief surfaced as tears . . . tears for her own mentor . . . her own holy father. The camerlengo's words seemed as appropriate for her father as they did for the Pope.

'Supreme father, counselor, friend.' The camerlengo's voice echoed dully around the ring. 'You told me when I was young that the voice in my heart was that of God. You told me I must follow it no matter what painful places it leads. I hear that voice now, asking of me impossible tasks. Give me strength. Bestow on me forgiveness. What I do . . . I do in the name of everything you believe. Amen.'

'Amen,' the guards whispered.

Amen, Father. Vittoria wiped her eyes.

The camerlengo stood slowly and stepped away from the tomb. 'Push the covering aside.'

The Swiss Guards hesitated. 'Signore,' one said, 'by law we are at your command.' He paused. 'We will do as you say . . .'

The camerlengo seemed to read the young man's mind. 'Someday I will ask your forgiveness for placing you in this position. Today I ask for your obedience. Vatican laws are established to protect this church. It is in that very spirit that I command you to break them now.'

There was a moment of silence and then the lead guard gave the order. The three men set down their flashlights on the floor, and their shadows leapt overhead. Lit now from beneath, the men advanced toward the tomb. Bracing their hands against the marble covering near the head of the tomb, they planted their feet and prepared to push. On signal, they all thrust, straining against the enormous slab. When the lid did not move at all, Vittoria found herself almost hoping it was too heavy She was suddenly fearful of what they would find inside.

The men pushed harder, and still the stone did not move.

'*Ancora*,' the camerlengo said, rolling up the sleeves of his cassock and preparing to push along with them. '*Ora!*' Everyone heaved.

Vittoria was about to offer her own help, but just then, the lid began to slide. The men dug in again, and with an almost primal growl of stone on stone, the lid rotated off the top of the tomb and came to rest at an angle – the Pope's carved head now pushed back into the niche and his feet extended out into the hallway.

Everyone stepped back.

Tentatively, a guard bent and retrieved his flashlight. Then he aimed it into the tomb. The beam seemed to tremble a moment, and then the guard held it steady. The other guards gathered one by one. Even in the darkness Vittoria sensed them recoil. In succession, they crossed themselves.

The camerlengo shuddered when he looked into the tomb, his shoulders dropping like weights. He stood a long moment before turning away.

Vittoria had feared the corpse's mouth might be clenched tight with *rigor mortis* and that she would have to suggest breaking the jaw to see the tongue. She now saw it would be unnecessary. The cheeks had collapsed, and the Pope's mouth gaped wide.

His tongue was black as death.

86

No light. No sound.

The Secret Archives were black.

Fear, Langdon now realized, was an intense motivator. Short of breath, he fumbled through the blackness toward the revolving door. He found the button on the wall and rammed his palm against it. Nothing happened. He tried again. The door was dead.

Spinning blind, he called out, but his voice emerged strangled. The peril of his predicament suddenly closed in around him. His lungs strained for oxygen as the adrenaline doubled his heart rate. He felt like someone had just punched him in the gut.

When he threw his weight into the door, for an instant he thought he felt the door start to turn. He pushed again, seeing stars. Now he realized it was the entire room turning, not the door. Staggering away, Langdon tripped over the base of a rolling ladder and fell hard. He tore his knee against the edge of a book stack. Swearing, he got up and groped for the ladder.

He found it. He had hoped it would be heavy wood or iron, but it was aluminum. He grabbed the ladder and held it like a battering ram. Then he ran through the dark at the glass wall. It was closer than he thought. The ladder hit head-on, bouncing off. From the feeble sound of the collision, Langdon knew he was going to need a hell of a lot more than an aluminum ladder to break this glass.

When he flashed on the semiautomatic, his hopes surged and then instantly fell. The weapon was gone. Olivetti had relieved him of it in the Pope's office, saying he did not want loaded weapons around with the camerlengo present. It made sense at the time.

Langdon called out again, making less sound than the last time.

Next he remembered the walkie-talkie the guard had left on the table outside the vault. *Why the hell didn't I bring it in!* As the purple stars began to dance before his eyes, Langdon forced himself to think. *You've been trapped before,* he told himself. *You survived worse. You were just a kid and you figured it out.* The crushing darkness came flooding in. *Think!*

Langdon lowered himself onto the floor. He rolled over on his back and laid his hands at his sides. The first step was to gain control.

Relax. Conserve.

No longer fighting gravity to pump blood, Langdon's heart began to slow. It was a trick swimmers used to re-oxygenate their blood between tightly scheduled races.

There is plenty of air in here, he told himself. *Plenty. Now think.* He waited, half-expecting the lights to come back on at any moment. They did not. As he lay there, able to breathe better now, an eerie resignation came across him. He felt peaceful. He fought it.

You will move, damn it! But where . . .

On Langdon's wrist, Mickey Mouse glowed happily as if enjoying the dark: 9.33 p.m. Half an hour until *Fire.* Langdon thought it felt a whole hell of a lot later. His mind, instead of coming up with a plan for escape, was suddenly demanding an explanation. *Who turned off the power? Was Rocher expanding his search? Wouldn't Olivetti have warned Rocher that I'm in here!* Langdon knew at this point it made no difference.

Opening his mouth wide and tipping back his head,

Langdon pulled the deepest breaths he could manage. Each breath burned a little less than the last. His head cleared. He reeled his thoughts in and forced the gears into motion.

Glass walls, he told himself. *But damn thick glass*.

He wondered if any of the books in here were stored in heavy, steel, fireproof file cabinets. Langdon had seen them from time to time in other archives but had seen none here. Besides, finding one in the dark could prove time-consuming. Not that he could lift one anyway, particularly in his present state.

How about the examination table? Langdon knew this vault, like the other, had an examination table in the center of the stacks. *So what!* He knew he couldn't lift it. Not to mention, even if he could drag it, he wouldn't get it far. The stacks were closely packed, the aisles between them far too narrow.

The aisles are too narrow . . .

Suddenly, Langdon knew.

With a burst of confidence, he jumped to his feet far too fast. Swaying in the fog of a head rush, he reached out in the dark for support. His hand found a stack. Waiting a moment, he forced himself to conserve. He would need all of his strength to do this.

Positioning himself against the book stack like a football player against a training sled, he planted his feet and pushed. *If I can somehow tip the shelf.* But it barely moved. He realigned and pushed again. His feet slipped backward on the floor. The stack creaked but did not move.

He needed leverage.

Finding the glass wall again, he placed one hand on it to guide him as he raced in the dark toward the far end of the vault. The back wall loomed suddenly, and he collided with it, crushing his shoulder. Cursing, Langdon circled the shelf and grabbed the stack at about eye level. Then, propping one leg on the glass behind him and another on the lower shelves, he started to climb. Books fell around him, fluttering into the darkness. He didn't care. Instinct for survival had long since overridden archival decorum. He sensed his equilibrium was hampered by the total darkness and closed his eyes, coaxing his brain to ignore visual input. He moved faster now. The air felt leaner the higher he went. He scrambled toward the upper shelves, stepping on books, trying to gain purchase, heaving himself upward. Then, like a rock climber conquering a rock face, Langdon grasped the top shelf. Stretching his legs out behind him, he walked his feet up the glass wall until he was almost horizontal.

Now or never, Robert, a voice urged. *Just like the leg press in the Harvard gym.*

With dizzying exertion, he planted his feet against the wall behind him, braced his arms and chest against the stack, and pushed. Nothing happened.

Fighting for air, he repositioned and tried again, extending his legs. Ever so slightly, the stack moved. He pushed again, and the stack rocked forward an inch or so and then back. Langdon took advantage of the motion, inhaling what felt like an oxygenless breath and heaving again. The shelf rocked farther.

Like a swing set, he told himself. *Keep the rhythm. A little more.*

Langdon rocked the shelf, extending his legs farther with each push. His quadriceps burned now, and he blocked the pain. The pendulum was in motion. *Three more pushes,* he urged himself.

It only took two.

There was an instant of weightless uncertainty. Then, with a thundering of books sliding off the shelves, Langdon and the shelf were falling forward.

Halfway to the ground, the shelf hit the stack next to it. Langdon hung on, throwing his weight forward, urging the second shelf to topple. There was a moment of motionless panic, and then, creaking under the weight, the second stack began to tip. Langdon was falling again.

Like enormous dominoes, the stacks began to topple, one after another. Metal on metal, books tumbling everywhere. Langdon held on as his inclined stack bounced downward like a ratchet on a jack. He wondered how many stacks there were in all. How much would they weigh? The glass at the far end was thick . . .

Langdon's stack had fallen almost to the horizontal when he heard what he was waiting for – a different kind of collision. Far off. At the end of the vault. The sharp smack of metal on glass. The vault around him shook, and Langdon knew the final stack, weighted down by the others, had hit the glass hard. The sound that followed was the most unwelcome sound Langdon had ever heard.

Silence.

There was no crashing of glass, only the resounding thud as the wall accepted the weight of the stacks now propped against it. He lay wide-eyed on the pile of books. Somewhere in the distance there was a creaking. Langdon would have held his breath to listen, but he had none left to hold.

One second. Two . . .

Then, as he teetered on the brink of unconsciousness, Langdon heard a distant yielding . . . a ripple spidering outward through the glass. Suddenly, like a cannon, the glass exploded. The stack beneath Langdon collapsed to the floor.

Like welcome rain on a desert, shards of glass tinkled downward in the dark. With a great sucking hiss, the air gushed in.

Thirty seconds later, in the Vatican Grottoes, Vittoria was standing before a corpse when the electronic squawk of a walkie-talkie broke the silence. The voice blaring out sounded short of breath. 'This is Robert Langdon! Can anyone hear me?'

Vittoria looked up. *Robert!* She could not believe how much she suddenly wished he were there.

The guards exchanged puzzled looks. One took a radio off his belt. 'Mr Langdon? You are on channel three. The commander is waiting to hear from you on channel one.'

'I know he's on channel one, damn it! I don't want to speak to him. I want the camerlengo. Now! Somebody find him for me.'

In the obscurity of the Secret Archives, Langdon stood amidst shattered glass and tried to catch his breath. He felt a warm liquid on his left hand and knew he was bleeding. The camerlengo's voice spoke at once, startling Langdon.

'This is Camerlengo Ventresca. What's going on?'

Langdon pressed the button, his heart still pounding. 'I think somebody just tried to kill me!'

There was a silence on the line.

Langdon tried to calm himself. 'I also know where the next killing is going to be.'

The voice that came back was not the camerlengo's.

387

It was Commander Olivetti's: 'Mr Langdon. Do not speak another word.'

87

Langdon's watch, now smeared with blood, read 9.41 p.m. as he ran across the Courtyard of the Belvedere and approached the fountain outside the Swiss Guard security center. His hand had stopped bleeding and now felt worse than it looked. As he arrived, it seemed everyone convened at once – Olivetti, Rocher, the camerlengo, Vittoria, and a handful of guards.

Vittoria hurried toward him immediately. 'Robert, you're hurt.'

Before Langdon could answer, Olivetti was before him. 'Mr Langdon, I'm relieved you're okay. I'm sorry about the crossed signals in the archives.'

'Crossed signals?' Langdon demanded. 'You knew damn well—'

'It was my fault,' Rocher said, stepping forward, sounding contrite. 'I had no idea you were in the archives. Portions of our white zones are cross-wired with that building. We were extending our search. I'm the one who killed power. If I had known . . '

'Robert,' Vittoria said, taking his wounded hand in hers and looking it over, 'the Pope was poisoned. The Illuminati killed him.'

Langdon heard the words, but they barely registered. He was saturated. All he could feel was the warmth of Vittoria's hands.

The camerlengo pulled a silk handkerchief from his

cassock and handed it to Langdon so he could clean himself. The man said nothing. His green eyes seemed filled with a new fire.

'Robert,' Vittoria pressed, 'you said you found where the next cardinal is going to be killed?'

Langdon felt flighty. 'I do, it's at the—'

'No,' Olivetti interrupted. 'Mr Langdon, when I asked you not to speak another word on the walkie-talkie, it was for a reason.' He turned to the handful of assembled Swiss Guards. 'Excuse us, gentlemen.'

The soldiers disappeared into the security center. No indignity. Only compliance.

Olivetti turned back to the remaining group. 'As much as it pains me to say this, the murder of our Pope is an act that could only have been accomplished with help from within these walls. For the good of all, we can trust no one. Including our guards.' He seemed to be suffering as he spoke the words.

Rocher looked anxious. 'Inside collusion implies—'

'Yes,' Olivetti said. 'The integrity of your search is compromised. And yet it is a gamble we must take. Keep looking.'

Rocher looked like he was about to say something, thought better of it, and left.

The camerlengo inhaled deeply. He had not said a word yet, and Langdon sensed a new rigor in the man, as if a turning point had been reached.

'Commander?' The camerlengo's tone was impermeable. 'I am going to break conclave.'

Olivetti pursed his lips, looking dour. 'I advise against it. We still have two hours and twenty minutes.'

'A heartbeat.'

Olivetti's tone was now challenging. 'What do you

intend to do? Evacuate the cardinals single-handedly?'

'I intend to save this church with whatever power God has given me. How I proceed is no longer your concern.'

Olivetti straightened. 'Whatever you intend to do . . ' He paused. 'I do not have the authority to restrain you. Particularly in light of my apparent failure as head of security. I ask only that you wait. Wait twenty minutes . . . until after ten o'clock. If Mr Langdon's information is correct, I may still have a chance to catch this assassin. There is still a chance to preserve protocol and decorum.'

'Decorum?' The camerlengo let out a choked laugh. 'We have long since passed propriety, commander. In case you hadn't noticed, this is war.'

A guard emerged from the security center and called out to the camerlengo, 'Signore, I just got word we have detained the BBC reporter, Mr Glick.'

The camerlengo nodded. 'Have both he and his camerawoman meet me outside the Sistine Chapel.'

Olivetti's eyes widened. 'What are you doing?'

'Twenty minutes, commander. That's all I'm giving you.' Then he was gone.

When Olivetti's Alfa Romeo tore out of Vatican City, this time there was no line of unmarked cars following him. In the back seat, Vittoria bandaged Langdon's hand with a first-aid kit she'd found in the glove box.

Olivetti stared straight ahead. 'Okay Mr. Langdon. Where are we going?'

88

Even with its siren now affixed and blaring, Olivetti's Alfa Romeo seemed to go unnoticed as it rocketed across the bridge into the heart of old Rome. All the traffic was moving in the other direction, toward the Vatican, as if the Holy See had suddenly become the hottest entertainment in Rome.

Langdon sat in the backseat, the questions whipping through his mind. He wondered about the killer, if they would catch him this time, if he would tell them what they needed to know, if it was already too late. How long before the camerlengo told the crowd in St Peter's Square they were in danger? The incident in the vault still nagged. *A mistake.*

Olivetti never touched the brakes as he snaked the howling Alfa Romeo toward the Church of Santa Maria della Vittoria. Langdon knew on any other day his knuckles would have been white. At the moment, however, he felt anesthetized. Only the throbbing in his hand reminded him where he was.

Overhead, the siren wailed. *Nothing like telling him we're coming*, Langdon thought. And yet they were making incredible time. He guessed Olivetti would kill the siren as they drew nearer.

Now with a moment to sit and reflect, Langdon felt a tinge of amazement as the news of the Pope's murder finally registered in his mind. The thought was inconceivable, and yet somehow it seemed a perfectly logical event. Infiltration had always been the Illuminati powerbase – rearrangements of power from within. And it was not as if Popes had never been murdered. Countless rumors of treachery abounded, although with no autopsy, none was ever confirmed. Until recently. Academics not long ago had gotten permission to X-ray the tomb of Pope Celestine V, who had allegedly died at the hands of his overeager successor, Boniface VIII. The researchers had hoped the X-ray might reveal some small hint of foul play – a broken bone perhaps. Incredibly, the X-ray had revealed a ten-inch nail driven into the Pope's skull.

Langdon now recalled a series of news clippings fellow Illuminati buffs had sent him years ago. At first he had thought the clippings were a prank, so he'd gone to the Harvard microfiche collection to confirm the articles were authentic. Incredibly, they were. He now kept them on his bulletin board as examples of how even respectable news organizations sometimes got carried away with Illuminati paranoia. Suddenly, the media's suspicions seemed a lot less paranoid. Langdon could see the articles clearly in his mind . . .

THE BRITISH BROADCASTING CORPORATION
June 14,1998

Pope John Paul I, who died in 1978, fell victim to a plot by the P2 Masonic Lodge . . . The secret society P2 decided to murder John Paul I when it saw he was determined to dismiss the American Archbishop Paul Marcinkus as President of the Vatican Bank. The Bank had been implicated in shady financial deals with the Masonic Lodge . . .

THE NEW YORK TIMES
August 24, 1998

Why was the late John Paul I wearing his day shirt in

bed? Why was it torn? The questions don't stop there. No medical investigations were made. Cardinal Villot forbade an autopsy on the grounds that no Pope was ever given a postmortem. And John Paul's medicines mysteriously vanished from his bedside, as did his glasses, slippers and his last will and testament.

LONDON DAILY MAIL
August 27, 1998

... a plot including a powerful, ruthless and illegal Masonic lodge with tentacles stretching into the Vatican.

The cellular in Vittoria's pocket rang, thankfully erasing the memories from Langdon's mind.

Vittoria answered, looking confused as to who might be calling her. Even from a few feet away, Langdon recognized the laserlike voice on the phone.

'Vittoria? This is Maximilian Kohler. Have you found the antimatter yet?'

'Max? You're okay?'

'I saw the news. There was no mention of CERN or the antimatter. This is good. What is happening?'

'We haven't located the canister yet. The situation is complex. Robert Langdon has been quite an asset. We have a lead on catching the man assassinating cardinals. Right now we are headed—'

'Ms Vetra,' Olivetti interrupted. 'You've said enough.'

She covered the receiver, clearly annoyed. 'Commander, this is the president of CERN. Certainly he has a right to—'

'He has a right,' Olivetti snapped, 'to be here handling this situation. You're on an open cellular line. You've said enough.'

Vittoria took a deep breath. 'Max?'

'I may have some information for you,' Max said. 'About your father . . . I may know who he told about the antimatter.'

Vittoria's expression clouded. 'Max, my father said he told no one.'

'I'm afraid, Vittoria, your father *did* tell someone. I need to check some security records. I will be in touch soon.' The line went dead.

Vittoria looked waxen as she returned the phone to her pocket.

'You okay?' Langdon asked.

Vittoria nodded, her trembling fingers revealing the lie.

'The church is near Piazza Barberini,' Olivetti said, killing the siren and checking his watch. 'We have nine minutes.'

When Langdon had first realized the location of the third marker, the position of the church had rung some distant bell for him. *Piazza Barberini*. Something about the name was familiar . . . something he could not place. Now Langdon realized what it was. The piazza was the sight of a controversial subway stop. Twenty years ago, construction of the subway terminal had created a stir among art historians who feared digging beneath Piazza Barberini might topple the multiton obelisk that stood in the center. City planners had removed the obelisk and replaced it with a small fountain called the *Triton*.

In Bernini's day, Langdon now realized, *Piazza Barberini had contained an obelisk!* Whatever doubts Langdon had felt that this was the location of the third marker now totally evaporated.

A block from the piazza, Olivetti turned into an alley, gunned the car halfway down, and skidded to a stop. He pulled off his suit jacket, rolled up his sleeves, and loaded his weapon.

'We can't risk your being recognized,' he said. 'You two were on television. I want you across the piazza, out of sight, watching the front entrance. I'm going in the back.' He produced a familiar pistol and handed it to Langdon. 'Just in case.'

Langdon frowned. It was the second time today he had been handed the gun. He slid it into his breast pocket. As he did, he realized he was still carrying the folio from *Diagramma*. He couldn't believe he had forgotten to leave it behind. He pictured the Vatican Curator collapsing in spasms of outrage at the thought of this priceless artifact being packed around Rome like some tourist map. Then Langdon thought of the mess of shattered glass and strewn documents that he'd left behind in the archives. The curator had other problems. *If the archives even survive the night . . .*

Olivetti got out of the car and motioned back up the alley. 'The piazza is that way. Keep your eyes open and don't let yourselves be seen.' He tapped the phone on his belt. 'Ms Vetra, let's retest our auto dial.'

Vittoria removed her phone and hit the auto dial number she and Olivetti had programmed at the Pantheon. Olivetti's phone vibrated in silent-ring mode on his belt.

The commander nodded. 'Good. If you see anything, I want to know.' He cocked his weapon. 'I'll be inside waiting. This heathen is mine.'

At that moment, very nearby, another cellular phone was ringing.

The Hassassin answered. 'Speak.'

'It is I,' the voice said. 'Janus.'

The Hassassin smiled. 'Hello, master.'

'Your position may be known. Someone is coming to stop you.'

'They are too late. I have already made the arrangements here.'

'Good. Make sure you escape alive. There is work yet to be done.'

'Those who stand in my way will die.'

'Those who stand in your way are knowledgeable.'

'You speak of an American scholar?'

'You are aware of him?'

The Hassassin chuckled. 'Cool-tempered but naïve. He spoke to me on the phone earlier. He is with a female who seems quite the opposite.' The killer felt a stirring of arousal as he recalled the fiery temperament of Leonardo Vetra's daughter.

There was a momentary silence on the line, the first hesitation the Hassassin had ever sensed from his Illuminati master. Finally, Janus spoke. 'Eliminate them if need be.'

The killer smiled. 'Consider it done.' He felt a warm anticipation spreading through his body. *Although the woman I may keep as a prize.*

89

War had broken out in St Peter's Square.

The piazza had exploded into a frenzy of aggression. Media trucks skidded into place like assault vehicles claiming beachheads. Reporters unfurled high-tech electronics like soldiers arming for battle. All around the perimeter of the square, networks jockeyed for position as they raced to erect the newest weapon in media wars – flat-screen displays.

Flat-screen displays were enormous video screens that could be assembled on top of trucks or portable scaffolding. The screens served as a kind of billboard advertisement for the network, broadcasting that network's coverage and corporate logo like a drive-in movie. If a screen were well-situated – in front of the action, for example – a competing network could not shoot the story without including an advertisement for their competitor.

The square was quickly becoming not only a multi-media extravaganza, but a frenzied public vigil. Onlookers poured in from all directions. Open space in the usually limitless square was fast becoming a valuable commodity. People clustered around the towering flat-screen displays, listening to live reports in stunned excitement.

Only a hundred yards away, inside the thick walls of St Peter's Basilica, the world was serene. Lieutenant Chartrand and three other guards moved through the darkness. Wearing their infrared goggles, they fanned out across the nave, swinging their detectors before them. The search of Vatican City's public access areas so far had yielded nothing.

'Better remove your goggles up here,' the senior guard said.

Chartrand was already doing it. They were nearing the Niche of the Palliums – the sunken area in the center of the basilica. It was lit by ninety-nine oil lamps, and the amplified infrared would have seared their eyes.

Chartrand enjoyed being out of the heavy goggles, and he stretched his neck as they descended into the sunken niche to scan the area. The room was beautiful . . . golden and glowing. He had not been down here yet.

It seemed every day since Chartrand had arrived in Vatican City he had learned some new Vatican mystery. These oil lamps were one of them. There were exactly ninety-nine lamps burning at all times. It was tradition. The clergy vigilantly refilled the lamps with sacred oils such that no lamp ever burned out. It was said they would burn until the end of time.

Or at least until midnight, Chartrand thought, feeling his mouth go dry again.

Chartrand swung his detector over the oil lamps. Nothing hidden in here. He was not surprised; the canister, according to the video feed, was hidden in a *dark* area.

As he moved across the niche, he came to a bulkhead grate covering a hole in the floor. The hole led to a steep and narrow stairway that went straight down. He had heard stories about what lay down there. Thankfully they would not have to descend. Rocher's orders were clear. *Search only the public access areas; ignore the white zones.*

'What's that smell?' he asked, turning away from the grate. The niche smelled intoxicatingly sweet.

'Fumes from the lamps,' one of them replied.

Chartrand was surprised. 'Smells more like cologne than kerosene.'

'It's not kerosene. These lamps are close to the papal

altar, so they take a special, ambiental mixture – ethanol, sugar, butane, and perfume.'

'Butane?' Chartrand eyed the lamps uneasily

The guard nodded. 'Don't spill any. Smells like heaven, but burns like hell.'

The guards had completed searching the Niche of the Palliums and were moving across the basilica again when their walkie-talkies went off.

It was an update. The guards listened in shock.

Apparently there were troubling new developments, which could not be shared on-air, but the camerlengo had decided to break tradition and enter conclave to address the cardinals. Never before in history had this been done. Then again, Chartrand realized, never before in history had the Vatican been sitting on what amounted to some sort of neoteric nuclear warhead.

Chartrand felt comforted to know the camerlengo was taking control. The camerlengo was the person inside Vatican City for whom Chartrand held the most respect. Some of the guards thought of the camerlengo as a *beato* – a religious zealot whose love of God bordered on obsession – but even they agreed ... when it came to fighting the enemies of God, the camerlengo was the one man who would stand up and play hardball.

The Swiss Guards had seen a lot of the camerlengo this week in preparation for conclave, and everyone had commented that the man seemed a bit rough around the edges, his verdant eyes a bit more intense than usual. Not surprisingly, they had all commented; not only was the camerlengo responsible for planning the sacred conclave, but he had to do it immediately on the heels of the loss of his mentor, the Pope.

Chartrand had only been at the Vatican a few months when he heard the story of the bomb that blew up the camerlengo's mother before the kid's very eyes. *A bomb in church . . . and now it's happening all over again.* Sadly, the authorities never caught the bastards who planted the bomb ... probably some anti-Christian hate group they said, and the case faded away. No wonder the camerlengo despised apathy.

A couple months back, on a peaceful afternoon inside Vatican City, Chartrand had bumped into the camerlengo coming across the grounds. The camerlengo had apparently recognized Chartrand as a new guard and invited him to accompany him on a stroll. They had talked about nothing in particular, and the camerlengo made Chartrand feel immediately at home.

'Father,' Chartrand said, 'may I ask you a strange question?'

The camerlengo smiled. 'Only if I may give you a strange answer.'

Chartrand laughed. 'I have asked every priest I know, and I still don't understand.'

'What troubles you?' The camerlengo led the way in short, quick strides, his frock kicking out in front of him as he walked. His black, crepe-sole shoes seemed befitting, Chartrand thought, like reflections of the man's essence ... modern but humble, and showing signs of wear.

Chartrand took a deep breath. 'I don't understand this *omnipotent-benevolent* thing.'

The camerlengo smiled. 'You've been reading Scripture.'

'I try.'

'You are confused because the Bible describes God as an omnipotent and benevolent deity.'

'Exactly.'

'Omnipotent-benevolent simply means that God is all-powerful *and* well-meaning.'

'I understand the concept. It's just . . . there seems to be a contradiction.'

'Yes. The contradiction is pain. Man's starvation, war, sickness . . .'

'Exactly!' Chartrand knew the camerlengo would understand. 'Terrible things happen in this world. Human tragedy seems like proof that God could not possibly be *both* all-powerful and well-meaning. If He *loves* us and has the *power* to change our situation, He would prevent our pain, wouldn't He?'

The camerlengo frowned. 'Would He?'

Chartrand felt uneasy. Had he overstepped his bounds? Was this one of those religious questions you just didn't ask? 'Well . . . if God loves us, and He can protect us, He would *have* to. It seems He is either omnipotent and uncaring, or benevolent and powerless to help.'

'Do you have children, Lieutenant?'

Chartrand flushed. 'No, signore.'

'Imagine you had an eight-year-old son . . . would you love him?'

'Of course.'

'Would you do everything in your power to prevent pain in his life?'

'Of course.'

'Would you let him skateboard?'

Chartrand did a double take. The camerlengo always seemed oddly 'in touch' for a clergyman. 'Yeah, I guess,' Chartrand said. 'Sure, I'd let him skateboard, but I'd tell him to be careful.'

'So as this child's father, you would give him some basic, good advice and then let him go off and make his own mistakes?'

'I wouldn't run behind him and mollycoddle him if that's what you mean.'

'But what if he fell and skinned his knee?'

'He would learn to be more careful.'

The camerlengo smiled. 'So although you have the *power* to interfere and prevent your child's pain, you would *choose* to show your love by letting him learn his own lessons?'

'Of course. Pain is part of growing up. It's how we learn.'

The camerlengo nodded. 'Exactly.'

90

Langdon and Vittoria observed Piazza Barberini from the shadows of a small alleyway on the western corner. The church was opposite them, a hazy cupola emerging from a faint cluster of buildings across the square. The night had brought with it a welcome cool, and Langdon was surprised to find the square deserted. Above them, through open windows, blaring televisions reminded Langdon where everyone had disappeared to.

'. . . no comment yet from the Vatican . . . Illuminati murders of two cardinals . . . satanic presence in Rome . . . speculation about further infiltration . . .'

The news had spread like Nero's fire. Rome sat riveted, as did the rest of the world. Langdon wondered if they would really be able to stop this runaway train. As he scanned the piazza and waited, Langdon realized that despite the encroachment of modern buildings, the piazza still looked remarkably elliptical. High above, like some sort of modern shrine to a bygone hero, an enormous neon sign blinked on the roof of a luxurious hotel. Vittoria had already pointed it out to Langdon. The sign seemed eerily befitting.

HOTEL BERNINI

'Five of ten,' Vittoria said, cat eyes darting around the square. No sooner had she spoken the words than she grabbed Langdon's arm and pulled him back into the shadows. She motioned into the center of the square.

Langdon followed her gaze. When he saw it, he stiffened.

Crossing in front of them, beneath a street lamp, two dark figures appeared. Both were cloaked, their heads covered with dark *mantles*, the traditional black covering of Catholic widows. Langdon would have guessed they were women, but he couldn't be sure in the dark. One looked elderly and moved as if in pain, hunched over. The other, larger and stronger, was helping.

'Give me the gun,' Vittoria said.

'You can't just—'

Fluid as a cat, Vittoria was in and out of his pocket once again. The gun glinted in her hand. Then, in absolute silence, as if her feet never touched the cobblestone, she was circling left in the shadows, arching across the square to approach the couple from the

403

rear. Langdon stood transfixed as Vittoria disappeared. Then, swearing to himself, he hurried after her.

The couple was moving slowly, and it was only a matter of half a minute before Langdon and Vittoria were positioned behind them, closing in from the rear. Vittoria concealed the gun beneath casually crossed arms in front of her, out of sight but accessible in a flash. She seemed to float faster and faster as the gap lessened, and Langdon battled to keep up. When his shoes scuffed a stone and sent it skittering, Vittoria shot him a sideways glare. But the couple did not seem to hear. They were talking.

At thirty feet, Langdon could start to hear voices. No words. Just faint murmurings. Beside him, Vittoria moved faster with every step. Her arms loosened before her, the gun starting to peek out. Twenty feet. The voices were clearer – one much louder than the other. Angry. Ranting. Langdon sensed it was the voice of an old woman. Gruff. Androgynous. He strained to hear what she was saying, but another voice cut the night.

'*Mi scusi!*' Vittoria's friendly tone lit the square like a torch.

Langdon tensed as the cloaked couple stopped short and began to turn. Vittoria kept striding toward them, even faster now, on a collision course. They would have no time to react. Langdon realized his own feet had stopped moving. From behind, he saw Vittoria's arms loosening, her hand coming free, the gun swinging forward. Then, over her shoulder, he saw a face, lit now in the street lamp. The panic surged to his legs, and he lunged forward. 'Vittoria no!'

Vittoria, however, seemed to exist a split second

ahead of him. In a motion as swift as it was casual, Vittoria's arms were raised again, the gun disappearing as she clutched herself like a woman on a chilly night. Langdon stumbled to her side, almost colliding with the cloaked couple before them.

'*Buona sera*,' Vittoria blurted, her voice startled with retreat.

Langdon exhaled in relief. Two elderly women stood before them scowling out from beneath their mantles. One was so old she could barely stand. The other was helping her. Both clutched rosaries. They seemed confused by the sudden interruption.

Vittoria smiled, although she looked shaken. '*Dov'è la chiesa Santa Maria della Vittoria?* Where is the Church of—'

The two women motioned in unison to a bulky silhouette of a building on an inclined street from the direction they had come. '*È là.*'

'*Grazie*,' Langdon said, putting his hands on Vittoria's shoulders and gently pulling her back. He couldn't believe they'd almost attacked a pair of old ladies.

'*Non si puó entrare*,' one woman warned. '*È chiusa temprano.*'

'Closed early?' Vittoria looked surprised. '*Perchè?*'

Both women explained at once. They sounded irate. Langdon understood only parts of the grumbling Italian. Apparently, the women had been inside the church fifteen minutes ago praying for the Vatican in its time of need, when some man had appeared and told them the church was closing early.

'*Hanno conosciuto l'uomo?*' Vittoria demanded, sounding tense. 'Did you know the man?'

The women shook their heads. The man was a

straniero crudo, they explained, and he had forcibly made everyone inside leave, even the young priest and janitor, who said they were calling the police. But the intruder had only laughed, telling them to be sure the police brought cameras.

Cameras? Langdon wondered.

The women clucked angrily and called the man a *bar-àrabo*. Then, grumbling, they continued on their way.

'Bar-àrabo?' Langdon asked Vittoria. 'A barbarian?'

Vittoria looked suddenly taut. 'Not quite. *Bar-àrabo* is derogatory wordplay. It means *Àrabo* . . . Arab.'

Langdon felt a shiver and turned toward the outline of the church. As he did, his eyes glimpsed something in the church's stained-glass windows. The image shot dread through his body.

Unaware, Vittoria removed her cell phone and pressed the auto dial. 'I'm warning Olivetti.'

Speechless, Langdon reached out and touched her arm. With a tremulous hand, he pointed to the church.

Vittoria let out a gasp.

Inside the building, glowing like evil eyes through the stained-glass windows . . . shone the growing flash of flames.

91

Langdon and Vittoria dashed to the main entrance of the church of Santa Maria della Vittoria and found the wooden door locked. Vittoria fired three shots from

Olivetti's semi-automatic into the ancient bolt, and it shattered.

The church had no anteroom, so the entirety of the sanctuary spread out in one gasping sweep as Langdon and Vittoria threw open the main door. The scene before them was so unexpected, so bizarre, that Langdon had to close his eyes and reopen them before his mind could take it all in.

The church was lavish baroque . . . gilded walls and altars. Dead center of the sanctuary, beneath the main cupola, wooden pews had been stacked high and were now ablaze in some sort of epic funeral pyre. A bonfire shooting high into the dome. As Langdon's eyes followed the inferno upward, the true horror of the scene descended like a bird of prey.

High overhead, from the left and right sides of the ceiling, hung two incensor cables – lines used for swinging frankincense vessels above the congregation. These lines, however, carried no incensors now. Nor were they swinging. They had been used for something else . . .

Suspended from the cables was a human being. A naked man. Each wrist had been connected to an opposing cable, and he had been hoisted almost to the point of being torn apart. His arms were outstretched in a spread-eagle as if he were nailed to some sort of invisible crucifix hovering within the house of God.

Langdon felt paralyzed as he stared upward. A moment later, he witnessed the final abomination. The old man was alive, and he raised his head. A pair of terrified eyes gazed down in a silent plea for help. On the man's chest was a scorched emblem. He had been branded. Langdon could not see it clearly, but he had little doubt what the marking said. As the flames climbed higher, lapping at the man's feet, the victim let out a cry of pain, his body trembling.

As if ignited by some unseen force, Langdon felt his body suddenly in motion, dashing down the main aisle toward the conflagration. His lungs filled with smoke as he closed in. Ten feet from the inferno, at a full sprint, Langdon hit a wall of heat. The skin on his face singed, and he fell back, shielding his eyes and landing hard on the marble floor. Staggering upright, he pressed forward again, hands raised in protection.

Instantly he knew. The fire was far too hot.

Moving back again, he scanned the chapel walls. *A heavy tapestry*, he thought. *If I can somehow smother the . . .* But he knew a tapestry was not to be found. *This is a baroque chapel, Robert, not some damn German castle! Think!* He forced his eyes back to the suspended man.

High above, smoke and flames swirled in the cupola. The incensor cables stretched outward from the man's wrists, rising to the ceiling where they passed through pulleys, and descended again to metal cleats on either side of the church. Langdon looked over at one of the cleats. It was high on the wall, but he knew if he could get to it and loosen one of the lines, the tension would slacken and the man would swing wide of the fire.

A sudden surge of flames crackled higher, and Langdon heard a piercing scream from above. The skin on the man's feet was starting to blister. The cardinal was being roasted alive. Langdon fixed his sights on the cleat and ran for it.

In the rear of the church, Vittoria clutched the back of a pew, trying to gather her senses. The image overhead was horrid. She forced her eyes away. *Do something!*

She wondered where Olivetti was. Had he seen the Hassassin? Had he caught him? Where were they now? Vittoria moved forward to help Langdon, but as she did, a sound stopped her.

The crackling of the flames was getting louder by the instant, but a second sound also cut the air. A metallic vibration. Nearby The repetitive pulse seemed to emanate from the end of the pews to her left. It was a stark rattle, like the ringing of a phone, but stony and hard. She clutched the gun firmly and moved down the row of pews. The sound grew louder. On. Off. A recurrent vibration.

As she approached the end of the aisle, she sensed the sound was coming from the floor just around the corner at the end of the pews. As she moved forward, gun outstretched in her right hand, she realized she was also holding something in her left hand – her cell phone. In her panic she had forgotten that outside she had used it to dial the commander ... setting off his phone's silent vibration feature as a warning. Vittoria raised her phone to her ear. It was still ringing. The commander had never answered. Suddenly, with rising fear, Vittoria sensed she knew what was making the sound. She stepped forward, trembling.

The entire church seemed to sink beneath her feet as her eyes met the lifeless form on the floor. No stream of liquid flowed from the body. No signs of violence tattooed the flesh. There was only the fearful geometry of the commander's head ... torqued backward, twisted 180 degrees in the wrong direction. Vittoria fought the images of her own father's mangled body

The phone on the commander's belt lay against the floor, vibrating over and over against the cold marble. Vittoria hung up her own phone, and the ringing stopped. In the silence, Vittoria heard a new sound. A breathing in the dark directly behind her.

She started to spin, gun raised, but she knew she was too late. A laser beam of heat screamed from the top of her skull to the soles of her feet as the killer's elbow crashed down on the back of her neck.

'Now you are mine,' a voice said.

Then, everything went black.

Across the sanctuary, on the left lateral wall, Langdon balanced atop a pew and scraped upward on the wall trying to reach the cleat. The cable was still six feet above his head. Cleats like these were common in churches and were placed high to prevent tampering. Langdon knew priests used wooden ladders called *piuòli* to access the cleats. The killer had obviously used the church's ladder to hoist his victim. *So where the hell is the ladder now!* Langdon looked down, searching the floor around him. He had a faint recollection of seeing a ladder in here somewhere. *But where?* A moment later his heart sank. He realized where he had seen it. He turned toward the raging fire. Sure enough, the ladder was high atop the blaze, engulfed in flames.

Filled now with desperation, Langdon scanned the entire church from his raised platform, looking for anything at all that could help him reach the cleat. As his eyes probed the church, he had a sudden realization.

Where the hell is Vittoria? She had disappeared. *Did she go for help?* Langdon screamed out her name, but there was no response. *And where is Olivetti!*

There was a howl of pain from above, and Langdon sensed he was already too late. As his eyes went skyward again and saw the slowly roasting victim,

Langdon had thoughts for only one thing. *Water. Lots of it. Put out the fire. At least lower the flames.* 'I need water, damn it!' he yelled out loud.

'That's next,' a voice growled from the back of the church.

Langdon wheeled, almost falling off the pews.

Striding up the side aisle directly toward him came a dark monster of a man. Even in the glow of the fire, his eyes burned black. Langdon recognized the gun in his hand as the one from his own jacket pocket . . . the one Vittoria had been carrying when they came in.

The sudden wave of panic that rose in Langdon was a frenzy of disjunct fears. His initial instinct was for Vittoria. What had this animal done to her? Was she hurt? Or *worse?* In the same instant, Langdon realized the man overhead was screaming louder. The cardinal would die. Helping him now was impossible. Then, as the Hassassin leveled the gun at Langdon's chest, Langdon's panic turned inward, his senses on overload. He reacted on instinct as the shot went off. Launching off the bench, Langdon sailed arms first over the sea of church pews.

When he hit the pews, he hit harder than he had imagined, immediately rolling to the floor. The marble cushioned his fall with all the grace of cold steel. Footsteps closed to his right. Langdon turned his body toward the front of the church and began scrambling for his life beneath the pews.

High above the chapel floor, Cardinal Guidera endured his last torturous moments of consciousness. As he looked down the length of his naked body, he saw the skin on his legs begin to blister and peel away. *I am in hell,* he decided. *God, why hast thou forsaken me?*

411

He knew this must be hell because he was looking at the brand on his chest upside down ... and yet, as if by the devil's magic, the word made perfect sense.

92

Three ballotings. No Pope.

Inside the Sistine Chapel, Cardinal Mortati had begun praying for a miracle. *Send us the candidates!* The delay had gone long enough. A *single* missing candidate, Mortati could understand. But all four? It left no options. Under these conditions, achieving a two-thirds majority would take an act of God Himself.

When the bolts on the outer door began to grind open, Mortati and the entire College of Cardinals wheeled in unison toward the entrance. Mortati knew this unsealing could mean only one thing. By law, the chapel door could only be unsealed for two reasons – to remove the very ill, or to admit late cardinals.

The preferiti are coming!

Mortati's heart soared. Conclave had been saved.

But when the door opened, the gasp that echoed through the chapel was not one of joy. Mortati stared in incredulous shock as the man walked in. For the first time in Vatican history, a *camerlengo* had just crossed the sacred threshold of conclave *after* sealing the doors.

What is he thinking!

The camerlengo strode to the altar and turned to address the thunderstruck audience. 'Signori,' he said, 'I have waited as long as I can. There is something you have a right to know.'

93

Langdon had no idea where he was going. Reflex was his only compass, driving him away from danger. His elbows and knees burned as he clambered beneath the pews. Still he clawed on. Somewhere a voice was telling him to move left. *If you can get to the main aisle, you can dash for the exit.* He knew it was impossible. *There's a wall of flames blocking the main aisle!* His mind hunting for options, Langdon scrambled blindly on. The footsteps closed faster now to his right.

When it happened, Langdon was unprepared. He had guessed he had another ten feet of pews until he reached the front of the church. He had guessed wrong. Without warning, the cover above him ran out. He froze for an instant, half exposed at the front of the church. Rising in the recess to his left, gargantuan from this vantage point, was the very thing that had brought him here. He had entirely forgotten. Bernini's *Ecstasy of St Teresa* rose up like some sort of pornographic still life . . . the saint on her back, arched in pleasure, mouth open in a moan, and over her, an angel pointing his spear of fire.

413

A bullet exploded in the pew over Langdon's head. He felt his body rise like a sprinter out of a gate. Fueled only by adrenaline, and barely conscious of his actions, he was suddenly running, hunched, head down, pounding across the front of the church to his right. As the bullets erupted behind him, Langdon dove yet again, sliding out of control across the marble floor before crashing in a heap against the railing of a niche on the right-hand wall.

It was then that he saw her. A crumpled heap near the back of the church. *Vittoria!* Her bare legs were twisted beneath her, but Langdon sensed somehow that she was breathing. He had no time to help her.

Immediately, the killer rounded the pews on the far left of the church and bore relentlessly down. Langdon knew in a heartbeat it was over. The killer raised the weapon, and Langdon did the only thing he could do. He rolled his body over the banister into the niche. As he hit the floor on the other side, the marble columns of the balustrade exploded in a storm of bullets.

Langdon felt like a cornered animal as he scrambled deeper into the semicircular niche. Rising before him, the niche's sole contents seemed ironically apropos – a single sarcophagus. *Mine perhaps*, Langdon thought. Even the casket itself seemed fitting. It was a *scàtola* – a small, unadorned, marble box. Burial on a budget. The casket was raised off the floor on two marble blocks, and Langdon eyed the opening beneath it, wondering if he could slide through.

Footsteps echoed behind him.

With no other option in sight, Langdon pressed himself to the floor and slithered toward the casket. Grabbing the two marble supports, one with each hand, he pulled like a breaststroker, dragging his torso

414

into the opening beneath the tomb. The gun went off.

Accompanying the roar of the gun, Langdon felt a sensation he had never felt in his life . . . a bullet sailing past his flesh. There was a hiss of wind, like the backlash of a whip, as the bullet just missed him and exploded in the marble with a puff of dust. Blood surging, Langdon heaved his body the rest of the way beneath the casket. Scrambling across the marble floor, he pulled himself out from beneath the casket and to the other side.

Dead end.

Langdon was now face to face with the rear wall of the niche. He had no doubt that this tiny space behind the tomb would become his grave. *And soon*, he realized, as he saw the barrel of the gun appear in the opening beneath the sarcophagus. The Hassassin held the weapon parallel with the floor, pointing directly at Langdon's midsection.

Impossible to miss.

Langdon felt a trace of self-preservation grip his unconscious mind. He twisted his body onto his stomach, parallel with the casket. Face down, he planted his hands flat on the floor, the glass cut from the archives pinching open with a stab. Ignoring the pain, he pushed. Driving his body upward in an awkward push-up, Langdon arched his stomach off the floor just as the gun went off. He could feel the shock wave of the bullets as they sailed beneath him and pulverized the porous travertine behind. Closing his eyes and straining against exhaustion, Langdon prayed for the thunder to stop.

And then it did.

The roar of gunfire was replaced with the cold click of an empty chamber.

Langdon opened his eyes slowly, almost fearful his eyelids would make a sound. Fighting the trembling pain, he held his position, arched like a cat. He didn't even dare breathe. His eardrums numbed by gunfire, Langdon listened for any hint of the killer's departure. Silence. He thought of Vittoria and ached to help her.

The sound that followed was deafening. Barely human. A guttural bellow of exertion.

The sarcophagus over Langdon's head suddenly seemed to rise on its side. Langdon collapsed on the floor as hundreds of pounds teetered toward him. Gravity overcame friction, and the lid was the first to go, sliding off the tomb and crashing to the floor beside him. The casket came next, rolling off its supports and toppling upside down toward Langdon.

As the box rolled, Langdon knew he would either be entombed in the hollow beneath it or crushed by one of the edges. Pulling in his legs and head, Langdon compacted his body and yanked his arms to his sides. Then he closed his eyes and awaited the sickening crush.

When it came, the entire floor shook beneath him. The upper rim landed only millimeters from the top of his head, rattling his teeth in their sockets. His right arm, which Langdon had been certain would be crushed, miraculously still felt intact. He opened his eyes to see a shaft of light. The right rim of the casket had not fallen all the way to the floor and was still propped partially on its supports. Directly overhead, though, Langdon found himself staring quite literally into the face of death.

The original occupant of the tomb was suspended above him, having adhered, as decaying bodies often did, to the bottom of the casket. The skeleton hovered a moment, like a tentative lover, and then with a sticky crackling, it succumbed to gravity and peeled away. The carcass rushed down to embrace him, raining putrid bones and dust into Langdon's eyes and mouth.

Before Langdon could react, a blind arm was slithering through the opening beneath the casket, sifting through the carcass like a hungry python. It groped until it found Langdon's neck and clamped down. Langdon tried to fight back against the iron fist now crushing his larynx, but he found his left sleeve pinched beneath the edge of the coffin. He had only one arm free, and the fight was a losing battle.

Langdon's legs bent in the only open space he had, his feet searching for the casket floor above him. He found it. Coiling, he planted his feet. Then, as the hand around his neck squeezed tighter, Langdon closed his eyes and extended his legs like a ram. The casket shifted, ever so slightly, but enough.

With a raw grinding, the sarcophagus slid off the supports and landed on the floor. The casket rim crashed onto the killer's arm, and there was a muffled scream of pain. The hand released Langdon's neck, twisting and jerking away into the dark. When the killer finally pulled his arm free, the casket fell with a conclusive thud against the flat marble floor.

Complete darkness. Again.

And silence.

There was no frustrated pounding outside the overturned sarcophagus. No prying to get in. Nothing. As Langdon lay in the dark amidst a pile of bones, he fought the closing darkness and turned his thoughts to her.

Vittoria. Are you alive?

If Langdon had known the truth – the horror to which Vittoria would soon awake – he would have wished for her sake that she were dead.

94

Sitting in the Sistine Chapel among his stunned colleagues, Cardinal Mortati tried to comprehend the words he was hearing. Before him, lit only by the candlelight, the camerlengo had just told a tale of such hatred and treachery that Mortati found himself trembling. The camerlengo spoke of kidnapped cardinals, branded cardinals, *murdered* cardinals. He spoke of the ancient Illuminati – a name that dredged up forgotten fears – and of their resurgence and vow of revenge against the church. With pain in his voice, the camerlengo spoke of his late Pope . . . the victim of an Illuminati poisoning. And finally, his words almost a whisper, he spoke of a deadly new technology, anti-matter, which in less than two hours threatened to destroy all of Vatican City.

When he was through, it was as if Satan himself had sucked the air from the room. Nobody could move. The camerlengo's words hung in the darkness.

The only sound Mortati could now hear was the anomalous hum of a television camera in back – an electronic presence no conclave in history had ever endured – but a presence demanded by the camerlengo. To the utter astonishment of the cardinals, the camerlengo had entered the Sistine Chapel with two BBC reporters – a man and a woman – and announced that they would be transmitting his solemn statement, *live* to the world.

Now, speaking directly to the camera, the camerlengo stepped forward. 'To the Illuminati,' he said, his voice deepening, 'and to those of science, let me say this.' He paused. 'You have won the war.'

The silence spread now to the deepest corners of the chapel. Mortati could hear the desperate thumping of his own heart.

'The wheels have been in motion for a long time,' the camerlengo said. 'Your victory has been inevitable. Never before has it been as obvious as it is at this moment. Science is the new God.'

What is he saying! Mortati thought. *Has he gone mad? The entire world is hearing this!*

'Medicine, electronic communications, space travel, genetic manipulation . . . these are the miracles about which we now tell our children. These are the miracles we herald as proof that science will bring us the answers. The ancient stories of immaculate conceptions, burning bushes, and parting seas are no longer relevant. God has become obsolete. Science has won the battle. We concede.'

A rustle of confusion and bewilderment swept through the chapel.

'But science's victory,' the camerlengo added, his voice intensifying, 'has cost every one of us. And it has cost us deeply.'

Silence.

'Science may have alleviated the miseries of disease and drudgery and provided an array of gadgetry for our entertainment and convenience, but it has left us in a world without wonder. Our sunsets have been reduced to wavelengths and frequencies. The

419

complexities of the universe have been shredded into mathematical equations. Even our self-worth as human beings has been destroyed. Science proclaims that Planet Earth and its inhabitants are a meaningless speck in the grand scheme. A cosmic accident.' He paused. 'Even the technology that promises to unite us, divides us. Each of us is now electronically connected to the globe, and yet we feel utterly alone. We are bombarded with violence, division, fracture, and betrayal. Skepticism has become a virtue. Cynicism and demand for proof has become enlightened thought. Is it any wonder that humans now feel more depressed and defeated than they have at any point in human history? Does science hold *anything* sacred? Science looks for answers by probing our unborn fetuses. Science even presumes to rearrange our own DNA. It shatters God's world into smaller and smaller pieces in quest of meaning . . . and all it finds is more questions.'

Mortati watched in awe. The camerlengo was almost hypnotic now. He had a physical strength in his movements and voice that Mortati had never witnessed on a Vatican altar. The man's voice was wrought with conviction and sadness.

'The ancient war between science and religion is over,' the camerlengo said. 'You have won. But you have not won fairly. You have not won by providing answers. You have won by so radically reorienting our society that the truths we once saw as signposts now seem inapplicable. Religion cannot keep up. Scientific growth is exponential. It feeds on itself like a virus. Every new breakthrough opens doors for new breakthroughs. Mankind took thousands of years to progress from the wheel to the car. Yet only decades from the car into space. Now we measure scientific progress in weeks. We are spinning out of control. The rift between us grows deeper and deeper, and as religion is left behind, people find themselves in a spiritual void. We cry out for meaning. And believe me, we *do* cry out. We see UFOs, engage in channeling, spirit contact, out-of-body experiences, mindquests – all these eccentric ideas have a scientific veneer, but they are unashamedly irrational. They are the desperate cry of the modern soul, lonely and tormented, crippled by its own enlightenment and its inability to accept meaning in anything removed from technology.'

Mortati could feel himself leaning forward in his seat. He and the other cardinals and people around the world were hanging on this priest's every utterance. The camerlengo spoke with no rhetoric or vitriol. No references to scripture or Jesus Christ. He spoke in modern terms, unadorned and pure. Somehow, as though the words were flowing from God himself, he spoke the modern language ... delivering the ancient message. In that moment, Mortati saw one of the reasons the late Pope held this young man so dear. In a world of apathy, cynicism, and technological deification, men like the camerlengo, realists who could speak to our souls like this man just had, were the church's only hope.

The camerlengo was talking more forcefully now. 'Science, you say, will save us. Science, I say, has destroyed us. Since the days of Galileo, the church has tried to slow the relentless march of science, sometimes with misguided means, but always with benevolent intention. Even so, the temptations are too great for man to resist. I warn you, look around yourselves. The promises of science have not been kept. Promises of efficiency and simplicity have bred nothing but pollution and chaos. We are a fractured and frantic species ... moving down a path of destruction.'

The camerlengo paused a long moment and then sharpened his eyes on the camera.

'Who is this God science? Who is the God who offers his people power but no moral framework to tell you how to use that power? What kind of God gives a child *fire* but does not warn the child of its dangers? The language of science comes with no signposts about good and bad. Science textbooks tell us how to create a nuclear reaction, and yet they contain no chapter asking us if it is a good or a bad idea.

'To science, I say this. The church is tired. We are exhausted from trying to be your signposts. Our resources are drying up from our campaign to be the voice of balance as you plow blindly on in your quest for smaller chips and larger profits. We ask not why you will not govern yourselves, but how can you? Your world moves so fast that if you stop even for an instant to consider the implications of your actions, someone more efficient will whip past you in a blur. So you move on. You proliferate weapons of mass destruction, but it is the Pope who travels the world beseeching leaders to use restraint. You clone living creatures, but it is the church reminding us to consider the moral implications of our actions. You encourage people to interact on phones, video screens, and computers, but it is the church who opens its doors and reminds us to commune in person as we were meant to do. You even murder unborn babies in the name of research that will save lives. Again, it is the church who points out the fallacy of this reasoning.

'And all the while, you proclaim the church is ignorant. But who is more ignorant? The man who cannot define lightning, or the man who does not respect its awesome power? This church is reaching out to you. Reaching out to everyone. And yet the more we reach, the more you push us away. Show me *proof* there is a God, you say. I say use your telescopes to look to the heavens, and tell me how there could *not* be a God!' The camerlengo had tears in his eyes now. 'You ask what does God look like. I say, where did that question come from? The answers are one and the same. Do you not see God in your science? How can you miss Him! You proclaim that even the slightest change in the force of gravity or the weight of an atom would have rendered our universe a lifeless mist rather than our magnificent sea of heavenly bodies, and yet you fail to see God's hand in *this*? Is it really so much easier to believe that we simply chose the right card from a deck of billions? Have we become so spiritually bankrupt that we would rather believe in mathematical impossibility than in a power greater than us?

'Whether or not you believe in God,' the camerlengo said, his voice deepening with deliberation, 'you must believe this. When we as a species abandon our trust in the power greater than us, we abandon our sense of accountability. Faith ... *all* faiths ... are admonitions that there is something we cannot understand, something to which we are accountable ... With faith we are accountable to each other, to ourselves, and to a higher truth. Religion is flawed, but only because *man* is flawed. If the outside world could see this church as I do ... looking beyond the ritual of these walls . . . they would see a modern miracle . . . a brotherhood of imperfect, simple souls wanting only to be a voice of compassion in a world spinning out of control.'

The camerlengo motioned out over the College of Cardinals, and the BBC camerawoman instinctively followed, panning the crowd.

'Are we obsolete?' the camerlengo asked. 'Are these men dinosaurs? Am I? Does the world really need a voice for the poor, the weak, the oppressed, the unborn child? Do we really need souls like these who, though imperfect, spend their lives imploring each of us to read the signposts of morality and not lose our way?'

Mortati now realized that the camerlengo, whether consciously or not, was making a brilliant move. By showing the cardinals, he was personalizing the church. Vatican City was no longer a building, it was *people* – people like the camerlengo who had spent their lives in the service of goodness.

'Tonight we are perched on a precipice,' the camerlengo said. 'None of us can afford to be apathetic. Whether you see this evil as Satan, corruption, or immorality . . . the dark force is alive and growing every day. Do not ignore it.' The camerlengo lowered his voice to a whisper, and the camera moved in. 'The force, though mighty, is not invincible. Goodness can prevail. Listen to your hearts. Listen to God. Together we can step back from this abyss.'

Now Mortati understood. This was the reason. Conclave had been violated, but this was the only way. It was a dramatic and desperate plea for help. The camerlengo was speaking to both his enemy and his friends now. He was entreating anyone, friend or foe, to see the light and stop this madness. Certainly some-one listening would realize the insanity of this plot and come forward.

The camerlengo knelt at the altar. 'Pray with me.'

The College of Cardinals dropped to their knees to join him in prayer. Outside in St Peter's Square and around the globe . . . a stunned world knelt with them.

95

The Hassassin arranged his unconscious trophy in the rear of the van and took a moment to admire her sprawled body. She was not as beautiful as the women he bought, and yet she had an animal strength that excited him. Her body was radiant, dewy with perspiration. She smelled of musk.

As the Hassassin stood there savoring his prize, he ignored the throb in his arm. The bruise from the falling sarcophagus, although painful, was insigni-ficant . . . well worth the compensation that lay before him. He took consolation in knowing the American who had done this to him was probably dead by now.

Gazing down at his incapacitated prisoner, the Hassassin visualized what lay ahead. He ran a palm up beneath her shirt. Her breasts felt perfect beneath her bra. *Yes*, he smiled. *You are more than worthy.* Fighting the urge to take her right there, he closed the door and drove off into the night.

There was no need to alert the press about *this* killing . . . the flames would do that for him.

* * *

At CERN, Sylvie sat stunned by the camerlengo's address. Never before had she felt so proud to be a Catholic and so ashamed to work at CERN. As she left the recreational wing, the mood in every single viewing room was dazed and somber. When she got back to Kohler's office, all seven phone lines were ringing. Media inquiries were never routed to Kohler's office, so the incoming calls could only be one thing.

Geld. Money calls.

Antimatter technology already had some takers.

Inside the Vatican, Gunther Glick was walking on air as he followed the camerlengo from the Sistine Chapel. Glick and Macri had just made *the* live transmission of the decade. And what a transmission it had been. The camerlengo had been spellbinding.

Now out in the hallway, the camerlengo turned to Glick and Macri. 'I have asked the Swiss Guard to assemble photos for you – photos of the branded cardinals as well as one of His late Holiness. I must warn you, these are not pleasant pictures. Ghastly burns. Blackened tongues. But I would like you to broadcast them to the world.'

Glick decided it must be perpetual Christmas inside Vatican City. *He wants me to broadcast an exclusive photo of the dead Pope?* 'Are you sure?' Glick asked, trying to keep the excitement from his voice.

The camerlengo nodded. 'The Swiss Guard will also provide you a live video feed of the antimatter canister as it counts down.'

Glick stared. *Christmas. Christmas. Christmas!*

'The Illuminati are about to find out,' the camerlengo declared, 'that they have grossly overplayed their hand.'

426

96

Like a recurring theme in some demonic symphony, the suffocating darkness had returned.

No light. No air. No exit.

Langdon lay trapped beneath the overturned sarcophagus and felt his mind careening dangerously close to the brink. Trying to drive his thoughts in any direction other than the crushing space around him, Langdon urged his mind toward some logical process ... mathematics, music, anything. But there was no room for calming thoughts. *I can't move! I can't breathe!*

The pinched sleeve of his jacket had thankfully come free when the casket fell, leaving Langdon now with two mobile arms. Even so, as he pressed upward on the ceiling of his tiny cell, he found it immovable. Oddly, he wished his sleeve were still caught. *At least it might create a crack for some air.*

As Langdon pushed against the roof above, his sleeve fell back to reveal the faint glow of an old friend. Mickey. The greenish cartoon face seemed mocking now.

Langdon probed the blackness for any other sign of light, but the casket rim was flush against the floor. Goddamn Italian perfectionists, he cursed, now imperiled by the same artistic excellence he taught his students to revere ... impeccable edges, faultless parallels, and of course, use only of the most seamless and resilient *Carrara* marble.

Precision can be suffocating.

'Lift the damn thing,' he said aloud, pressing harder through the tangle of bones. The box shifted slightly. Setting his jaw, he heaved again. The box felt like a boulder, but this time it raised a quarter of an inch. A fleeting glimmer of light surrounded him, and then the casket thudded back down. Langdon lay panting in the dark. He tried to use his legs to lift as he had before, but now that the sarcophagus had fallen flat, there was no room even to straighten his knees.

As the claustrophobic panic closed in, Langdon was overcome by images of the sarcophagus shrinking around him. Squeezed by delirium, he fought the illusion with every logical shred of intellect he had.

'Sarcophagus,' he stated aloud, with as much academic sterility as he could muster. But even erudition seemed to be his enemy today. *Sarcophagus is from the Greek 'sarx' meaning 'flesh', and 'phagein' meaning 'to eat'. I'm trapped in a box literally designed to 'eat flesh'.*

Images of flesh eaten from bone only served as a grim reminder that Langdon lay covered in human remains. The notion brought nausea and chills. But it also brought an idea.

Fumbling blindly around the coffin, Langdon found a shard of bone. A rib maybe? He didn't care. All he wanted was a wedge. If he could lift the box, even a crack, and slide the bone fragment beneath the rim, then maybe enough air could . . .

Reaching across his body and wedging the tapered end of the bone into the crack between the floor and the coffin, Langdon reached up with his other hand and heaved skyward. The box did not move. Not even slightly. He tried again. For a moment, it seemed to tremble slightly, but that was all.

With the fetid stench and lack of oxygen choking the strength from his body, Langdon realized he only had time for one more effort. He also knew he would need both arms.

Regrouping, he placed the tapered edge of the bone against the crack, and shifting his body, he wedged the bone against his shoulder, pinning it in place. Careful not to dislodge it, he raised both hands above him. As the stifling confine began to smother him, he felt a welling of intensified panic. It was the second time today he had been trapped with no air. Hollering aloud, Langdon thrust upward in one explosive motion. The casket jostled off the floor for an instant. But long enough. The bone shard he had braced against his shoulder slipped outward into the widening crack. When the casket fell again, the bone shattered. But this time Langdon could see the casket was propped up. A tiny slit of light showed beneath the rim.

Exhausted, Langdon collapsed. Hoping the strangling sensation in his throat would pass, he waited. But it only worsened as the seconds passed. Whatever air was coming through the slit seemed imperceptible. Langdon wondered if it would be enough to keep him alive. And if so, for how long? If he passed out, who would know he was even in there?

With arms like lead, Langdon raised his watch again: 10.12 p.m. Fighting trembling fingers, he fumbled with the watch and made his final play. He twisted one of the tiny dials and pressed a button.

As consciousness faded, and the walls squeezed closer, Langdon felt the old fears sweep over him. He tried to imagine, as he had so many times, that he was in an open field. The image he conjured, however, was no help. The nightmare that had haunted him since his youth came crashing back . . .

* * *

The flowers here are like paintings, *the child thought,*
laughing as he ran across the meadow. He wished his parents
had come along. But his parents were busy pitching camp.

'Don't explore too far, ' his mother had said.

He had pretended not to hear as he bounded off into the
woods.

Now, traversing this glorious field, the boy came across a
pile of fieldstones. He figured it must be the foundation of an
old homestead. He would not go near it. He knew better.
Besides, his eyes had been drawn to something else – a
brilliant lady's slipper – the rarest and most beautiful
flower in New Hampshire. He had only ever seen them in
books.

Excited, the boy moved toward the flower. He knelt down.
The ground beneath him felt mulchy and hollow. He realized
his flower had found an extra fertile spot. It was growing
from a patch of rotting wood.

Thrilled by the thought of taking home his prize, the boy
reached out . . . fingers extending toward the stem.

He never reached it.

With a sickening crack, the earth gave way.

In the three seconds of dizzying terror as he fell, the boy
knew he would die. Plummeting downward, he braced for
the bone-crushing collision. When it came, there was no
pain. Only softness.

And cold.

He hit the deep liquid face first, plunging into a narrow
blackness. Spinning disoriented somersaults, he groped the
sheer walls that enclosed him on all sides. Somehow, as if by
instinct, he sputtered to the surface.

Light.

Faint. Above him. Miles above him, it seemed.

His arms clawed at the water, searching the walls of the
hollow for something to grab onto. Only smooth stone. He

*had fallen through an abandoned well covering.
He screamed for help, but his cries reverberated in the tight
shaft. He called out again and again. Above him, the tattered
hole grew dim.*

Night fell.

*Time seemed to contort in the darkness. Numbness set in
as he treaded water in the depths of the chasm, calling, crying out. He was tormented by visions of the walls collapsing
in, burying him alive. His arms ached with fatigue. A few
times he thought he heard voices. He shouted out, but his
own voice was muted . . . like a dream.*

*As the night wore on, the shaft deepened. The walls
inched quietly inward. The boy pressed out against the
enclosure, pushing it away. Exhausted, he wanted to give
up. And yet he felt the water buoy him, cooling his burning
fears until he was numb.*

*When the rescue team arrived, they found the boy barely
conscious. He had been treading water for five hours. Two
days later, the* Boston Globe *ran a front-page story called
'The Little Swimmer That Could.'*

97

The Hassassin smiled as he pulled his van into the
mammoth stone structure overlooking the Tiber River.
He carried his prize up and up . . . spiraling higher in
the stone tunnel, grateful his load was slender.

He arrived at the door.

The Church of Illumination, he gloated. *The ancient
Illuminati meeting room. Who would have imagined it to be
here?*

431

Inside, he placed her on a plush divan. Then he expertly bound her arms behind her back and tied her feet. He knew that what he longed for would have to wait until his final task was finished. *Water*.

Still, he thought, he had a moment for indulgence. Kneeling beside her, he ran his hand along her thigh. It was smooth. Higher. His dark fingers snaked beneath the cuff of her shorts. Higher.

He stopped. *Patience*, he told himself, feeling aroused. *There is work to be done*.

He walked for a moment out onto the chamber's high stone balcony. The evening breeze slowly cooled his ardor. Far below the Tiber raged. He raised his eyes to the dome of St Peter's, three quarters of a mile away, naked under the glare of hundreds of press lights.

'Your final hour,' he said aloud, picturing the thousands of Muslims slaughtered during the Crusades. 'At midnight you will meet your God.'

Behind him, the woman stirred. The Hassassin turned. He considered letting her wake up. Seeing terror in a woman's eyes was his ultimate aphrodisiac.

He opted for prudence. It would be better if she remained unconscious while he was gone. Although she was tied and would never escape, the Hassassin did not want to return and find her exhausted from struggling. *I want your strength preserved . . . for me.*

Lifting her head slightly, he placed his palm beneath her neck and found the hollow directly beneath her skull. The crown/meridian pressure point was one he had used countless times. With crushing force, he drove his thumb into the soft cartilage and felt it depress. The woman slumped instantly. *Twenty minutes*, he thought. She would be a tantalizing end to a perfect day. After she had served him and died doing it, he would stand on the balcony and watch the midnight Vatican fireworks.

Leaving his prize unconscious on the couch, the Hassassin went downstairs into a torchlit dungeon. The final task. He walked to the table and revered the sacred, metal forms that had been left there for him.

Water. It was his last.

Removing a torch from the wall as he had done three times already, he began heating the end. When the end of the object was white hot, he carried it to the cell.

Inside, a single man stood in silence. Old and alone.

'Cardinal Baggia,' the killer hissed. 'Have you prayed yet?'

The Italian's eyes were fearless. 'Only for your soul.'

98

The six *pompieri* firemen who responded to the fire at the Church of Santa Maria Della Vittoria extinguished the bonfire with blasts of Halon gas. Water was cheaper, but the steam it created would have ruined the frescoes in the chapel, and the Vatican paid Roman *pompieri* a healthy stipend for swift and prudent service in all Vatican-owned buildings.

Pompieri, by the nature of their work, witnessed tragedy almost daily, but the execution in this church was something none of them would ever forget. Part crucifixion, part hanging, part burning at the stake, the scene was something dredged from a Gothic nightmare.

Unfortunately, the press, as usual, had arrived before the fire department. They'd shot plenty of video before the *pompieri* cleared the church. When the firemen finally cut the victim down and laid him on the floor, there was no doubt who the man was.

'*Cardinale Guidera,*' one whispered. '*Di Barcellona.*'

The victim was nude. The lower half of his body was crimson-black, blood oozing through gaping cracks in his thighs. His shinbones were exposed. One fireman vomited. Another went outside to breathe.

The true horror, though, was the symbol seared on the cardinal's chest. The squad chief circled the corpse in awestruck dread. *Lavoro del diavolo,* he said to himself. *Satan himself did this.* He crossed himself for the first time since childhood.

'*Un' altro corpo!*' someone yelled. One of the firemen had found another body.

The second victim was a man the chief recognized immediately. The austere commander of the Swiss Guard was a man for whom few public law enforcement officials had any affection. The chief called the Vatican, but all the circuits were busy. He knew it didn't matter. The Swiss Guard would hear about this on television in a matter of minutes.

As the chief surveyed the damage, trying to recreate what possibly could have gone on here, he saw a niche riddled with bullet holes. A coffin had been rolled off its supports and fallen upside down in an apparent struggle. It was a mess. *That's for the police and Holy See to deal with,* the chief thought, turning away.

As he turned, though, he stopped. Coming from the coffin he heard a sound. It was not a sound any fireman ever liked to hear.

'*Bomba!*' he cried out. '*Tutti fuori!*'

When the bomb squad rolled the coffin over, they discovered the source of the electronic beeping. They stared, confused.

'*Mèdico!*' one finally screamed. '*Mèdico!*'

99

'Any word from Olivetti?' the camerlengo asked, looking drained as Rocher escorted him back from the Sistine Chapel to the Pope's office.

'No, signore. I am fearing the worst.'

When they reached the Pope's office, the camerlengo's voice was heavy. 'Captain, there is nothing more I can do here tonight. I fear I have done too much already. I am going into this office to pray. I do not wish to be disturbed. The rest is in God's hands.'

'Yes, signore.'

'The hour is late, Captain. Find that canister.'

'Our search continues.' Rocher hesitated. 'The weapon proves to be too well hidden.'

The camerlengo winced, as if he could not think of it. 'Yes. At exactly 11.15 p.m., if the church is still in peril, I want you to evacuate the cardinals. I am putting their safety in your hands. I ask only one thing. Let these men proceed from this place with dignity. Let them exit into St Peter's Square and stand side by side with the rest of the world. I do not want the last image of this church to be frightened old men sneaking out a back door.'

'Very good, signore. And you? Shall I come for you at 11.15 as well?'

'There will be no need.'

'Signore?'

'I will leave when the spirit moves me.'

Rocher wondered if the camerlengo intended to go down with the ship.

The camerlengo opened the door to the Pope's office and entered. 'Actually . . .' he said, turning. 'There is one thing.'

'Signore?'

'There seems to be a chill in this office tonight. I am trembling.'

'The electric heat is out. Let me lay you a fire.'

The camerlengo smiled tiredly. 'Thank you. Thank you, very much.'

Rocher exited the Pope's office where he had left the camerlengo praying by firelight in front of a small statue of the Blessed Mother Mary. It was an eerie sight. A black shadow kneeling in the flickering glow. As Rocher headed down the hall, a guard appeared, running toward him. Even by candlelight Rocher recognized Lieutenant Chartrand. Young, green, and eager.

'Captain,' Chartrand called, holding out a cellular phone. 'I think the camerlengo's address may have worked. We've got a caller here who says he has information that can help us. He phoned on one of the Vatican's private extensions. I have no idea how he got the number.'

Rocher stopped. 'What?'

'He will only speak to the ranking officer.'

'Any word from Olivetti?'

'No, sir.'

He took the receiver. 'This is Captain Rocher. I am ranking officer here.'

'Rocher,' the voice said. 'I will explain to you who I am. Then I will tell you what you are going to do next.'

When the caller stopped talking and hung up, Rocher stood stunned. He now knew from whom he was taking orders.

Back at CERN, Sylvie Baudeloque was frantically trying to keep track of all the licensing inquiries coming in on Kohler's voice mail. When the private line on the director's desk began to ring, Sylvie jumped. Nobody had that number. She answered.

'Yes?'

'Ms Baudeloque? This is Director Kohler. Contact my pilot. My jet is to be ready in five minutes.'

100

Robert Langdon had no idea where he was or how long he had been unconscious when he opened his eyes and found himself staring up at the underside of a baroque, frescoed cupola. Smoke drifted overhead. Something was covering his mouth. An oxygen mask. He pulled it off. There was a terrible smell in the room – like burning flesh.

Langdon winced at the pounding in his head. He tried to sit up. A man in white was kneeling beside him.

'*Riposati!*' the man said, easing Langdon onto his back again. '*Sono il paramédico.*'

Langdon succumbed, his head spiraling like the smoke overhead. *What the hell happened?* Wispy feelings of panic sifted through his mind.

'*Sórcio salvatore*,' the paramedic said. 'Mouse ... savior.'

Langdon felt even more lost. *Mouse savior?*

The man motioned to the Mickey Mouse watch on Langdon's wrist. Langdon's thoughts began to clear. He remembered setting the alarm. As he stared absently at the watch face, Langdon also noted the hour. 10.28 p.m.

He sat bolt upright.

Then, it all came back.

Langdon stood near the main altar with the fire chief and a few of his men. They had been rattling him with questions. Langdon wasn't listening. He had questions of his own. His whole body ached, but he knew he needed to act immediately.

A *pompiero* approached Langdon across the church. 'I checked again, sir. The only bodies we found are Cardinal Guidera and the Swiss Guard commander. There's no sign of a woman here.'

'*Grazie*,' Langdon said, unsure whether he was relieved or horrified. He knew he had seen Vittoria unconscious on the floor. Now she was gone. The only explanation he came up with was not a comforting one. The killer had not been subtle on the phone. *A woman of spirit. I am aroused. Perhaps before this night is over, I will find you. And when I do . . .*

Langdon looked around. 'Where is the Swiss Guard?'

'Still no contact. Vatican lines are jammed.'

Langdon felt overwhelmed and alone. Olivetti was dead. The cardinal was dead. Vittoria was missing. A half hour of his life had disappeared in a blink.

Outside, Langdon could hear the press swarming.

He suspected footage of the third cardinal's horrific death would no doubt air soon, if it hadn't already. Langdon hoped the camerlengo had long since assumed the worst and taken action. *Evacuate the damn Vatican! Enough games! We lose!*

Langdon suddenly realized that all of the catalysts that had been driving him – helping to save Vatican City, rescuing the four cardinals, coming face to face with the brotherhood he had studied for years – all of these things had evaporated from his mind. The war was lost. A new compulsion had ignited within him. It was simple. Stark. Primal.

Find Vittoria.

He felt an unexpected emptiness inside. Langdon had often heard that intense situations could unite two people in ways that decades together often did not. He now believed it. In Vittoria's absence he felt something he had not felt in years. Loneliness. The pain gave him strength.

Pushing all else from his mind, Langdon mustered his concentration. He prayed that the Hassassin would take care of business before pleasure. Otherwise, Langdon knew he was already too late. *No*, he told himself, *you have time.* Vittoria's captor still had work to do. He had to surface one last time before disappearing forever.

The last altar of science, Langdon thought. The killer had one final task. *Earth. Air. Fire. Water.*

He looked at his watch. Thirty minutes. Langdon moved past the firemen toward Bernini's *Ecstasy of St Teresa*. This time, as he stared at Bernini's marker, Langdon had no doubt what he was looking for.

Let angels guide you on your lofty quest . . .

Directly over the recumbent saint, against a

backdrop of gilded flame, hovered Bernini's angel. The angel's hand clutched a pointed spear of fire. Langdon's eyes followed the direction of the shaft, arching toward the right side of the church. His eyes hit the wall. He scanned the spot where the spear was pointing. There was nothing there. Langdon knew, of course, the spear was pointing far beyond the wall, into the night, somewhere across Rome.

'What direction is that?' Langdon asked, turning and addressing the chief with a newfound determination.

'Direction?' The chief glanced where Langdon was pointing. He sounded confused. 'I don't know ... west, I think.'

'What churches are in that direction?'

The chief's puzzlement seemed to deepen. 'Dozens. Why?'

Langdon frowned. Of course there were dozens. 'I need a city map. Right away.'

The chief sent someone running out to the fire truck for a map. Langdon turned back to the statue. *Earth ... Air ... Fire ... VITTORIA.*

The final marker is Water, he told himself. *Bernini's Water*. It was in a church out there somewhere. A needle in a haystack. He spurred his mind through all the Bernini works he could recall. *I need a tribute to Water!*

Langdon flashed on Bernini's statue of *Triton* – the Greek God of the sea. Then he realized it was located in the square outside this very church, in entirely the wrong direction. He forced himself to think. *What figure would Bernini have carved as a glorification of water? Neptune and Tritone?* Unfortunately that statue was in London's Victoria & Albert Museum.

'Signore?' A fireman ran in with a map.

Langdon thanked him and spread it out on the altar. He immediately realized he had asked the right people; the fire department's map of Rome was as detailed as any Langdon had ever seen. 'Where are we now?'

The man pointed. 'Next to Piazza Barberini.'

Langdon looked at the angel's spear again to get his bearings. The chief had estimated correctly. According to the map, the spear was pointing west. Langdon traced a line from his current location west across the map. Almost instantly his hopes began to sink. It seemed that with every inch his finger traveled, he passed yet another building marked by a tiny black cross. *Churches.* The city was riddled with them. Finally, Langdon's finger ran out of churches and trailed off into the suburbs of Rome. He exhaled and stepped back from the map. *Damn.*

Surveying the whole of Rome, Langdon's eyes touched down on the three churches where the first three cardinals had been killed. *The Chigi Chapel . . . St Peter's . . . here . . .*

Seeing them all laid out before him now, Langdon noted an oddity in their locations. Somehow he had imagined the churches would be scattered randomly across Rome. But they most definitely were not. Improbably, the three churches seemed to be separated systematically, in an enormous city-wide triangle. Langdon double-checked. He was not imagining things. *'Penna,'* he said suddenly, without looking up.

Someone handed him a ballpoint pen.

Langdon circled the three churches. His pulse quickened. He triple-checked his markings. *A symmetrical triangle!*

Langdon's first thought was for the Great Seal on the one-dollar bill – the triangle containing the all-seeing eye. But it didn't make sense. He had marked only *three* points. There were supposed to be four in all.

So where the hell is Water? Langdon knew that anywhere he placed the fourth point, the triangle would be destroyed. The only option to retain the symmetry was to place the fourth marker inside the triangle, at the center. He looked at the spot on the map. Nothing. The idea bothered him anyway. The four elements of science were considered *equal*. Water was not special; Water would not be at the *center* of the others.

Still, his instinct told him the systematic arrangement could not possibly be accidental. *I'm not yet seeing the whole picture.* There was only one alternative. The four points did not make a triangle; they made some other shape.

Langdon looked at the map. *A square, perhaps?* Although a square made no symbolic sense, squares were symmetrical at least. Langdon put his finger on the map at one of the points that would turn the triangle into a square. He saw immediately that a perfect square was impossible. The angles of the original triangle were oblique and created more of a distorted quadrilateral.

As he studied the other possible points around the triangle, something unexpected happened. He noticed that the line he had drawn earlier to indicate the direction of the angel's spear passed perfectly through one of the possibilities. Stupefied, Langdon circled that point. He was now looking at four ink marks on the map, arranged in somewhat of an awkward, kitelike diamond.

He frowned. Diamonds were not an Illuminati symbol either. He paused. *Then again* . . .

For an instant Langdon flashed on the famed Illuminati Diamond. The thought, of course, was ridiculous. He dismissed it. Besides, this diamond was oblong – like a kite – hardly an example of the flawless symmetry for which the Illuminati Diamond was revered.

When he leaned in to examine where he had placed the final mark, Langdon was surprised to find that the fourth point lay dead center of Rome's famed Piazza Navona. He knew the piazza contained a major church, but he had already traced his finger through that piazza and considered the church there. To the best of his knowledge it contained no Bernini works. The church was called Saint Agnes in Agony, named for St Agnes, a ravishing teenage virgin banished to a life of sexual slavery for refusing to renounce her faith.

There must be something in that church! Langdon racked his brain, picturing the inside of the church. He could think of no Bernini works at all inside, much less anything to do with *water*. The arrangement on the map was bothering him too. A diamond. It was far too accurate to be coincidence, but it was not accurate enough to make any sense. *A kite?* Langdon wondered if he had chosen the wrong point. *What am I missing!*

The answer took another thirty seconds to hit him, but when it did, Langdon felt an exhilaration like nothing he had ever experienced in his academic career.

The Illuminati genius, it seemed, would never cease.

The shape he was looking at was not intended as a diamond at all. The four points only formed a diamond because Langdon had connected *adjacent* points. *The Illuminati believe in opposites!* Connecting opposite vertices with his pen, Langdon's fingers were trembling. There before him on the map was a giant cruciform. *It's a cross!* The four elements of science unfolded before his eyes . . . sprawled across Rome in an enormous, city-wide cross.

As he stared in wonder, a line of poetry rang in his mind . . . like an old friend with a new face.

'Cross Rome the mystic elements unfold . . .

'Cross Rome . . .

The fog began to clear. Langdon saw that the answer had been in front of him all night! The Illuminati poem had been telling him *how* the altars were laid out. A cross!

'Cross Rome the mystic elements unfold!

It was cunning wordplay. Langdon had originally read the word *'Cross* as an abbreviation of *Across.* He assumed it was poetic license intended to retain the meter of the poem. But it was so much more than that! Another hidden clue.

The cruciform on the map, Langdon realized, was the ultimate Illuminati duality. It was a religious symbol formed by elements of science. Galileo's path of Illumination was a tribute to both science *and* God!

The rest of the puzzle fell into place almost immediately.

Piazza Navona.

Dead center of Piazza Navona, outside the church of St Agnes in Agony, Bernini had forged one of his most celebrated sculptures. Everyone who came to Rome went to see it.

The Fountain of the Four Rivers!

A flawless tribute to water, Bernini's *Fountain of the*

Four Rivers glorified the four major rivers of the Old World – The Nile, Ganges, Danube, and Rio Plata.

Water, Langdon thought. *The final marker.* It was perfect.

And even more perfect, Langdon realized, the cherry on the cake, was that high atop Bernini's fountain stood a towering obelisk.

Leaving confused firemen in his wake, Langdon ran across the church in the direction of Olivetti's lifeless body.

10.31 p.m., he thought. *Plenty of time.* It was the first instant all day that Langdon felt ahead of the game.

Kneeling beside Olivetti, out of sight behind some pews, Langdon discreetly took possession of the commander's semiautomatic and walkie-talkie. Langdon knew he would call for help, but this was not the place to do it. The final altar of science needed to remain a secret for now. The media and fire department racing with sirens blaring to Piazza Navona would be no help at all.

Without a word, Langdon slipped out the door and skirted the press, who were now entering the church in droves. He crossed Piazza Barberini. In the shadows he turned on the walkie-talkie. He tried to hail Vatican City but heard nothing but static. He was either out of range or the transmitter needed some kind of authorization code. Langdon adjusted the complex dials and buttons to no avail. Abruptly, he realized his plan to get help was not going to work. He spun, looking for a pay phone. None. Vatican circuits were jammed anyway.

He was alone.

Feeling his initial surge of confidence decay,

Langdon stood a moment and took stock of his pitiful state – covered in bone dust, cut, deliriously exhausted, and hungry

Langdon glanced back at the church. Smoke spiraled over the cupola, lit by the media lights and fire trucks. He wondered if he should go back and get help. Instinct warned him however that extra help, especially untrained help, would be nothing but a liability. *If the Hassassin sees us coming* . . . He thought of Vittoria and knew this would be his final chance to face her captor.

Piazza Navona, he thought, knowing he could get there in plenty of time and stake it out. He scanned the area for a taxi, but the streets were almost entirely deserted. Even the taxi drivers, it seemed, had dropped everything to find a television. Piazza Navona was only about a mile away but Langdon had no intention of wasting precious energy on foot. He glanced back at the church, wondering if he could borrow a vehicle from someone.

A fire truck? A press van? Be serious.

Sensing options and minutes slipping away, Langdon made his decision. Pulling the gun from his pocket, he committed an act so out of character that he suspected his soul must now be possessed. Running over to a lone Citroën sedan idling at a stoplight, Langdon pointed the weapon through the driver's open window. *'Fuori!'* he yelled.

The trembling man got out.

Langdon jumped behind the wheel and hit the gas.

101

Gunther Glick sat on a bench in a holding tank inside the office of the Swiss Guard. He prayed to every god he could think of. *Please let this NOT be a dream.* It had been the scoop of his life. The scoop of anyone's life. Every reporter on earth wished he were Glick right now. *You are awake,* he told himself *And you are a star. Dan Rather is crying right now.*

Macri was beside him, looking a little bit stunned. Glick didn't blame her. In addition to exclusively broadcasting the camerlengo's address, she and Glick had provided the world with gruesome photos of the cardinals and of the Pope – *that tongue!* – as well as a live video feed of the antimatter canister counting down. *Incredible!*

Of course, all of that had all been at the camerlengo's behest, so that was not the reason Glick and Macri were now locked in a Swiss Guard holding tank. It had been Glick's daring addendum to their coverage that the guards had not appreciated. Glick knew the conversation on which he had just reported was not intended for his ears, but this was his moment in the sun. *Another Glick scoop!*

'The 11th Hour Samaritan?' Macri groaned on the bench beside him, clearly unimpressed.

Glick smiled. 'Brilliant, wasn't it?'

'Brilliantly dumb.'

She's just jealous, Glick knew. Shortly after the camerlengo's address, Glick had again, by chance, been in the right place at the right time. He'd overheard Rocher giving new orders to his men. Apparently Rocher had received a phone call from a mysterious individual who Rocher claimed had critical information regarding the current crisis. Rocher was talking as if this man could help them and was advising his guards to prepare for the guest's arrival.

Although the information was clearly private, Glick had acted as any dedicated reporter would – without honor. He'd found a dark corner, ordered Macri to fire up her remote camera, and he'd reported the news.

'Shocking new developments in God's city,' he had announced, squinting his eyes for added intensity. Then he'd gone on to say that a mystery guest was coming to Vatican City to save the day. *The 11th Hour Samaritan*, Glick had called him – a perfect name for the faceless man appearing at the last moment to do a good deed. The other networks had picked up the catchy sound bite, and Glick was yet again immortalized.

I'm brilliant, he mused. *Peter Jennings just jumped off a bridge.*

Of course Glick had not stopped there. While he had the world's attention, he had thrown in a little of his own conspiracy theory for good measure.

Brilliant. Utterly brilliant.

'You screwed us,' Macri said. 'You totally blew it.'

'What do you mean? I was great!'

Macri stared disbelievingly. 'Former President George Bush? An Illuminatus?'

Glick smiled. How much more obvious could it be? George Bush was a well-documented, 33rd-degree Mason, *and* he was the head of the CIA when the agency closed their Illuminati investigation for lack of evidence. And all those speeches about 'a thousand points of light' and a 'New World Order' . . . Bush was obviously Illuminati.

'And that bit about CERN?' Macri chided. 'You are going to have a very big line of lawyers outside your door tomorrow.'

'CERN? Oh come on! It's so obvious! Think about it! The Illuminati disappear off the face of the earth in the 1950s at about the same time CERN is *founded*. CERN is a haven for the most enlightened people on earth. Tons of private funding. They build a weapon that can destroy the church, and oops! . . . they *lose* it!'

'So you tell the world that CERN is the new home base of the Illuminati?'

'Obviously! Brotherhoods don't just disappear. The Illuminati had to go *somewhere*. CERN is a perfect place for them to hide. I'm not saying everyone at CERN is Illuminati. It's probably like a huge Masonic lodge, where most people are innocent, but the upper echelons—'

'Have you ever heard of slander, Glick? Liability?'

'Have you ever heard of real journalism!'

'Journalism? You were pulling bullshit out of thin air! I should have turned off the camera! And what the hell was that crap about CERN's corporate logo? Satanic symbology? Have you lost your mind?'

Glick smiled. Macri's jealousy was definitely showing. The CERN logo had been the most brilliant coup of all. Ever since the camerlengo's address, all the networks were talking about CERN and anti-matter. Some stations were showing the CERN corporate logo as a backdrop. The logo seemed standard enough – two intersecting circles represent-ing two particle accelerators, and five tangential lines representing particle injection tubes. The whole world was staring at this logo, but it had been Glick, a bit of a symbologist himself, who had first seen the Illuminati symbology hidden in it.

'You're not a symbologist,' Macri chided, 'you're just one lucky-ass reporter. You should have left the symbology to the Harvard guy.'

'The Harvard guy missed it,' Glick said.

The Illuminati significance in this logo is so obvious!

He was beaming inside. Although CERN had lots of accelerators, their logo showed only two. *Two is the Illuminati number of duality.* Although most accelerators had only one injection tube, the logo showed five. *Five is the number of the Illuminati pentagram.* Then had come the coup – the most brilliant point of all. Glick pointed out that the logo contained a large numeral '6' – clearly formed by one of the lines and circles – and when the logo was rotated, another six appeared . . . and then another. The logo contained three sixes! 666! The devil's number! The mark of the beast!

Glick was a genius.

Macri looked ready to slug him.

The jealousy would pass, Glick knew, his mind now wandering to another thought. If CERN was Illuminati headquarters, was CERN where the Illuminati kept their infamous Illuminati Diamond? Glick had read about it on the Internet – *'a flawless diamond, born of the ancient elements with such perfection that all those who saw it could only stand in wonder.'*

Glick wondered if the secret whereabouts of the Illuminati Diamond might be yet another mystery he could unveil tonight.

102

Piazza Navona. *Fountain of the Four Rivers*.

Nights in Rome, like those in the desert, can be surprisingly cool, even after a warm day. Langdon was huddled now on the fringes of Piazza Navona, pulling his jacket around him. Like the distant white noise of traffic, a cacophony of news reports echoed across the city. He checked his watch. Fifteen minutes. He was grateful for a few moments of rest.

The piazza was deserted. Bernini's masterful fountain sizzled before him with a fearful sorcery. The foaming pool sent a magical mist upward, lit from beneath by underwater floodlights. Langdon sensed a cool electricity in the air.

The fountain's most arresting quality was its height. The central core alone was over twenty feet tall – a rugged mountain of travertine marble riddled with caves and grottoes through which the water churned. The entire mound was draped with pagan figures. Atop this stood an obelisk that climbed another forty feet. Langdon let his eyes climb. On the obelisk's tip, a faint shadow blotted the sky, a lone pigeon perched silently.

A cross, Langdon thought, still amazed by the arrangement of the markers across Rome. Bernini's *Fountain of the Four Rivers* was the last altar of science. Only hours ago Langdon had been standing in the Pantheon convinced the Path of Illumination had been broken and he would never get this far. It had been a foolish blunder. In fact, the entire path was intact. *Earth, Air, Fire, Water*. And Langdon had followed it . . . from beginning to end.

Not quite to the end, he reminded himself. The path had *five* stops, not four. This fourth marker fountain somehow pointed to the ultimate destiny – the Illuminati's sacred lair – the Church of Illumination. Langdon wondered if the lair were still standing. He wondered if that was where the Hassassin had taken Vittoria.

Langdon found his eyes probing the figures in the fountain, looking for any clue as to the direction of the lair. *Let angels guide you on your lofty quest.* Almost immediately though, he was overcome by an unsettling awareness. This fountain contained no angels whatsoever. It certainly contained none Langdon could see from where he was standing . . . and none he had ever seen in the past. *The Fountain of the Four Rivers* was a pagan work. The carvings were all profane – humans, animals, even an awkward armadillo. An angel here would stick out like a sore thumb.

Is this the wrong place? He considered the cruciform arrangement of the four obelisks. He clenched his fists. *This fountain is perfect.*

It was only 10.46 p.m. when a black van emerged from the alleyway on the far side of the piazza. Langdon would not have given it a second look except that the van drove with no headlights. Like a shark patrolling a moonlit bay the vehicle circled the perimeter of the piazza.

Langdon hunkered lower, crouched in the shadows beside the huge stairway leading up to the Church of St Agnes in Agony. He gazed out at the piazza, his pulse climbing.

After making two complete circuits, the van banked inward toward Bernini's fountain. It pulled abreast of the basin, moving laterally along the rim until its side was flush with the fountain. Then it parked, its sliding door positioned only inches above the churning water.

Mist billowed.

Langdon felt an uneasy premonition. Had the Hassassin arrived early? Had he come in a van? Langdon had imagined the killer escorting his last victim across the piazza on foot, like he had at St Peter's, giving Langdon an open shot. But if the Hassassin had arrived in a van, the rules had just changed.

Suddenly, the van's side door slid open.

On the floor of the van, contorted in agony, lay a naked man. The man was wrapped in yards of heavy chains. He thrashed against the iron links, but the chains were too heavy. One of the links bisected the man's mouth like a horse's bit, stifling his cries for help. It was then that Langdon saw the second figure, moving around behind the prisoner in the dark, as though making final preparations.

Langdon knew he had only seconds to act.

Taking the gun, he slipped off his jacket and dropped it on the ground. He didn't want the added encumbrance of a tweed jacket, nor did he have any intention of taking Galileo's *Diagramma* anywhere near the water. The document would stay here where it was safe and dry.

Langdon scrambled to his right. Circling the perimeter of the fountain, he positioned himself directly opposite the van. The fountain's massive centerpiece obscured his view. Standing, he ran directly toward the basin. He hoped the thundering water was drowning his footsteps. When he reached the fountain, he climbed over the rim and dropped into the foaming pool.

The water was waist deep and like ice. Langdon grit his teeth and plowed through the water. The bottom was slippery, made doubly treacherous by a stratum of coins thrown for good luck. Langdon sensed he would need more than good luck. As the mist rose all around him, he wondered if it was the cold or the fear that was causing the gun in his hand to shake.

He reached the interior of the fountain and circled back to his left. He waded hard, clinging to the cover of the marble forms. Hiding himself behind the huge carved form of a horse, Langdon peered out. The van was only fifteen feet away. The Hassassin was crouched on the floor of the van, hands planted on the cardinal's chain-clad body, preparing to roll him out the open door into the fountain.

Waist-deep in water, Robert Langdon raised his gun and stepped out of the mist, feeling like some sort of aquatic cowboy making a final stand. 'Don't move.' His voice was steadier than the gun.

The Hassassin looked up. For a moment he seemed confused, as though he had seen a ghost. Then his lips curled into an evil smile. He raised his arms in submission. 'And so it goes.'

'Get out of the van.'

'You look wet.'

'You're early.'

'I am eager to return to my prize.'

Langdon leveled the gun. 'I won't hesitate to shoot.'

'You've already hesitated.'

Langdon felt his finger tighten on the trigger. The cardinal lay motionless now. He looked exhausted, moribund. 'Untie him.'

'Forget him. You've come for the woman. Do not pretend otherwise.'

454

Langdon fought the urge to end it right there. 'Where is she?'

'Somewhere safe. Awaiting my return.'

She's alive. Langdon felt a ray of hope. 'At the Church of Illumination?'

The killer smiled. 'You will never find its location.'

Langdon was incredulous. *The lair is still standing.* He aimed the gun. 'Where?'

'The location has remained secret for centuries. Even to me it was only revealed recently. I would die before I break that trust.'

'I can find it without you.'

'An arrogant thought.'

Langdon motioned to the fountain. 'I've come this far.'

'So have many. The final step is the hardest.'

Langdon stepped closer, his footing tentative beneath the water. The Hassassin looked remarkably calm, squatting there in the back of the van with his arms raised over his head. Langdon aimed at his chest, wondering if he should simply shoot and be done with it. *No. He knows where Vittoria is. He knows where the antimatter is. I need information!*

From the darkness of the van the Hassassin gazed out at his aggressor and couldn't help but feel an amused pity. The American was brave, that he had proven. But he was also untrained. That he had also proven. Valor without expertise was suicide. There were rules of survival. Ancient rules. And the American was breaking all of them.

You had the advantage – the element of surprise. You squandered it.

The American was indecisive . . . hoping for backup

most likely ... or perhaps a slip of the tongue that would reveal critical information.

Never interrogate before you disable your prey. A cornered enemy is a deadly enemy.

The American was talking again. Probing. Maneuvering.

The killer almost laughed aloud. *This is not one of your Hollywood movies ... there will be no long discussions at gunpoint before the final shoot-out. This is the end. Now.*

Without breaking eye contact, the killer inched his hands across the ceiling of the van until he found what he was looking for. Staring dead ahead, he grasped it.

Then he made his play.

The motion was utterly unexpected. For an instant, Langdon thought the laws of physics had ceased to exist. The killer seemed to hang weightless in the air as his legs shot out from beneath him, his boots driving into the cardinal's side and launching the chain-laden body out the door. The cardinal splashed down, sending up a sheet of spray.

Water dousing his face, Langdon realized too late what had happened. The killer had grasped one of the van's roll bars and used it to swing outward. Now the Hassassin was sailing toward him, feet-first through the spray.

Langdon pulled the trigger, and the silencer spat. The bullet exploded through the toe of the Hassassin's left boot. Instantly Langdon felt the soles of the Hassassin's boots connect with his chest, driving him back with a crushing kick.

The two men splashed down in a spray of blood and water.

As the icy liquid engulfed Langdon's body, his first

cognition was pain. Survival instinct came next. He realized he was no longer holding his weapon. It had been knocked away. Diving deep, he groped along the slimy bottom. His hand gripped metal. A handful of coins. He dropped them. Opening his eyes, Langdon scanned the glowing basin. The water churned around him like a frigid Jacuzzi.

Despite the instinct to breathe, fear kept him on the bottom. Always moving. He did not know from where the next assault would come. He needed to find the gun! His hands groped desperately in front of him.

You have the advantage, he told himself. *You are in your element.* Even in a soaked turtleneck Langdon was an agile swimmer. *Water is your element.*

When Langdon's fingers found metal a second time, he was certain his luck had changed. The object in his hand was no handful of coins. He gripped it and tried to pull it toward him, but when he did, he found himself gliding through the water. The object was stationary.

Langdon realized even before he coasted over the cardinal's writhing body that he had grasped part of the metal chain that was weighing the man down. Langdon hovered a moment, immobilized by the sight of the terrified face staring up at him from the floor of the fountain.

Jolted by the life in the man's eyes, Langdon reached down and grabbed the chains, trying to heave him toward the surface. The body came slowly . . . like an anchor. Langdon pulled harder. When the cardinal's head broke the surface, the old man gasped a few sucking, desperate breaths. Then, violently, his body rolled, causing Langdon to lose his grip on the slippery chains. Like a stone, Baggia went down again and disappeared beneath the foaming water.

Langdon dove, eyes wide in the liquid murkiness. He found the cardinal. This time, when Langdon grabbed on, the chains across Baggia's chest shifted . . . parting to reveal a further wickedness . . . a word stamped in seared flesh.

An instant later, two boots strode into view. One was gushing blood.

103

As a water polo player, Robert Langdon had endured more than his fair share of underwater battles. The competitive savagery that raged beneath the surface of a water polo pool, away from the eyes of the referees, could rival even the ugliest wrestling match. Langdon had been kicked, scratched, held, and even bitten once by a frustrated defenseman from whom Langdon had continuously twisted away.

Now, though, thrashing in the frigid water of Bernini's fountain, Langdon knew he was a long way from the Harvard pool. He was fighting not for a game, but for his life. This was the second time they had battled. No referees here. No rematches. The arms driving his face toward the bottom of the basin thrust with a force that left no doubt that it intended to kill.

Langdon instinctively spun like a torpedo. *Break the hold!* But the grip torqued him back, his attacker enjoying an advantage no water polo defenseman ever had – two feet on solid ground. Langdon contorted, trying to get his own feet beneath him. The Hassassin seemed to be favoring one arm ... but nonetheless, his grip held firm.

It was then that Langdon knew he was not coming up. He did the only thing he could think of to do. He stopped trying to surface. *If you can't go north, go east.* Marshalling the last of his strength, Langdon dolphin-kicked his legs and pulled his arms beneath him in an awkward butterfly stroke. His body lurched forward.

The sudden switch in direction seemed to take the Hassassin off guard. Langdon's lateral motion dragged his captor's arms sideways, compromising his balance. The man's grip faltered, and Langdon kicked again. The sensation felt like a towline had snapped. Suddenly Langdon was free. Blowing the stale air from his lungs, Langdon clawed for the surface. A single breath was all he got. With crashing force the Hassassin was on top of him again, palms on his shoulders, all of his weight bearing down. Langdon scrambled to plant his feet beneath him but the Hassassin's leg swung out, cutting Langdon down.

He went under again.

Langdon's muscles burned as he twisted beneath the water. This time his maneuvers were in vain. Through the bubbling water, Langdon scanned the bottom, looking for the gun. Everything was blurred.

The bubbles were denser here. A blinding light flashed in his face as the killer wrestled him deeper, toward a submerged spotlight bolted on the floor of the fountain. Langdon reached out, grabbing the canister. It was hot. Langdon tried to pull himself free, but the contraption was mounted on hinges and pivoted in his hand. His leverage was instantly lost.

The Hassassin drove him deeper still.

It was then Langdon saw it. Poking out from under the coins directly beneath his face. A narrow, black cylinder. *The silencer of Olivetti's gun!* Langdon reached out, but as his fingers wrapped around the cylinder, he did not feel metal, he felt plastic. When he pulled, the flexible rubber hose came flopping toward him like a flimsy snake. It was about two feet long with a jet of bubbles surging from the end. Langdon had not found the gun at all. It was one of the fountain's many harmless *spumanti* . . . bubble makers.

Only a few feet away Cardinal Baggia felt his soul straining to leave his body. Although he had prepared for this moment his entire life, he had never imagined the end would be like this. His physical shell was in agony . . . burned, bruised, and held underwater by an immovable weight. He reminded himself that this suffering was nothing compared to what Jesus had endured.

He died for my sins . . .

Baggia could hear the thrashing of a battle raging nearby. He could not bear the thought of it. His captor was about to extinguish yet another life . . . the man with kind eyes, the man who had tried to help.

As the pain mounted, Baggia lay on his back and stared up through the water at the black sky above him. For a moment he thought he saw stars.

It was time.

Releasing all fear and doubt, Baggia opened his mouth and expelled what he knew would be his final breath. He watched his spirit gurgle heavenward in a burst of transparent bubbles. Then, reflexively, he gasped. The water poured in like icy daggers to his sides. The pain lasted only a few seconds.

Then . . . peace.

The Hassassin ignored the burning in his foot and focused on the drowning American, whom he now held pinned beneath him in the churning water. *Finish it fully*. He tightened his grip, knowing *this* time Robert Langdon would not survive. As he predicted, his victim's struggling became weaker and weaker.

Suddenly Langdon's body went rigid. He began to shake wildly.

Yes, the Hassassin mused. *The rigors. When the water first hits the lungs*. The rigors, he knew, would last about five seconds.

They lasted six.

Then, exactly as the Hassassin expected, his victim went suddenly flaccid. Like a great deflating balloon, Robert Langdon fell limp. It was over. The Hassassin held him down for another thirty seconds to let the water flood all of his pulmonary tissue. Gradually, he felt Langdon's body sink, on its own accord, to the bottom. Finally, the Hassassin let go. The media would find a double surprise in the *Fountain of the Four Rivers*.

'*Tabban!*' the Hassassin swore, clambering out of the fountain and looking at his bleeding toe. The tip of his boot was shredded, and the front of his big toe had been sheared off. Angry at his own carelessness, he tore the cuff from his pant leg and rammed the fabric into the toe of his boot. Pain shot up his leg. *'Ibn al-kalb!'* He clenched his fists and rammed the cloth deeper. The bleeding slowed until it was only a trickle.

Turning his thoughts from pain to pleasure, the Hassassin got into his van. His work in Rome was done. He knew exactly what would soothe his discomfort. Vittoria Vetra was bound and waiting. The Hassassin, even cold and wet, felt himself stiffen.

I have earned my reward.

Across town Vittoria awoke in pain. She was on her back. All of her muscles felt like stone. Tight. Brittle. Her arms hurt. When she tried to move, she felt spasms in her shoulders. It took her a moment to comprehend her hands were tied behind her back. Her initial reaction was confusion. *Am I dreaming?* But when she tried to lift her head, the pain at the base of her skull informed her of her wakefulness.

Confusion transforming to fear, she scanned her surroundings. She was in a crude, stone room – large and well-furnished, lit by torches. Some kind of ancient meeting hall. Old-fashioned benches sat in a circle nearby.

Vittoria felt a breeze, cold now on her skin. Nearby, a set of double doors stood open, beyond them a balcony. Through the slits in the balustrade, Vittoria could have sworn she saw the Vatican.

104

Robert Langdon lay on a bed of coins at the bottom of the *Fountain of the Four Rivers*. His mouth was still wrapped around the plastic hose. The air being pumped through the *spumanti* tube to froth the fountain had been polluted by the pump, and his throat burned. He was not complaining, though. He was alive.

He was not sure how accurate his imitation of a drowning man had been, but having been around water his entire life, Langdon had certainly heard accounts. He had done his best. Near the end, he had even blown all the air from his lungs and stopped breathing so that his muscle mass would carry his body to the floor..

Thankfully, the Hassassin had bought it and let go.

Now, resting on the bottom of the fountain, Langdon had waited as long as he could wait. He was about to start choking. He wondered if the Hassassin was still out there. Taking an acrid breath from the tube, Langdon let go and swam across the bottom of the fountain until he found the smooth swell of the central core. Silently, he followed it upward, surfacing out of sight, in the shadows beneath the huge marble figures.

The van was gone.

That was all Langdon needed to see. Pulling a long breath of fresh air back into his lungs, he scrambled back toward where Cardinal Baggia had gone down. Langdon knew the man would be unconscious now, and chances of revival were slim, but he had to try. When Langdon found the body, he planted his feet on either side, reached down, and grabbed the chains wrapped around the cardinal. Then Langdon pulled. When the cardinal broke water, Langdon could see the eyes were already rolled upward, bulging. Not a good sign. There was no breath or pulse.

Knowing he could never get the body up and over the fountain rim, Langdon lugged Cardinal Baggia through the water and into the hollow beneath the central mound of marble. Here the water became shallow and there was an inclined ledge. Langdon dragged the naked body up onto the ledge as far as he could. Not far.

Then he went to work. Compressing the cardinal's chain-clad chest, Langdon pumped the water from his lungs. Then he began CPR. Counting carefully. Deliberately. Resisting the instinct to blow too hard and too fast. For three minutes Langdon tried to revive the old man. After five minutes, Langdon knew it was over.

Il preferito. The man who would be Pope. Lying dead before him.

Somehow, even now, prostrate in the shadows on the semisubmerged ledge, Cardinal Baggia retained an air of quiet dignity. The water lapped softly across his chest, seeming almost remorseful . . . as if asking forgiveness for being the man's ultimate killer . . . as if trying to cleanse the scalded wound that bore its name.

Gently, Langdon ran a hand across the man's face and closed his upturned eyes. As he did, he felt an exhausted shudder of tears well from within. It startled him. Then, for the first time in years, Langdon cried.

105

The fog of weary emotion lifted slowly as Langdon waded away from the dead cardinal, back into deep water. Depleted and alone in the fountain, Langdon half-expected to collapse. But instead, he felt a new compulsion rising within him. Undeniable. Frantic. He sensed his muscles hardening with an unexpected grit. His mind, as though ignoring the pain in his heart, forced aside the past and brought into focus the single, desperate task ahead.

Find the Illuminati lair. Help Vittoria.

Turning now to the mountainous core of Bernini's fountain, Langdon summoned hope and launched himself into his quest for the final Illuminati marker. He knew somewhere on this gnarled mass of figures was a clue that pointed to the lair. As Langdon scanned the fountain, though, his hope withered quickly. The words of the *segno* seemed to gurgle mockingly all around him. *Let angels guide you on your lofty quest.* Langdon glared at the carved forms before him. *The fountain is pagan! It has no damn angels anywhere!*

When Langdon completed his fruitless search of the core, his eyes instinctively climbed the towering stone pillar. *Four markers,* he thought, *spread across Rome in a giant cross.*

Scanning the hieroglyphics covering the obelisk, he wondered if perhaps there were a clue hidden in the Egyptian symbology He immediately dismissed the idea. The hieroglyphs predated Bernini by centuries, and hieroglyphs had not even been decipherable until the Rosetta Stone was discovered.

Still, Langdon ventured, maybe Bernini had carved an additional symbol? One that would go unnoticed among all the hieroglyphs?

Feeling a shimmer of hope, Langdon circumnavigated the fountain one more time and studied all four façades of the obelisk. It took him two minutes, and when he reached the end of the final face, his hopes sank. Nothing in the hieroglyphs stood out as any kind of addition. Certainly no angels.

Langdon checked his watch. It was eleven on the dot. He couldn't tell whether time was flying or crawling. Images of Vittoria and the Hassassin started to swirl hauntingly as Langdon clambered his way around the fountain, the frustration mounting as he frantically completed yet another fruitless circle. Beaten and exhausted, Langdon felt ready to collapse. He threw back his head to scream into the night.

The sound jammed in his throat.

Langdon was staring straight up the obelisk. The object perched at the very top was one he had seen earlier and ignored. Now, however, it stopped him short. It was not an angel. Far from it. In fact, he had not even perceived it as *part* of Bernini's fountain. He thought it was a living creature, another one of the city's scavengers perched on a lofty tower.

A pigeon.

Langdon squinted skyward at the object, his vision blurred by the glowing mist around him. It was a pigeon, wasn't it? He could clearly see the head and beak silhouetted against a cluster of stars. And yet the bird had not budged since Langdon's arrival, even with the battle below. The bird sat now exactly as it had been when Langdon entered the square. It was perched high atop the obelisk, gazing calmly westward.

Langdon stared at it a moment and then plunged his hand into the fountain and grabbed a fistful of coins. He hurled the coins skyward. They clattered across the upper levels of the granite obelisk. The bird did not budge. He tried again. This time, one of the coins hit the mark. A faint sound of metal on metal clanged across the square.

The damned pigeon was bronze.

You're looking for an angel, not a pigeon, a voice reminded him. But it was too late. Langdon had made the connection. He realized the bird was not a pigeon at all.

It was a dove.

Barely aware of his own actions, Langdon splashed toward the center of the fountain and began scrambling up the travertine mountain, clambering over huge arms and heads, pulling himself higher. Halfway to the base of the obelisk, he emerged from the mist and could see the head of the bird more clearly.

There was no doubt. It was a dove. The bird's deceptively dark color was the result of Rome's pollution tarnishing the original bronze. Then the significance hit him. He had seen a pair of doves earlier today at the Pantheon. A *pair* of doves carried no meaning. This dove, however, was alone.

The lone dove is the pagan symbol for the Angel of Peace.

The truth almost lifted Langdon the rest of the way to the obelisk. Bernini had chosen the *pagan* symbol for the angel so he could disguise it in a pagan fountain. *Let angels guide you on your lofty quest. The dove is the angel!* Langdon could think of no more lofty perch for the Illuminati's final marker than atop this obelisk.

The bird was looking west. Langdon tried to follow

467

its gaze, but he could not see over the buildings. He climbed higher. A quote from St Gregory of Nyssa emerged from his memory most unexpectedly. *As the soul becomes enlightened ... it takes the beautiful shape of the dove.*

Langdon rose heavenward. Toward the dove. He was almost flying now. He reached the platform from which the obelisk rose and could climb no higher. With one look around, though, he knew he didn't have to. All of Rome spread out before him. The view was stunning.

To his left, the chaotic media lights surrounding St Peter's. To his right, the smoking cupola of Santa Maria della Vittoria. In front of him in the distance, Piazza del Popolo. Beneath him, the fourth and final point. A giant cross of obelisks.

Trembling, Langdon looked to the dove overhead. He turned and faced the proper direction, and then he lowered his eyes to the skyline.

In an instant he saw it.

So obvious. So clear. So deviously simple.

Staring at it now, Langdon could not believe the Illuminati lair had stayed hidden for so many years. The entire city seemed to fade away as he looked out at the monstrous stone structure across the river in front of him. The building was as famous as any in Rome. It stood on the banks of the Tiber River diagonally adjacent to the Vatican. The building's geometry was stark – a circular castle, within a square fortress, and then, outside its walls, surrounding the entire structure, a park in the shape of a *pentagram*.

The ancient stone ramparts before him were dramatically lit by soft floodlights. High atop the castle stood the mammoth bronze angel. The angel pointed his sword downward at the exact center of the castle. And as if that were not enough, leading solely and directly to the castle's main entrance stood the famous Bridge of Angels ... a dramatic approachway adorned by twelve towering angels carved by none other than Bernini himself.

In a final breathtaking revelation, Langdon realized Bernini's city-wide cross of obelisks marked the fortress in perfect Illuminati fashion; the cross's central arm passed *directly* through the center of the castle's bridge, dividing it into two equal halves.

Langdon retrieved his tweed coat, holding it away from his dripping body Then he jumped into the stolen sedan and rammed his soggy shoe into the accelerator, speeding off into the night.

106

It was 11.07 p.m. Langdon's car raced through the Roman night. Speeding down Lungotevere Tor Di Nona, parallel with the river, Langdon could now see his destination rising like a mountain to his right.

Castel Sant' Angelo. Castle of the Angel.

Without warning, the turnoff to the narrow Bridge of Angels – Ponte Sant' Angelo – appeared suddenly. Langdon slammed on his brakes and swerved. He turned in time, but the bridge was barricaded. He skidded ten feet and collided with a series of short cement pillars blocking his way. Langdon lurched forward as the vehicle stalled, wheezing and shuddering. He had forgotten the Bridge of Angels, in order to preserve it, was now zoned pedestrians only

Shaken, Langdon staggered from the crumpled car, wishing now he had chosen one of the other routes. He felt chilled, shivering from the fountain. He donned his Harris tweed over his damp shirt, grateful for Harris's trademark double lining. The *Diagramma* folio would remain dry. Before him, across the bridge, the stone fortress rose like a mountain. Aching and depleted, Langdon broke into a loping run.

On both sides of him now, like a gauntlet of escorts, a procession of Bernini angels whipped past, funneling him toward his final destination. *Let angels guide you on your lofty quest.* The castle seemed to rise as he advanced, an unscalable peak, more intimidating to him even than St Peter's. He sprinted toward the bastion, running on fumes, gazing upward at the citadel's circular core as it shot skyward to a gargantuan, sword-wielding angel.

The castle appeared deserted.

Langdon knew through the centuries the building had been used by the Vatican as a tomb, a fortress, a papal hideout, a prison for enemies of the church, and a museum. Apparently, the castle had other tenants as well – the Illuminati. Somehow it made eerie sense. Although the castle was property of the Vatican, it was used only sporadically, and Bernini had made numerous renovations to it over the years. The building was now rumored to be honeycombed with secret entries, passageways, and hidden chambers. Langdon had little doubt that the angel and surrounding pentagonal park were Bernini's doing as well.

Arriving at the castle's elephantine double doors, Langdon shoved them hard. Not surprisingly, they were immovable. Two iron knockers hung at eye level.

Langdon didn't bother. He stepped back, his eyes climbing the sheer outer wall. These ramparts had fended off armies of Berbers, heathens, and Moors. Somehow he sensed his chances of breaking in were slim.

Vittoria, Langdon thought. *Are you in there?*

Langdon hurried around the outer wall. *There must be another entrance!*

Rounding the second bulwark to the west, Langdon arrived breathless in a small parking area off Lungotere Angelo. On this wall he found a second castle entrance, a drawbridge-type ingress, raised and sealed shut. Langdon gazed upward again.

The only lights on the castle were exterior floods illuminating the façade. All the tiny windows inside seemed black. Langdon's eyes climbed higher. At the very peak of the central tower, a hundred feet above, directly beneath the angel's sword, a single balcony protruded. The marble parapet seemed to shimmer slightly, as if the room beyond it were aglow with torchlight. Langdon paused, his soaked body shivering suddenly. A shadow? He waited, straining. Then he saw it again. His spine prickled. *Someone is up there!*

'Vittoria!' he called out, unable to help himself, but his voice was swallowed by the raging Tiber behind him. He wheeled in circles, wondering where the hell the Swiss Guard were. Had they even heard his transmission?

Across the lot a large media truck was parked. Langdon ran toward it. A paunchy man in headphones sat in the cabin adjusting levers. Langdon rapped on the side of the truck. The man jumped, saw Langdon's dripping clothes, and yanked off his headset.

'What's the worry, mate?' His accent was Australian.

'I need your phone.' Langdon was frenzied.

The man shrugged. 'No dial tone. Been trying all night. Circuits are packed.'

Langdon swore aloud. 'Have you seen anyone go in there?' He pointed to the drawbridge.

'Actually, yeah. A black van's been going in and out all night.'

Langdon felt a brick hit the bottom of his stomach.

'Lucky bastard,' the Aussie said, gazing up at the tower, and then frowning at his obstructed view of the Vatican. 'I bet the view from up there is perfect. I couldn't get through the traffic in St Peter's, so I'm shooting from here.'

Langdon wasn't listening. He was looking for options.

'What do you say?' the Australian said. 'This 11th Hour Samaritan for real?'

Langdon turned. 'The what?'

'You didn't hear? The Captain of the Swiss Guard got a call from somebody who claims to have some primo info. The guy's flying in right now. All I know is if he saves the day . . . there go the ratings!' The man laughed.

Langdon was suddenly confused. A good Samaritan flying in to help? Did the person somehow know where the antimatter was? Then why didn't he just *tell* the Swiss Guard? Why was he coming in person? Something was odd, but Langdon didn't have time to figure out what.

'Hey,' the Aussie said, studying Langdon more closely. 'Ain't you that guy I saw on TV? Trying to save that cardinal in St Peter's Square?'

Langdon did not answer. His eyes had suddenly locked on a contraption attached to the top of the truck

– a satellite dish on a collapsible appendage. Langdon looked at the castle again. The outer rampart was fifty feet tall. The inner fortress climbed farther still. A shelled defense. The top was impossibly high from here, but maybe if he could clear the first wall . . .

Langdon spun to the newsman and pointed to the satellite arm. 'How high does that go?'

'Huh?' The man looked confused. 'Fifteen meters. Why?'

'Move the truck. Park next to the wall. I need help.'

'What are you talking about?'

Langdon explained.

The Aussie's eyes went wide. 'Are you insane? That's a two-hundred-thousand-dollar telescoping extension. Not a ladder!'

'You want ratings? I've got information that will make your day.' Langdon was desperate.

'Information worth two hundred grand?'

Langdon told him what he would reveal in exchange for the favor.

Ninety seconds later, Robert Langdon was gripping the top of the satellite arm wavering in the breeze fifty feet off the ground. Leaning out, he grabbed the top of the first bulwark, dragged himself onto the wall, and dropped onto the castle's lower bastion.

'Now keep your bargain!' the Aussie called up. 'Where is he?'

Langdon felt guilt-ridden for revealing this information, but a deal was a deal. Besides, the Hassassin would probably call the press anyway. 'Piazza Navona,' Langdon shouted. 'He's in the fountain.'

The Aussie lowered his satellite dish and peeled out after the scoop of his career.

* * *

In a stone chamber high above the city, the Hassassin removed his soaking boots and bandaged his wounded toe. There was pain, but not so much that he couldn't enjoy himself.

He turned to his prize.

She was in the corner of the room, on her back on a rudimentary divan, hands tied behind her, mouth gagged. The Hassassin moved toward her. She was awake now. This pleased him. Surprisingly, in her eyes, he saw fire instead of fear.

The fear will come.

107

Robert Langdon dashed around the outer bulwark of the castle, grateful for the glow of the floodlights. As he circled the wall, the courtyard beneath him looked like a museum of ancient warfare – catapults, stacks of marble cannonballs, and an arsenal of fearful contraptions. Parts of the castle were open to tourists during the day, and the courtyard had been partially restored to its original state.

Langdon's eyes crossed the courtyard to the central core of the fortress. The circular citadel shot skyward 107 feet to the bronze angel above. The balcony at the top still glowed from within. Langdon wanted to call out but knew better. He would have to find a way in.

He checked his watch.

11.12 p.m.

Dashing down the stone ramp that hugged the inside of the wall, Langdon descended to the courtyard. Back on ground level, he ran through shadows, clockwise around the fort. He passed three porticos, but all of them were permanently sealed. *How did the Hassassin get in?* Langdon pushed on. He passed two modern entrances, but they were padlocked from the outside. *Not here.* He kept running.

Langdon had circled almost the entire building when he saw a gravel drive cutting across the courtyard in front of him. At one end, on the outer wall of the castle, he saw the back of the gated drawbridge leading back outside. At the other end, the drive disappeared into the fortress. The drive seemed to enter a kind of tunnel – a gaping entry in the central core. *Il traforo!* Langdon had read about this castle's *traforo*, a giant spiral ramp that circled up inside the fort, used by commanders on horseback to ride from top to bottom rapidly. *The Hassassin drove up!* The gate blocking the tunnel was raised, ushering Langdon in. He felt almost exuberant as he ran toward the tunnel. But as he reached the opening, his excitement disappeared.

The tunnel spiraled *down*.

The wrong way. This section of the *traforo* apparently descended to the dungeons, not to the top.

Standing at the mouth of a dark bore that seemed to twist endlessly deeper into the earth, Langdon hesitated, looking up again at the balcony. He could swear he saw motion up there. *Decide!* With no other options, he dashed down into the tunnel.

High overhead, the Hassassin stood over his prey. He ran a hand across her arm. Her skin was like cream. The anticipation of exploring her bodily treasures was inebriating. How many ways could he violate her?

The Hassassin knew he deserved this woman. He had served Janus well. She was a spoil of war, and when he was finished with her, he would pull her from the divan and force her to her knees. She would service him again. *The ultimate submission.* Then, at the moment of his own climax, he would slit her throat.

Ghayat assa'adah, they called it. *The ultimate pleasure.*

Afterward, basking in his glory, he would stand on the balcony and savor the culmination of the Illuminati triumph . . . a revenge desired by so many for so long.

The tunnel grew darker. Langdon descended.

After one complete turn into the earth, the light was all but gone. The tunnel leveled out, and Langdon slowed, sensing by the echo of his footfalls that he had just entered a larger chamber. Before him in the murkiness, he thought he saw glimmers of light . . . fuzzy reflections in the ambient gleam. He moved forward, reaching out his hand. He found smooth surfaces. Chrome and glass. It was a vehicle. He groped the surface, found a door, and opened it.

The vehicle's interior dome-light flashed on. He stepped back and recognized the black van immediately. Feeling a surge of loathing, he stared a moment, then he dove in, rooting around in hopes of finding a weapon to replace the one he'd lost in the fountain. He found none. He did, however, find Vittoria's cell phone. It was shattered and useless. The sight of it filled Langdon with fear. He prayed he was not too late.

He reached up and turned on the van's headlights. The room around him blazed into existence, harsh shadows in a simple chamber. Langdon guessed the room was once used for horses and ammunition. It was also a dead end.

No exit. *I came the wrong way!*

At the end of his rope, Langdon jumped from the van and scanned the walls around him. No doorways. No gates. He thought of the angel over the tunnel entrance and wondered if it had been a coincidence. *No!* He thought of the killer's words at the fountain. *She is in the Church of Illumination ... awaiting my return.* Langdon had come too far to fail now. His heart was pounding. Frustration and hatred were starting to cripple his senses.

When he saw the blood on the floor, Langdon's first thought was for Vittoria. But as his eyes followed the stains, he realized they were bloody footprints. The strides were long. The splotches of blood were only on the left foot. *The Hassassin!*

Langdon followed the footprints toward the corner of the room, his sprawling shadow growing fainter. He felt more and more puzzled with every step. The bloody prints looked as though they walked directly into the corner of the room and then disappeared.

When Langdon arrived in the corner, he could not believe his eyes. The granite block in the floor here was not a square like the others. He was looking at another signpost. The block was carved into a perfect pentagram, arranged with the tip pointing into the corner. Ingeniously concealed by overlapping walls, a narrow slit in the stone served as an exit. Langdon slid through. He was in a passage. In front of him were the remains of a wooden barrier that had once been blocking this tunnel.

Beyond it there was light.

Langdon was running now. He clambered over the

wood and headed for the light. The passage quickly opened into another, larger chamber. Here a single torch flickered on the wall. Langdon was in a section of the castle that had no electricity ... a section no tourists would ever see. The room would have been frightful in daylight, but the torch made it even more gruesome.

Il prigione.

There were a dozen tiny jail cells, the iron bars on most eroded away. One of the larger cells, however, remained intact, and on the floor Langdon saw something that almost stopped his heart. Black robes and red sashes on the floor. *This is where he held the cardinals!*

Near the cell was an iron doorway in the wall. The door was ajar and beyond it Langdon could see some sort of passage. He ran toward it. But Langdon stopped before he got there. The trail of blood did not enter the passage. When Langdon saw the words carved over the archway, he knew why.

Il Passetto.

He was stunned. He had heard of this tunnel many times, never knowing where exactly the entrance was. *Il Passetto* – The Little Passage – was a slender, three-quarter-mile tunnel built between Castle St Angelo and the Vatican. It had been used by various Popes to escape to safety during sieges of the Vatican ... as well as by a few less pious Popes to secretly visit mistresses or oversee the torture of their enemies. Nowadays both ends of the tunnel were supposedly sealed with impenetrable locks whose keys were kept in some Vatican vault. Langdon suddenly feared he knew how the Illuminati had been moving in and out of the Vatican. He found himself wondering *who* on the inside had betrayed the church and coughed up the keys. *Olivetti? One of the Swiss Guard?* None of it mattered anymore.

The blood on the floor led to the opposite end of the prison. Langdon followed. Here, a rusty gate hung draped with chains. The lock had been removed and the gate stood ajar. Beyond the gate was a steep ascension of spiral stairs. The floor here was also marked with a pentagramal block. Langdon stared at the block, trembling, wondering if Bernini himself had held the chisel that had shaped these chunks. Overhead, the archway was adorned with a tiny carved cherub. This was it.

The trail of blood curved up the stairs.

Before ascending, Langdon knew he needed a weapon, any weapon. He found a four-foot section of iron bar near one of the cells. It had a sharp, splintered end. Although absurdly heavy, it was the best he could do. He hoped the element of surprise, combined with the Hassassin's wound, would be enough to tip the scales in his advantage. Most of all, though, he hoped he was not too late.

The staircase's spiral treads were worn and twisted steeply upward. Langdon ascended, listening for sounds. None. As he climbed, the light from the prison area faded away. He ascended into the total darkness, keeping one hand on the wall. Higher. In the blackness, Langdon sensed the ghost of Galileo, climbing these very stairs, eager to share his visions of heaven with other men of science and faith.

Langdon was still in a state of shock over the location of the lair. The Illuminati meeting hall was in a building owned by the Vatican. No doubt while the Vatican guards were out searching basements and homes of well-known scientists, the Illuminati were meeting *here* . . . right under the Vatican's nose. It suddenly seemed so perfect. Bernini, as head architect of renovations here, would have had unlimited access to this structure . . . remodeling it to his own specifications with no questions asked. How many secret entries had Bernini added? How many subtle embellishments pointing the way?

The Church of Illumination. Langdon knew he was close.

As the stairs began narrowing, Langdon felt the passage closing around him. The shadows of history were whispering in the dark, but he moved on. When he saw the horizontal shaft of light before him, he realized he was standing a few steps beneath a landing, where the glow of torchlight spilled out beneath the threshold of a door in front of him. Silently he moved up.

Langdon had no idea where in the castle he was right now, but he knew he had climbed far enough to be near the peak. He pictured the mammoth angel atop the castle and suspected it was directly overhead.

Watch over me, angel, he thought, gripping the bar. Then, silently, he reached for the door.

On the divan, Vittoria's arms ached. When she had first awoken to find them tied behind her back, she'd thought she might be able to relax and work her hands free. But time had run out. The beast had returned. Now he was standing over her, his chest bare and powerful, scarred from battles he had endured. His eyes looked like two black slits as he stared down at her body. Vittoria sensed he was imagining the deeds he was about to perform. Slowly, as if to taunt her, the

Hassassin removed his soaking belt and dropped it on the floor.

Vittoria felt a loathing horror. She closed her eyes. When she opened them again, the Hassassin had produced a switchblade knife. He snapped it open directly in front of her face.

Vittoria saw her own terrified reflection in the steel.

The Hassassin turned the blade over and ran the back of it across her belly. The icy metal gave her chills. With a contemptuous stare, he slipped the blade below the waistline of her shorts. She inhaled. He moved back and forth, slowly, dangerously . . . lower. Then he leaned forward, his hot breath whispering in her ear.

'This blade cut out your father's eye.'

Vittoria knew in that instant that she was capable of killing.

The Hassassin turned the blade again and began sawing upward through the fabric of her khaki shorts. Suddenly, he stopped, looking up. Someone was in the room.

'Get away from her,' a deep voice growled from the doorway.

Vittoria could not see who had spoken, but she recognized the voice. *Robert! He's alive!*

The Hassassin looked as if he had seen a ghost. 'Mr Langdon, you must have a guardian angel.'

108

In the split second it took Langdon to take in his surroundings, he realized he was in a sacred place.

The embellishments in the oblong room, though old and faded, were replete with familiar symbology. Pentagram tiles. Planet frescoes. Doves. Pyramids.

The Church of Illumination. Simple and pure. He had arrived.

Directly in front of him, framed in the opening of the balcony, stood the Hassassin. He was bare chested, standing over Vittoria, who lay bound but very much alive. Langdon felt a wave of relief to see her. For an instant, their eyes met, and a torrent of emotions flowed – gratitude, desperation, and regret.

'So we meet yet again,' the Hassassin said. He looked at the bar in Langdon's hand and laughed out loud. 'And this time you come for me with *that*?'

'Untie her.'

The Hassassin put the knife to Vittoria's throat. 'I will kill her.'

Langdon had no doubt the Hassassin was capable of such an act. He forced a calm into his voice. 'I imagine she would welcome it ... considering the alternative.'

The Hassassin smiled at the insult. 'You're right. She has much to offer. It would be a waste.'

Langdon stepped forward, grasping the rusted bar, and aimed the splintered end directly at the Hassassin. The cut on his hand bit sharply. 'Let her go.'

The Hassassin seemed for a moment to be considering it. Exhaling, he dropped his shoulders. It was a clear motion of surrender, and yet at that exact instant the Hassassin's arm seemed to accelerate unexpectedly. There was a blur of dark muscle, and a blade suddenly came tearing through the air toward Langdon's chest.

Whether it was instinct or exhaustion that buckled

Langdon's knees at that moment, he didn't know, but the knife sailed past his left ear and clattered to the floor behind him. The Hassassin seemed unfazed. He smiled at Langdon, who was kneeling now, holding the metal bar. The killer stepped away from Vittoria and moved toward Langdon like a stalking lion.

As Langdon scrambled to his feet, lifting the bar again, his wet turtleneck and pants felt suddenly more restrictive. The Hassassin, half-clothed, seemed to move much faster, the wound on his foot apparently not slowing him at all. Langdon sensed this was a man accustomed to pain. For the first time in his life, Langdon wished he were holding a very big gun.

The Hassassin circled slowly, as if enjoying himself, always just out of reach, moving toward the knife on the floor. Langdon cut him off. Then the killer moved back toward Vittoria. Again Langdon cut him off.

'There's still time,' Langdon ventured. 'Tell me where the canister is. The Vatican will pay more than the Illuminati ever could.'

'You are naïve.'

Langdon jabbed with the bar. The Hassassin dodged. He navigated around a bench, holding the weapon in front of him, trying to corner the Hassassin in the oval room. *This damn room has no corners!* Oddly, the Hassassin did not seem interested in attacking or fleeing. He was simply playing Langdon's game. Coolly waiting.

Waiting for what? The killer kept circling, a master at positioning himself. It was like an endless game of chess. The weapon in Langdon's hand was getting heavy, and he suddenly sensed he knew what the Hassassin was waiting for. *He's tiring me out.* It was working, too. Langdon was hit by a surge of weariness, the adrenaline alone no longer enough to keep him alert. He knew he had to make a move.

The Hassassin seemed to read Langdon's mind, shifting again, as if intentionally leading Langdon toward a table in the middle of the room. Langdon could tell there was something on the table. Something glinted in the torchlight. *A weapon?* Langdon kept his eyes focused on the Hassassin and maneuvered himself closer to the table. When the Hassassin cast a long, guileless glance at the table, Langdon tried to fight the obvious bait. But instinct overruled. He stole a glance. The damage was done.

It was not a weapon at all. The sight momentarily riveted him.

On the table lay a rudimentary copper chest, crusted with ancient patina. The chest was a pentagon. The lid lay open. Arranged inside in five padded compartments were five brands. The brands were forged of iron – large embossing tools with stout handles of wood. Langdon had no doubt what they said.

ILLUMINATI, EARTH, AIR, FIRE, WATER.

Langdon snapped his head back up, fearing the Hassassin would lunge. He did not. The killer was waiting, almost as if he were refreshed by the game. Langdon fought to recover his focus, locking eyes again with his quarry, thrusting with the pipe. But the image of the box hung in his mind. Although the brands themselves were mesmerizing – artifacts few Illuminati scholars even believed existed – Langdon suddenly realized there had been something *else* about the box that had ignited a wave of foreboding within. As the Hassassin maneuvered again, Langdon stole another glance downward.

My God!

In the chest, the five brands sat in compartments around the outer edge. But in the *center*, there was another compartment. This partition was empty, but it clearly was intended to hold another brand ... a brand much larger than the others, and perfectly square.

The attack was a blur.

The Hassassin swooped toward him like a bird of prey. Langdon, his concentration having been masterfully diverted, tried to counter, but the pipe felt like a tree trunk in his hands. His parry was too slow. The Hassassin dodged. As Langdon tried to retract the bar, the Hassassin's hands shot out and grabbed it. The man's grip was strong, his injured arm seeming no longer to affect him. Violently, the two men struggled. Langdon felt the bar ripped away, and a searing pain shot through his palm. An instant later, Langdon was staring into the splintered point of the weapon. The hunter had become the hunted.

Langdon felt like he'd been hit by a cyclone. The Hassassin circled, smiling now, backing Langdon against the wall. 'What is your American *adàgio*?' he chided. 'Something about curiosity and the cat?'

Langdon could barely focus. He cursed his carelessness as the Hassassin moved in. Nothing was making sense. *A sixth Illuminati brand?* In frustration he blurted, 'I've never read anything about a *sixth* Illuminati brand!'

'I think you probably have.' The killer chuckled as he herded Langdon around the oval wall.

Langdon was lost. He most certainly had not. There were *five* Illuminati brands. He backed up, searching the room for any weapon at all.

'A perfect union of the ancient elements,' the

Hassassin said. 'The final brand is the most brilliant of all. I'm afraid you will never see it, though.'

Langdon sensed he would not be seeing much of anything in a moment. He kept backing up, searching the room for an option. 'And you've seen this final brand?' Langdon demanded, trying to buy time.

'Someday perhaps they will honor me. As I prove myself.' He jabbed at Langdon, as if enjoying a game.

Langdon slid backward again. He had the feeling the Hassassin was directing him around the wall toward some unseen destination. *Where?* Langdon could not afford to look behind him. 'The brand?' he demanded. 'Where is it?'

'Not here. Janus is apparently the only one who holds it.'

'Janus?' Langdon did not recognize the name.

'The Illuminati leader. He is arriving shortly.'

'The Illuminati leader is coming *here*?'

'To perform the final branding.'

Langdon shot a frightened glance to Vittoria. She looked strangely calm, her eyes closed to the world around her, her lungs pulling slowly . . . deeply. Was she the final victim? Was *he*?

'Such conceit,' the Hassassin sneered, watching Langdon's eyes. 'The two of you are nothing. You will die, of course, that is for certain. But the final victim of whom I speak is a truly dangerous enemy.'

Langdon tried to make sense of the Hassassin's words. A dangerous enemy? The top cardinals were all dead. The Pope was dead. The Illuminati had wiped them all out. Langdon found the answer in the vacuum of the Hassassin's eyes.

The camerlengo.

Camerlengo Ventresca was the one man who had

been a beacon of hope for the world through this entire tribulation. The camerlengo had done more to condemn the Illuminati tonight than decades of conspiracy theorists. Apparently he would pay the price. He was the Illuminati's final target.

'You'll never get to him,' Langdon challenged.

'Not I,' the Hassassin replied, forcing Langdon farther back around the wall. 'That honor is reserved for Janus himself.'

'The Illuminati leader *himself* intends to brand the camerlengo?'

'Power has its privileges.'

'But no one could possibly get into Vatican City right now!'

The Hassassin looked smug. 'Not unless he had an appointment.'

Langdon was confused. The only person expected at the Vatican right now was the person the press was calling the 11th Hour Samaritan – the person Rocher said had information that could save—

Langdon stopped short. *Good God!*

The Hassassin smirked, clearly enjoying Langdon's sickening cognition. 'I too wondered how Janus would gain entrance. Then in the van I heard the radio – a report about an 11th hour Samaritan.' He smiled. 'The Vatican will welcome Janus with open arms.'

Langdon almost stumbled backward. *Janus is the Samaritan!* It was an unthinkable deception. The Illuminati leader would get a royal escort directly to the camerlengo's chambers. *But how did Janus fool Rocher? Or was Rocher somehow involved?* Langdon felt a chill. Ever since he had almost suffocated in the secret archives, Langdon had not entirely trusted Rocher.

The Hassassin jabbed suddenly, nicking Langdon in the side.

Langdon jumped back, his temper flaring. 'Janus will never get out alive!'

The Hassassin shrugged. 'Some causes are worth dying for.'

Langdon sensed the killer was serious. Janus coming to Vatican City on a *suicide* mission? A question of honor? For an instant, Langdon's mind took in the entire terrifying cycle. The Illuminati plot had come full circle. The priest whom the Illuminati had inadvertently brought to power by killing the Pope had emerged as a worthy adversary. In a final act of defiance, the Illuminati leader would destroy him.

Suddenly, Langdon felt the wall behind him disappear. There was a rush of cool air, and he staggered backward into the night. *The balcony!* He now realized what the Hassassin had in mind.

Langdon immediately sensed the precipice behind him – a hundred-foot drop to the courtyard below. He had seen it on his way in. The Hassassin wasted no time. With a violent surge, he lunged. The spear sliced toward Langdon's midsection. Langdon skidded back, and the point came up short, catching only his shirt. Again the point came at him. Langdon slid farther back, feeling the banister right behind him. Certain the next jab would kill him, Langdon attempted the absurd. Spinning to one side, he reached out and grabbed the shaft, sending a jolt of pain through his palm. Langdon held on.

The Hassassin seemed unfazed. They strained for a moment against one another, face to face, the Hassassin's breath fetid in Langdon's nostrils. The bar began to slip. The Hassassin was too strong. In a final act of desperation, Langdon stretched out his leg, dangerously off balance as he tried to ram his foot down on the Hassassin's injured toe. But the man was a professional and adjusted to protect his weakness.

Langdon had just played his final card. And he knew he had lost the hand.

The Hassassin's arms exploded upward, driving Langdon back against the railing. Langdon sensed nothing but empty space behind him as the railing hit just beneath his buttocks. The Hassassin held the bar crosswise and drove it into Langdon's chest. Langdon's back arched over the chasm.

'*Ma'assalamah*,' the Hassassin sneered. 'Good-bye.'

With a merciless glare, the Hassassin gave a final shove. Langdon's center of gravity shifted, and his feet swung up off the floor. With only one hope of survival, Langdon grabbed on to the railing as he went over. His left hand slipped, but his right hand held on. He ended up hanging upside down by his legs and one hand . . . straining to hold on.

Looming over him, the Hassassin raised the bar overhead, preparing to bring it crashing down. As the bar began to accelerate, Langdon saw a vision. Perhaps it was the imminence of death or simply blind fear, but in that moment, he sensed a sudden aura surrounding the Hassassin. A glowing effulgence seemed to swell out of nothing behind him . . . like an incoming fireball.

Halfway through his swing, the Hassassin dropped the bar and screamed in agony.

The iron bar clattered past Langdon out into the night. The Hassassin spun away from him, and Langdon saw a blistering torch burn on the killer's back. Langdon pulled himself up to see Vittoria, eyes flaring, now facing the Hassassin.

Vittoria waved a torch in front of her, the vengeance in her face resplendent in the flames. How she had escaped, Langdon did not know or care. He began scrambling back up over the banister.

The battle would be short. The Hassassin was a deadly match. Screaming with rage, the killer lunged for her. She tried to dodge, but the man was on her, holding the torch and about to wrestle it away. Langdon did not wait. Leaping off the banister, Langdon jabbed his clenched fist into the blistered burn on the Hassassin's back.

The scream seemed to echo all the way to the Vatican.

The Hassassin froze a moment, his back arched in anguish. He let go of the torch, and Vittoria thrust it hard into his face. There was a hiss of flesh as his left eye sizzled. He screamed again, raising his hands to his face.

'Eye for an eye,' Vittoria hissed. This time she swung the torch like a bat, and when it connected, the Hassassin stumbled back against the railing. Langdon and Vittoria went for him at the same instant, both heaving and pushing. The Hassassin's body sailed backward over the banister into the night. There was no scream. The only sound was the crack of his spine as he landed spread-eagle on a pile of cannonballs far below.

Langdon turned and stared at Vittoria in bewilderment. Slackened ropes hung off her midsection and shoulders. Her eyes blazed like an inferno.

'Houdini knew yoga.'

109

Meanwhile, in St Peter's Square, the wall of Swiss Guards yelled orders and fanned outward, trying to push the crowds back to a safer distance. It was no use. The crowd was too dense and seemed far more interested in the Vatican's impending doom than in their own safety. The towering media screens in the square were now transmitting a live countdown of the antimatter canister – a direct feed from the Swiss Guard security monitor – compliments of the camerlengo. Unfortunately, the image of the canister counting down was doing nothing to repel the crowds. The people in the square apparently looked at the tiny droplet of liquid suspended in the canister and decided it was not as menacing as they had thought. They could also see the countdown clock now – a little under forty-five minutes until detonation. Plenty of time to stay and watch.

Nonetheless, the Swiss Guards unanimously agreed that the camerlengo's bold decision to address the world with the truth and then provide the media with actual *visuals* of Illuminati treachery had been a savvy maneuver. The Illuminati had no doubt expected the Vatican to be their usual reticent selves in the face of adversity. Not tonight. Camerlengo Carlo Ventresca had proven himself a commanding foe.

Inside the Sistine Chapel, Cardinal Mortati was getting restless. It was past 11.15 p.m. Many of the cardinals were continuing to pray, but others had clustered around the exit, clearly unsettled by the hour. Some of the cardinals began pounding on the door with their fists.

Outside the door Lieutenant Chartrand heard the pounding and didn't know what to do. He checked his watch. It was time. Captain Rocher had given strict orders that the cardinals were not to be let out until he gave the word. The pounding on the door became more intense, and Chartrand felt uneasy. He wondered if the captain had simply forgotten. The captain had been acting very erratic since his mysterious phone call.

Chartrand pulled out his walkie-talkie. 'Captain? Chartrand here. It is past time. Should I open the Sistine?'

'That door stays shut. I believe I already gave you that order.'

'Yes, sir, I just—'

'Our guest is arriving shortly. Take a few men upstairs, and guard the door of the Pope's office. The camerlengo is not to go *anywhere*.'

'I'm sorry, sir?'

'What is it that you don't understand, Lieutenant?'

'Nothing, sir. I am on my way.'

Upstairs in the Office of the Pope, the camerlengo stared in quiet meditation at the fire. *Give me strength, God. Bring us a miracle.* He poked at the coals, wondering if he would survive the night.

110

Eleven-twenty-three p.m.

Vittoria stood trembling on the balcony of Castle St

Angelo, staring out across Rome, her eyes moist with tears. She wanted badly to embrace Robert Langdon, but she could not. Her body felt anesthetized. Readjusting. Taking stock. The man who had killed her father lay far below, dead, and she had almost been a victim as well.

When Langdon's hand touched her shoulder, the infusion of warmth seemed to magically shatter the ice. Her body shuddered back to life. The fog lifted, and she turned. Robert looked like hell – wet and matted – he had obviously been through purgatory to come rescue her.

'Thank you . . .' she whispered.

Langdon gave an exhausted smile and reminded her that it was *she* who deserved thanks – her ability to practically dislocate her shoulders had just saved them both. Vittoria wiped her eyes. She could have stood there forever with him, but the reprieve was short-lived.

'We need to get out of here,' Langdon said.

Vittoria's mind was elsewhere. She was staring out toward the Vatican. The world's smallest country looked unsettlingly close, glowing white under a barrage of media lights. To her shock, much of St Peter's Square was still packed with people! The Swiss Guard had apparently been able to clear only about a hundred and fifty feet back – the area directly in front of the basilica – less than one-third of the square. The shell of congestion encompassing the square was compacted now, those at the safer distances pressing for a closer look, trapping the others inside. *They are too close!* Vittoria thought. *Much too close!*

'I'm going back in,' Langdon said flatly.

Vittoria turned, incredulous. 'Into the *Vatican*?'

Langdon told her about the Samaritan, and how it was a ploy. The Illuminati leader, a man named Janus, was actually coming himself to brand the camerlengo. A final Illuminati act of domination.

'Nobody in Vatican City knows,' Langdon said. 'I have no way to contact them, and this guy is arriving any minute. I have to warn the guards before they let him in.'

'But you'll never get through the crowd!'

Langdon's voice was confident. 'There's a way. Trust me.'

Vittoria sensed once again that the historian knew something she did not. 'I'm coming.'

'No. Why risk both—'

'I have to find a way to get those people out of there! They're in incredible dange—'

Just then, the balcony they were standing on began to shake. A deafening rumble shook the whole castle. Then a white light from the direction of St Peter's blinded them. Vittoria had only one thought. *Oh my God! The antimatter annihilated early!*

But instead of an explosion, a huge cheer went up from the crowd. Vittoria squinted into the light. It was a barrage of media lights from the square, now trained, it seemed, on them! Everyone was turned their way, hollering and pointing. The rumble grew louder. The air in the square seemed suddenly joyous.

Langdon looked baffled. 'What the devil—'

The sky overhead roared.

Emerging from behind the tower, without warning, came the papal helicopter. It thundered fifty feet above them, on a beeline for Vatican City. As it passed overhead, radiant in the media lights, the castle trembled. The lights followed the helicopter as it passed by, and

Langdon and Vittoria were suddenly again in the dark.

Vittoria had the uneasy feeling they were too late as they watched the mammoth machine slow to a stop over St Peter's Square. Kicking up a cloud of dust, the chopper dropped onto the open portion of the square between the crowd and the basilica, touching down at the bottom of the basilica's staircase.

'Talk about an entrance,' Vittoria said. Against the white marble, she could see a tiny speck of a person emerge from the Vatican and move toward the chopper. She would never have recognized the figure except for the bright red beret on his head. 'Red carpet greeting. That's Rocher.'

Langdon pounded his fist on the banister. 'Somebody's got to warn them!' He turned to go.

Vittoria caught his arm. 'Wait!' She had just seen something else, something her eyes refused to believe. Fingers trembling, she pointed toward the chopper. Even from this distance, there was no mistaking. Descending the gangplank was another figure . . . a figure who moved so uniquely that it could only be one man. Although the figure was seated, he accelerated across the open square with effortless control and startling speed.

A king on an electric throne.

It was Maximilian Kohler.

111

Kohler was sickened by the opulence of the Hallway of the Belvedere. The gold leaf in the ceiling alone

495

probably could have funded a year's worth of cancer research. Rocher led Kohler up a handicapped ramp on a circuitous route into the Apostolic Palace.

'No elevator?' Kohler demanded.

'No power.' Rocher motioned to the candles burning around them in the darkened building. 'Part of our search tactic.'

'Tactics which no doubt failed.'

Rocher nodded.

Kohler broke into another coughing fit and knew it might be one of his last. It was not an entirely unwelcome thought.

When they reached the top floor and started down the hallway toward the Pope's office, four Swiss Guards ran toward them, looking troubled. 'Captain, what are you doing up here? I thought this man had information that—'

'He will only speak to the camerlengo.'

The guards recoiled, looking suspicious.

'Tell the camerlengo,' Rocher said forcefully, 'that the director of CERN, Maximilian Kohler, is here to see him. Immediately.'

'Yes, sir!' One of the guards ran off in the direction of the camerlengo's office. The others stood their ground. They studied Rocher, looking uneasy. 'Just one moment, captain. We will announce your guest.'

Kohler, however, did not stop. He turned sharply and maneuvered his chair around the sentinels.

The guards spun and broke into a jog beside him. '*Fermati!* Sir! Stop!'

Kohler felt repugnance for them. Not even the most elite security force in the world was immune to the pity everyone felt for cripples. Had Kohler been a healthy man, the guards would have tackled him.

Cripples are powerless, Kohler thought. *Or so the world believes.*

Kohler knew he had very little time to accomplish what he had come for. He also knew he might die here tonight. He was surprised how little he cared. Death was a price he was ready to pay. He had endured too much in his life to have his work destroyed by someone like Camerlengo Ventresca.

'*Signore!*' the guards shouted, running ahead and forming a line across the hallway '*You must stop!*' One of them pulled a sidearm and aimed it at Kohler.

Kohler stopped.

Rocher stepped in, looking contrite. 'Mr Kohler, please. It will only be a moment. No one enters the Office of the Pope unannounced.'

Kohler could see in Rocher's eyes that he had no choice but to wait. *Fine*, Kohler thought. *We wait.*

The guards, cruelly it seemed, had stopped Kohler next to a full-length gilded mirror. The sight of his own twisted form repulsed Kohler. The ancient rage brimmed yet again to the surface. It empowered him. He was among the enemy now. *These* were the people who had robbed him of his dignity. These were the people. Because of *them* he had never felt the touch of a woman . . . had never stood tall to accept an award. *What truth do these people possess? What proof damn it! A book of ancient fables? Promises of miracles to come? Science creates miracles every day!*

Kohler stared a moment into his own stony eyes. *Tonight I may die at the hands of religion*, he thought. *But it will not be the first time.*

For a moment, he was eleven years old again, lying in his bed in his parents' Frankfurt mansion. The sheets beneath him were Europe's finest linen, but they were soaked with sweat. Young Max felt like he was on fire, the pain wracking his body unimaginable. Kneeling beside his bed, where they had been for two days, were his mother and father. They were praying.

In the shadows stood three of Frankfurt's best doctors.

'I urge you to reconsider!' one of the doctors said. 'Look at the boy! His fever is increasing. He is in terrible pain. And danger!'

But Max knew his mother's reply before she even said it. '*Gott wird ihn beschuetzen.*'

Yes, Max thought. *God will protect me.* The conviction in his mother's voice gave him strength. *God will protect me.*

An hour later, Max felt like his whole body was being crushed beneath a car. He could not even breathe to cry.

'Your son is in great suffering,' another doctor said. 'Let me at least ease his pain. I have in my bag a simple injection of—'

'*Ruhe, bitte!*' Max's father silenced the doctor without ever opening his eyes. He simply kept praying.

'Father, please!' Max wanted to scream. 'Let them stop the pain!' But his words were lost in a spasm of coughing.

An hour later, the pain had worsened.

'Your son could become paralyzed,' one of the doctors scolded. 'Or even die! We have medicines that will help!'

Frau and Herr Kohler would not allow it. They did not believe in medicine. Who were they to interfere with God's master plan? They prayed harder. After all, God had blessed them with this boy, why would God take the child away? His mother whispered to Max to be strong. She explained that God was testing him . . . like the Bible story of Abraham . . . a test of his faith.

Max tried to have faith, but the pain was excruciating.

'I cannot watch this!' one of the doctors finally said, running from the room.

By dawn, Max was barely conscious. Every muscle in his body spasmed in agony. *Where is Jesus?* he wondered. *Doesn't he love me?* Max felt the life slipping from his body.

His mother had fallen asleep at the bedside, her hands still clasped over him. Max's father stood across the room at the window staring out at the dawn. He seemed to be in a trance. Max could hear the low mumble of his ceaseless prayers for mercy.

It was then that Max sensed the figure hovering over him. *An angel?* Max could barely see. His eyes were swollen shut. The figure whispered in his ear, but it was not the voice of an angel. Max recognized it as one of the doctors . . . the one who had sat in the corner for two days, never leaving, begging Max's parents to let him administer some new drug from England.

'I will never forgive myself,' the doctor whispered, 'if I do not do this.' Then the doctor gently took Max's frail arm. 'I wish I had done it sooner.'

Max felt a tiny prick in his arm – barely discernible through the pain.

Then the doctor quietly packed his things. Before he left, he put a hand on Max's forehead. 'This will save your life. I have great faith in the power of medicine.'

Within minutes, Max felt as if some sort of magic spirit were flowing through his veins. The warmth spread through his body numbing his pain. Finally, for the first time in days, Max slept.

When the fever broke, his mother and father proclaimed a miracle of God. But when it became evident that their son was crippled, they became despondent. They wheeled their son into the church and begged the priest for counseling.

'It was only by the grace of God,' the priest told them, 'that this boy survived.'

Max listened, saying nothing.

'But our son cannot walk!' Frau Kohler was weeping.

The priest nodded sadly 'Yes. It seems God has punished him for not having enough faith.'

'Mr Kohler?' It was the Swiss Guard who had run ahead. 'The camerlengo says he will grant you audience.'

Kohler grunted, accelerating again down the hall.

'He is surprised by your visit,' the guard said.

'I'm sure.' Kohler rolled on. 'I would like to see him alone.'

'Impossible,' the guard said. 'No one—'

'Lieutenant,' Rocher barked. 'The meeting will be as Mr Kohler wishes.'

The guard stared in obvious disbelief.

Outside the door to the Pope's office, Rocher allowed his guards to take standard precautions before letting Kohler in. Their handheld metal detector was rendered worthless by the myriad of electronic devices on Kohler's wheelchair. The guards frisked him but were obviously too ashamed of his disability to do it properly. They never found the revolver affixed beneath his chair. Nor did they relieve him of the other object . . . the one that Kohler knew would bring

500

unforgettable closure to this evening's chain of events.

When Kohler entered the Pope's office, Camerlengo Ventresca was alone, kneeling in prayer beside a dying fire. He did not open his eyes.

'Mr Kohler,' the camerlengo said. 'Have you come to make me a martyr?'

112

All the while, the narrow tunnel called *Il Passetto* stretched out before Langdon and Vittoria as they dashed toward Vatican City. The torch in Langdon's hand threw only enough light to see a few yards ahead. The walls were close on either side, and the ceiling low. The air smelled dank. Langdon raced on into the darkness with Vittoria close at his heels.

The tunnel inclined steeply as it left the Castle St Angelo, proceeding upward into the underside of a stone bastion that looked like a Roman aqueduct. There, the tunnel leveled out and began its secret course toward Vatican City.

As Langdon ran, his thoughts turned over and over in a kaleidoscope of confounding images – Kohler, Janus, the Hassassin, Rocher . . . a sixth brand? *I'm sure you've heard about the sixth brand*, the killer had said. *The most brilliant of all.* Langdon was quite certain he had *not*. Even in conspiracy theory lore, Langdon could think of no references to any sixth brand. Real or imagined. There were rumors of a gold bullion and a flawless Illuminati Diamond but never any mention of a sixth brand.

'Kohler can't be Janus!' Vittoria declared as they ran down the interior of the dike. 'It's impossible!'

Impossible was one word Langdon had stopped using tonight. 'I don't know,' Langdon yelled as they ran. 'Kohler has a serious grudge, and he also has some serious influence.'

'This crisis has made CERN look like monsters! Max would *never* do anything to damage CERN's reputation!'

On one count, Langdon knew CERN had taken a public beating tonight, all because of the Illuminati's insistence on making this a public spectacle. And yet, he wondered how much CERN had *really* been damaged. Criticism from the church was nothing new for CERN. In fact, the more Langdon thought about it, the more he wondered if this crisis might actually *benefit* CERN. If publicity were the game, then antimatter was the jackpot winner tonight. The entire planet was talking about it.

'You know what promoter P. T. Barnum said,' Langdon called over his shoulder. '"I don't care what you say about me, just spell my name right!" I bet people are already secretly lining up to license antimatter technology. And after they see its true power at midnight tonight . . .'

'Illogical,' Vittoria said. 'Publicizing scientific breakthroughs is not about showing destructive power! This is *terrible* for antimatter, trust me!'

Langdon's torch was fading now. 'Then maybe it's all much simpler than that. Maybe Kohler gambled that the Vatican would keep the antimatter a secret – refusing to empower the Illuminati by confirming the weapon's existence. Kohler expected the Vatican to be their usual tight-lipped selves about the threat, but the camerlengo changed the rules.'

Vittoria was silent as they dashed down the tunnel.

Suddenly the scenario was making more sense to Langdon. 'Yes! Kohler never counted on the camerlengo's reaction. The camerlengo broke the Vatican tradition of secrecy and went public about the crisis. He was dead honest. He put the anti-matter on TV, for God's sake. It was a brilliant response, and Kohler never expected it. And the irony of the whole thing is that the Illuminati attack back-fired. It inadvertently produced a new church leader in the camerlengo. And now Kohler is coming to kill him!'

'Max is a bastard,' Vittoria declared, 'but he is not a murderer. And he would *never* have been involved in my father's assassination.'

In Langdon's mind, it was Kohler's voice that answered. *Leonardo was considered dangerous by many purists at CERN. Fusing science and God is the ultimate scientific blasphemy.* 'Maybe Kohler found out about the antimatter project weeks ago and didn't like the religious implications.'

'So he *killed* my father over it? Ridiculous! Besides, Max Kohler would never have *known* the project existed.'

'While you were gone, maybe your father broke down and consulted Kohler, asking for guidance. You yourself said your father was concerned about the moral implications of creating such a deadly substance.'

'Asking moral guidance from Maximilian Kohler?' Vittoria snorted. 'I don't think so!'

The tunnel banked slightly westward. The faster they ran, the dimmer Langdon's torch became. He

503

began to fear what the place would look like if the light went out. Black.

'Besides,' Vittoria argued, 'why would Kohler have bothered to call you in this morning and ask for help if *he* is behind the whole thing?'

Langdon had already considered it. 'By calling me, Kohler covered his bases. He made sure no one would accuse him of nonaction in the face of crisis. He probably never expected us to get this far.'

The thought of being *used* by Kohler incensed Langdon. Langdon's involvement had given the Illuminati a level of credibility. His credentials and publications had been quoted all night by the media, and as ridiculous as it was, the presence of a Harvard professor in Vatican City had somehow raised the whole emergency beyond the scope of paranoid delusion and convinced skeptics around the world that the Illuminati brotherhood was not only a historical fact, but a force to be reckoned with.

'That BBC reporter,' Langdon said, 'thinks CERN is the new Illuminati lair.'

'What!' Vittoria stumbled behind him. She pulled herself up and ran on. 'He *said* that!?'

'On air. He likened CERN to the Masonic lodges – an innocent organization unknowingly harboring the Illuminati brotherhood within.'

'My God, this is going to destroy CERN.'

Langdon was not so sure. Either way, the theory suddenly seemed less far-fetched. CERN was the ultimate scientific haven. It was home to scientists from over a dozen countries. They seemed to have endless private funding. And Maximilian Kohler was their director.

Kohler is Janus.

'If Kohler's not involved,' Langdon challenged, 'then what is he doing here?'

'Probably trying to stop this madness. Show support. Maybe he really is acting as the Samaritan! He could have found out who knew about the anti-matter project and has come to share information.'

'The killer said he was coming to brand the camerlengo.'

'Listen to yourself! It would be a suicide mission. Max would never get out alive.'

Langdon considered it. *Maybe that was the point.*

The outline of a steel gate loomed ahead, blocking their progress down the tunnel. Langdon's heart almost stopped. When they approached, however, they found the ancient lock hanging open. The gate swung freely.

Langdon breathed a sigh of relief, realizing as he had suspected, that the ancient tunnel was in use. Recently. As in today. He now had little doubt that four terrified cardinals had been secreted through here earlier.

They ran on. Langdon could now hear the sounds of chaos to his left. It was St Peter's Square. They were getting close.

They hit another gate, this one heavier. It too was unlocked. The sound of St Peter's Square faded behind them now, and Langdon sensed they had passed through the outer wall of Vatican City. He wondered where inside the Vatican this ancient passage would conclude. *In the gardens? In the basilica? In the papal residence?*

Then, without warning, the tunnel ended.

The cumbrous door blocking their way was a thick

wall of riveted iron. Even by the last flickers of his torch, Langdon could see that the portal was perfectly smooth – no handles, no knobs, no keyholes, no hinges. No entry.

He felt a surge of panic. In architect-speak, this rare kind of door was called a *senza chiave* – a one-way portal, used for security, and only operable from one side – the *other* side. Langdon's hope dimmed to black . . . along with the torch in his hand.

He looked at his watch. Mickey glowed.

11.29 p.m.

With a scream of frustration, Langdon swung the torch and started pounding on the door.

113

Something was wrong.

Lieutenant Chartrand stood outside the Pope's office and sensed in the uneasy stance of the soldier standing with him that they shared the same anxiety. The private meeting they were shielding, Rocher had said, could save the Vatican from destruction. So Chartrand wondered why his protective instincts were tingling. And why was Rocher acting so strangely?

Something definitely was awry.

Captain Rocher stood to Chartrand's right, staring dead ahead, his sharp gaze uncharacteristically distant. Chartrand barely recognized the captain. Rocher had not been himself in the last hour. His decisions made no sense.

Someone should be present inside this meeting!

Chartrand thought. He had heard Maximilian Kohler bolt the door after he entered. *Why had Rocher permitted this?*

But there was so much more bothering Chartrand. *The cardinals.* The cardinals were still locked in the Sistine Chapel. This was absolute insanity. The camerlengo had wanted them evacuated fifteen minutes ago! Rocher had overruled the decision and not informed the camerlengo. Chartrand had expressed concern, and Rocher had almost taken off his head. Chain of command was never questioned in the Swiss Guard, and Rocher was now top dog.

Half an hour, Rocher thought, discreetly checking his Swiss chronometer in the dim light of the candelabra lighting the hall. *Please hurry.*

Chartrand wished he could hear what was happening on the other side of the doors. Still, he knew there was no one he would rather have handling this crisis than the camerlengo. The man had been tested beyond reason tonight, and he had not flinched. He had confronted the problem head-on ... truthful, candid, shining like an example to all. Chartrand felt proud right now to be a Catholic. The Illuminati had made a mistake when they challenged Camerlengo Ventresca.

At that moment, however, Chartrand's thoughts were jolted by an unexpected sound. A banging. It was coming from down the hall. The pounding was distant and muffled, but incessant. Rocher looked up. The captain turned to Chartrand and motioned down the hall. Chartrand understood. He turned on his flashlight and took off to investigate.

The banging was more desperate now. Chartrand ran thirty yards down the corridor to an intersection. The noise seemed to be coming from around the corner, beyond the Sala Clementina. Chartrand felt perplexed. There was only one room back there – the Pope's private library. His Holiness's private library had been locked since the Pope's death. Nobody could possibly be in there!

Chartrand hurried down the second corridor, turned another corner, and rushed to the library door. The wooden portico was diminutive, but it stood in the dark like a dour sentinel. The banging was coming from somewhere inside. Chartrand hesitated. He had never been inside the private library. Few had. No one was allowed in without an escort by the Pope himself.

Tentatively, Chartrand reached for the doorknob and turned. As he had imagined, the door was locked. He put his ear to the door. The banging was louder. Then he heard something else. *Voices! Someone calling out!*

He could not make out the words, but he could hear the panic in their shouts. Was someone trapped in the library? Had the Swiss Guard not properly evacuated the building? Chartrand hesitated, wondering if he should go back and consult Rocher. The hell with that. Chartrand had been trained to make decisions, and he would make one now. He pulled out his side arm and fired a single shot into the door latch. The wood exploded, and the door swung open.

Beyond the threshold Chartrand saw nothing but blackness. He shone his flashlight. The room was rectangular – oriental carpets, high oak shelves packed with books, a stitched leather couch, and a marble fireplace. Chartrand had heard stories of this place – three thousand ancient volumes side by side with hundreds of current magazines and periodicals, anything His Holiness requested. The coffee table was covered with journals of science and politics.

The banging was clearer now. Chartrand shone his light across the room toward the sound. On the far wall, beyond the sitting area, was a huge door made of iron. It looked impenetrable as a vault. It had four mammoth locks. The tiny etched letters dead center of the door took Chartrand's breath away.

IL PASSETTO

Chartrand stared. *The Pope's secret escape route!* Chartrand had certainly heard of *Il Passetto*, and he had even heard rumors that it had once had an entrance here in the library, but the tunnel had not been used in ages! *Who could be banging on the other side?*

Chartrand took his flashlight and rapped on the door. There was a muffled exultation from the other side. The banging stopped, and the voices yelled louder. Chartrand could barely make out their words through the barricade.

'. . . Kohler . . . lie . . . camerlengo . . .'

'Who is that?' Chartrand yelled.

'. . . ert Langdon . . . Vittoria Ve . . .'

Chartrand understood enough to be confused. *I thought you were dead!*

'. . . the door,' the voices yelled. 'Open . . .!'

Chartrand looked at the iron barrier and knew he would need dynamite to get through there. 'Impossible!' he yelled. 'Too thick!'

'. . . meeting . . . stop . . . erlegno . . . danger . . .'

Despite his training on the hazards of panic, Chartrand felt a sudden rush of fear at the last few words. Had he understood correctly? Heart pounding, he turned to run back to the office. As he turned, though, he stalled. His gaze had fallen to something on the door ... something more shocking even than the message coming from beyond it. Emerging from the keyholes of each of the door's massive locks were *keys*. Chartrand stared. The *keys* were here? He blinked in disbelief. The keys to this door were supposed to be in a vault someplace! This passage was never used – not for centuries!

Chartrand dropped his flashlight on the floor. He grabbed the first key and turned. The mechanism was rusted and stiff, but it still worked. Someone had opened it recently. Chartrand worked the next lock. And the next. When the last bolt slid aside, Chartrand pulled. The slab of iron creaked open. He grabbed his light and shone it into the passage.

Robert Langdon and Vittoria Vetra looked like apparitions as they staggered into the library. Both were ragged and tired, but they were very much alive.

'What is this!' Chartrand demanded. 'What's going on! Where did you come from?'

'Where's Max Kohler?' Langdon demanded.

Chartrand pointed. 'In a private meeting with the camer—'

Langdon and Vittoria pushed past him and ran down the darkened hall. Chartrand turned, instinctively raising his gun at their backs. He quickly lowered it and ran after them. Rocher apparently heard them coming, because as they arrived outside the Pope's office, Rocher had spread his legs in a protective stance and was leveling his gun at them. '*Alt!*'

'The camerlengo is in danger!' Langdon yelled, raising his arms in surrender as he slid to a stop. 'Open the door! Max Kohler is going to kill the camerlengo!'

Rocher looked angry.

'Open the door!' Vittoria said. 'Hurry!'

But it was too late.

From inside the Pope's office came a bloodcurdling scream. It was the camerlengo.

114

The confrontation lasted only seconds.

Camerlengo Ventresca was still screaming when Chartrand stepped past Rocher and blew open the door of the Pope's office. The guards dashed in. Langdon and Vittoria ran in behind them.

The scene before them was staggering.

The chamber was lit only by candlelight and a dying fire. Kohler was near the fireplace, standing awkwardly in front of his wheelchair. He brandished a pistol, aimed at the camerlengo, who lay on the floor at his feet, writhing in agony. The camerlengo's cassock was torn open, and his bare chest was seared black. Langdon could not make out the symbol from across the room, but a large, square brand lay on the floor near Kohler. The metal still glowed red.

Two of the Swiss Guards acted without hesitation. They opened fire. The bullets smashed into Kohler's chest, driving him backward. Kohler collapsed into his wheelchair, his chest gurgling blood. His gun went skittering across the floor.

Langdon stood stunned in the doorway.

Vittoria seemed paralyzed. 'Max . . .' she whispered.

The camerlengo, still twisting on the floor, rolled toward Rocher, and with the trancelike terror of the early witch hunts, pointed his index finger at Rocher and yelled a single word. 'ILLUMINATUS!'

'You bastard,' Rocher said, running at him. 'You sanctimonious bas—'

This time it was Chartrand who reacted on instinct, putting three bullets in Rocher's back. The captain fell face first on the tile floor and slid lifeless through his own blood. Chartrand and the guards dashed immediately to the camerlengo, who lay clutching himself, convulsing in pain.

Both guards let out exclamations of horror when they saw the symbol seared on the camerlengo's chest. The second guard saw the brand upside down and immediately staggered backward with fear in his eyes. Chartrand, looking equally overwhelmed by the symbol, pulled the camerlengo's torn cassock up over the burn, shielding it from view.

Langdon felt delirious as he moved across the room. Through a mist of insanity and violence, he tried to make sense of what he was seeing. A crippled scientist, in a final act of symbolic dominance, had flown into Vatican City and branded the church's highest official. *Some things are worth dying for*, the Hassassin had said. Langdon wondered how a handicapped man could possibly have overpowered the camerlengo. Then again, Kohler had a gun. *It doesn't matter how he did it! Kohler accomplished his mission!*

Langdon moved toward the gruesome scene. The camerlengo was being attended, and Langdon felt himself drawn toward the smoking brand on the floor near Kohler's wheelchair. *The sixth brand?* The closer Langdon got, the more confused he became. The brand seemed to be a perfect square, quite large, and had obviously come from the sacred center

512

compartment of the chest in the Illuminati Lair. *A sixth and final brand*, the Hassassin had said. *The most brilliant of all.*

Langdon knelt beside Kohler and reached for the object. The metal still radiated heat. Grasping the wooden handle, Langdon picked it up. He was not sure what he expected to see, but it most certainly was not this.

Langdon stared a long, confused moment. Nothing was making sense. Why had the guards cried out in horror when they saw this? It was a square of meaningless squiggles. *The most brilliant of all?* It was symmetrical, Langdon could tell as he rotated it in his hand, but it was gibberish.

When he felt a hand on his shoulder, Langdon looked up, expecting Vittoria. The hand, however, was covered with blood. It belonged to Maximilian Kohler, who was reaching out from his wheelchair.

Langdon dropped the brand and staggered to his feet. *Kohler's still alive!*

Slumped in his wheelchair, the dying director was still breathing, albeit barely, sucking in sputtering gasps. Kohler's eyes met Langdon's, and it was the same stony gaze that had greeted Langdon at CERN earlier that day. The eyes looked even harder in death, the loathing and enmity rising to the surface.

The scientist's body quivered, and Langdon sensed he was trying to move. Everyone else in the room was focused on the camerlengo, and Langdon wanted to call out, but he could not react. He was transfixed by the intensity radiating from Kohler in these final seconds of his life. The director, with tremulous effort, lifted his arm and pulled a small device off the arm of his wheelchair. It was the size of a matchbox. He held it out, quivering. For an instant, Langdon feared Kohler had a weapon. But it was something else.

'G-give . . .' Kohler's final words were a gurgling whisper. 'G-give this . . . to the m-media.' Kohler collapsed motionless, and the device fell in his lap.

Shocked, Langdon stared at the device. It was electronic. The words SONY RUVI were printed across the front. Langdon recognized it as one of those new ultra-miniature, palm-held camcorders. *The balls on this guy!* he thought. Kohler had apparently recorded some sort of final suicide message he wanted the media to broadcast . . . no doubt some sermon about the importance of science and the evils of religion. Langdon decided he had done enough for this man's cause tonight. Before Chartrand saw Kohler's camcorder, Langdon slipped it into his deepest jacket pocket. *Kohler's final message can rot in hell!*

It was the voice of the camerlengo that broke the silence. He was trying to sit up. 'The cardinals,' he gasped to Chartrand.

'Still in the Sistine Chapel!' Chartrand exclaimed. 'Captain Rocher ordered—'

'Evacuate . . . now. Everyone.'

Chartrand sent one of the other guards running off to let the cardinals out.

The camerlengo grimaced in pain. 'Helicopter . . . out front . . . get me to a hospital.'

115

In St Peter's Square, the Swiss Guard pilot sat in the cockpit of the parked Vatican helicopter and rubbed his temples. The chaos in the square around him was so loud that it drowned out the sound of his idling rotors. This was no solemn candlelight vigil. He was amazed a riot had not broken out yet.

With less than twenty-five minutes left until midnight, the people were still packed together, some praying, some weeping for the church, others screaming obscenities and proclaiming that this was what the church deserved, still others chanting apocalyptic Bible verses.

The pilot's head pounded as the media lights glinted off his windshield. He squinted out at the clamorous masses. Banners waved over the crowd.

ANTIMATTER IS THE ANTICHRIST!
SCIENTIST=SATANIST
WHERE IS YOUR GOD NOW?

The pilot groaned, his headache worsening. He half considered grabbing the windshield's vinyl covering and putting it up so he wouldn't have to watch, but he knew he would be airborne in a matter of minutes. Lieutenant Chartrand had just radioed with terrible news. The camerlengo had been attacked by

Maximilian Kohler and seriously injured. Chartrand, the American, and the woman were carrying the camerlengo out now so he could be evacuated to a hospital.

The pilot felt personally responsible for the attack. He reprimanded himself for not acting on his gut. Earlier, when he had picked up Kohler at the airport, he had sensed something in the scientist's dead eyes. He couldn't place it, but he didn't like it. Not that it mattered. Rocher was running the show, and Rocher insisted *this* was the guy. Rocher had apparently been wrong.

A new clamor arose from the crowd, and the pilot looked over to see a line of cardinals processing solemnly out of the Vatican onto St Peter's Square. The cardinals' relief to be leaving ground zero seemed to be quickly overcome by looks of bewilderment at the spectacle now going on outside the church.

The crowd noise intensified yet again. The pilot's head pounded. He needed an aspirin. Maybe three. He didn't like to fly on medication, but a few aspirin would certainly be less debilitating than this raging headache. He reached for the first-aid kit, kept with assorted maps and manuals in a cargo box bolted between the two front seats. When he tried to open the box, though, he found it locked. He looked around for the key and then finally gave up. Tonight was clearly not his lucky night. He went back to massaging his temples.

Inside the darkened basilica, Langdon, Vittoria, and the two guards strained breathlessly toward the main exit. Unable to find anything more suitable, the four of them were transporting the wounded camerlengo on a narrow table, balancing the inert body between them as though on a stretcher. Outside the doors, the faint roar of human chaos was now audible. The camerlengo teetered on the brink of unconsciousness.

Time was running out.

116

It was 11.39 p.m. when Langdon stepped with the others from St Peter's Basilica. The glare that hit his eyes was searing. The media lights shone off the white marble like sunlight off a snowy tundra. Langdon squinted, trying to find refuge behind the façade's enormous columns, but the light came from all directions. In front of him, a collage of massive video screens rose above the crowd.

Standing there atop the magnificent stairs that spilled down to the piazza below, Langdon felt like a reluctant player on the world's biggest stage. Somewhere beyond the glaring lights, Langdon heard an idling helicopter and the roar of a hundred thousand voices. To their left, a procession of cardinals was now evacuating onto the square. They all stopped in apparent distress to see the scene now unfolding on the staircase.

'Careful now,' Chartrand urged, sounding focused as the group began descending the stairs toward the helicopter.

Langdon felt like they were moving underwater. His arms ached from the weight of the camerlengo and the table. He wondered how the moment could get much less dignified. Then he saw the answer. The two BBC reporters had apparently been crossing the open square on their way back to the press area. But now, with the roar of the crowd, they had turned. Glick and Macri were now running back toward them. Macri's camera was raised and rolling. *Here come the vultures*, Langdon thought.

'*Alt!*' Chartrand yelled. 'Get back!'

But the reporters kept coming. Langdon guessed the other networks would take about six seconds to pick up this live BBC feed again. He was wrong. They took two. As if connected by some sort of universal consciousness, every last media screen in the piazza cut away from their countdown clocks and their Vatican experts and began transmitting the same picture – a jiggling action footage swooping up the Vatican stairs. Now, everywhere Langdon looked, he saw the camerlengo's limp body in a Technicolor close-up.

This is wrong! Langdon thought. He wanted to run down the stairs and interfere, but he could not. It wouldn't have helped anyway. Whether it was the roar of the crowd or the cool night air that caused it, Langdon would never know, but at that moment, the inconceivable occurred.

Like a man awakening from a nightmare, the camerlengo's eyes shot open and he sat bolt upright. Taken entirely by surprise, Langdon and the others fumbled with the shifting weight. The front of the table dipped. The camerlengo began to slide. They tried to recover by setting the table down, but it was too late. The camerlengo slid off the front. Incredibly, he did not fall. His feet hit the marble, and he swayed upright. He stood a moment, looking disoriented, and then, before anyone could stop him, he lurched forward, staggering down the stairs toward Macri.

'*No!*' Langdon screamed.

Chartrand rushed forward, trying to reign in the camerlengo. But the camerlengo turned on him, wild-eyed, crazed. 'Leave me!'

Chartrand jumped back.

The scene went from bad to worse. The camerlengo's torn cassock, having been only laid over his chest by Chartrand, began to slip lower. For a moment, Langdon thought the garment might hold, but that moment passed. The cassock let go, sliding off his shoulders down around his waist.

The gasp that went up from the crowd seemed to travel around the globe and back in an instant. Cameras rolled, flashbulbs exploded. On media screens everywhere, the image of the camerlengo's branded chest was projected, towering and in grisly detail. Some screens were even freezing the image and rotating it 180 degrees.

The ultimate Illuminati victory.

Langdon stared at the brand on the screens. Although it was the imprint of the square brand he had held earlier, the symbol *now* made sense. Perfect sense. The marking's awesome power hit Langdon like a train.

Orientation. Langdon had forgotten the first rule of symbology. *When is a square not a square?* He had also forgotten that iron brands, just like rubber stamps, never looked like their imprints. They were in reverse. Langdon had been looking at the brand's *negative*!

As the chaos grew, an old Illuminati quote echoed with new meaning: 'A flawless diamond, born of the ancient elements with such perfection that

all those who saw it could only stare in wonder.'
Langdon knew now the myth was true.
Earth, Air, Fire, Water.
The Illuminati Diamond.

117

Robert Langdon had little doubt that the chaos and hysteria coursing through St Peter's Square at this very instant exceeded anything Vatican Hill had ever witnessed. No battle, no crucifixion, no pilgrimage, no mystical vision ... nothing in the shrine's 2,000-year history could possibly match the scope and drama of this very moment.

As the tragedy unfolded, Langdon felt oddly separate, as if hovering there beside Vittoria at the top of the stairs. The action seemed to distend, as if in a time warp, all the insanity slowing to a crawl ...

The branded camerlengo ... raving for the world to see ...

The Illuminati Diamond . . . unveiled in its diabolical genius . . .

The countdown clock registering the final twenty minutes of Vatican history . . .

The drama, however, had only just begun.

The camerlengo, as if in some sort of post-traumatic trance, seemed suddenly puissant, possessed by demons. He began babbling, whispering to unseen spirits, looking up at the sky and raising his arms to God.

'Speak!' the camerlengo yelled to the heavens. 'Yes, I hear you!'

In that moment, Langdon understood. His heart dropped like a rock.

Vittoria apparently understood too. She went white. 'He's in shock,' she said. 'He's hallucinating. He thinks he's talking to God!'

Somebody's got to stop this, Langdon thought. It was a wretched and embarrassing end. *Get this man to a hospital!*

Below them on the stairs, Chinita Macri was poised and filming, apparently having located her ideal vantage point. The images she filmed appeared instantly across the square behind her on media screens . . . like endless drive-in movies all playing the same grisly tragedy.

The whole scene felt epic. The camerlengo, in his torn cassock, with the scorched brand on his chest, looked like some sort of battered champion who had overcome the rings of hell for this one moment of revelation. He bellowed to the heavens.

'*Ti sento, Dio!* I hear you, God!'

Chartrand backed off, a look of awe on his face.

The hush that fell across the crowd was instant and

absolute. For a moment it was as if the silence had fallen across the entire planet . . . everyone in front of their TVs rigid, a communal holding of breath.

The camerlengo stood on the stairs, before the world, and held out his arms. He looked almost Christlike, bare and wounded before the world. He raised his arms to the heavens and, looking up, exclaimed, '*Grazie! Grazie, Dio!*'

The silence of the masses never broke.

'*Grazie, Dio!*' the camerlengo cried out again. Like the sun breaking through a stormy sky, a look of joy spread across his face. '*Grazie, Dio!*'

Thank you, God? Langdon stared in wonder.

The camerlengo was radiant now, his eerie transformation complete. He looked up at the sky, still nodding furiously. He shouted to the heavens, 'Upon this rock I will build my church!'

Langdon knew the words, but he had no idea why the camerlengo could possibly be shouting them.

The camerlengo turned back to the crowd and bellowed again into the night. 'Upon this rock I will build my church!' Then he raised his hands to the sky and laughed out loud. '*Grazie, Dio! Grazie!*'

The man had clearly gone mad.

The world watched, spellbound.

The culmination, however, was something no one expected.

With a final joyous exultation, the camerlengo turned and dashed back into St Peter's Basilica.

118

Eleven-forty-two p.m.

The frenzied convoy that plunged back into the basilica to retrieve the camerlengo was not one Langdon had ever imagined he would be part of . . . much less leading. But he had been closest to the door and had acted on instinct.

He'll die in here, Langdon thought, sprinting over the threshold into the darkened void. 'Camerlengo! Stop!'

The wall of blackness that hit Langdon was absolute. His pupils were contracted from the glare outside, and his field of vision now extended no farther than a few feet before his face. He skidded to a stop. Somewhere in the blackness ahead, he heard the camerlengo's cassock rustle as the priest ran blindly into the abyss.

Vittoria and the guards arrived immediately. Flashlights came on, but the lights were almost dead now and did not even begin to probe the depths of the basilica before them. The beams swept back and forth, revealing only columns and bare floor. The camerlengo was nowhere to be seen.

'Camerlengo!' Chartrand yelled, fear in his voice. 'Wait! Signore!'

A commotion in the doorway behind them caused everyone to turn. Chinita Macri's large frame lurched through the entry. Her camera was shouldered, and the glowing red light on top revealed that it was still transmitting. Glick was running behind her, microphone in hand, yelling for her to slow down.

Langdon could not believe these two. *This is not the time!*

'Out!' Chartrand snapped. 'This is not for your eyes!'

But Macri and Glick kept coming.

'Chinita!' Glick sounded fearful now. 'This is suicide! I'm not coming!'

Macri ignored him. She threw a switch on her camera. The spotlight on top glared to life, blinding everyone.

Langdon shielded his face and turned away in pain. *Damn it!* When he looked up, though, the church around them was illuminated for thirty yards.

At that moment the camerlengo's voice echoed somewhere in the distance. 'Upon this rock I will build my church!'

Macri wheeled her camera toward the sound. Far off, in the grayness at the end of the spotlight's reach, black fabric billowed, revealing a familiar form running down the main aisle of the basilica.

There was a fleeting instant of hesitation as everyone's eyes took in the bizarre image. Then the dam broke. Chartrand pushed past Langdon and sprinted after the camerlengo. Langdon took off next. Then the guards and Vittoria.

Macri brought up the rear, lighting everyone's way and transmitting the sepulchral chase to the world. An unwilling Glick cursed aloud as he tagged along, fumbling through a terrified blow-by-blow commentary.

The main aisle of St Peter's Basilica, Lieutenant Chartrand had once figured out, was longer than an Olympic soccer field. Tonight, however, it felt like twice that. As the guard sprinted after the camerlengo, he wondered where the man was headed. The camerlengo was clearly in shock, delirious no doubt from his physical trauma and bearing witness to the horrific massacre in the Pope's office.

Somewhere up ahead, beyond the reach of the BBC spotlight, the camerlengo's voice rang out joyously. 'Upon this rock I will build my church!'

Chartrand knew the man was shouting Scripture – Matthew 16:18, if Chartrand recalled correctly. *Upon this rock I will build my church*. It was an almost cruelly inapt inspiration – the church was about to be destroyed. Surely the camerlengo had gone mad.

Or had he?

For a fleeting instant, Chartrand's soul fluttered. Holy visions and divine messages had always seemed like wishful delusions to him – the product of over-zealous minds hearing what they wanted to hear – God did not interact *directly*!

A moment later, though, as if the Holy Spirit Himself had descended to persuade Chartrand of His power, Chartrand had a vision.

Fifty yards ahead, in the center of the church, a ghost appeared . . . a diaphanous, glowing outline. The pale shape was that of the half-naked camerlengo. The specter seemed transparent, radiating light. Chartrand staggered to a stop, feeling a knot tighten in his chest. *The camerlengo is glowing!* The body seemed to shine brighter now. Then, it began to sink . . . deeper and deeper, until it disappeared as if by magic into the blackness of the floor.

Langdon had seen the phantom also. For a moment, he too thought he had witnessed a magical vision. But as he passed the stunned Chartrand and ran toward the spot where the camerlengo had disappeared, he realized what had just happened. The camerlengo had arrived at the Niche of the Palliums – the sunken chamber lit by ninety-nine oil lamps. The lamps in the niche shone up from beneath, illuminating him like a ghost. Then, as the camerlengo descended the stairs into the light, he had seemed to disappear beneath the floor.

Langdon arrived breathless at the rim overlooking the sunken room. He peered down the stairs. At the bottom, lit by the golden glow of oil lamps, the camerlengo dashed across the marble chamber toward the set of glass doors that led to the room holding the famous golden box.

What is he doing? Langdon wondered. *Certainly he can't think the golden box—*

The camerlengo yanked open the doors and ran inside. Oddly though, he totally ignored the golden box, rushing right past it. Five feet beyond the box, he dropped to his knees and began struggling to lift an iron grate embedded in the floor.

Langdon watched in horror, now realizing where the camerlengo was headed. *Good God, no!* He dashed down the stairs after him. 'Father! Don't!'

As Langdon opened the glass doors and ran toward the camerlengo, he saw the camerlengo heave on the grate. The hinged, iron bulkhead fell open with a deafening crash, revealing a narrow shaft and a steep stairway that dropped into nothingness. As the camerlengo moved toward the hole, Langdon grabbed his bare shoulders and pulled him back. The man's skin was slippery with sweat, but Langdon held on.

The camerlengo wheeled, obviously startled. 'What are you doing!'

Langdon was surprised when their eyes met. The

camerlengo no longer had the glazed look of a man in a trance. His eyes were keen, glistening with a lucid determination. The brand on his chest looked excruciating.

'Father,' Langdon urged, as calmly as possible, 'you can't go down there. We need to evacuate.'

'My son,' the camerlengo said, his voice eerily sane. 'I have just had a message. I know—'

'Camerlengo!' It was Chartrand and the others. They came dashing down the stairs into the room, lit by Macri's camera.

When Chartrand saw the open grate in the floor, his eyes filled with dread. He crossed himself and shot Langdon a thankful look for having stopped the camerlengo. Langdon understood; he had read enough about Vatican architecture to know what lay beneath that grate. It was the most sacred place in all of Christendom. *Terra Santa.* Holy Ground. Some called it the Necropolis. Some called it the Catacombs. According to accounts from the select few clergy who had descended over the years, the Necropolis was a dark maze of subterranean crypts that could swallow a visitor whole if he lost his way. It was not the kind of place through which they wanted to be chasing the camerlengo.

'Signore,' Chartrand pleaded. 'You're in shock. We need to leave this place. You cannot go down there. It's suicide.'

The camerlengo seemed suddenly stoic. He reached out and put a quiet hand on Chartrand's shoulder. 'Thank you for your concern and service. I cannot tell you how. I cannot tell you I understand. But I have had a revelation. I know where the antimatter is.'

Everyone stared.

The camerlengo turned to the group. 'Upon this rock I will build my church. That was the message. The meaning is clear.'

Langdon was still unable to comprehend the camerlengo's conviction that he had spoken to God, much less that he had deciphered the message. *Upon this rock I will build my church?* They were the words spoken by Jesus when he chose Peter as his first apostle. What did they have to do with anything?

Macri moved in for a closer shot. Glick was mute, as if shell-shocked.

The camerlengo spoke quickly now. 'The Illuminati have placed their tool of destruction on the very cornerstone of this church. At the foundation.' He motioned down the stairs. 'On the very rock upon which this church was built. And I know where that rock is.'

Langdon was certain the time had come to overpower the camerlengo and carry him off. As lucid as he seemed, the priest was talking nonsense. *A rock? The cornerstone in the foundation?* The stairway before them didn't lead to the foundation, it led to the necropolis! 'The quote is a metaphor, Father! There is no actual *rock*!'

The camerlengo looked strangely sad. 'There *is* a rock, my son.' He pointed into the hole. '*Pietro è la pietra.*'

Langdon froze. In an instant it all came clear.

The austere simplicity of it gave him chills. As Langdon stood there with the others, staring down the long staircase, he realized that there was indeed a rock buried in the darkness beneath this church.

Pietro è la pietra. Peter is the rock.

Peter's faith in God was so steadfast that Jesus

called Peter 'the rock' – the unwavering disciple on whose shoulders Jesus would build his church. On this very location, Langdon realized – Vatican Hill – Peter had been crucified and buried. The early Christians built a small shrine over his tomb. As Christianity spread, the shrine got bigger, layer upon layer, culminating in this colossal basilica. The entire Catholic faith had been built, quite literally, upon St Peter. The rock.

'The antimatter is on St Peter's tomb,' the camerlengo said, his voice crystalline.

Despite the seemingly supernatural origin of the information, Langdon sensed a stark logic in it. Placing the antimatter on St Peter's tomb seemed painfully obvious now. The Illuminati, in an act of symbolic defiance, had located the antimatter at the core of Christendom, both literally and figuratively. *The ultimate infiltration.*

'And if you all need worldly proof,' the camerlengo said, sounding impatient now, 'I just found that grate unlocked.' He pointed to the open bulkhead in the floor. 'It is *never* unlocked. Someone has been down there . . . *recently.*'

Everyone stared into the hole.

An instant later, with deceptive agility, the camerlengo spun, grabbed an oil lamp, and headed for the opening.

119

The stone steps declined steeply into the earth.
I'm going to die down here, Vittoria thought, gripping

the heavy rope banister as she bounded down the cramped passageway behind the others. Although Langdon had made a move to stop the camerlengo from entering the shaft, Chartrand had intervened, grabbing Langdon and holding on. Apparently, the young guard was now convinced the camerlengo knew what he was doing.

After a brief scuffle, Langdon had freed himself and pursued the camerlengo with Chartrand close on his heels. Instinctively, Vittoria had dashed after them.

Now she was racing headlong down a precipitous grade where any misplaced step could mean a deadly fall. Far below, she could see the golden glow of the camerlengo's oil lamp. Behind her, Vittoria could hear the BBC reporters hurrying to keep up. The camera spotlight threw gnarled shadows beyond her down the shaft, illuminating Chartrand and Langdon. Vittoria could scarcely believe the world was bearing witness to this insanity. *Turn off the damn camera!* Then again, she knew the light was the only reason any of them could see where they were going.

As the bizarre chase continued, Vittoria's thoughts whipped like a tempest. What could the camerlengo possibly do down here? Even if he found the anti-matter? There was no time!

Vittoria was surprised to find her intuition now telling her the camerlengo was probably right. Placing the antimatter three stories beneath the earth seemed an almost noble and merciful choice. Deep under-ground – much as in Z-lab – an antimatter annihilation would be partially contained. There would be no heat blast, no flying shrapnel to injure onlookers, just a biblical opening of the earth and a towering basilica crumbling into a crater.

Was this Kohler's one act of decency? Sparing lives? Vittoria still could not fathom the director's involvement. She could accept his hatred of religion ... but this awesome conspiracy seemed beyond him. Was Kohler's loathing really this profound? Destruction of the Vatican? Hiring an assassin? The murders of her father, the Pope, and four cardinals? It seemed unthinkable. And how had Kohler managed all this treachery within the Vatican walls? *Rocher was Kohler's inside man*, Vittoria told herself. *Rocher was an Illuminatus*. No doubt Captain Rocher had keys to everything – the Pope's chambers, *Il Passetto*, the Necropolis, St Peter's tomb, all of it. He could have placed the antimatter on St Peter's tomb – a highly restricted locale – and then commanded his guards not to waste time searching the Vatican's restricted areas. Rocher *knew* nobody would ever find the canister.

But Rocher never counted on the camerlengo's message from above.

The message. This was the leap of faith Vittoria was still struggling to accept. Had God actually *communicated* with the camerlengo? Vittoria's gut said no, and yet hers was the science of entanglement physics – the study of interconnectedness. She witnessed miraculous communications every day – twin sea-turtle eggs separated and placed in labs thousands of miles apart hatching at the same instant ... acres of jellyfish pulsating in perfect rhythm as if of a single mind. *There are invisible lines of communication everywhere*, she thought.

But between God and man?

Vittoria wished her father were there to give her faith. He had once explained divine communication to her in scientific terms, and he had made her believe.

531

She still remembered the day she had seen him praying and asked him, 'Father, why do you bother to pray? God cannot answer you.'

Leonardo Vetra had looked up from his meditations with a paternal smile. 'My daughter the skeptic. So you don't believe God speaks to man? Let me put it in your language.' He took a model of the human brain down from a shelf and set it in front of her. 'As you probably know, Vittoria, human beings normally use a very small percentage of their brain power. However, if you put them in emotionally charged situations – like physical trauma, extreme joy or fear, deep meditation – all of a sudden their neurons start firing like crazy, resulting in massively enhanced mental clarity.'

'So what?' Vittoria said. 'Just because you think clearly doesn't mean you talk to God.'

'Aha!' Vetra exclaimed. 'And yet remarkable solutions to seemingly impossible problems often occur in these moments of clarity. It's what gurus call higher consciousness. Biologists call it altered states. Psychologists call it super-sentience.' He paused. 'And Christians call it answered prayer.' Smiling broadly, he added, 'Sometimes, divine revelation simply means adjusting your brain to hear what your heart already knows.'

Now, as she dashed down, headlong into the dark, Vittoria sensed perhaps her father was right. Was it so hard to believe that the camerlengo's trauma had put his mind in a state where he had simply 'realized' the antimatter's location?

Each of us is a God, Buddha had said. *Each of us knows all. We need only open our minds to hear our own wisdom.*

It was in that moment of clarity, as Vittoria plunged deeper into the earth, that she felt her own mind open

. . . her own wisdom surface. She sensed now without a doubt what the camerlengo's intentions were. Her awareness brought with it a fear like nothing she had ever known.

'Camerlengo, no!' she shouted down the passage. 'You don't understand!' Vittoria pictured the multitudes of people surrounding Vatican City, and her blood ran cold. 'If you bring the antimatter up . . . everyone will *die!*'

Langdon was leaping three steps at a time now, gaining ground. The passage was cramped, but he felt no claustrophobia. His once debilitating fear was overshadowed by a far deeper dread.

'Camerlengo!' Langdon felt himself closing the gap on the lantern's glow 'You must leave the antimatter where it is! There's no other choice!'

Even as Langdon spoke the words, he could not believe them. Not only had he accepted the camerlengo's divine revelation of the antimatter's location, but he was lobbying for the destruction of St Peter's Basilica – one of the greatest architectural feats on earth . . . as well as all of the art inside.

But the people outside . . . it's the only way.

It seemed a cruel irony that the only way to save the people now was to destroy the church. Langdon figured the Illuminati were amused by the symbolism.

The air coming up from the bottom of the tunnel was cool and dank. Somewhere down here was the sacred *necropolis* . . . burial place of St Peter and countless other early Christians. Langdon felt a chill, hoping this was not a suicide mission.

Suddenly, the camerlengo's lantern seemed to halt. Langdon closed on him fast.

The end of the stairs loomed abruptly from out of the shadows. A wrought-iron gate with three embossed skulls blocked the bottom of the stairs. The camerlengo was there, pulling the gate open. Langdon leapt, pushing the gate shut, blocking the camerlengo's way. The others came thundering down the stairs, everyone ghostly white in the BBC spotlight . . . especially *Glick*, who was looking more pasty with every step.

Chartrand grabbed Langdon. 'Let the camerlengo pass!'

'No!' Vittoria said from above, breathless. 'We must evacuate right now! You *cannot* take the anti-matter out of here! If you bring it up, everyone outside will *die*!'

The camerlengo's voice was remarkably calm. 'All of you . . . we must trust. We have little time.'

'You don't understand,' Vittoria said. 'An explosion at ground level will be much worse than one down here!'

The camerlengo looked at her, his green eyes resplendently sane. 'Who said anything about an explosion at ground level?'

Vittoria stared. 'You're *leaving* it down here?'

The camerlengo's certitude was hypnotic. 'There will be no more death tonight.'

'Father, but—'

'Please . . . some *faith*.' The camerlengo's voice plunged to a compelling hush. 'I am not asking any-one to join me. You are all free to go. All I am asking is that you not interfere with His bidding. Let me do what I have been called to do.' The camerlengo's stare intensified. 'I am to save this church. And I *can*. I swear on my life.'

The silence that followed might as well have been thunder.

120

Eleven fifty-one p.m.

Necropolis literally means *City of the Dead*.

Nothing Robert Langdon had ever read about this place prepared him for the sight of it. The colossal subterranean hollow was filled with crumbling mausoleums, like small houses on the floor of a cave. The air smelled lifeless. An awkward grid of narrow walkways wound between the decaying memorials, most of which were fractured brick with marble platings. Like columns of dust, countless pillars of unexcavated earth rose up, supporting a dirt sky, which hung low over the penumbral hamlet.

City of the dead, Langdon thought, feeling trapped between academic wonder and raw fear. He and the others dashed deeper down the winding passages. *Did I make the wrong choice?*

Chartrand had been the first to fall under the camerlengo's spell, yanking open the gate and declaring his faith in the camerlengo. Glick and Macri, at the camerlengo's suggestion, had nobly agreed to provide light to the quest, although considering what accolades awaited them if they got out of here alive, their motivations were certainly suspect. Vittoria had been the least eager of all, and Langdon had seen in her eyes a wariness that looked, unsettlingly, a lot like female intuition.

It's too late now, he thought, he and Vittoria dashing after the others. *We're committed.*

Vittoria was silent, but Langdon knew they were thinking the same thing. *Nine minutes is not enough time to get the hell out of Vatican City if the camerlengo is wrong.*

As they ran on through the mausoleums, Langdon felt his legs tiring, noting to his surprise that the group was ascending a steady incline. The explanation, when it dawned on him, sent shivers to his core. The topography beneath his feet was that of Christ's time. He was running up the original Vatican Hill! Langdon had heard Vatican scholars claim that St Peter's tomb was near the *top* of Vatican Hill, and he had always wondered how they knew. Now he understood. *The damn hill is still here!*

Langdon felt like he was running through the pages of history. Somewhere ahead was St Peter's tomb – *the* Christian relic. It was hard to imagine that the original grave had been marked only with a modest shrine. Not any more. As Peter's eminence spread, new shrines were built on top of the old, and now, the homage stretched 440 feet overhead to the top of Michelangelo's dome, the apex positioned directly over the original tomb within a fraction of an inch.

They continued ascending the sinuous passages. Langdon checked his watch. *Eight minutes.* He was beginning to wonder if he and Vittoria would be joining the deceased here permanently.

'Look out!' Glick yelled from behind them. 'Snake holes!'

Langdon saw it in time. A series of small holes riddled the path before them. He leapt, just clearing them.

Vittoria jumped too, barely avoiding the narrow hollows. She looked uneasy as they ran on. '*Snake* holes?'

'*Snack* holes, actually,' Langdon corrected. 'Trust me, you don't want to know.' The holes, he had just realized, were *libation tubes*. The early Christians had believed in the resurrection of the flesh, and they'd used the holes to literally 'feed the dead' by pouring milk and honey into crypts beneath the floor.

The camerlengo felt weak.

He dashed onward, his legs finding strength in his duty to God and man. *Almost there.* He was in incredible pain. *The mind can bring so much more pain than the body.* Still he felt tired. He knew he had precious little time.

'I will save your church, Father. I swear it.'

Despite the BBC lights behind him, for which he was grateful, the camerlengo carried his oil lamp high. *I am a beacon in the darkness. I am the light.* The lamp sloshed as he ran, and for an instant he feared the flammable oil might spill and burn him. He had experienced enough burned flesh for one evening.

As he approached the top of the hill, he was drenched in sweat, barely able to breathe. But when he emerged over the crest, he felt reborn. He staggered onto the flat piece of earth where he had stood many times. Here the path ended. The necropolis came to an abrupt halt at a wall of earth. A tiny marker read: *Mausoleum S.*

La tomba di San Pietro.

Before him, at waist level, was an opening in the wall. There was no gilded plaque here. No fanfare. Just a simple hole in the wall, beyond which lay a small grotto and a meager, crumbling sarcophagus. The camerlengo gazed into the hole and smiled in exhaustion. He could hear the others coming up the hill behind him. He set down his oil lamp and knelt to pray.

Thank you, God. It is almost over.

Outside in the square, surrounded by astounded cardinals, Cardinal Mortati stared up at the media screen and watched the drama unfold in the crypt below. He no longer knew what to believe. Had the entire world just witnessed what *he* had seen? Had God truly spoken to the camerlengo? Was the antimatter really going to appear on St Peter's—

'Look!' A gasp went up from the throngs.

'There!' Everyone was suddenly pointing at the screen. 'It's a miracle!'

Mortati looked up. The camera angle was unsteady, but it was clear enough. The image was unforgettable.

Filmed from behind, the camerlengo was kneeling in prayer on the earthen floor. In front of him was a rough-hewn hole in the wall. Inside the hollow, among the rubble of ancient stone, was a terra cotta casket. Although Mortati had seen the coffin only once in his life, he knew beyond a doubt what it contained.

San Pietro.

Mortati was not naïve enough to think that the shouts of joy and amazement now thundering through the crowd were exaltations from bearing witness to one of Christianity's most sacred relics. St Peter's tomb was not what had people falling to their knees in spontaneous prayer and thanksgiving. It was the object on *top* of his tomb.

The antimatter canister. It was there . . . where it had

been all day ... hiding in the darkness of the Necropolis. Sleek. Relentless. Deadly. The camerlengo's revelation was correct.

Mortati stared in wonder at the transparent cylinder. The globule of liquid still hovered at its core. The grotto around the canister blinked red as the LED counted down into its final five minutes of life.

Also sitting on the tomb, inches away from the canister, was the wireless Swiss Guard security camera that had been pointed at the canister and transmitting all along.

Mortati crossed himself, certain this was the most frightful image he had seen in his entire life. He realized, a moment later, however, that it was about to get worse.

The camerlengo stood suddenly. He grabbed the antimatter in his hands and wheeled toward the others. His face showing total focus. He pushed past the others and began descending the Necropolis the way he had come, running down the hill.

The camera caught Vittoria Vetra, frozen in terror. 'Where are you going! Camerlengo! I thought you said—'

'Have faith!' he exclaimed as he ran off.

Vittoria spun toward Langdon. 'What do we do?'

Robert Langdon tried to stop the camerlengo, but Chartrand was running interference now, apparently trusting the camerlengo's conviction.

The picture coming from the BBC camera was like a roller coaster ride now, winding, twisting. Fleeting freeze-frames of confusion and terror as the chaotic cortege stumbled through the shadows back toward the Necropolis entrance.

Out in the square, Mortati let out a fearful gasp. 'Is he bringing that up *here*?'

On televisions all over the world, larger than life, the camerlengo raced upward out of the Necropolis with the antimatter before him. 'There will be no more death tonight!'

But the camerlengo was wrong.

121

The camerlengo erupted through the doors of St Peter's Basilica at exactly 11.56 p.m. He staggered into the dazzling glare of the world spotlight, carrying the antimatter before him like some sort of numinous offering. Through burning eyes he could see his own form, half-naked and wounded, towering like a giant on the media screens around the square. The roar that went up from the crowd in St Peter's Square was like none the camerlengo had ever heard– crying, scream-ing, chanting, praying ... a mix of veneration and terror.

Deliver us from evil, he whispered.

He felt totally depleted from his race out of the Necropolis. It had almost ended in disaster. Robert Langdon and Vittoria Vetra had wanted to intercept him, to throw the canister back into its subterranean hiding place, to run outside for cover. *Blind fools!*

The camerlengo realized now, with fearful clarity, that on any other night, he would never have won the race. Tonight, however, God again had been with him. Robert Langdon, on the verge of overtaking the camerlengo, had been grabbed by Chartrand, ever trusting and dutiful to the camerlengo's demands for faith. The reporters, of course, were spellbound and lugging too much equipment to interfere.

The Lord works in mysterious ways.

The camerlengo could hear the others behind him now . . . see them on the screens, closing in. Mustering the last of his physical strength, he raised the anti-matter high over his head. Then, throwing back his bare shoulders in an act of defiance to the Illuminati brand on his chest, he dashed down the stairs.

There was one final act.

Godspeed, he thought. *Godspeed.*

Four minutes . . .

Langdon could barely see as he burst out of the basilica. Again the sea of media lights bore into his retinas. All he could make out was the murky outline of the camerlengo, directly ahead of him, running down the stairs. For an instant, refulgent in his halo of media lights, the camerlengo looked celestial, like some kind of modern deity. His cassock was at his waist like a shroud. His body was scarred and wounded by the hands of his enemies, and still he endured. The camerlengo ran on, standing tall, calling out to the world to have faith, running toward the masses carrying this weapon of destruction.

Langdon ran down the stairs after him. *What is he doing? He will kill them all!*

'Satan's work,' the camerlengo screamed, 'has no place in the House of God!' He ran on toward a now terrified crowd.

'Father!' Langdon screamed, behind him. 'There's nowhere to go!'

'Look to the heavens! We forget to look to the heavens!'

In that moment, as Langdon saw where the camerlengo was headed, the glorious truth came flooding all around him. Although Langdon could not see it on account of the lights, he knew their salvation was directly overhead.

A star-filled Italian sky. *The escape route.*

The helicopter the camerlengo had summoned to take him to the hospital sat dead ahead, pilot already in the cockpit, blades already humming in neutral. As the camerlengo ran toward it, Langdon felt a sudden overwhelming exhilaration.

The thoughts that tore through Langdon's mind came as a torrent . . .

First he pictured the wide-open expanse of the Mediterranean Sea. How far was it? Five miles? Ten? He knew the beach at *Fiumocino* was only about seven minutes by train. But by helicopter, 200 miles an hour, no stops . . . If they could fly the canister far enough out to sea, and drop it . . . There were other options too, he realized, feeling almost weightless as he ran. *La Cava Romana!* The marble quarries north of the city were less than three miles away. How large were they? Two square miles? Certainly they were deserted at this hour! Dropping the canister *there* . . .

'Everyone back!' the camerlengo yelled. His chest ached as he ran. 'Get away! Now!'

The Swiss Guard standing around the chopper stood slack-jawed as the camerlengo approached them.

'Back!' the priest screamed.

The guards moved back.

With the entire world watching in wonder, the camerlengo ran around the chopper to the pilot's door and yanked it open. 'Out, son! Now!'

The guard jumped out.

The camerlengo looked at the high cockpit seat and knew that in his exhausted state, he would need both hands to pull himself up. He turned to the pilot, trembling beside him, and thrust the canister into his hands. 'Hold this. Hand it back when I'm in.'

As the camerlengo pulled himself up, he could hear Robert Langdon yelling excitedly, running toward the craft. *Now you understand*, the camerlengo thought. *Now you have faith!*

The camerlengo pulled himself up into the cockpit, adjusted a few familiar levers, and then turned back to his window for the canister.

But the guard to whom he had given the canister stood empty-handed. 'He took it!' the guard yelled.

The camerlengo felt his heart seize. 'Who!'

The guard pointed. 'Him!'

Robert Langdon was surprised by how heavy the canister was. He ran to the other side of the chopper and jumped in the rear compartment where he and Vittoria had sat only hours ago. He left the door open and buckled himself in. Then he yelled to the camerlengo in the front seat.

'Fly, Father!'

The camerlengo craned back at Langdon, his face bloodless with dread. 'What are you doing!'

'*You* fly! I'll throw!' Langdon barked. 'There's no time! Just fly the blessed chopper!'

The camerlengo seemed momentarily paralyzed, the media lights glaring through the cockpit darkening

543

the creases in his face. 'I can do this alone,' he whispered. 'I am *supposed* to do this alone.'

Langdon wasn't listening. *Fly!* he heard himself screaming. *Now! I'm here to help you!* Langdon looked down at the canister and felt his breath catch in his throat when he saw the numbers. '*Three* minutes, Father! *Three!*'

The number seemed to stun the camerlengo back to sobriety. Without hesitation, he turned back to the controls. With a grinding roar, the helicopter lifted off.

Through a swirl of dust, Langdon could see Vittoria running toward the chopper. Their eyes met, and then she dropped away like a sinking stone.

122

Inside the chopper, the whine of the engines and the gale from the open door assaulted Langdon's senses with a deafening chaos. He steadied himself against the magnified drag of gravity as the camerlengo accelerated the craft straight up. The glow of St Peter's Square shrank beneath them until it was an amorphous glowing ellipse radiating in a sea of city lights.

The antimatter canister felt like deadweight in Langdon's hands. He held tighter, his palms slick now with sweat and blood. Inside the trap, the globule of antimatter hovered calmly, pulsing red in the glow of the LED countdown clock.

'Two minutes!' Langdon yelled, wondering where the camerlengo intended to drop the canister.

The city lights beneath them spread out in all directions. In the distance to the west, Langdon could see the twinkling delineation of the Mediterranean coast – a jagged border of luminescence beyond which spread an endless dark expanse of nothingness. The sea looked farther now than Langdon had imagined. Moreover, the concentration of lights at the coast was a stark reminder that even far out at sea an explosion might have devastating effects. Langdon had not even considered the effects of a ten-kiloton tidal wave hitting the coast.

When Langdon turned and looked straight ahead through the cockpit window, he was more hopeful. Directly in front of them, the rolling shadows of the Roman foothills loomed in the night. The hills were spotted with lights – the villas of the very wealthy – but a mile or so north, the hills grew dark. There were no lights at all – just a huge pocket of blackness. Nothing.

The quarries! Langdon thought. *La Cava Romana!*

Staring intently at the barren pocket of land, Langdon sensed that it was plenty large enough. It seemed close, too. Much closer than the ocean. Excitement surged through him. This was obviously where the camerlengo planned to take the antimatter! The chopper was pointing directly toward it! The quarries! Oddly, however, as the engines strained louder and the chopper hurtled through the air, Langdon could see that the quarries were not getting any closer. Bewildered, he shot a glance out the side door to get his bearings. What he saw doused his excitement in a wave of panic. Directly beneath them, thousands of feet straight down, glowed the media lights in St Peter's Square.

We're still over the Vatican!

'Camerlengo!' Langdon choked. 'Go forward! We're high *enough*! You've got to start moving forward! We can't drop the canister back over Vatican City!'

The camerlengo did not reply. He appeared to be concentrating on flying the craft.

'We've got less than *two* minutes!' Langdon shouted, holding up the canister. 'I can see them! *La Cava Romana!* A couple of miles north! We don't have—'

'No,' the camerlengo said. 'It's far too dangerous. I'm sorry.' As the chopper continued to claw heavenward, the camerlengo turned and gave Langdon a mournful smile. 'I wish you had not come, my friend. You have made the ultimate sacrifice.'

Langdon looked in the camerlengo's exhausted eyes and suddenly understood. His blood turned to ice. 'But . . . there must be *somewhere* we can go!'

'*Up*,' the camerlengo replied, his voice resigned. 'It's the only guarantee.'

Langdon could barely think. He had entirely misinterpreted the camerlengo's plan. *Look to the heavens!*

Heaven, Langdon now realized, was literally where he was headed. The camerlengo had never intended to drop the antimatter. He was simply getting it as far away from Vatican City as humanly possible.

This was a one-way trip.

123

In St Peter's Square, Vittoria Vetra stared upward. The helicopter was a speck now, the media lights no longer reaching it. Even the pounding of the rotors had faded to a distant hum. It seemed, in that instant, that the entire world was focused upward, silenced in anticipation, necks craned to the heavens . . . all peoples, all faiths . . . all hearts beating as one.

Vittoria's emotions were a cyclone of twisting agonies. As the helicopter disappeared from sight, she pictured Robert's face, rising above her. *What had he been thinking? Didn't he understand?*

Around the square, television cameras probed the darkness, waiting. A sea of faces stared heavenward, united in a silent countdown. The media screens all flickered the same tranquil scene . . . a Roman sky illuminated with brilliant stars. Vittoria felt the tears begin to well.

Behind her on the marble escarpment, 161 cardinals stared up in silent awe. Some folded their hands in prayer. Most stood motionless, transfixed. Some wept. The seconds ticked past.

In homes, bars, businesses, airports, hospitals around the world, souls were joined in universal witness. Men and women locked hands. Others held their children. Time seemed to hover in limbo, souls suspended in unison.

Then, cruelly, the bells of St Peter's began to toll.

Vittoria let the tears come.

Then . . . with the whole world watching . . . time ran out.

The dead silence of the event was the most terrifying of all.

High above Vatican City, a pinpoint of light appeared in the sky. For a fleeting instant, a new heavenly body had been born . . . a speck of light as pure and white as anyone had ever seen.

Then it happened.

A flash. The point billowed, as if feeding on itself, unraveling across the sky in a dilating radius of blinding white. It shot out in all directions, accelerating with incomprehensible speed, gobbling up the dark. As the sphere of light grew, it intensified, like a burgeoning fiend preparing to consume the entire sky. It raced downward, toward them, picking up speed.

Blinded, the multitudes of starkly lit human faces gasped as one, shielding their eyes, crying out in strangled fear.

As the light roared out in all directions, the unimaginable occurred. As if bound by God's own will, the surging radius seemed to hit a wall. It was as if the explosion were contained somehow in a giant glass sphere. The light rebounded inward, sharpening, rippling across itself. The wave appeared to have reached a predetermined diameter and hovered there. For that instant, a perfect and silent sphere of light glowed over Rome. Night had become day.

Then it hit.

The concussion was deep and hollow – a thunderous shock wave from above. It descended on them like the wrath of hell, shaking the granite foundation of Vatican City, knocking the breath out of people's lungs, sending others stumbling backward. The reverberation circled the colonnade, followed by a sudden torrent of warm air. The wind tore through the square, letting out a sepulchral moan as it whistled through the columns and buffeted the walls. Dust swirled overhead as people huddled ... witnesses to Armageddon.

Then, as fast as it appeared, the sphere imploded,

sucking back in on itself, crushing inward to the tiny point of light from which it had come.

124

Never before had so many been so silent.

The faces in St Peter's Square, one by one, averted their eyes from the darkening sky and turned downward, each person in his or her own private moment of wonder. The media lights followed suit, dropping their beams back to earth as if out of reverence for the blackness now settling upon them. It seemed for a moment the entire world was bowing its head in unison.

Cardinal Mortati knelt to pray, and the other cardinals joined him. The Swiss Guard lowered their long swords and stood numb. No one spoke. No one moved. Everywhere, hearts shuddered with spontaneous emotion. Bereavement. Fear. Wonder. Belief. And a dread-filled respect for the new and awesome power they had just witnessed.

Vittoria Vetra stood trembling at the foot of the basilica's sweeping stairs. She closed her eyes. Through the tempest of emotions now coursing through her blood, a single word tolled like a distant bell. Pristine. Cruel. She forced it away. And yet the word echoed. Again she drove it back. The pain was too great. She tried to lose herself in the images that blazed in other's minds ... antimatter's mind-boggling power ... the Vatican's deliverance ... the camerlengo ... feats of bravery ... miracles ...

selflessness. And still the word echoed ... tolling through the chaos with a stinging loneliness.

Robert.

He had come for her at Castle St Angelo.

He had saved her.

And now he had been destroyed by *her* creation.

As Cardinal Mortati prayed, he wondered if he too would hear God's voice as the camerlengo had. *Does one need to believe in miracles to experience them?* Mortati was a modern man in an ancient faith. Miracles had never played a part in his belief. Certainly his faith spoke of miracles ... bleeding palms, ascensions from the dead, imprints on shrouds ... and yet, Mortati's rational mind had always justified these accounts as part of the myth. They were simply the result of man's greatest weakness – his *need* for proof. Miracles were nothing but stories we all clung to because we *wished* they were true.

And yet ...

Am I so modern that I cannot accept what my eyes have just witnessed? It was a miracle, was it not? Yes! God, with a few whispered words in the camerlengo's ear, had intervened and saved this church. Why was this so hard to believe? What would it say about God if God had done nothing? That the Almighty did not care? That He was powerless to stop it? *A miracle was the only possible response!*

As Mortati knelt in wonder, he prayed for the camerlengo's soul. He gave thanks to the young chamberlain who, even in his youthful years, had opened this old man's eyes to the miracles of unquestioning faith.

Incredibly, though, Mortati never suspected the

extent to which his faith was about to be tested . . .

The silence of St Peter's Square broke with a ripple at first. The ripple grew to a murmur. And then, suddenly, to a roar. Without warning, the multitudes were crying out as one.

'Look! Look!'

Mortati opened his eyes and turned to the crowd. Everyone was pointing behind him, toward the front of St Peter's Basilica. Their faces were white. Some fell to their knees. Some fainted. Some burst into uncontrollable sobs.

'Look! Look!'

Mortati turned, bewildered, following their outstretched hands. They were pointing to the uppermost level of the basilica, the rooftop terrace, where huge statues of Christ and his apostles watched over the crowd.

There, on the right of Jesus, arms outstretched to the world . . . stood Camerlengo Carlo Ventresca.

125

Robert Langdon was no longer falling.

There was no more terror. No pain. Not even the sound of the racing wind. There was only the soft sound of lapping water, as though he were comfortably asleep on a beach.

In a paradox of self-awareness, Langdon sensed this was death. He felt glad for it. He allowed the drifting numbness to possess him entirely. He let it carry him wherever it was he would go. His pain and fear had been anesthetized, and he did not wish it back at any price. His final memory had been one that could only have been conjured in hell.

Take me. Please . . .

But the lapping that lulled in him a far-off sense of peace was also pulling him back. It was trying to awaken him from a dream. *No! Let me be!* He did not want to awaken. He sensed demons gathering on the perimeter of his bliss, pounding to shatter his rapture. Fuzzy images swirled. Voices yelled. Wind churned. *No, please!* The more he fought, the more the fury filtered through.

Then, harshly, he was living it all again . . .

The helicopter was in a dizzying dead climb. He was trapped inside. Beyond the open door, the lights of Rome looked farther away with every passing second. His survival instinct told him to jettison the canister right now. Langdon knew it would take less than twenty seconds for the canister to fall half a mile. But it would be falling toward a city of people.

Higher! Higher!

Langdon wondered how high they were now. Small prop planes, he knew, flew at altitudes of about four miles. This helicopter *had* to be at a good fraction of that by now. *Two miles up? Three?* There was still a chance. If they timed the drop perfectly, the canister would fall only partway toward earth, exploding a safe distance over the ground and away from the chopper. Langdon looked out at the city sprawling below them.

'And if you calculate incorrectly?' the camerlengo said.

Langdon turned, startled. The camerlengo was not

even looking at him, apparently having read Langdon's thoughts from the ghostly reflection in the windshield. Oddly, the camerlengo was no longer engrossed in his controls. His hands were not even on the throttle. The chopper, it seemed, was now in some sort of autopilot mode, locked in a climb. The camerlengo reached above his head, to the ceiling of the cockpit, fishing behind a cable-housing, where he removed a key, taped there out of view.

Langdon watched in bewilderment as the camerlengo quickly unlocked the metal cargo box bolted between the seats. He removed some sort of large, black, nylon pack. He laid it on the seat next to him. Langdon's thoughts churned. The camerlengo's movements seemed composed, as if he had a solution.

'Give me the canister,' the camerlengo said, his tone serene.

Langdon did not know what to think anymore. He thrust the canister to the camerlengo. 'Ninety seconds!'

What the camerlengo did with the antimatter took Langdon totally by surprise. Holding the canister carefully in his hands, the camerlengo placed it inside the cargo box. Then he closed the heavy lid and used the key to lock it tight.

'What are you doing!' Langdon demanded.

'Leading us from temptation.' The camerlengo threw the key out the open window.

As the key tumbled into the night, Langdon felt his soul falling with it.

The camerlengo then took the nylon pack and slipped his arms through the straps. He fastened a waist clamp around his stomach and cinched it all down like a backpack. He turned to a dumbstruck Robert Langdon.

'I'm sorry,' the camerlengo said. 'It wasn't supposed to happen this way.' Then he opened his door and hurled himself into the night.

The image burned in Langdon's unconscious mind, and with it came the pain. Real pain. Physical pain. Aching. Searing. He begged to be taken, to let it end, but as the water lapped louder in his ears, new images began to flash. His hell had only just begun. He saw bits and pieces. Scattered frames of sheer panic. He lay halfway between death and nightmare, begging for deliverance, but the pictures grew brighter in his mind.

The antimatter canister was locked out of reach. It counted relentlessly downward as the chopper shot upward. *Fifty seconds.* Higher. Higher. Langdon spun wildly in the cabin, trying to make sense of what he had just seen. *Forty-five seconds.* He dug under seats searching for another parachute. *Forty seconds.* There was none! There had to be an option! *Thirty-five seconds.* He raced to the open doorway of the chopper and stood in the raging wind, gazing down at the lights of Rome below. *Thirty-two seconds.*

And then he made the choice.

The unbelievable choice . . .

With no parachute, Robert Langdon had jumped out the door. As the night swallowed his tumbling body, the helicopter seemed to rocket off above him, the sound of its rotors evaporating in the deafening rush of his own free fall.

As he plummeted toward earth, Robert Langdon felt something he had not experienced since his years on the high dive – the inexorable pull of gravity during a dead drop. The faster he fell, the harder the earth seemed to pull, sucking him down. This time, however, the drop was not fifty feet into a pool. The drop was thousands of feet into a city – an endless expanse of pavement and concrete.

Somewhere in the torrent of wind and desperation, Kohler's voice echoed from the grave . . . words he had spoken earlier this morning standing at CERN's free-fall tube. *One square yard of drag will slow a falling body almost twenty per cent.* Twenty per cent, Langdon now realized, was not even close to what one would need to survive a fall like this. Nonetheless, more out of paralysis than hope, he clenched in his hands the sole object he had grabbed from the chopper on his way out the door. It was an odd memento, but it was one that for a fleeting instant had given him hope.

The windshield tarp had been lying in the back of the helicopter. It was a concave rectangle – about four yards by two – like a huge fitted sheet . . . the crudest approximation of a parachute imaginable. It had no harness, only bungie loops at either end for fastening it to the curvature of the windshield. Langdon had grabbed it, slid his hands through the loops, held on, and leapt out into the void.

His last great act of youthful defiance.

No illusions of life beyond this moment.

Langdon fell like a rock. Feet first. Arms raised. His hands gripping the loops. The tarp billowed like a mushroom overhead. The wind tore past him violently.

As he plummeted toward earth, there was a deep explosion somewhere above him. It seemed farther off than he had expected. Almost instantly, the shock wave hit. He felt the breath crushed from his lungs.

There was a sudden warmth in the air all around him. He fought to hold on. A wall of heat raced down from above. The top of the tarp began to smolder . . . but held.

Langdon rocketed downward, on the edge of a billowing shroud of light, feeling like a surfer trying to outrun a thousand-foot tidal wave. Then suddenly, the heat receded.

He was falling again through the dark coolness.

For an instant, Langdon felt hope. A moment later, though, that hope faded like the withdrawing heat above. Despite his straining arms assuring him that the tarp was slowing his fall, the wind still tore past his body with deafening velocity. Langdon had no doubt he was still moving too fast to survive the fall. He would be crushed when he hit the ground.

Mathematical figures tumbled through his brain, but he was too numb to make sense of them . . . *one square yard of drag . . . 20 per cent reduction of speed*. All Langdon could figure was that the tarp over his head was big enough to slow him more than 20 per cent. Unfortunately, though, he could tell from the wind whipping past him that whatever good the tarp was doing was not enough. He was still falling fast . . . there would be no surviving the impact on the waiting sea of concrete.

Beneath him, the lights of Rome spread out in all directions. The city looked like an enormous starlit sky that Langdon was falling into. The perfect expanse of stars was marred only by a dark strip that split the city in two – a wide, unlit ribbon that wound through the dots of light like a fat snake. Langdon stared down at the meandering swatch of black.

Suddenly, like the surging crest of an unexpected wave, hope filled him again.

With almost maniacal vigor, Langdon yanked down hard with his right hand on the canopy. The tarp suddenly flapped louder, billowing, cutting right to find the path of least resistance. Langdon felt himself drifting sideways. He pulled again, harder, ignoring the pain in his palm. The tarp flared, and Langdon sensed his body sliding laterally. Not much. But *some*! He looked beneath him again, to the sinuous serpent of black. It was off to the right, but he was still pretty high. Had he waited too long? He pulled with all his might and accepted somehow that it was now in the hands of God. He focused hard on the widest part of the serpent and . . . for the first time in his life, prayed for a miracle.

The rest was a blur.

The darkness rushing up beneath him . . . the diving instincts coming back . . . the reflexive locking of his spine and pointing of the toes . . . the inflating of his lungs to protect his vital organs . . . the flexing of his legs into a battering ram . . . and finally . . . the thankfulness that the winding Tiber River was raging . . . making its waters frothy and air-filled . . . and three times softer than standing water.

Then there was impact . . . and blackness.

It had been the thundering sound of the flapping canopy that drew the group's eyes away from the fireball in the sky. The sky above Rome had been filled with sights tonight . . . a skyrocketing helicopter, an enormous explosion, and now this strange object that had plummeted into the churning waters of the Tiber River, directly off the shore of the river's tiny island, Isola Tiberina.

Ever since the island had been used to quarantine the sick during the Roman plague of A.D. 1656, it had been thought to have mystic healing properties. For this reason, the island had later become the site for Rome's Hospital Tiberina.

The body was battered when they pulled it onto shore. The man still had a faint pulse, which was amazing, they thought. They wondered if it was Isola Tiberina's mythical reputation for healing that had somehow kept his heart pumping. Minutes later, when the man began coughing and slowly regained consciousness, the group decided the island must indeed be magical.

126

Cardinal Mortati knew there were no words in any language that could have added to the mystery of this moment. The silence of the vision over St Peter's Square sang louder than any chorus of angels.

As he stared up at Camerlengo Ventresca, Mortati felt the paralyzing collision of his heart and mind. The vision seemed real, tangible. And yet . . . how could it be? Everyone had seen the camerlengo get in the helicopter. They had all witnessed the ball of light in the sky. And now, somehow, the camerlengo stood high above them on the rooftop terrace. Transported by angels? Reincarnated by the hand of God?

This is impossible . . .

Mortati's heart wanted nothing more than to believe, but his mind cried out for reason. And yet all around him, the cardinals stared up, obviously seeing what he was seeing, paralyzed with wonder.

It was the camerlengo. There was no doubt. But he looked different somehow. Divine. As if he had been purified. A spirit? A man? His white flesh shone in the spotlights with an incorporeal weightlessness.

In the square there was crying, cheering, spontaneous applause. A group of nuns fell to their knees and wailed *saetas*. A pulsing grew from in the crowd. Suddenly, the entire square was chanting the camerlengo's name. The cardinals, some with tears rolling down their faces, joined in. Mortati looked around him and tried to comprehend. *Is this really happening?*

Camerlengo Carlo Ventresca stood on the rooftop terrace of St Peter's Basilica and looked down over the multitudes of people staring up at him. Was he awake or dreaming? He felt transformed, otherworldly. He wondered if it was his body or just his spirit that had floated down from heaven toward the soft, darkened expanse of the Vatican City Gardens . . . alighting like a silent angel on the deserted lawns, his black parachute shrouded from the madness by the towering shadow of St Peter's Basilica. He wondered if it was his body or his spirit that had possessed the strength to climb the ancient Stairway of Medallions to the rooftop terrace where he now stood.

He felt as light as a ghost.

Although the people below were chanting his name, he knew it was not *him* they were cheering. They were cheering from impulsive joy, the same kind of joy he felt every day of his life as he pondered the Almighty. They were experiencing what each of them had always longed for ... an assurance of the beyond ... a substantiation of the power of the Creator.

Camerlengo Ventresca had prayed all his life for this moment, and still, even *he* could not fathom that God had found a way to make it manifest. He wanted to cry out to them. *Your God is a living God! Behold the miracles all around you!*

He stood there a while, numb and yet feeling more than he had ever felt. When, at last, the spirit moved him, he bowed his head and stepped back from the edge.

Alone now, he knelt on the roof, and prayed.

127

The images around him blurred, drifting in and out. Langdon's eyes slowly began to focus. His legs ached, and his body felt like it had been run over by a truck. He was lying on his side on the ground. Something stunk, like bile. He could still hear the incessant sound of lapping water. It no longer sounded peaceful to him. There were other sounds too – talking close around him. He saw blurry white forms. Were they all wearing white? Langdon decided he was either in an asylum or heaven. From the burning in his throat, Langdon decided it could not be heaven.

'*He's finished vomiting,*' one man said in Italian. '*Turn him.*' The voice was firm and professional.

Langdon felt hands slowly rolling him onto his back. His head swam. He tried to sit up, but the hands gently forced him back down. His body submitted.

Then Langdon felt someone going through his pockets, removing items.

Then he passed out cold.

Dr Jacobus was not a religious man; the science of medicine had bred that from him long ago. And yet, the events in Vatican City tonight had put his systematic logic to the test. *Now bodies are falling from the sky?*

Dr Jacobus felt the pulse of the bedraggled man they had just pulled from the Tiber River. The doctor decided that God himself had hand-delivered this one to safety. The concussion of hitting the water had knocked the victim unconscious, and if it had not been for Jacobus and his crew standing out on the shore watching the spectacle in the sky, this falling soul would surely have gone unnoticed and drowned.

'*É Americano,*' a nurse said, going through the man's wallet after they pulled him to dry land.

American? Romans often joked that Americans had gotten so abundant in Rome that hamburgers should become the official Italian food. *But Americans falling from the sky?* Jacobus flicked a penlight in the man's eyes, testing his dilation. 'Sir? Can you hear me? Do you know where you are?'

The man was unconscious again. Jacobus was not surprised. The man had vomited a lot of water after Jacobus had performed CPR.

'*Si chiama Robert Langdon,*' the nurse said, reading the man's driver's license.

The group assembled on the dock all stopped short.

'*Impossibile!*' Jacobus declared. Robert Langdon was the man from the television – the American professor who had been helping the Vatican. Jacobus had seen Mr Langdon, only minutes ago, getting into a helicopter in St Peter's Square and flying miles up into the air. Jacobus and the others had run out to the dock to witness the antimatter explosion – a tremendous sphere of light like nothing any of them had ever seen. *How could this be the same man!*

'It's him!' the nurse exclaimed, brushing his soaked hair back. 'And I recognize his tweed coat!'

Suddenly someone was yelling from the hospital entryway. It was one of the patients. She was screaming, going mad, holding her portable radio to the sky and praising God. Apparently Camerlengo Ventresca had just miraculously appeared on the roof of the Vatican.

Dr Jacobus decided, when his shift got off at 8 a.m., he was going straight to church.

The lights over Langdon's head were brighter now, sterile. He was on some kind of examination table. He smelled astringents, strange chemicals. Someone had just given him an injection, and they had removed his clothes.

Definitely not gypsies, he decided in his semiconscious delirium. *Aliens, perhaps?* Yes, he had heard about things like this. Fortunately these beings would not harm him. All they wanted were his—

'Not on your life!' Langdon sat bolt upright, eyes flying open.

'*Attento!*' one of the creatures yelled, steadying him. His badge read Dr Jacobus. He looked remarkably human.

Langdon stammered, 'I . . . thought . . .'

'Easy, Mr Langdon. You're in a hospital.'

The fog began to lift. Langdon felt a wave of relief. He hated hospitals, but they certainly beat aliens harvesting his testicles.

'My name is Dr Jacobus,' the man said. He explained what had just happened. 'You are very lucky to be alive.'

Langdon did not feel lucky. He could barely make sense of his own memories . . . the helicopter . . . the camerlengo. His body ached everywhere. They gave him some water, and he rinsed out his mouth. They placed a new gauze on his palm.

'Where are my clothes?' Langdon asked. He was wearing a paper robe.

One of the nurses motioned to a dripping wad of shredded khaki and tweed on the counter. 'They were soaked. We had to cut them off you.'

Langdon looked at his shredded Harris tweed and frowned.

'You had some Kleenex in your pocket,' the nurse said.

It was then that Langdon saw the ravaged shreds of parchment clinging all over the lining of his jacket. The folio from Galileo's *Diagramma*. The last copy on earth had just dissolved. He was too numb to know how to react. He just stared.

'We saved your personal items.' She held up a plastic bin. 'Wallet, camcorder, and pen. I dried the camcorder off the best I could.'

'I don't own a camcorder.'

The nurse frowned and held out the bin. Langdon looked at the contents. Along with his wallet and pen was a tiny Sony RUVI camcorder. He recalled it now. Kohler had handed it to him and asked him to give it to the media.

'We found it in your pocket. I think you'll need a new one, though.' The nurse flipped open the two-inch screen on the back. 'Your viewer is cracked.' Then she brightened. 'The sound still works, though. Barely.' She held the device up to her ear. 'Keeps playing something over and over.' She listened a moment and then scowled, handing it to Langdon. 'Two guys arguing, I think.'

Puzzled, Langdon took the camcorder and held it to his ear. The voices were pinched and metallic, but they were discernible. One close. One far away. Langdon recognized them both.

Sitting there in his paper gown, Langdon listened in amazement to the conversation. Although he couldn't see what was happening, when he heard the shocking finale, he was thankful he had been spared the visual.

My God!

As the conversation began playing again from the beginning, Langdon lowered the camcorder from his ear and sat in appalled mystification. The antimatter . . . the helicopter . . . Langdon's mind now kicked into gear.

But that means . . .

He wanted to vomit again. With a rising fury of disorientation and rage, Langdon got off the table and stood on shaky legs.

'Mr Langdon!' the doctor said, trying to stop him.

'I need some clothes,' Langdon demanded, feeling the draft on his rear from the backless gown.

'But, you need to rest.'

'I'm checking out. Now. I need some clothes.'

'But, sir, you—'

'Now!'

Everyone exchanged bewildered looks. 'We have no clothes,' the doctor said. 'Perhaps tomorrow a friend could bring you some.'

Langdon drew a slow patient breath and locked

eyes with the doctor. 'Dr Jacobus, I am walking out your door right now. I need clothes. I am going to Vatican City. One does not go to Vatican City with one's ass hanging out. Do I make myself clear?'

Dr Jacobus swallowed hard. 'Get this man something to wear.'

When Langdon limped out of Hospital Tiberina, he felt like an overgrown Cub Scout. He was wearing a blue paramedic's jumpsuit that zipped up the front and was adorned with cloth badges that apparently depicted his numerous qualifications.

The woman accompanying him was heavyset and wore a similar suit. The doctor had assured Langdon she would get him to the Vatican in record time.

'*Molto traffico*,' Langdon said, reminding her that the area around the Vatican was packed with cars and people.

The woman looked unconcerned. She pointed proudly to one of her patches. '*Sono conducente di ambulanza.*'

'*Ambulanza?*' That explained it. Langdon felt like he could use an ambulance ride.

The woman led him around the side of the building. On an outcropping over the water was a cement deck where her vehicle sat waiting. When Langdon saw the vehicle he stopped in his tracks. It was an aging medevac chopper. The hull read *Aero-Ambulanza*.

He hung his head.

The woman smiled. 'Fly Vatican City. Very fast.'

128

The College of Cardinals bristled with ebullience and electricity as they streamed back into the Sistine Chapel. In contrast, Mortati felt in himself a rising confusion he thought might lift him off the floor and carry him away. He believed in the ancient miracles of the Scriptures, and yet what he had just *witnessed* in person was something he could not possibly comprehend. After a lifetime of devotion, seventy-nine years, Mortati knew these events should ignite in him a pious exuberance ... a fervent and living faith. And yet all he felt was a growing spectral unease. Something did not feel right.

'Signore Mortati!' a Swiss Guard yelled, running down the hall.

'We have gone to the roof as you asked. The camerlengo is ... *flesh*! He is a true man! He is not a spirit! He is exactly as we knew him!'

'Did he *speak* to you?'

'He kneels in silent prayer! We are afraid to touch him!'

Mortati was at a loss. 'Tell him ... his cardinals await.'

'Signore, because he is a *man* ...' the guard hesitated.

'What is it?'

'His chest ... he is burned. Should we bind his wounds? He must be in pain.'

Mortati considered it. Nothing in his lifetime of service to the church had prepared him for this situation. 'He is a man, so serve him as a man. Bathe him. Bind his wounds. Dress him in fresh robes. We await his arrival in the Sistine Chapel.'

The guard ran off.

Mortati headed for the chapel. The rest of the cardinals were inside now. As he walked down the hall, he saw Vittoria Vetra slumped alone on a bench at the foot of the Royal Staircase. He could see the pain and loneliness of her loss and wanted to go to her, but he knew it would have to wait. He had work to do . . . although he had no idea what that work could possibly be.

Mortati entered the chapel. There was a riotous excitement. He closed the door. *God help me.*

Hospital Tiberina's twin-rotor *Aero-Ambulanza* circled in behind Vatican City, and Langdon clenched his teeth, swearing to God this was the very last helicopter ride of his life.

After convincing the pilot that the rules governing Vatican airspace were the least of the Vatican's concerns right now, he guided her in, unseen, over the rear wall, and landed them on the Vatican's helipad.

'*Grazie,*' he said, lowering himself painfully onto the ground. She blew him a kiss and quickly took off, disappearing back over the wall and into the night.

Langdon exhaled, trying to clear his head, hoping to make sense of what he was about to do. With the camcorder in hand, he boarded the same golf cart he had ridden earlier that day. It had not been charged, and the battery-meter registered close to empty. Langdon drove without headlights to conserve power.

He also preferred no one see him coming.

At the back of the Sistine Chapel, Cardinal Mortati stood in a daze as he watched the pandemonium before him.

'It was a miracle!' one of the cardinals shouted. 'The work of God!'

'Yes!' others exclaimed. 'God has made His will manifest!'

'The camerlengo will be our Pope!' another shouted. 'He is not a cardinal, but God has sent a miraculous sign!'

'Yes!' someone agreed. 'The laws of conclave are *man's* laws. God's will is before us! I call for a balloting immediately!'

'A balloting?' Mortati demanded, moving toward them. 'I believe that is *my* job.'

Everyone turned.

Mortati could sense the cardinals studying him. They seemed distant, at a loss, offended by his sobriety. Mortati longed to feel his heart swept up in the miraculous exultation he saw in the faces around him. But he was not. He felt an inexplicable pain in his soul ... an aching sadness he could not explain. He had vowed to guide these proceedings with purity of soul, and this hesitancy was something he could not deny.

'My friends,' Mortati said, stepping to the altar. His voice did not seem his own. 'I suspect I will struggle for the rest of my days with the meaning of what I have witnessed tonight. And yet, what you are suggesting regarding the camerlengo ... it cannot possibly be God's will.'

The room fell silent.

'How ... can you say that?' one of the cardinals finally demanded. 'The camerlengo *saved* the church. God spoke to the camerlengo directly! The man survived death itself! What sign do we need!'

'The camerlengo is coming to us now,' Mortati said.

'Let us wait. Let us hear him before we have a balloting. There may be an explanation.'

'An explanation?'

'As your Great Elector, I have vowed to uphold the laws of conclave. You are no doubt aware that by Holy Law the camerlengo is ineligible for election to the papacy. He is not a cardinal. He is a priest ... a chamberlain. There is also the question of his inadequate age.' Mortati felt the stares hardening. 'By even allowing a balloting, I would be requesting that you endorse a man who Vatican Law proclaims ineligible. I would be asking each of you to break a sacred oath.'

'But what happened here tonight,' someone stammered, 'it *certainly* transcends our laws!'

'Does it?' Mortati boomed, not even knowing now where his words were coming from. 'Is it God's will that we discard the rules of the church? Is it God's will that we abandon reason and give ourselves over to frenzy?'

'But did you not see what *we* saw?' another challenged angrily. 'How can you presume to question that kind of power!'

Mortati's voice bellowed now with a resonance he had never known. 'I am not questioning God's power! It is *God* who gave us reason and circumspection! It is God we serve by exercising prudence!'

129

In the hallway outside the Sistine Chapel, Vittoria Vetra sat benumbed on a bench at the foot of the

Royal Staircase. When she saw the figure coming through the rear door, she wondered if she were seeing another spirit. He was bandaged, limping, and wearing some kind of medical suit.

She stood . . . unable to believe the vision. 'Ro . . . bert?'

He never answered. He strode directly to her and wrapped her in his arms. When he pressed his lips to hers, it was an impulsive, longing kiss filled with thankfulness.

Vittoria felt the tears coming. 'Oh, God . . . oh, thank God . . .'

He kissed her again, more passionately, and she pressed against him, losing herself in his embrace. Their bodies locked, as if they had known each other for years. She forgot the fear and pain. She closed her eyes, weightless in the moment.

'It is God's will!' someone was yelling, his voice echoing in the Sistine Chapel. 'Who but the *chosen* one could have survived that diabolical explosion?'

'Me,' a voice reverberated from the back of the chapel.

Mortati and the others turned in wonder at the bedraggled form coming up the center aisle. 'Mr . . . *Langdon*?'

Without a word, Langdon walked slowly to the front of the chapel. Vittoria Vetra entered too. Then two guards hurried in, pushing a cart with a large television on it. Langdon waited while they plugged it in, facing the cardinals. Then Langdon motioned for the guards to leave. They did, closing the door behind them.

Now it was only Langdon, Vittoria, and the

cardinals. Langdon plugged the Sony RUVI's output into the television. Then he pressed PLAY.

The television blared to life.

The scene that materialized before the cardinals revealed the Pope's office. The video had been awkwardly filmed, as if by hidden camera. Off center on the screen the camerlengo stood in the dimness, in front of a fire. Although he appeared to be talking directly to the camera, it quickly became evident that he was speaking to someone else – whoever was making this video. Langdon told them the video was filmed by Maximilian Kohler, the director of CERN. Only an hour ago Kohler had secretly recorded his meeting with the camerlengo by using a tiny camcorder covertly mounted under the arm of his wheelchair.

Mortati and the cardinals watched in bewilderment. Although the conversation was already in progress, Langdon did not bother to rewind. Apparently, whatever Langdon wanted the cardinals to see was coming up . . .

'Leonardo Vetra kept diaries?' the camerlengo was saying. 'I suppose that is good news for CERN. If the diaries contain his processes for creating antimatter—'

'They don't,' Kohler said. 'You will be relieved to know those processes died with Leonardo. However, his diaries spoke of something else. *You.*'

The camerlengo looked troubled. 'I don't understand.'

'They described a meeting Leonardo had last month. With *you.*'

The camerlengo hesitated, then looked toward the door. 'Rocher should not have granted you access without consulting me. How did you get in here?'

'Rocher knows the truth. I called earlier and told him what you have done.'

'What *I* have done? Whatever story you told him, Rocher is a Swiss Guard and far too faithful to this church to believe a bitter scientist over his camerlengo.'

'Actually, he is too faithful *not* to believe. He is so faithful that despite the evidence that one of his loyal guards had betrayed the church, he refused to accept it. All day long he has been searching for another explanation.'

'So you gave him one.'

'The truth. Shocking as it was.'

'If Rocher believed you, he would have arrested me.'

'No. I wouldn't let him. I offered him my silence in exchange for this meeting.'

The camerlengo let out an odd laugh. 'You plan to *blackmail* the church with a story that no one will possibly believe?'

'I have no need of blackmail. I simply want to hear the truth from your lips. Leonardo Vetra was a friend.'

The camerlengo said nothing. He simply stared down at Kohler.

'Try this,' Kohler snapped. 'About a month ago, Leonardo Vetra contacted you requesting an urgent audience with the Pope – an audience you granted because the Pope was an admirer of Leonardo's work and because Leonardo said it was an emergency.'

The camerlengo turned to the fire. He said nothing.

'Leonardo came to the Vatican in great secrecy. He was betraying his daughter's confidence by coming here, a fact that troubled him deeply, but he felt he had

572

no choice. His research had left him deeply conflicted and in need of spiritual guidance from the church. In a private meeting, he told you and the Pope that he had made a scientific discovery with profound religious implications. He had *proved* Genesis was physically possible, and that intense sources of energy – what Vetra called *God* – could duplicate the moment of Creation.'

Silence.

'The Pope was stunned,' Kohler continued. 'He wanted Leonardo to go public. His Holiness thought this discovery might begin to bridge the gap between science and religion – one of the Pope's life dreams. Then Leonardo explained to you the downside – the reason he required the church's guidance. It seemed his Creation experiment, exactly as your Bible predicts, produced everything in pairs. Opposites. Light *and* dark. Vetra found himself, in addition to creating matter, creating *antimatter*. Shall I go on?'

The camerlengo was silent. He bent down and stoked the coals.

'After Leonardo Vetra came here,' Kohler said, '*you* came to CERN to see his work. Leonardo's diaries said you made a personal trip to his lab.'

The camerlengo looked up.

Kohler went on. 'The Pope could not travel without attracting media attention, so he sent *you*. Leonardo gave you a secret tour of his lab. He showed you an antimatter annihilation – the Big Bang – the power of Creation. He also showed you a large specimen he kept locked away as proof that his new process could produce antimatter on a large scale. You were in awe. You returned to Vatican City to report to the Pope what you had witnessed.'

The camerlengo sighed. 'And what is it that troubles you? That I would respect Leonardo's confidentiality by pretending before the world tonight that I knew nothing of antimatter?'

'No! It troubles me that Leonardo Vetra practically *proved* the existence of your God, and you had him murdered!'

The camerlengo turned now, his face revealing nothing.

The only sound was the crackle of the fire.

Suddenly, the camera jiggled, and Kohler's arm appeared in the frame. He leaned forward, seeming to struggle with something affixed beneath his wheelchair. When he sat back down, he held a pistol out before him. The camera angle was a chilling one ... looking from behind ... down the length of the outstretched gun ... directly at the camerlengo.

Kohler said, 'Confess your sins, Father. Now.'

The camerlengo looked startled. 'You will never get out of here alive.'

'Death would be a welcome relief from the misery your faith has put me through since I was a boy.' Kohler held the gun with both hands now. 'I am giving you a choice. Confess your sins ... or die right now.'

The camerlengo glanced toward the door.

'Rocher is outside,' Kohler challenged. 'He too is prepared to kill you.'

'Rocher is a sworn protector of th—'

'Rocher let me in here. *Armed.* He is sickened by your lies. You have a single option. Confess to me. I have to hear it from your very lips.'

The camerlengo hesitated.

Kohler cocked his gun. 'Do you really doubt I will kill you?'

'No matter what I tell you,' the camerlengo said, 'a man like you will never understand.'

'Try me.'

The camerlengo stood still for a moment, a dominant silhouette in the dim light of the fire. When he spoke, his words echoed with a dignity more suited to the glorious recounting of altruism than that of a confession.

'Since the beginning of time,' the camerlengo said, 'this church has fought the enemies of God. Sometimes with words. Sometimes with swords. And we have always survived.'

The camerlengo radiated conviction.

'But the demons of the past,' he continued, 'were demons of fire and abomination . . . *they* were enemies we could fight – enemies who inspired *fear*. Yet Satan is shrewd. As time passed, he cast off his diabolical countenance for a new face . . . the face of pure reason. Transparent and insidious, but soulless all the same.' The camerlengo's voice flashed sudden anger – an almost maniacal transition. 'Tell me, Mr Kohler! How can the church condemn that which makes logical sense to our minds! How can we decry that which is now the very foundation of our society! Each time the church raises its voice in warning, *you* shout back, calling us ignorant. Paranoid. Controlling! And so your evil grows. Shrouded in a veil of self-righteous intellectualism. It spreads like a cancer. Sanctified by the miracles of its own technology. Deifying itself! Until we no longer suspect you are anything but pure goodness. Science has come to save us from our sickness, hunger, and pain! Behold science – the new God of endless miracles, omnipotent and benevolent! Ignore the weapons and the chaos. Forget the fractured loneliness and endless peril. Science is here!' The camerlengo stepped toward the gun. 'But I have seen Satan's face lurking ... I have seen the peril ...'

'What are you talking about! Vetra's science practically *proved* the existence of your God! He was your ally!'

'Ally? Science and religion are not in this together! We do not seek the same God, you and I! Who is your God? One of protons, masses, and particle charges? How does your God *inspire*? How does your God reach into the hearts of man and remind him he is accountable to a greater power! Remind him that he is accountable to his fellow man! Vetra was misguided. His work was not religious, it was *sacrilegious*! Man cannot put God's Creation in a test tube and wave it around for the world to see! This does not glorify God, it *demeans* God!' The camerlengo was clawing at his body now, his voice manic.

'And so you had Leonardo Vetra killed!'

'For the church! For all mankind! The madness of it! Man is not ready to hold the power of Creation in his hands. God in a test tube? A droplet of liquid that can vaporize an entire city? He had to be stopped!' The camerlengo fell abruptly silent. He looked away, back toward the fire. He seemed to be contemplating his options.

Kohler's hands leveled the gun. 'You have confessed. You have no escape.'

The camerlengo laughed sadly. 'Don't you see. Confessing your sins *is* the escape.' He looked toward the door. 'When God is on your side, you have options a man like you could never comprehend.' With his words still hanging in the air, the camerlengo grabbed the neck of his cassock and violently tore it open, revealing his bare chest.

Kohler jolted, obviously startled. 'What are you doing!'

The camerlengo did not reply. He stepped backward, toward the fireplace, and removed an object from the glowing embers.

'Stop!' Kohler demanded, his gun still leveled. 'What are you doing!'

When the camerlengo turned, he was holding a red-hot brand. The Illuminati Diamond. The man's eyes looked wild suddenly. 'I had intended to do this all alone.' His voice seethed with a feral intensity. 'But now . . . I see God meant for you to be here. *You* are my salvation.'

Before Kohler could react, the camerlengo closed his eyes, arched his back, and rammed the red hot brand into the center of his own chest. His flesh hissed. '*Mother Mary! Blessed Mother . . . Behold your son!*' He screamed out in agony.

Kohler lurched into the frame now . . . standing awkwardly on his feet, gun wavering wildly before him.

The camerlengo screamed louder, teetering in shock. He threw the brand at Kohler's feet. Then the priest collapsed on the floor, writhing in agony.

What happened next was a blur.

There was a great flurry onscreen as the Swiss Guard burst into the room. The soundtrack exploded with gunfire. Kohler clutched his chest, blown backward, bleeding, falling into his wheelchair.

'No!' Rocher called, trying to stop his guards from firing on Kohler.

The camerlengo, still writhing on the floor, rolled

and pointed frantically at Rocher. *'Illuminatus!'*

'You bastard,' Rocher yelled, running at him. 'You sanctimonious bas—'

Chartrand cut him down with three bullets. Rocher slid dead across the floor.

Then the guards ran to the wounded camerlengo, gathering around him. As they huddled, the video caught the face of a dazed Robert Langdon, kneeling beside the wheelchair, looking at the brand. Then, the entire frame began lurching wildly. Kohler had regained consciousness and was detaching the tiny camcorder from its holder under the arm of the wheelchair. Then he tried to hand the camcorder to Langdon.

'G-give . . .' Kohler gasped. 'G-give this to the m-media.'

Then the screen went blank.

130

The camerlengo began to feel the fog of wonder and adrenaline dissipating. As the Swiss Guard helped him down the Royal Staircase toward the Sistine Chapel, the camerlengo heard singing in St Peter's Square and he knew that mountains had been moved.

Grazie Dio.

He had prayed for strength, and God had given it to him. At moments when he had doubted, God had spoken. *Yours is a Holy mission*, God had said. *I will give you strength*. Even with God's strength, the camerlengo had felt fear, questioning the righteousness of his path.

If not you, God had challenged, *then WHO?*
If not now, then WHEN?
If not this way, then HOW?

Jesus, God reminded him, had saved them all . . . saved them from their own apathy. With two deeds, Jesus had opened their eyes. Horror and Hope. The crucifixion and the resurrection. He had changed the world.

But that was millennia ago. Time had eroded the miracle. People had forgotten. They had turned to false idols – techno-deities and miracles of the mind. *What about miracles of the heart!*

The camerlengo had often prayed to God to show him how to make the people believe again. But God had been silent. It was not until the camerlengo's moment of deepest darkness that God had come to him. *Oh, the horror of that night!*

The camerlengo could still remember lying on the floor in tattered nightclothes, clawing at his own flesh, trying to purge his soul of the pain brought on by a vile truth he had just learned. *It cannot be!* he had screamed. And yet he knew it was. The deception tore at him like the fires of hell. The bishop who had taken him in, the man who had been like a father to him, the clergyman whom the camerlengo had stood beside while he rose to the papacy . . . was a fraud. A common sinner. Lying to the world about a deed so traitorous at its core that the camerlengo doubted even God could forgive it. 'Your *vow!*' the camerlengo had screamed at the Pope. 'You broke your vow to God! *You,* of all men!'

The Pope had tried to explain himself, but the camerlengo could not listen. He had run out, staggering blindly through the hallways, vomiting, tearing at his own skin, until he found himself bloody and alone, lying on the cold earthen floor before St Peter's tomb. *Mother Mary, what do I do?* It was in that moment of pain and betrayal, as the camerlengo lay devastated in the Necropolis, praying for God to take him from this faithless world, that God had come.

The voice in his head resounded like peals of thunder. *'Did you vow to serve your God?'*

'Yes!' the camerlengo cried out.

'Would you die for your God?'

'Yes! Take me now!'

'Would you die for your church?'

'Yes! Please deliver me!'

'But would you die for . . . mankind?'

It was in the silence that followed that the camerlengo felt himself falling into the abyss. He tumbled farther, faster, out of control. And yet he knew the answer. He had always known.

'Yes!' he shouted into the madness. 'I would die for man! Like your son, I would die for them!'

Hours later, the camerlengo still lay shivering on his floor. He saw his mother's face. *God has plans for you,* she was saying. The camerlengo plunged deeper into madness. It was then God had spoken again. This time with silence. But the camerlengo understood. *Restore their faith.*

If not me . . . then who?

If not now . . . then when?

As the guards unbolted the door of the Sistine Chapel, Camerlengo Carlo Ventresca felt the power moving in his veins . . . exactly as it had when he was a boy. God had chosen him. Long ago.

His will be done.

The camerlengo felt reborn. The Swiss Guard had bandaged his chest, bathed him, and dressed him in a fresh white linen robe. They had also given him an injection of morphine for the burn. The camerlengo wished they had not given him painkillers. *Jesus endured his pain for three days before ascending!* He could already feel the drug uprooting his senses . . . a dizzying undertow.

As he walked into the chapel, he was not at all surprised to see the cardinals staring at him in wonder. *They are in awe of God*, he reminded himself. *Not of me, but how God works THROUGH me.* As he moved up the center aisle, he saw bewilderment in every face. And yet, with each new face he passed, he sensed something *else* in their eyes. What was it? The camerlengo had tried to imagine how they would receive him tonight. Joyfully? Reverently? He tried to read their eyes and saw neither emotion.

It was then the camerlengo looked at the altar and saw Robert Langdon.

131

Camerlengo Carlo Ventresca stood in the aisle of the Sistine Chapel. The cardinals were all standing near the front of the church, turned, staring at him. Robert Langdon was on the altar beside a television that was on endless loop, playing a scene the camerlengo recognized but could not imagine how it had come to be. Vittoria Vetra stood beside him, her face drawn.

The camerlengo closed his eyes for a moment,

hoping the morphine was making him hallucinate and that when he opened them the scene might be different. But it was not.

They knew.

Oddly, he felt no fear. *Show me the way, Father. Give me the words that I can make them see Your vision.*

But the camerlengo heard no reply.

Father, We have come too far together to fail now.

Silence.

They do not understand what We have done.

The camerlengo did not know whose voice he heard in his own mind, but the message was stark.

And the truth shall set you free . . .

And so it was that Camerlengo Carlo Ventresca held his head high as he walked toward the front of the Sistine Chapel. As he moved toward the cardinals, not even the diffused light of the candles could soften the eyes boring into him. *Explain yourself*, the faces said. *Make sense of this madness. Tell us our fears are wrong!*

Truth, the camerlengo told himself. *Only truth*. There were too many secrets in these walls . . . one so dark it had driven him to madness. *But from the madness had come the light.*

'If you could give your own soul to save millions,' the camerlengo said, as he moved down the aisle, '*would* you?'

The faces in the chapel simply stared. No one moved. No one spoke. Beyond the walls, the joyous strains of song could be heard in the square.

The camerlengo walked toward them. 'Which is the greater sin? Killing one's enemy? Or standing idle while your true love is strangled?' *They are singing in St Peter's Square!* The camerlengo stopped for a moment and gazed up at the ceiling of the Sistine. Michelangelo's God was staring down from the darkened vault . . . and He seemed pleased.

'I could no longer stand by,' the camerlengo said. Still, as he drew nearer, he saw no flicker of understanding in anyone's eyes. Didn't they see the radiant simplicity of his deeds? Didn't they see the utter necessity!

It had been so pure.

The Illuminati. Science and Satan as one.

Resurrect the ancient fear. Then crush it.

Horror and Hope. Make them believe again.

Tonight, the power of the Illuminati had been unleashed anew . . . and with glorious consequence. The apathy had evaporated. The fear had shot out across the world like a bolt of lightning, uniting the people. And then God's majesty had vanquished the darkness.

I could not stand idly by!

The inspiration had been God's own – appearing like a beacon in the camerlengo's night of agony. *Oh, this faithless world! Someone must deliver them. You. If not you, who? You have been saved for a reason. Show them the old demons. Remind them of their fear. Apathy is death. Without darkness, there is no light. Without evil, there is no good. Make them choose. Dark or light. Where is the fear? Where are the heroes? If not now, when?*

The camerlengo walked up the center aisle directly toward the crowd of standing cardinals. He felt like Moses as the sea of red sashes and caps parted before him, allowing him to pass. On the altar, Robert Langdon switched off the television, took Vittoria's hand, and relinquished the altar. The fact that Robert Langdon had survived, the camerlengo knew, could only have been God's will. God had saved Robert Langdon. The camerlengo wondered why.

The voice that broke the silence was the voice of the only woman in the Sistine Chapel. 'You *killed* my father?' she said, stepping forward.

When the camerlengo turned to Vittoria Vetra, the look on her face was one he could not quite understand – pain yes, but *anger*? Certainly she must understand. Her father's genius was deadly. He had to be stopped. For the good of Mankind.

'He was doing God's work,' Vittoria said.

'God's work is not done in a lab. It is done in the heart.'

'My father's heart was pure! And his research proved—'

'His research proved yet again that man's mind is progressing faster than his soul!' The camerlengo's voice was sharper than he had expected. He lowered his voice. 'If a man as spiritual as your father could create a weapon like the one we saw tonight, imagine what an ordinary man will do with his technology.'

'A man like *you*?'

The camerlengo took a deep breath. Did she not see? Man's morality was not advancing as fast as man's science. Mankind was not spiritually evolved enough for the powers he possessed. *We have never created a weapon we have not used!* And yet he knew that antimatter was nothing – another weapon in man's already burgeoning arsenal. Man could already destroy. Man learned to kill long ago. *And his mother's blood rained down.* Leonardo Vetra's genius was dangerous for another reason.

'For centuries,' the camerlengo said, 'the church has stood by while science picked away at religion bit by bit. Debunking miracles. Training the mind to overcome the heart. Condemning religion as the opiate of the masses. They denounce God as a hallucination – a delusional crutch for those too weak to accept that life is meaningless. I could not stand by while science presumed to harness the power of God himself! *Proof,* you say? Yes, proof of science's ignorance! What is wrong with the admission that something exists beyond our understanding? The day science substantiates God in a lab is the day people stop needing faith!'

'You mean the day they stop needing the *church,*' Vittoria challenged, moving toward him. 'Doubt is your last shred of control. It is *doubt* that brings souls to you. Our need to know that life has meaning. Man's insecurity and need for an enlightened soul assuring him everything is part of a master plan. But the church is not the only enlightened soul on the planet! We all seek God in different ways. What are you afraid of? That God will show himself somewhere *other* than inside these walls? That people will find him in their own lives and leave your antiquated rituals behind? Religions evolve! The mind finds answers, the heart grapples with new truths. My father was on *your* quest! A parallel path! Why couldn't you see that? God is not some omnipotent authority looking down from above, threatening to throw us into a pit of fire if we disobey. God is the energy that flows through the synapses of our nervous system and the chambers of our hearts! God is in all things!'

'*Except* science,' the camerlengo fired back, his eyes showing only pity. 'Science, by definition, is soulless. Divorced from the heart. Intellectual miracles like antimatter arrive in this world with no ethical instructions attached. This in itself is perilous! But when science heralds its Godless pursuits as the enlightened path? Promising answers to questions whose beauty is that they have no answers?' He shook his head. 'No.'

There was a moment of silence. The camerlengo felt suddenly tired as he returned Vittoria's unbending stare. This was not how it was supposed to be. *Is this God's final test?*

It was Mortati who broke the spell. 'The *preferiti*,' he said in a horrified whisper. 'Baggia and the others. Please tell me you did not . . .'

The camerlengo turned to him, surprised by the pain in his voice. Certainly *Mortati* could understand. Headlines carried science's miracles every day. How long had it been for religion? Centuries? Religion needed a miracle! Something to awaken a sleeping world. Bring them back to the path of righteousness. Restore faith. The *preferiti* were not leaders anyway, they were transformers – liberals prepared to embrace the new world and abandon the old ways! This was the only way. A new leader. Young. Powerful. Vibrant. Miraculous. The *preferiti* served the church far more effectively in death than they ever could alive. Horror and Hope. *Offer four souls to save millions.* The world would remember them forever as martyrs. The church would raise glorious tribute to their names. *How many thousands have died for the glory of God? They are only four.*

'The *preferiti*,' Mortati repeated.

'I shared their pain,' the camerlengo defended, motioning to his chest. 'And I too would die for God, but my work is only just begun. They are singing in St Peter's Square!'

The camerlengo saw the horror in Mortati's eyes and again felt confused. Was it the morphine? Mortati was looking at him as if the camerlengo himself had killed these men with his bare hands. *I would do even that for God*, the camerlengo thought, and yet he had not. The deeds had been carried out by the Hassassin – a heathen soul tricked into thinking he was doing the work of the Illuminati. *I am Janus*, the camerlengo had told him. *I will prove my power*. And he had. The Hassassin's hatred had made him God's pawn.

'Listen to the singing,' the camerlengo said, smiling, his own heart rejoicing. 'Nothing unites hearts like the presence of evil. Burn a church and the community rises up, holding hands, singing hymns of defiance as they rebuild. Look how they flock tonight. Fear has brought them home. Forge modern demons for modern man. Apathy is dead. Show them the face of evil – Satanists lurking among us – running our governments, our banks, our schools, threatening to obliterate the very House of God with their misguided science. Depravity runs deep. Man must be vigilant. Seek the goodness. *Become* the goodness!'

In the silence, the camerlengo hoped they now understood. The Illuminati had not resurfaced. The Illuminati were long deceased. Only their myth was alive. The camerlengo had resurrected the Illuminati as a reminder. Those who knew the Illuminati history relived their evil. Those who did not, had learned of it and were amazed how blind they had been. The ancient demons had been resurrected to awaken an indifferent world.

'But . . . the brands?' Mortati's voice was stiff with outrage.

The camerlengo did not answer. Mortati had no way of knowing, but the brands had been confiscated by the Vatican over a century ago. They had been locked away, forgotten and dust covered, in the Papal Vault – the Pope's private reliquary, deep within his Borgia apartments. The Papal Vault contained those items the church deemed too dangerous for anyone's eyes except the Pope's.

Why did they hide that which inspired fear? Fear brought people to God!

The vault's key was passed down from Pope to Pope. Camerlengo Carlo Ventresca had purloined the key and ventured inside; the myth of what the vault contained was bewitching – including the original manuscript for the fourteen unpublished books of the Bible known as the *Apocrypha* and the location of the tomb of the Virgin Mary. In addition to these, the camerlengo had found the Illuminati Collection – all the secrets the church had uncovered after banishing the group from Rome ... their contemptible Path of Illumination ... the cunning deceit of the Vatican's head artist, Bernini ... Europe's top scientists mocking religion as they secretly assembled in the Vatican's own Castle St Angelo. The collection included a pentagon box containing iron brands, one of them the mythical Illuminati Diamond. This was a part of Vatican history the ancients thought best forgotten. The camerlengo, however, had disagreed.

'But the *antimatter* ...' Vittoria demanded. 'You risked destroying the Vatican!'

'There is no risk when God is at your side,' the camerlengo said. 'This cause was His.'

'You're insane!' she seethed.

'Millions were saved.'

'People were *killed*!'

'Souls were saved.'

'Tell that to my father and Max Kohler!'

'CERN's arrogance needed to be revealed. A droplet of liquid that can vaporize a half mile? And you call me mad?' The camerlengo felt a rage rising in him. Did they think his was a simple charge? 'Those who *believe* undergo great tests for God! God asked Abraham to sacrifice his child! God commanded Jesus to endure crucifixion! And so we hang the symbol of the crucifix before our eyes – bloody painful, agonizing – to remind us of evil's power! To keep our hearts vigilant! The scars on Jesus' body are a living reminder of the powers of darkness! My scars are a living reminder! Evil lives, but the power of God will overcome!'

His shouts echoed off the back wall of the Sistine Chapel and then a profound silence fell. Time seemed to stop. Michelangelo's *Last Judgment* rose ominously behind him . . . Jesus casting sinners into hell. Tears brimmed in Mortati's eyes.

'What have you done, Carlo?' Mortati asked in a whisper. He closed his eyes, and a tear rolled. 'His *Holiness?*'

A collective sigh of pain went up, as if everyone in the room had forgotten until that very moment. The Pope. Poisoned.

'A vile liar,' the camerlengo said.

Mortati looked shattered. 'What do you mean? He was honest! He . . . loved you.'

'And I him.' *Oh, how I loved him! But the deceit! The broken vows to God!*

The camerlengo knew they did not understand right now, but they *would*. When he told them, they would see! His Holiness was the most nefarious deceiver the church had ever seen. The camerlengo still remembered that terrible night. He had returned from his trip to CERN with news of Vetra's *Genesis* and

589

of antimatter's horrific power. The camerlengo was certain the Pope would see the perils, but the Holy Father saw only hope in Vetra's breakthrough. He even suggested the Vatican *fund* Vetra's work as a gesture of goodwill toward spiritually based scientific research.

Madness! The church investing in research that threatened to make the church obsolete? Work that spawned weapons of mass destruction? The bomb that had killed his mother . . .

'But . . . you can't!' the camerlengo had exclaimed.

'I owe a deep debt to science,' the Pope had replied. 'Something I have hidden my entire life. Science gave me a gift when I was a young man. A gift I have never forgotten.'

'I don't understand. What does science have to offer a man of *God*?'

'It is complicated,' the Pope had said. 'I will need time to make you understand. But first, there is a simple fact about me that you must know. I have kept it hidden all these years. I believe it is time I told you.'

Then the Pope had told him the astonishing truth.

132

The camerlengo lay curled in a ball on the dirt floor in front of St Peter's tomb. The Necropolis was cold, but it helped clot the blood flowing from the wounds he had torn at his own flesh. His Holiness would not find him here. Nobody would find him here . . .

'It is complicated,' the Pope's voice echoed in his

mind. 'I will need time to make you understand . . .'

But the camerlengo knew no amount of time could make him understand.

Liar! I believed in you! GOD believed in you!

With a single sentence, the Pope had brought the camerlengo's world crashing down around him. Everything the camerlengo had ever believed about his mentor was shattered before his eyes. The truth drilled into the camerlengo's heart with such force that he staggered backward out of the Pope's office and vomited in the hallway.

'Wait!' the Pope had cried, chasing after him. 'Please let me explain!'

But the camerlengo ran off. How could His Holiness expect him to endure any more? Oh, the wretched depravity of it! What if someone else found out? Imagine the desecration to the church! Did the Pope's holy vows mean nothing?

The madness came quickly, screaming in his ears, until he awoke before St Peter's tomb. It was then that God came to him with an awesome fierceness.

YOURS IS A VENGEFUL GOD!

Together, they made their plans. Together they would protect the church. Together they would restore faith to this faithless world. Evil was everywhere. And yet the world had become immune! Together they would unveil the darkness for the world to see . . . and God would overcome! Horror and Hope. Then the world would believe!

God's first test had been less horrible than the camerlengo imagined. Sneaking into the Papal bed chambers . . . filling his syringe . . . covering the deceiver's mouth as his body spasmed into death. In the moonlight, the camerlengo could see in the

Pope's wild eyes there was something he wanted to say.

But it was too late.

The Pope had said enough.

133

'The Pope fathered a child.'

Inside the Sistine Chapel, the camerlengo stood unwavering as he spoke. Five solitary words of astonishing disclosure. The entire assembly seemed to recoil in unison. The cardinals' accusing miens evaporated into aghast stares, as if every soul in the room were praying the camerlengo was wrong.

The Pope fathered a child.

Langdon felt the shock wave hit him too. Vittoria's hand, tight in his, jolted, while Langdon's mind, already numb with unanswered questions, wrestled to find a center of gravity.

The camerlengo's utterance seemed like it would hang forever in the air above them. Even in the camerlengo's frenzied eyes, Langdon could see pure conviction. Langdon wanted to disengage, tell himself he was lost in some grotesque nightmare, soon to wake up in a world that made sense.

'This must be a lie!' one of the cardinals yelled.

'I will not believe it!' another protested. 'His Holiness was as devout a man as ever lived!'

It was Mortati who spoke next, his voice thin with devastation. 'My friends. What the camerlengo says is true.' Every cardinal in the chapel spun as though

Mortati had just shouted an obscenity. 'The Pope indeed fathered a child.'

The cardinals blanched with dread.

The camerlengo looked stunned. 'You *knew*? But . . . how could you possibly know this?'

Mortati sighed. 'When His Holiness was elected . . . *I* was the Devil's Advocate.'

There was a communal gasp.

Langdon understood. This meant the information was probably true. The infamous 'Devil's Advocate' was *the* authority when it came to scandalous information inside the Vatican. Skeletons in a Pope's closet were dangerous, and prior to elections, secret inquiries into a candidate's background were carried out by a lone cardinal who served as the 'Devil's Advocate' – that individual responsible for unearthing reasons why the eligible cardinals should *not* become Pope. The Devil's Advocate was appointed in advance by the reigning Pope in preparation for his own death. The Devil's Advocate was never supposed to reveal his identity. *Ever*.

'*I* was the Devil's Advocate,' Mortati repeated. 'That is how I found out.'

Mouths dropped. Apparently tonight was a night when all the rules were going out the window.

The camerlengo felt his heart filling with rage. 'And you . . . told *no one*?'

'I confronted His Holiness,' Mortati said. 'And he confessed. He explained the entire story and asked only that I let my heart guide my decision as to whether or not to reveal his secret.'

'And your heart told you to *bury* the information?'

'He was the runaway favorite for the papacy. People

loved him. The scandal would have hurt the church deeply.'

'But he fathered a *child*! He broke his sacred vow of celibacy!' The camerlengo was screaming now. He could hear his mother's voice. *A promise to God is the most important promise of all. Never break a promise to God.* 'The Pope broke his vow!'

Mortati looked delirious with angst. 'Carlo, his love . . . was *chaste*. He had broken no vow. He didn't explain it to you?'

'Explain what?' The camerlengo remembered running out of the Pope's office while the Pope was calling to him. *Let me explain!*

Slowly, sadly, Mortati let the tale unfold. Many years ago, the Pope, when he was still just a priest, had fallen in love with a young nun. Both of them had taken vows of celibacy and never even considered breaking their covenant with God. Still, as they fell deeper in love, although they could resist the temptations of the flesh, they both found themselves longing for something they never expected – to participate in God's ultimate miracle of creation – a child. *Their* child. The yearning, especially in her, became overwhelming. Still, God came first. A year later, when the frustration had reached almost unbearable proportions, she came to him in a whirl of excitement. She had just read an article about a new miracle of science – a process by which two people, without ever having sexual relations, could have a child. She sensed this was a sign from God. The priest could see the happiness in her eyes and agreed. A year later she had a child through the miracle of artificial insemination . . .

'This cannot . . . be true,' the camerlengo said, panicked, hoping it was the morphine washing over his senses. Certainly he was hearing things.

Mortati now had tears in his eyes. 'Carlo, this is why His Holiness has always had an affection for the sciences. He felt he owed a debt to science. Science let him experience the joys of fatherhood without breaking his vow of celibacy. His Holiness told me he had no regrets except one – that his advancing stature in the church prohibited him from being with the woman he loved and seeing his infant grow up.'

Camerlengo Carlo Ventresca felt the madness setting in again. He wanted to claw at his flesh. *How could I have known?*

'The Pope committed no sin, Carlo. He was chaste.'

'But . . .' The camerlengo searched his anguished mind for any kind of rationale. 'Think of the jeopardy . . . of his deeds.' His voice felt weak. 'What if this whore of his came forward? Or, heaven forbid, his *child*? Imagine the shame the church would endure.'

Mortati's voice was tremulous. 'The child has *already* come forward.'

Everything stopped.

'Carlo . . . ?' Mortati crumbled. 'His Holiness's child . . . is *you*.'

At that moment, the camerlengo could feel the fire of faith dim in his heart. He stood trembling on the altar, framed by Michelangelo's towering *Last Judgment*. He knew he had just glimpsed hell itself. He opened his mouth to speak, but his lips wavered, soundless.

'Don't you see?' Mortati choked. '*That* is why His Holiness came to you in the hospital in Palermo when you were a boy. *That* is why he took you in and raised you. The nun he loved was Maria . . . your mother. She left the nunnery to raise you, but she never abandoned

595

her strict devotion to God. When the Pope heard she had died in an explosion and that you, his son, had miraculously survived . . . he swore to God he would never leave you alone again. Carlo, your parents were both virgins. They kept their vows to God. And still they found a way to bring you into the world. You were their miraculous child.'

The camerlengo covered his ears, trying to block out the words. He stood paralyzed on the altar. Then, with his world yanked from beneath him, he fell violently to his knees and let out a wail of anguish.

Seconds. Minutes. Hours.

Time seemed to have lost all meaning inside the four walls of the chapel. Vittoria felt herself slowly breaking free of the paralysis that seemed to have gripped them all. She let go of Langdon's hand and began moving through the crowd of cardinals. The chapel door seemed miles away and she felt like she was moving underwater . . . slow motion.

As she maneuvered through the robes, her motion seemed to pull others from their trance. Some of the cardinals began to pray. Others wept. Some turned to watch her go, their blank expressions turning slowly to a foreboding cognition as she moved toward the door. She had almost reached the back of the crowd when a hand caught her arm. The touch was frail but resolute. She turned, face to face with a wizened cardinal. His visage was clouded by fear.

'No,' the man whispered. 'You cannot.'

Vittoria stared, incredulous.

Another cardinal was at her side now. 'We must think before we act.'

And another. 'The pain this could cause . . .'

Vittoria was surrounded. She looked at them all, stunned. 'But these deeds here today, tonight . . . certainly the world should know the truth.'

'My heart agrees,' the wizened cardinal said, still holding her arm, 'and yet it is a path from which there is no return. We must consider the shattered hopes. The cynicism. How could the people *ever* trust again?'

Suddenly, more cardinals seemed to be blocking her way. There was a wall of black robes before her. 'Listen to the people in the square,' one said. 'What will this do to their hearts? We must exercise prudence.'

'We need time to think and pray,' another said. 'We must act with foresight. The repercussions of this . . .'

'He killed my father!' Vittoria said. 'He killed his *own* father!'

'I'm certain he will pay for his sins,' the cardinal holding her arm said sadly.

Vittoria was certain too, and she intended to *ensure* he paid. She tried to push toward the door again, but the cardinals huddled closer, their faces frightened.

'What are you going to do?' she exclaimed. '*Kill* me?'

The old men blanched, and Vittoria immediately regretted her words. She could see these men were gentle souls. They had seen enough violence tonight. They meant no threat. They were simply trapped. Scared. Trying to get their bearings.

'I want . . .' the wizened cardinal said, '. . . to do what is right.'

'Then you will let her out,' a deep voice declared behind her. The words were calm but absolute. Robert Langdon arrived at her side, and she felt his hand take hers. 'Ms Vetra and I are leaving this chapel. Right now.'

Faltering, hesitant, the cardinals began to step aside.

'Wait!' It was Mortati. He moved toward them now, down the center aisle, leaving the camerlengo alone and defeated on the altar. Mortati looked older all of a sudden, wearied beyond his years. His motion was burdened with shame. He arrived, putting a hand on Langdon's shoulder and one on Vittoria's as well. Vittoria felt sincerity in his touch. The man's eyes were more tearful now.

'*Of course* you are free to go,' Mortati said. 'Of course.' The man paused, his grief almost tangible. 'I ask only this . . .' He stared down at his feet a long moment then back up at Vittoria and Langdon. 'Let *me* do it. I will go into the square right now and find a way. I will tell them. I don't know how . . . but I will find a way. The church's confession should come from within. Our failures should be our own to expose.'

Mortati turned sadly back toward the altar. 'Carlo, you have brought this church to a disastrous juncture.' He paused, looking around. The altar was bare.

There was a rustle of cloth down the side aisle, and the door clicked shut.

The camerlengo was gone.

134

Camerlengo Ventresca's white robe billowed as he moved down the hallway away from the Sistine Chapel. The Swiss Guards had seemed perplexed when he emerged all alone from the chapel and told them he needed a moment of solitude. But they had obeyed, letting him go.

Now as he rounded the corner and left their sight, the camerlengo felt a maelstrom of emotions like nothing he thought possible in human experience. He had poisoned the man he called 'Holy Father,' the man who addressed him as 'my son.' The camerlengo had always believed the words 'father' and 'son' were religious tradition, but now he knew the diabolical truth – the words had been *literal*.

Like that fateful night weeks ago, the camerlengo now felt himself reeling madly through the darkness.

It was raining the morning the Vatican staff banged on the camerlengo's door, awakening him from a fitful sleep. The Pope, they said, was not answering his door or his phone. The clergy were frightened. The camerlengo was the only one who could enter the Pope's chambers unannounced.

The camerlengo entered alone to find the Pope, as he was the night before, twisted and dead in his bed. His Holiness's face looked like that of Satan. His tongue black like death. The Devil himself had been sleeping in the Pope's bed.

The camerlengo felt no remorse. God had spoken.

Nobody would see the treachery . . . not yet. That would come later.

He announced the terrible news – His Holiness was dead of a stroke. Then the camerlengo prepared for conclave.

Mother Maria's voice was whispering in his ear. 'Never break a promise to God.'

'I hear you, Mother,' he replied. 'It is a faithless

world. They need to be brought back to the path of righteousness. Horror and Hope. It is the only way.'

'Yes,' she said. 'If not you . . . then who? Who will lead the church out of darkness?'

Certainly not one of the *preferiti*. They were old . . . walking death . . . liberals who would follow the Pope, endorsing science in his memory, seeking modern followers by abandoning the ancient ways. Old men desperately behind the times, pathetically pretending they were not. They would fail, of course. The church's strength was its tradition, not its transience. The whole world was transitory. The church did not need to change, it simply needed to remind the world it was relevant! Evil lives! God will overcome!

The church needed a leader. Old men do not inspire! Jesus inspired! Young, vibrant, powerful . . . *MIRACULOUS*.

'Enjoy your tea,' the camerlengo told the four *preferiti*, leaving them in the Pope's private library before conclave. 'Your guide will be here soon.'

The *preferiti* thanked him, all abuzz that they had been offered a chance to enter the famed Passetto. Most uncommon! The camerlengo, before leaving them, had unlocked the door to the Passetto, and exactly on schedule, the door had opened, and a foreign-looking priest with a torch had ushered the excited *preferiti* in.

The men had never come out.

They will be the Horror. I will be the Hope.

No . . . I am the horror.

The camerlengo staggered now through the darkness

600

of St Peter's Basilica. Somehow, through the insanity and guilt, through the images of his father, through the pain and revelation, even through the pull of the morphine . . . he had found a brilliant clarity. A sense of destiny. *I know my purpose,* he thought, awed by the lucidity of it.

From the beginning, nothing tonight had gone exactly as he had planned. Unforeseen obstacles had presented themselves, but the camerlengo had adapted, making bold adjustments. Still, he had never imagined tonight would end this way, and yet now he saw the preordained majesty of it.

It could end no other way.

Oh, what terror he had felt in the Sistine Chapel, wondering if God had forsaken him! *Oh, what deeds He had ordained!* He had fallen to his knees, awash with doubt, his ears straining for the voice of God but hearing only silence. He had begged for a sign. Guidance. Direction. Was this God's will? The church destroyed by scandal and abomination? No! *God* was the one who had willed the camerlengo to act! *Hadn't He?*

Then he had seen it. Sitting on the altar. A sign. Divine communication – something ordinary seen in an extraordinary light. The crucifix. Humble, wooden. Jesus on the cross. In that moment, it had all come clear . . the camerlengo was not alone. He would never be alone.

This was His will . . . His meaning.

God had always asked great sacrifice of those he loved most. Why had the camerlengo been so slow to understand? Was he too fearful? Too humble? It made no difference. God had found a way. The camerlengo even understood now why Robert Langdon had been saved. It was to bring the truth. To compel this ending.

This was the sole path to the church's salvation!

The camerlengo felt like he was floating as he descended into the Niche of the Palliums. The surge of morphine seemed relentless now, but he knew God was guiding him.

In the distance, he could hear the cardinals clamoring in confusion as they poured from the chapel, yelling commands to the Swiss Guard.

But they would never find him. Not in time.

The camerlengo felt himself drawn ... faster ... descending the stairs into the sunken area where the ninety-nine oil lamps shone brightly. God was returning him to Holy Ground. The camerlengo moved toward the grate covering the hole that led down to the Necropolis. The Necropolis is where this night would end. In the sacred darkness below. He lifted an oil lamp, preparing to descend.

But as he moved across the Niche, the camerlengo paused. Something about this felt wrong. How did this serve God? A solitary and silent end? *Jesus* had suffered before the eyes of the entire world. Surely this could not be God's will! The camerlengo listened for the voice of his God, but heard only the blurring buzz of drugs.

'*Carlo.*' It was his mother. '*God has plans for you.*'

Bewildered, the camerlengo kept moving.

Then, without warning, God arrived.

The camerlengo stopped short, staring. The light of the ninety-nine oil lanterns had thrown the camerlengo's shadow on the marble wall beside him. Giant and fearful. A hazy form surrounded by golden light. With flames flickering all around him, the camerlengo looked like an angel ascending to heaven. He stood a moment, raising his arms to his sides, watching his own image. Then he turned, looking back up the stairs.

God's meaning was clear.

Three minutes had passed in the chaotic hallways outside the Sistine Chapel, and still nobody could locate the camerlengo. It was as if the man had been swallowed up by the night. Mortati was about to demand a full-scale search of Vatican City when a roar of jubilation erupted outside in St Peter's Square. The spontaneous celebration of the crowd was tumultuous. The cardinals all exchanged startled looks.

Mortati closed his eyes. 'God help us.'

For the second time that evening, the College of Cardinals flooded onto St Peter's Square. Langdon and Vittoria were swept up in the jostling crowd of cardinals, and they too emerged into the night air. The media lights and cameras were all pivoted toward the basilica. And there, having just stepped onto the sacred Papal Balcony located in the exact center of the towering façade, Camerlengo Carlo Ventresca stood with his arms raised to the heavens. Even far away, he looked like purity incarnate. A figurine. Dressed in white. Flooded with light.

The energy in the square seemed to grow like a cresting wave, and all at once the Swiss Guard barriers gave way. The masses streamed toward the basilica in a euphoric torrent of humanity. The onslaught rushed forward – people crying, singing, media cameras flashing. Pandemonium. As the people flooded in around the front of the basilica, the chaos intensified, until it seemed nothing could stop it.

And then something did.

High above, the camerlengo made the smallest of gestures. He folded his hands before him. Then he bowed his head in silent prayer. One by one, then dozens by dozens, then hundreds by hundreds, the people bowed their heads along with him.

The square fell silent . . . as if a spell had been cast.

In his mind, swirling and distant now, the camerlengo's prayers were a torrent of hopes and sorrows . . . *forgive me, Father . . . Mother . . . full of grace . . . you are the church . . . may you understand this sacrifice of your only begotten son.*

Oh, my Jesus . . . save us from the fires of hell . . . take all souls to heaven, especially those most in need of thy mercy . . .

The camerlengo did not open his eyes to see the throngs below him, the television cameras, the whole world watching. He could feel it in his soul. Even in his anguish, the unity of the moment was intoxicating. It was as if a connective web had shot out in all directions around the globe. In front of televisions, at home, and in cars, the world prayed as one. Like synapses of a giant heart all firing in tandem, the people reached for God, in dozens of languages, in hundreds of countries. The words they whispered were newborn and yet as familiar to them as their own voices . . . ancient truths . . . imprinted on the soul.

The consonance felt eternal.

As the silence lifted, the joyous strains of singing began to rise again.

He knew the moment had come.

Most Holy Trinity, I offer Thee the most precious Body, Blood, Soul . . . in reparation for the outrages, sacrileges, and indifferences . . .

The camerlengo already felt the physical pain setting in. It was spreading across his skin like a plague, making him want to claw at his flesh like he had weeks ago when God had first come to him. *Do not forget what pain Jesus endured.* He could taste the fumes now in his throat. Not even the morphine could dull the bite.

My work here is done.

The Horror was his. The Hope was theirs.

In the Niche of the Palliums, the camerlengo had followed God's will and anointed his body. His hair. His face. His linen robe. His flesh. He was soaking now with the sacred, vitreous oils from the lamps. They smelled sweet like his mother, but they burned. *His* would be a merciful ascension. Miraculous and swift. And he would leave behind not scandal . . . but a new strength and wonder.

He slipped his hand into the pocket of his robe and fingered the small, golden lighter he had brought with him from the Pallium *incendiario.*

He whispered a verse from Judgments. *And when the flame went up toward heaven, the angel of the Lord ascended in the flame.*

He positioned his thumb.

They were singing in St Peter's Square . . .

The vision the world witnessed no one would ever forget.

High above on the balcony, like a soul tearing free of its corporeal restrains, a luminous pyre of flame erupted from the camerlengo's center. The fire shot upward, engulfing his entire body instantly. He did not scream. He raised his arms over his head and looked toward heaven. The conflagration roared around him, entirely shrouding his body in a column of light. It raged for what seemed like an eternity, the whole world bearing witness. The light flared brighter and brighter. Then, gradually, the flames dissipated. The camerlengo was gone. Whether he had collapsed behind the balustrade or evaporated into thin air was impossible to tell. All that was left was a cloud of smoke spiraling skyward over Vatican City.

135

Dawn came late to Rome.

An early rainstorm had washed the crowds from St Peter's Square. The media stayed on, huddling under umbrellas and in vans, commentating on the evening's events. Across the world, churches overflowed. It was a time of reflection and discussion . . . in all religions. Questions abounded, and yet the answers seemed only to bring deeper questions. Thus far, the Vatican had remained silent, issuing no statement whatsoever.

Deep in the Vatican Grottoes, Cardinal Mortati knelt alone before the open sarcophagus. He reached in and closed the old man's blackened mouth. His Holiness looked peaceful now. In quiet repose for eternity.

At Mortati's feet was a golden urn, heavy with ashes. Mortati had gathered the ashes himself and brought them here. 'A chance for forgiveness,' he said to His Holiness; laying the urn inside the sarcophagus at the Pope's side. 'No love is greater than that of a father for His son.' Mortati tucked the urn out of sight beneath the papal robes. He knew this sacred grotto was reserved exclusively for the relics of Popes, but somehow Mortati sensed this was appropriate.

'Signore?' someone said, entering the grottoes. It was Lieutenant Chartrand. He was accompanied by three Swiss Guards. 'They are ready for you in conclave.'

Mortati nodded. 'In a moment.' He gazed one last time into the sarcophagus before him, and then stood up. He turned to the guards. 'It is time for His Holiness to have the peace he has earned.'

The guards came forward and with enormous effort slid the lid of the Pope's sarcophagus back into place. It thundered shut with finality.

Mortati was alone as he crossed the Borgia Courtyard toward the Sistine Chapel. A damp breeze tossed his robe. A fellow cardinal emerged from the Apostolic Palace and strode beside him.

'May I have the honor of escorting you to conclave, signore?'

'The honor is mine.'

'Signore,' the cardinal said, looking troubled. 'The college owes you an apology for last night. We were blinded by—'

'Please,' Mortati replied. 'Our minds sometimes see what our hearts wish were true.'

The cardinal was silent a long time. Finally he spoke. 'Have you been told? You are no longer our Great Elector.'

Mortati smiled. 'Yes. I thank God for small blessings.'

'The college insisted you be eligible.'

'It seems charity is not dead in the church.'

'You are a wise man. You would lead us well.'

'I am an old man. I would lead you briefly.'

They both laughed.

As they reached the end of the Borgia Courtyard, the cardinal hesitated. He turned to Mortati with a troubled mystification, as if the precarious awe of the night before had slipped back into his heart.

'Were you aware,' the cardinal whispered, 'that we found no remains on the balcony?'

Mortati smiled. 'Perhaps the rain washed them away.'

The man looked to the stormy heavens. 'Yes, perhaps . . .'

136

The midmorning sky still hung heavy with clouds as the Sistine Chapel's chimney gave up its first faint puffs of white smoke. The pearly wisps curled upward toward the firmament and slowly dissipated.

Far below, in St Peter's Square, reporter Gunther Glick watched in reflective silence. The final chapter . . .

Chinita Macri approached him from behind and hoisted her camera onto her shoulder. 'It's time,' she said.

Glick nodded dolefully. He turned toward her, smoothed his hair, and took a deep breath. *My last transmission*, he thought. A small crowd had gathered around them to watch.

'Live in sixty seconds,' Macri announced.

Glick glanced over his shoulder at the roof of the Sistine Chapel behind him. 'Can you get the smoke?'

Macri patiently nodded. 'I know how to frame a shot, Gunther.'

Glick felt dumb. Of course she did. Macri's performance behind the camera last night had probably won her the Pulitzer. *His* performance, on the other hand . . . he didn't want to think about it. He was sure the BBC would let him go; no doubt they would have legal troubles from numerous powerful entities . . . CERN and George Bush among them.

'You look good,' Chinita patronized, looking out from behind her camera now with a hint of concern. 'I wonder if I might offer you . . .' She hesitated, holding her tongue.

'Some *advice*?'

Macri sighed. 'I was only going to say that there's no need to go out with a bang.'

'I know,' he said. 'You want a straight wrap.'

'The straightest in history. I'm trusting you.'

Glick smiled. *A straight wrap? Is she crazy?* A story like last night's deserved so much more. A twist. A final bombshell. An unforeseen revelation of shocking truth.

Fortunately, Glick had just the ticket waiting in the wings . . .

'You're on in . . . five . . . four . . . three . . .'

As Chinita Macri looked through her camera, she sensed a sly glint in Glick's eye. *I was insane to let him do this*, she thought. *What was I thinking?*

But the moment for second thoughts had passed. They were on.

'Live from Vatican City' Glick announced on cue, 'this is Gunther Glick reporting.' He gave the camera a solemn stare as the white smoke rose behind him from the Sistine Chapel. 'Ladies and gentlemen, it is now *official*. Cardinal Saverio Mortati, a seventy-nine-year-old progressive, has just been elected the next Pope of Vatican City. Although an unlikely candidate, Mortati was chosen by an unprecedented *unanimous* vote by the College of Cardinals.'

As Macri watched him, she began to breathe easier. Glick seemed surprisingly professional today. Even austere. For the first time in his life, Glick actually looked and sounded somewhat like a newsman.

'And as we reported earlier,' Glick added, his voice intensifying perfectly, 'the Vatican has yet to offer *any* statement whatsoever regarding the miraculous events of last night.'

Good. Chinita's nervousness waned some more. *So far, so good.*

Glick's expression grew sorrowful now. 'And though last night was a night of wonder, it was also a night of tragedy. Four cardinals perished in yesterday's conflict, along with Commander Olivetti and Captain Rocher of the Swiss Guard, both in the line of duty. Other casualties include Leonardo Vetra, the renowned CERN physicist and pioneer of antimatter technology, as well as Maximilian Kohler, the director of CERN, who apparently came to Vatican City in an effort to help but reportedly passed away in the process. No official report has been issued yet on Mr Kohler's death, but conjecture is that he died due to complications brought on by a long-time illness.'

Macri nodded. The report was going perfectly. Just as they discussed.

'And in the wake of the explosion in the sky over the Vatican last night, CERN's antimatter technology has become *the* hot topic among scientists, sparking excitement and controversy. A statement read by Mr Kohler's assistant in Geneva, Sylvie Baudeloque, announced this morning that CERN's board of directors, although enthusiastic about antimatter's potential, are suspending all research and licensing until further inquiries into its safety can be examined.'

Excellent, Macri thought. *Home stretch.*

'Notably absent from our screens tonight,' Glick reported, 'is the face of Robert Langdon, the Harvard professor who came to Vatican City yesterday to lend his expertise during this Illuminati crisis. Although originally thought to have perished in the antimatter blast, we now have reports that Langdon was spotted in St Peter's Square *after* the explosion. How he got there is still speculation, although a spokesman from Hospital Tiberina claims that Mr Langdon fell out of the sky into the Tiber River shortly after midnight, was treated, and released.' Glick arched his eyebrows at the camera. 'And if *that* is true . . . it was indeed a night of miracles.'

Perfect ending! Macri felt herself smiling broadly. *Flawless wrap! Now sign off!*

But Glick did not sign off. Instead, he paused a moment and then stepped toward the camera. He had a mysterious smile. 'But before we sign off . . .'

No!

'. . . I would like to invite a guest to join me.'

Chinita's hands froze on the camera. *A guest? What the hell is he doing? What guest! Sign off!* But she knew it was too late. Glick had committed.

611

'The man I am about to introduce,' Glick said, 'is an American . . . a renowned scholar.'

Chinita hesitated. She held her breath as Glick turned to the small crowd around them and motioned for his guest to step forward. Macri said a silent prayer. *Please tell me he somehow located Robert Langdon . . . and not some Illuminati-conspiracy nutcase.*

But as Glick's guest stepped out, Macri's heart sank. It was not Robert Langdon at all. It was a bald man in blue jeans and a flannel shirt. He had a cane and thick glasses. Macri felt terror. *Nutcase!*

'May I introduce,' Glick announced, 'the renowned Vatican scholar from De Paul University in Chicago. Dr Joseph Vanek.'

Macri now hesitated as the man joined Glick on camera. This was no conspiracy buff; Macri had actually *heard* of this guy.

'Dr Vanek,' Glick said. 'You have some rather startling information to share with us regarding last night's conclave.'

'I do indeed,' Vanek said. 'After a night of such surprises, it is hard to imagine there are any surprises left . . . and yet . . .' He paused.

Glick smiled. 'And yet, there is a strange twist to all this.'

Vanek nodded. 'Yes. As perplexing as this will sound, I believe the College of Cardinals unknowingly elected *two* Popes this weekend.'

Macri almost dropped the camera.

Glick gave a shrewd smile. 'Two Popes, you say?'

The scholar nodded. 'Yes. I should first say that I have spent my life studying the laws of papal election. Conclave judicature is extremely complex, and much of it is now forgotten or ignored as obsolete. Even the

Great Elector is probably not aware of what I am about to reveal. Nonetheless . . . according to the ancient forgotten laws put forth in the *Romano Pontifici Eligendo, Numero 63* . . . balloting is not the *only* method by which a Pope can be elected. There is another, more *divine* method. It is called "Acclamation by Adoration."' He paused. 'And it happened last night.'

Glick gave his guest a riveted look. 'Please, go on.'

'As you may recall,' the scholar continued, 'last night, when Camerlengo Carlo Ventresca was standing on the roof of the basilica, all of the cardinals below began calling out his name in unison.'

'Yes, I recall.'

'With that image in mind, allow me to read verbatim from the ancient electoral laws.' The man pulled some papers from his pocket, cleared his throat, and began to read. ' "Election by Adoration occurs when . . . all the cardinals, as if by inspiration of the Holy Spirit, freely and spontaneously, unanimously and aloud, proclaim one individual's name." '

Glick smiled. 'So you're saying that last night, when the cardinals chanted Carlo Ventresca's name together, they actually *elected* him Pope?'

'They did indeed. Furthermore, the law states that Election by Adoration supercedes the cardinal eligibility requirement and permits *any* clergyman – ordained priest, bishop, or cardinal – to be elected. So, as you can see, the camerlengo was perfectly qualified for papal election by this procedure.' Dr Vanek looked directly into the camera now 'The facts are these . . . Carlo Ventresca was elected Pope last night. He reigned for just under seventeen minutes. And had he not ascended miraculously into a pillar of fire, he would now be buried in the Vatican Grottoes along with the other Popes.'

'Thank you, doctor.' Glick turned to Macri with a mischievous wink. 'Most illuminating . . .'

137

High atop the steps of the Roman Coliseum, Vittoria laughed and called down to him. 'Robert, hurry up! I knew I should have married a younger man!' Her smile was magic.

He struggled to keep up, but his legs felt like stone. 'Wait,' he begged. 'Please . . .'

There was a pounding in his head.

Robert Langdon awoke with a start.

Darkness.

He lay still for a long time in the foreign softness of the bed, unable to figure out where he was. The pillows were goose down, oversized and wonderful. The air smelled of potpourri. Across the room, two glass doors stood open to a lavish balcony, where a light breeze played beneath a glistening cloud-swept moon. Langdon tried to remember how he had gotten here . . . and where *here* was.

Surreal wisps of memory sifted back into his consciousness . . .

A pyre of mystical fire . . . an angel materializing from out of the crowd . . . her soft hand taking his and leading him into the night . . . guiding his exhausted, battered body through the streets . . . leading him here . . . to this suite . . . propping him half-sleeping in a scalding hot shower . . .

*leading him to this bed . . . and watching over him as he fell
asleep like the dead.*

In the dimness now, Langdon could see a second
bed. The sheets were tousled, but the bed was empty.
From one of the adjoining rooms, he could hear the
faint, steady stream of a shower.

As he gazed at Vittoria's bed, he saw a boldly
embroidered seal on her pillowcase. It read: HOTEL
BERNINI. Langdon had to smile. Vittoria had chosen
well. Old World luxury overlooking Bernini's Triton
Fountain . . . there was no more fitting hotel in all of
Rome.

As Langdon lay there, he heard a pounding and
realized what had awoken him. Someone was knocking at the door. It grew louder.

Confused, Langdon got up. *Nobody knows we're here,*
he thought, feeling a trace of uneasiness. Donning a
luxuriant Hotel Bernini robe, he walked out of the bedroom into the suite's foyer. He stood a moment at the
heavy oak door, and then pulled it open.

A powerful man adorned in lavish purple and
yellow regalia stared down at him. 'I am Lieutenant
Chartrand,' the man said. 'Vatican Swiss Guard.'

Langdon knew full well who he was. 'How . . . how
did you find us?'

'I saw you leave the square last night. I followed
you. I'm relieved you're still here.'

Langdon felt a sudden anxiety, wondering if the cardinals had sent Chartrand to escort Langdon and
Vittoria back to Vatican City. After all, the two of them
were the only two people beyond the College of
Cardinals who knew the *truth.* They were a liability.

'His Holiness asked me to give this to you,'
Chartrand said, handing over an envelope sealed with

the Vatican signet. Langdon opened the envelope and read the handwritten note.

Mr Langdon and Ms Vetra,

Although it is my profound desire to request your discretion in the matters of the past 24 hours, I cannot possibly presume to ask more of you than you have already given. I therefore humbly retreat hoping only that you let your hearts guide you in this matter. The world seems a better place today . . . maybe the questions are more powerful than the answers.

My door is always open,

His Holiness, Saverio Mortati

Langdon read the message twice. The College of Cardinals had obviously chosen a noble and munificent leader.

Before Langdon could say anything, Chartrand produced a small package. 'A token of thanks from His Holiness.'

Langdon took the package. It was heavy, wrapped in brown paper.

'By his decree,' Chartrand said, 'this artifact is on indefinite loan to you from the sacred Papal Vault. His Holiness asks only that in your last will and testament you ensure it finds its way home.'

Langdon opened the package and was struck speechless. It was the brand. *The Illuminati Diamond.*

Chartrand smiled. 'May peace be with you.' He turned to go.

'Thank . . . you,' Langdon managed, his hands trembling around the precious gift.

The guard hesitated in the hall. 'Mr Langdon, may I ask you something?'

'Of course.'

'My fellow guards and I are curious. Those last few minutes . . . what *happened* up there in the helicopter?'

Langdon felt a rush of anxiety. He knew this moment was coming – the moment of truth. He and Vittoria had talked about it last night as they stole away from St Peter's Square. And they had made their decision. Even before the Pope's note.

Vittoria's father had dreamed his antimatter discovery would bring about a spiritual awakening. Last night's events were no doubt not what he had intended, but the undeniable fact remained . . . at this moment, around the world, people were considering God in ways they never had before. How long the magic would last, Langdon and Vittoria had no idea, but they knew they could never shatter the wonderment with scandal and doubt. *The Lord works in strange ways*, Langdon told himself, wondering wryly if maybe . . . just maybe . . . yesterday had been God's will after all.

'Mr Langdon?' Chartrand repeated. 'I was asking about the helicopter?'

Langdon gave a sad smile. 'Yes, I know . . .' He felt the words flow not from his mind but from his heart. 'Perhaps it was the shock of the fall . . . but my memory . . . it seems . . . it's all a blur . . .'

Chartrand slumped. 'You remember *nothing*?'

Langdon sighed. 'I fear it will remain a mystery forever.'

When Robert Langdon returned to the bedroom, the vision awaiting him stopped him in his tracks. Vittoria stood on the balcony, her back to the railing, her eyes gazing deeply at him. She looked like a heavenly apparition . . . a radiant silhouette with the moon behind her. She could have been a Roman goddess, enshrouded in her white terrycloth robe, the drawstring cinched tight, accentuating her slender curves. Behind her, a pale mist hung like a halo over Bernini's Triton Fountain.

Langdon felt wildly drawn to her . . . more than to any woman in his life. Quietly, he laid the Illuminati Diamond and the Pope's letter on his bedside table. There would be time to explain all of that later. He went to her on the balcony.

Vittoria looked happy to see him. 'You're awake,' she said, in a coy whisper. '*Finally.*'

Langdon smiled. 'Long day.'

She ran a hand through her luxuriant hair, the neck of her robe falling open slightly 'And now . . . I suppose you want your reward.'

The comment took Langdon off guard. 'I'm . . . sorry?'

'We're adults, Robert. You can admit it. You feel a longing. I see it in your eyes. A deep, carnal hunger.' She smiled. 'I feel it too. And that craving is about to be satisfied.'

'It is?' He felt emboldened and took a step toward her.

'*Completely.*' She held up a room-service menu. 'I ordered everything they've got.'

The feast was sumptuous. They dined together by moonlight . . . sitting on their balcony . . . savoring *frisée*, truffles, and risotto. They sipped *Dolcetto* wine and talked late into the night.

618

Langdon did not need to be a symbologist to read the signs Vittoria was sending him. During dessert of boysenberry cream with *savoiardi* and steaming *Romcaffé*, Vittoria pressed her bare legs against his beneath the table and fixed him with a sultry stare. She seemed to be willing him to set down his fork and carry her off in his arms.

But Langdon did nothing. He remained the perfect gentleman. *Two can play at this game*, he thought, hiding a roguish smile.

When all the food was eaten, Langdon retired to the edge of his bed where he sat alone, turning the Illuminati Diamond over and over in his hands, making repeated comments about the miracle of its symmetry. Vittoria stared at him, her confusion growing to an obvious frustration.

'You find that ambigram terribly interesting, don't you?' she demanded.

Langdon nodded. 'Mesmerizing.'

'Would you say it's the most interesting thing in this room?'

Langdon scratched his head, making a show of pondering it. 'Well, there is *one* thing that interests me more.'

She smiled and took a step toward him. 'That being?'

'How you disproved that Einstein theory using tuna fish.'

Vittoria threw up her hands. '*Dio mio!* Enough with the tuna fish! Don't play with me, I'm warning you.'

Langdon grinned. 'Maybe for your *next* experiment, you could study flounders and prove the earth is flat.'

Vittoria was steaming now, but the first faint hints of an exasperated smile appeared on her lips. 'For your information, professor, my next experiment will make scientific history. I plan to prove neutrinos have mass.'

'Neutrinos have *mass*?' Langdon shot her a stunned look. 'I didn't even know they were Catholic!'

With one fluid motion, she was on him, pinning him down. 'I hope you believe in life after death, Robert Langdon.' Vittoria was laughing as she straddled him, her hands holding him down, her eyes ablaze with a mischievous fire.

'Actually,' he choked, laughing harder now, 'I've always had trouble picturing anything beyond this world.'

'Really? So you've never had a religious experience? A perfect moment of glorious rapture?'

Langdon shook his head. 'No, and I seriously doubt I'm the kind of man who could ever *have* a religious experience.'

Vittoria slipped off her robe. 'You've never been to bed with a yoga master, have you?'

THE END

DAN BROWN
DECEPTION POINT

You may have cracked the code, but can you keep your cool?

When a new NASA satellite detects evidence of an astonishingly rare object buried deep in the Arctic ice, the floundering space agency proclaims a much-needed victory...a victory that has profound implications for U.S. space policy and the impending presidential election.

With the Oval Office in the balance, the President dispatches White House Intelligence analyst Rachel Sexton to the Arctic to verify the authenticity of the find. Accompanied by a team of experts, including the charismatic academic Michael Tolland, Rachel uncovers the unthinkable — evidence of scientific trickery — a bold deception that threatens to plunge the world into controversy.

'An excellent thriller... a big yet believable story unfolding at breakneck pace, with convincing settings and just the right blend of likeable and hateful characters'
Publishers Weekly

'Brown proves once again that he is among the most intelligent and dynamic of authors in the thriller genre'
Library Journal

0552 14919 5

DAN BROWN

THE DA VINCI CODE

'Fascinating and absorbing...
A great, riveting read.
I loved this book'

Harlan Coben

The bestselling thriller of all time

Harvard professor Robert Langdon receives an urgent late-night phone call while on business in Paris: the elderly curator of the Louvre has been brutally murdered inside the museum. Alongside the body, police have found a series of baffling codes. As Langdon and a gifted French cryptologist, Sophie Neveu, begin to sort through the bizarre riddles, they are stunned to find a trail that leads to the works of Leonardo Da Vinci – and suggests the answer to a mystery that stretches deep into the vault of history.

Unless Langdon and Neveu can decipher the labyrinthine code and quickly assemble the pieces of the puzzle, a stunning historical truth will be lost forever...

0 552 14951 9

SPECIAL ILLUSTRATED COLLECTOR'S EDITION ALSO AVAILABLE

Go behind the scenes of a modern classic

In this exclusive edition Dan Brown allows the reader behind the scenes of the novel, incorporating over 150 photographs and illustrations throughout the text, showing the rich historical tapestry from which he drew his inspiration. The visual sources, which provide both the backdrop and the stimulus for the novel's action, are revealed for the first time and uniquely complement the reading experience.

0 593 05425 3

DAN BROWN

DIGITAL FORTRESS

HIS ACTION-PACKED FIRST NOVEL

Can you crack the code?

When the National Security Agency's invincible code-breaking machine encounters a mysterious code it cannot break, the agency calls in its head cryptographer, Susan Fletcher, a brilliant, beautiful mathematician. What she uncovers sends shock waves through the corridors of power. The NSA is being held hostage – not by guns or bombs, but by a code so complex that if released would cripple U.S. intelligence.

Caught in an accelerating tempest of secrecy and lies, Fletcher battles to save the agency she believes in. Betrayed on all sides, she finds herself fighting not only for her country but for her life, and in the end, for the life of the man she loves...

0 552 16169 6